THEIR SECRETS MADE THEM PAWNS IN A GAME THAT COULD CHECKMATE THE NATION

LYNN CARLISLE: Nationally-known anchorwoman. Young, beautiful, haunted by a tragic past, trapped in a secret life she can't escape. . . .

STEPHEN BROWNELL: Secretary of State. He alone was privy to the secret summit meeting . . . and to the danger of having Seymour Clayton in the driver's seat.

SEYMOUR CLAYTON: Vice President. Suddenly thrust into the nation's number one job, he downed shot after shot—his instability, a well-kept secret.

WILSON McAVEE: CIA Director. The Intelligence Czar would stop at nothing to protect his vast, hidden domain.

JAY HILLER: Fierce idealism led to his break with the CIA. The First Lady's desperate plea brought him back—and set him on the perilous track that led from the corridors of power into the deadly heart of . . .

The Foxbat Spiral

The Foxbat Spiral

Mal Karman

A DELL BOOK

To My Parents

Published by
Dell Publishing Co., Inc.
1 Dag Hammarskjold Plaza
New York, New York 10017

Copyright © 1980 by Mal Karman

All rights reserved. No part of this book may be reproduced or transmitted in any form or by any means, electronic or mechanical, including photocopying, recording or by any information storage and retrieval system, without the written permission of the Publisher, except where permitted by law.

Dell ® TM 681510, Dell Publishing Co., Inc.

ISBN: 0-440-12582-0

Printed in the United States of America

First printing—June 1980

The author would like to thank the following
people who helped along the way:

Dick Ashcraft, Diane Cleaver, Alex Goldman,
Maude Honemann, Barbara Lowenstein,
Joe Salinaro, Kathy Sagan, Marty Schram,
Naomi Segal, Jack Warner.

Chapter 1

Thousands who had waited for him in the midst of downtown Atlanta's pre-Christmas pandemonium now surrounded the entrance of the St. Mark's Hotel armed with packages, balloons, and cameras. The balloons had been the idea of Mark Kinstrey, the P.T. Barnum of White House press secretaries, who figured every balloon was worth a handshake—and every handshake, ultimately, a vote.

But to the Secret Service agents assigned to escort the visiting President it was public relations lunacy. It was difficult enough managing safety with large crowds. How many breaking balloons would sound like gunshots today, and how many times would they resist the impulse to throw the Chief Executive to the ground and cover him with their bodies while newsmen recorded their nervous paranoia for the morning papers?

In the hotel lobby, two television monitors issued the command to Please Stand By, and the corps of media people waiting there did exactly that—chain-smoking while they jawed with one another, horsing around like a group of college kids at a frat party, and boasting with swelling pride about certain details each of them had in their preview stories that were missed by *The New York Times*.

Kinstrey paced about anxiously, checking his watch against a clipboard itinerary. It read 2:53P–8 Dec.

"Hey, Mark!" grumbled one reporter. "How about it? An hour ago you said he'd be here in half an hour."

"Gimme a break, Tony," the press secretary pleaded. "I'm not hiding him in my shorts. He'll be here soon. Just hang on."

"I got a deadline you know. We're a *daily*."

Kinstrey heaved a deep, mournful sigh and muttered to himself as he stepped over thick black television cables, which snaked across the plush carpeting.

During the ride from the airport Royce looked over the front page of the *Atlanta Constitution*. There were stories about an auto fatality of a fifty-nine-year-old television newsman, a memorial service commemorating the forty-second anniversary of Pearl Harbor, and a new cold wave that was expected over the East. All depressing news, he thought, as the armor-plated presidential limousine, surrounded by a shield of six advance cars and eight police motorcycles, turned down Peachtree Street and burrowed the last 150 yards to the hotel through traffic.

It had taken eighty-five minutes longer than anticipated to drive from the airport but the President had refused to have streets roped off for him during the holiday shopping rush. The motorcade had to stop for red lights, and he willingly waited in traffic.

To the Secret Service, this refusal of special treatment was nothing short of outrageous, causing unnecessary risk and requiring enormous precautions. But they were powerless when it came to changing the President's mind. So potentially dangerous locations were shored up with extra manpower, and almost every other building along the presidential route had at least one local law-enforcement officer at the entrance. Elsewhere, sharpshooter agents with high-powered binoculars scanned the crowds on the street and the parade-watchers waving from windows.

Royce refused to give up his plan to be "just another man in the street," and during his first three years in office, he had reaped the political rewards of his philosophy. As the most popular president in twenty years, he was supported by an impressive coalition of rich and poor, black and white, liberal and conservative.

"I must be doing something right," he kidded reporters from time to time. "As soon as you find out what it is, please let me know."

As the presidential car slowed to a halt, Franklin Zones and Bill Schiano, the two secret service agents guarding the Chief Executive, tried to speed him from the limo through the crowd, but he wouldn't be hurried.

"These people are concerned Americans," he would often say admonishingly when plunging headlong into crowds. "They deserve at least a few minutes of my time."

At fifty-four, he had rugged good looks: a straight nose, prominent cheekbones, and a broad, winning smile that—mixed with style and good humor—commanded his share of female admirers, whom he did little to discourage.

Royce stepped onto the red, white, and blue carpeting that spread out on the sidewalk like an elongated American flag and moved slowly along the yellow police barricades, chatting easily and shaking every extended hand in sight. His ease of manner belied the pressing matters of state that he bore with him.

He embraced an elderly woman in a wheelchair who said she had waited five hours to see him, he then asked if he could send her something for Christmas, and wondered at the same time what he would open with on the twenty-first when he met with the leaders of Communist China and the Soviet Union in Helsinki.

Above a wide brown awning covering the main entrance of Atlanta's oldest first-class hotel hung a large tricolored banner. It read: "President Royce—The People's Choice." Royce saw it out of the corner of his eye as he exchanged greetings with a young couple. He smiled to himself. Mark Kinstrey didn't waste a minute getting in punches for the reelection campaign.

A couple of balloons burst and Agent Zones grimaced. He was tense, and his tension had to be subordinated in favor of courtesy. But as far as the President was concerned the reception couldn't have been better.

Eduardo Morales watched Royce from a window in the penthouse suite the way a hawk surveys a field mouse. Ever since Royce took office Morales had witnessed the dream of a permanent return to his homeland slip further out of his reach with each passing day. He had planned for today ever so carefully, had carried out the design in his mind a thousand times. Failure had taught him to do so.

His mind raced back over the years of frustration. He remembered the arguments in the streets, the secret meetings and mobilization. He could see bombs exploding in neighborhoods and the ensuing evacuations; could feel the betrayal, and even taste defeat and humiliation in the black beans, fried plantain, and coffee.

Once he and others like him had been soldiers. But the political stanchions had turned over and now they were to be swept away like so much rubble. Once part of a movement dedicated to changing the face of the world, they were now expected to vanish without a trace. And so it all came down to one day—and finally, one hour—for him and for the four men with him in the room. It had taken years to make the plan a reality. It was clear they would never get a second chance. Though the scheme was much more elaborate and dangerous than any before, this time there would be one important difference: They would not fail.

Morales remained fixed at the window, watching the President shuffle through the crowd and finally disappear under the brown awning into the building.

"He's inside. Get ready!" he snapped.

Diego Saldise leapt behind a television camera and framed three elegant Tudor-style arm chairs in the monitor. Carlos Lopes and Armando Rodriguez each put on a dark blue television news jacket with the station call letters WFFV. Michael Callejo unscrewed the side panel of the camera and, from its cavity, removed two handguns and several pieces of an Ingram-L machine gun. Quickly he locked it together, slammed a bullet clip to the magazine, and stashed the weapons in the television equipment case.

Morales felt their activity behind him keeping time with his own feverish pulse. His olive skin flushed and he gnawed anxiously on the fleshy part of his upper lip. Had anything been overlooked? What if there were last minute changes? Would they still be able to bring it off?

Yes, yes, he thought impatiently and dismissed it from his mind. His anxiety surprised him.

At the main entrance to the lobby Secret Service man Franklin Zones stopped for a situation report from one of the shift leaders. He knew the advance team had been in Atlanta for ten days and had gone over the St. Mark's like a bloodhound. But as he got older he became more cautious and took nothing for granted. Thus he was relieved to hear that the situation was stable, about twenty-three hundred on hand, with no unusual incidents.

The advance team had done its job. Files in the Protective Research Section had been studied to make sure no one in the area was considered a potential threat. The agents also had consulted the Atlanta Police Department and the local field office of the FBI, and when the Bufiles had produced the name of one man—a part-time electrician who had written Royce a threatening note—he was immediately placed under surveillance.

Mike Popfinger, supervising agent of the White House detail, had selected the St. Mark's over other hotels because it had only two entrances and could easily be secured. The catwalks and balconies were a problem—they looked onto the floors below affording unobstructed views—but that drawback could be overcome by moving the President to the penthouse.

Elevator housings and cables had to be checked. Firemen were called in to assess hazards and escape routes. Names of hotel personnel were run through security files. Twenty-four agents and one-hundred-eighty uniformed police were assigned to secure the area in and around the hotel.

Agents at each entrance checked all who entered individually as packs of television reporters with hardware—cameras, monitors, microphones, sound recorders—were setting off metal-detection devices.

The east wing of the penthouse was partitioned off from the President's suite in the west wing by a double wall. The rest of the west wing was cleared and its corridors and suites completely scoured. Phones were checked for taps and explosive devices, as were vents and air ducts. Agents went over lamps, clocks, heaters, room refrigerators, TVs, toilets, rugs, shower heads, and faucets and checked for false walls. Bulletproof glass was installed in every window.

Uniformed police brought in dogs, and the Technical Services Division of the Secret Service covered every foot of space on the parade route, from manholes in the street to hotel bathrooms.

When the deputy told Agent Zones in a low hurried voice, "The building's clean," he said it with a certain amount of surety.

"The limo is at Alpha Two," Zones replied. "Have it rechecked for the ride back to the airport."

The deputy nodded. "There'll be no hotel traffic in the penthouse during the television interview," he quickly added. "They're broadcasting it to the lobby, and we'll be watching on our own set of monitors. Anyone going to or from the presidential suite will have to use the west elevator. It's programmed to go lobby-to-penthouse direct. There's double security at all stations, as well as uniformed on every floor."

Zones shook his head approvingly and rubbed his eyes. He walked across the lobby and felt a little fatigued. It got harder each time. Maybe he would think about retiring and starting a normal life. Hell, normal life? After his first three years on the job, his marriage had disintegrated; in the nine years since, he hadn't even had time for a steady girl friend.

He had protected diplomats, heads of state, and First Families since the Fords. But it was always the kooks who caused him the most concern, like the nut who had tried to crash through the White House gate with a grenade wired to his body. And while his reflexes were just a half-second slower than in his prime, he was occasionally short-tempered and jumpy.

Earlier, he had even snapped at Bill Schiano when the younger agent had asked him about personal goals. Swallowing some coffee that was really too hot to swallow, Zones had run a hand through his thinning crewcut and muttered irritably, "Screw personal goals. In this job you don't even have time to take a crap—you hold it in for national security."

Now a more subdued Zones joined Schiano and the President, who was welcomed at the elevators by his press secretary, Mark Kinstrey.

"No orchestra?" Royce said to him wryly.

Kinstrey smiled. He knew that meant the President was pleased.

"We couldn't get the tuba through the doors," he quipped.

Unmindful of their conversation, a couple of news correspondents shouted questions at the Chief Executive while a few privileged photojournalists jockeyed for position and clicked off photographs as fast as they could trigger the film advance.

The camera noise made Zones and Schiano impatient, and when they tried to hustle the President into the elevator, he said a little fretfully, "Give these hardworking photographers a minute to get their pictures."

Kinstrey sensed the agents' anxiety and, after tactfully checking his watch, quietly confessed to the President, "Maybe you should go right up. You're slated for a brief press conference in the lobby following the interview, then the mayoral dinner party, and we *are* running late. . . ."

Royce touched Kinstrey's arm in a way that reassured him about the time schedule.

A minute later, the elevator doors of the west penthouse flew open and Franklin Zones, preceding the President there to ensure safety, was met by two agents securing the wing.

"Situation stable," one of them said. "The TV group is inside."

"Okay. Take it back down," Zones barked, nodding at the elevator. "And send him up." Then he hurried to the door of the penthouse suite and burst in like a house detective.

Eduardo Morales and the others sprang to attention. They smiled and greeted him warmly.

Zones looked at them sharply.

"Over here," he said, gesturing to a spot on the blue carpet alongside a sofa.

Diego Saldise stepped before him and spread his legs as Zones began frisking him.

Lopes issued a mild protest. "They checked us downstairs."

"I'm checking you upstairs," the agent said curtly. And he made certain he had performed his job. But when Zones frisked the fifth man, Armando Rodriguez, he felt a heavy metal object in the breast jacket pocket that momentarily caused his heart to flutter. It felt like a gun.

Rodriguez smiled apologetically as the agent pulled an omnidirectional mike from the dark blue WFFV news jacket.

"Don't ever aim this at one of us," Zones said grimly. "We might not know what it is at first."

Rodriguez put a nervous hand to the back of his neck and nodded. He had unnecessarily aroused suspicion.

Zones looked over the rest of the suite, especially the floral bouquets. Then without a word he retreated to the hallway. A moment later, President John Quinlan Royce, accompanied by Zones and Schiano, entered, Royce's hand extending a greeting.

* * *

Ten minutes passed and Mark Kinstrey was still pacing in front of the television monitors in the downstairs lobby, keeping company with a kind of artless statue typical of hotels. He was a lean six-footer of about thirty-five with a bony face, prominent jaw, and bright red hair that caused White House correspondents to nickname him Wile E. Coyote, a name he accepted with good humor.

But now Kinstrey became increasingly irritated as press people again reminded him of deadlines. Finally he summoned an assistant and said, "Pump some alcohol into these jokers so they'll forget what time it is. Get them thinking about Jack Daniels instead of John Royce—which shouldn't be too difficult. You know these characters, if it's free they'll drink it."

Then Kinstrey went to a phone and dialed the penthouse suite. It rang a dozen times. When no one answered he grew anxious. He found the deputy Secret Service agent near the lobby entrance and said in a worried voice, "I can't get anyone to answer the phone in the President's suite. Try them for me, will you?"

The deputy lifted an arm to his mouth and appeared to mutter into his sleeve—where the microphone to a small plastic-tubed walkie-talkie was hidden.

The agent listened anxiously for Zones's reply in the tiny speaker affixed to his ear. There was none.

Then he tried Schiano. When he got no answer, he immediately broadcast a signal alert.

In a matter of seconds a dozen agents had hurried to the west elevator, the one the President had ridden to the top. Kinstrey pushed the call button several times but the elevator did not budge from the penthouse level. What was going on?

The sense of urgency multiplied. They had to get up there.

For security they had sealed the President from the rest of the hotel. But in so doing they had also sealed themselves off. The only direct access was the one lobby-to-penthouse lift, and, inexplicably, it was caught on the top floor.

On the roof of the St. Mark's, a Secret Service agent was astonished to see a helicopter circle the building and then hover overhead as if preparing to land.

He grabbed a high-powered rifle and frantically called over the walkie-talkie, "What the hell's going on? There's a chopper coming down on me!"

The voice that came back over the intercom was strained. "We've lost communication with the President and the elevator's not responding. Wave that eggbeater off and try to get down to the penthouse!"

The agent signaled the helicopter to move on. When it did not follow the order immediately, he fired a warning shot.

The thunderous rattle of the copter engines obliterated the sound of a return volley. Tiny charges blew out of a weapon in the sky and slammed into the agent's back and neck as he raced toward a stairwell door, tumbling him onto the coarse gravel coating of the roof.

When John Quinlan Royce followed agents Schiano and Zones into the penthouse suite, Eduardo Morales was—for a brief moment—a little disarmed to finally have his prey within reach. And yet here he was, the tall sandy-haired liberal from the keystone state.

Morales sized him up, nervous and excited, like a wolf before a chicken coop. Now it was only a question of seizing the right moment. . . .

"Gentlemen, I'm sorry we're so late," the President said as he went about the room shaking hands, "but

I've always found it impossible to rush through Atlanta."

"Impossible to rush *anywhere* this time of year," replied Carlos Lopes with a television-handsome grin.

The President smiled and said complacently, "And yet everybody's always rushing. No one wants to take an extra minute to slow down and relax." Then with a faint trace of impatience he said to his Secret Service men, "I'll bet you fellas are as tired of seeing me as I am of you. Why don't you take a breather. Go out in the hallway and have a smoke. Leave us to our chat."

When Zones immediately started to protest, the President threw up his hands to cut him off and said playfully, but with a slight edge, "I know you men have your doubts, but believe me, I'm capable of answering a couple of tough questions on my own."

Morales was secretly delighted with how easily Royce was playing into his hands. With a little luck a shoot-out would be avoided. He decided to play it coyly, to ensure an easy target. "Are you sure, Mr. President, that you won't need your men for moral support in case our questions become too overbearing."

Royce responded by urging Zones and Schiano out the door with a pained smile, saying "Thanks, fellas. I'll shout if I need help with an answer."

Unable to hide their displeasure but unwilling to create a scene in front of the press, the agents reluctantly stepped into the hallway, and stationed themselves by the door.

Feeling once more his own man, Royce turned his attention to the huge assortment of flowers lined up near the sofa and remarked disdainfully, "Looks like the Jefferson Memorial in July. Please, if you've got family or friends who appreciate flowers, help yourselves to the arboretum."

Diego Saldise and Michael Callejo thanked him, and Callejo opened a television-equipment case. Rodriguez directed Royce behind the podium set up for the interview and Morales drew the drapes.

"It's such a beautiful day," Royce said with a sigh. "Can't we leave the drapes open? My Secret Service buddies keep me locked up like a gerbil and I haven't seen the sun in a week."

In another second he had his answer. Callejo held the machine gun pointed at his chest. Rodriguez and Lopes drew seven-clip .45-caliber handguns.

Royce's face caved in. He was stunned. He had at times been aware of the vulnerability of his office but until now it had always been an abstract vulnerability. He never imagined he would experience danger first hand.

Saldise opened the door and said, "Hey, fellas, can you come in. The President needs your help."

Zones and Schiano hurried in together. Schiano's reflexes were so acute that he had already drawn his gun from his jacket when the first bullet hit his wrist and shattered the bone. The next three tore into his chest and stomach.

Zones was caught from the side by two shots. One struck him just below the eye, the second cut cleanly through his forehead and emptied his brain.

Schiano collapsed at the President's feet, his eyes locked open in a shuddering, lifeless mask.

Royce shrank in shock at the cold-blooded horror, his wide disbelieving eyes riveted in their sockets, staring down at a dark viscous fluid seeping into the blue carpet from the body on the floor. He was shaken, overcome by a nightmare that with each passing moment sank deeper and deeper into the abyss of impossibility. It was the last reaction he was consciously aware of for some time. Later, when the presence of his abductors became a certainty, he would try to recall the beginning and would only remember Schiano's unblinking eyes.

Callejo pulled Royce to his feet and led him to a corner of the room. He placed a noose of thick cord around the President's neck and secured the machine-gun to the noose with duct tape so that the gun barrel pointed at his throat. There would be no need to lose precious seconds aiming. All Callejo needed to do to blow Royce's head off was pull the trigger.

At that moment, the phone in the suite began ringing.

Morales and the others ignored it and gathered their arsenal, quickly but with precision, assuring the perfection of the plan, leaving no cigarette ash, no breath on window glass, no fingerprint, no minute clue to their existence.

At 3:48 P.M., it was going the way they had expected.

In the hotel lobby, the Secret Service deputy prepared for the worst. "Try to get up on the north and south elevators and break through to the west wing," he cried. "Use the four stair-wells. Get to the top and blow out the doors if you have to."

Several agents raced to his order. Then he rebroadcast a general alert and sent out an emergency call to the command post for air support.

On the penthouse floor, Eduardo Morales shoved a Tudor-style chair against the door of the west elevator to keep it from closing. He climbed on the seat and removed an aluminium panel from the elevator ceiling which Carlos Lopes placed on the floor. Callejo and Rodriguez waited anxiously alongside the President, who seemed to have gone into shock, staring incomprehendingly at the activity before him.

Morales boosted himself through the opening onto the top of the elevator cabin. In the darkened shaft, five thick cables surrounded him—illuminated only by a thin stream of yellow light from the elevator. He shinnied up an auxiliary cable to a maintenance access door leading to the roof.

Periodically the door of the elevator on the penthouse floor started to close, only to slam into the buttressing chair and spring open again. It reminded them there would be others not far behind.

Frustrated by their sudden impotence, Secret Service agents in the lobby charged up stairwells and mounted the north and south elevators rather than wait for the hotel manager to produce a programming key that would take them directly to the penthouse. Three Secret Service agents rode the north elevator to the top, losing valuable time to intermediate stops along the way. Four agents rode the south elevator. When a hotel guest on the seventeenth floor tried to get on, one anxious Secret Service man shoved him back into the hallway shouting "Emergency!"

The north elevator reached the penthouse level first. Three agents rushed down the hallway, forcing a startled chambermaid into a doorwell.

At the end of the corridor one of them shoved a few Mini-mite explosives underneath the first of two locked steel reinforced partitions while the others rousted hotel guests from the suites in close proximity. Two rooms were unoccupied, in the third was a man shaving, in the fourth an odd couple—a short, fat businessman in a rumpled suit and a six-foot-four redhead wearing a short skirt and knee-high rattlesnake boots.

"Down the hall!" the agent shouted at them.

"Who the hell are you? Who the hell are you?" the businessman screamed over and over. "I'll have you . . ."

The rest of what he said was lost in the roar of an explosion. Three charges detonated and blew the partition off its guide tracks in the wall.

Michael Callejo heard the blast as he quickly removed the noose from the President's neck and ordered him through the opening in the ceiling of the elevator. Armando Rodriguez, who had climbed up before him, helped pull Royce through. Then Callejo followed.

Morales and Saldise lowered a rescue harness from the roof into the elevator shaft. Rodriguez slipped it over the President's shoulders and strapped him in under the armpits. Then the two men above hoisted him up.

There was a second explosion—much nearer than the first—warning Callejo and Rodriguez that the Secret Service agents had broken through to the west wing. Rodriguez, who had fought wars in the mountains of South America, had no trouble scaling the auxiliary elevator cable. As he reached the roof, he heard shouts rising from the hallway and quickly lowered the rescue harness to his comrade.

Callejo clung to the harness and was being pulled toward the roof when a Secret Service man, gun drawn, cautiously zeroed in on the west elevator. He sprang at the door, expecting a barrage of gunfire rather than the Tudor-style chair and the aluminum ceiling panel that Callejo had not had time to replace.

The agent looked overhead, his eyes not quite adjusting to the darkness of the elevator shaft. He could barely make out the faint shadow of a man reaching for the access door to the roof.

"Halt!" he shouted. And when the order was ignored, he fired four times, the bullets ricocheting through the elevator shaft with a deafening ring. But Callejo was pulled up safely and when he again had a firm grip on his gun, he leaned back into the elevator shaft and fired a wild shower of bullets from the Ingram-L, though none found a mark.

The gunfire greeted several agents who closed in on the elevator—it was only a momentary deterrent to them. One immediately hoisted himself through the opening in the ceiling to the elevator shaft and started to scale an auxiliary cable.

Now the five assailants raced with their captive across the roof of the hotel to a waiting helicopter, past the slain body of the Secret Service man who had been gunned down.

When the first agent climbed from the elevator shaft, he fired a shot from some distance away. Diego Saldise returned the volley, but Callejo angrily swung the President around to display to his would-be rescuers the compromising position they held him in.

Even at a great distance it was obvious the hostage was John Quinlan Royce. The agent lowered his weapon. There could be no attempts at heroics without endangering the President's life.

As Eduardo Morales, his companions, and the President climbed aboard the chopper, the engine spurted and kicked in and the big overhead blades cut through the air. Seconds later they were airborne.

Chapter 2

Bulletins of the kidnapping spread almost instantly from Atlanta to all major U.S. cities to the global centers all across the continents. The media ferreted out the most remote corners of the world to disseminate the story. Thousands of reporters descended on Washington and Atlanta. Television stations cancelled regular programming in favor of marathon news shows. Newspapers increased their press runs. Magazines rushed special issues to the stands. With the exception of some movie houses, entertainment and sporting events were cancelled. Federal courts closed. Wall Street immediately shut down to prevent the bottom from dropping out. The business world slowed while everyone hovered over their televisions. And though department stores remained open—it was the height of the Christmas season—few came to shop.

Three federal investigators from separate branches of the intelligence community tore apart the St. Mark's Hotel and picked for clues in the lobby and penthouse suite. Unfortunately, they were more adept at picking at each other.

The FBI claimed jurisdiction over kidnappings, the CIA assumed a foreign nation was attempting to overthrow the United States, while the Secret Service sought retribution. All three were unaccustomed to sharing information.

The prevailing reaction across the nation was stunned disbelief. How could anyone snatch up the President of the United States like a bag of jewels and make off like a thief in the night?

It was not uncommon to hear someone say, "I heard it, I saw the report on TV, I read about it, but I still don't believe it."

People spoke to complete strangers on the street, seeking answers to the unanswerable: Who were the kidnappers and what would they demand?

With the exception of Vice President Seymour Clayton, whose job it was to reassure the nation, most politicians avoided speculation and the media. One who did not was Senator Perry Jedlicker, a conservative Republican from Arizona, who said, "It is shocking and dreadful that a thing like this could happen in a free country." But Jedlicker didn't stop there. In the same breath he added, "This is another in a series of crimes against democracy by a group of cowardly extremists who find encouragement in the permissive society that John Royce advocates.

"And the Secret Service's slow reflexes in detecting something afoul at the St. Mark's Hotel is not unlike the President's own reactions in dealing with our foreign adversaries. . . ."

Members of the Senate and the House were appalled but for the most part refrained from engaging in battle in the press.

However, Senator Richard Wainwright of Oregon in a little less than two years in office had made an enemy of the powerful Jedlicker and replied to the television cameras: "Senator Jedlicker's remarks demonstrate an overt lack of sensitivity and understanding of even the most basic current events as well as the principles of democracy and indicate beyond a doubt that the wrong man was kidnapped."

* * *

It is never clear why certain individuals among the nation's leaders respond to a crisis with aggression and daring, while others seem to lose their judgment and stability. But sometimes, as in this case, the two reactions are indistinguishable—and an insurmountable problem grows to an impossibility. Who can say why? It was as though the country had become so mystified by the boldness of the kidnapping that it could not react with logic. The one man who was supposed to was Jay Marvin Hiller.

Jay Hiller slammed down the telephone receiver as if he were hammering a nail.

"That's the twenty-ninth fucking idiot to get through to me on the kidnapping," he spewed. "This one swears he has proof the *Republicans* did it. Get somebody to screen these calls. I don't need assholes on the phone—there's enough of them around here!"

Hiller was like a storm—a swarming, threatening body of black clouds that swept into a room with a fury, demanding attention.

It was a defense cultivated in his adolescence. Never knowing when his coarse, muscular, (now-aging) form would suddenly tremble and break down into a sweating, weak-kneed asthmatic's body, when his eyes would feel literally sucked into the center of his skull and air would become so precious and so desperately necessary, Hiller had reinforced a habit of speaking any time he was physically able. With little regard for protocol, he would quickly fashion the words before another unmerciful attack, doing so loudly, so as not to have to repeat, and plainly, so no one would ask him to.

But he was really more like the *eye* of a storm—and

what moved around him was usually much more lethal than what people chose to focus on.

Jay Hiller's reputation had preceded him to the Operations Center of the new General Office Building. The GOB was the epitome of the modern government superstructures of the eighties. Big even by Washington standards, it sprawled across six city blocks, a football-field-and-a-half wide, its four stories and triplet towers of dark green glass—each eleven stories tall—providing 1.7 million square feet of working space. Minicabs on the first floor shuttled workers to various parts of the building. Entrance to restricted sectors was monitored by multicombination locks, plastic computer cards, and telescreening devices.

The Op Center, located in the Blue Wing on the second floor, had the appearance of an insurance company—windowless, shadowless, charmless—except for the old Telex machines that rumbled in unison in one corner and a large digital clock with red and green numerals marking government time.

Like most new federal offices, it was airport-modern. Thirty desks, each with computer keyboard and telescreens and Lucite "burn baskets," were illuminated by soft green full-spectrum lighting. Half the desks were occupied by agents rechecking meagre leads, digging for new ones, and poring over tons of intelligence reports.

Whether it was because of the magnitude of the crime or his own notoriety Hiller wasn't sure, but he noticed that no one had made an effort to welcome him on the job.

An orange blip moved across the radar screen, illuminating Jay Hiller's granite features. He still retained the brutal attractiveness of early manhood—a sharply-defined mouth and a Marlon Brando nose that looked like it had been broken in two places. But there was no denying the pallor—a slightly whitish flesh tone—in his face.

Three heavy lines creased his forehead, the bottom line intersecting with a tiny crab's-leg wrinkle that looked like an upside-down check mark between his brows. He had heard many say that, along with his soulful brown eyes, it gave warmth to an otherwise austere countenance. But in the mirror it had a different effect. Along with a slightly thinning head of black woolly hair, it was the unmistakable mark of middle age. That, in itself, was not precursory. What troubled Hiller was a persistent feeling that he had wasted his youth.

Now he leaned over the technician's shoulder and watched in dismay as a radar videotape made only hours earlier showed a small orange light—the escape helicopter—on the radar screen. It had started as a single radar tracking signal just west of Macon, Georgia, and mysteriously multiplied into two orange blips. Then the blips had crisscrossed and become three, crisscrossed again and become four.

"Son of a bitch, they set up decoy craft to jam the tracking system," Hiller exclaimed. "Which is Number One?"

The technician shook his head. "I think it's this one, but I can't be sure. They've slipped under the radar defense screen a few times and we lost 'em."

Over a sloping desert of sunburned earth that stretched toward the first pastel shades of sunset, four helicopters suddenly dropped from the sky, hummingbirds coming to rest, their humming engines shutting down.

In spite of the hour, the heat from the afternoon sun

still rose off the parched face of the landscape. There was an oppressive midday humidity, painful to breathe. Blindfolded, with hands before him, President Royce felt it the moment he stepped from the helicopter. It was as incongruous with the Christmas chill in Atlanta as this fallow wilderness, pocked with divots and a lunar-like absence of life, was with the roof of the St. Mark's Hotel.

The day had started routinely for him around a fireplace in the White House, where political advisors kicked around reelection strategies and campaign slogans, hoping to find one to highlight all his major accomplishments: restoring the public's lost confidence in government; inducing several billion-dollar corporations to build low-rent housing in exchange for tax incentives (something his critics called "a socialist martini with a capitalist olive"); and proposing a World Food Bank, which the wealthy nations of the globe were now studying.

Royce's political rise had been, to say the least, meteoric and daring, stunning even those who had thought that some day with a little luck he just might make a run for the White House. But even the most optimistic in his camp would have admitted his lower-middle-class background, a construction worker's son, while looking good on paper might not have enough "snob appeal" with the prime movers of his party.

Supporters had vigorously cheered his "leadership with imagination." Critics tried to shrug him off as "another upstart political greenhorn." But after only two years as a Pennsylvania state assemblyman and one term as governor, he did the unthinkable by challenging a Democratic incumbent for the presidential nomination.

It was a gutsy, almost adolescently nervy thing to do, especially when party elders cautioned him to wait four more years and run with the party's blessing.

"I can't wait," Royce confessed to the Democratic national chairman. "It's like asking a man who's dying of thirst to wait for a drink."

He was impatient with slow progress and appealed to the voters as a man who could make things happen. Though not a gruff arm-twister, he used the media shrewdly, creating the impression that the incumbent was forever tangled in bureaurcracy while he could simply cut through it.

In the space of half a day, all that was as far away from him now as the summit meeting, Finland, and Helsinki.

In his winter suit Royce immediately began to perspire in the humid air. Still somewhat dazed, he tried to compose himself. Finally he asked that his jacket be removed. Eduardo Morales nodded and Michael Callejo removed the blindfold, the bond, and the noose and gun from the President's throat. Then Royce peeled the jacket off himself.

He was astonished at what was before him. To his eyes, the land—a dark reddish clay full of upturned roots and debris—looked like something from another planet. The closest thing to it he had ever seen was a burned-out forest.

His mind began to work again. He considered confronting his captors, demanding to know what they planned to do, insisting on reason and logic as if he were in a Cabinet meeting. But as sure as he was his questions would sound ludicrous, there were others in his head he was afraid to even form. Not fifty yards behind him was one such question.

Like a great godlike relic that primitive tribes might have worshipped, seeming even more alien as it cast long black shadows with its huge, mysterious body, a Galaxy C-7 cargo plane camped in absolute stillness. Its belly hung open like an animal whose guts had been methodically emptied by a surgeon.

Morales and Callejo moved Royce toward the plane, which had obscured something even more flabbergasting—three waiting F-25 Eagle jets equipped with forward-and-aft infrared scanners and electro-optical viewing systems to improve low-level flying capabilities.

The President was stunned. "American planes!" he thought incredulously. "A domestic plot? No! This can't be—none of it makes sense."

His mind raced feverishly, and he was gripped by a sudden frenzy. All at once it was agonizing not knowing if he would live or how he would die. He was keenly aware he had been elected to office in a zero-numbered year. Every President elected at twenty-year intervals in zero-numbered years since 1840 had died while serving.

A wave of fear broke over him, and his fear made him flush red with deep feelings of shame. Finally he calmed down and he thought of Phyllis and wished she had had a child. It was a subject he had given a lot of thought to in recent years. Now she would be alone.

The sun just now touching the horizon was the color of blood. Without knowing why, it made Eduardo Morales remember his brother.

He stopped walking and shaded his eyes. Then with obvious reference to their hostage, he spoke tersely in Spanish with Callejo.

"Take him in. Make him comfortable. And remember, he isn't here to be tortured for our past mistakes—there's time for that if need be. But don't overdo the comfort. He isn't on holiday either, and we are through serving others."

Morales was a formidable man with wide shoulders, a thick neck like a bull's, and dark, heavy features. His brows swept above his clever black eyes in a serpentine manner, as if they were protecting a bank of secrets. He had an abruptness about him that hinted at a precariously harnessed rage.

Until now Morales had had to be content with little victories—breaking terrorist sympathizers out of prison or coolly murdering low-ranking officials from the Dominican Republic, Cuba, and Chile during celebrated visits to Latin American countries.

The precision with which they had thus far carried out their plan was a long way from those meager rewards and from the pitiful beginnings marked by the utter unpreparedness of a toy army of neophyte soldiers—merchants, farmers, physicians, artists, musicians, and laborers—who exuded the blind faith of fools.

One such soldier had been Manuel Morales, Eduardo's brother. He had lost his life in the damp fields, murdered by those he had trusted and who had sworn their loyalty.

In the nearly twenty-four years since then, Eduardo Morales had learned to have faith only in himself. That is why he could now scoff privately at those would-be revolutionaries who had ridiculed and laughed at him, especially the tailor in the old community who had loved to play the role of shaman and had predicted disaster.

Morales smiled to himself. He was the natural leader, the most reliable, the most precise of these men. Now more than ever he believed anything could be made to happen. Here was living proof. He would not make the same mistake as his brother.

Michael Callejo was half a foot shorter than Morales but the most fierce looking of Royce's captors. He was sallow-faced, with sunken cheeks and eyes and a cruel mouth partly covered over by the thick black hairs of a full moustache.

As he coaxed Royce up the stairwell to the cockpit of the jet nearest the C-7, he too noticed the blood red sun and savored the command he had over his charge. It was partial payment for false promises and the anguish of twenty months in a foreign jail. He had escaped but it had cost him two fingers and part of his left hand which he himself had amputated with a bushknife to slip free of his shackles.

Callejo had fought as a soldier of fortune in South America in the sixties with a band of guerrillas determined to check the spread of communism. Later, along with Armando Rodriguez, who had been a freedom fighter in the mountains of Bolivia, and Carlos Lopes and Diego Saldise, Callejo began running supply and weapon drops out of Nicaragua for guerrilla operations in Central America and the Caribbean.

His first act of retaliation for the months in prison was to blow up a commercial airliner with seventy-six civilians aboard. That and his act of self-mutilation secretly earned him among his peers the nickname El Carnívore.

As Royce entered the aircraft he looked back just long enough to see that the four helicopters which had brought him here had already vanished. What he didn't see was that they had disappeared inside the belly of the cargo plane.

Almost in unison the engines of the sister ships roared like a chorus, joined a moment later by the quaking basso hum of the cargo plane, which caused the windows in the jets to vibrate.

Four minutes and twenty seconds later, just about

at twilight, the last of the aircraft was climbing. The one bearing John Quinlan Royce streaked toward the dying light of day; the others flew in different directions: north, northeast, east.

Morales leaned back in his seat and looked out the window. He no longer thought about his brother. Or how smoothly everything had gone. Or how he planned to further unsettle America. His only thoughts now were of reaching Foxbat.

Chapter 3

The afternoon advanced but still the sun baked the tiny Mexican village of Las Cumbres, defying everything that is known about late autumn.

Behind fences chickens snapped at seedlings, and pigs slept in corn mush. A donkey stood in the dirt road before a white adobe church, flicking insects with its tail. One woman sang a Spanish love song while she scrubbed clay pots and cleaned fish. Another called several beautiful dark children to her feet and fed them tamales and hot *atole* and offered some to a neighbor who was bent over a porcelain washbowl with her family's clothes.

Here the dark eyes and shy, kind smiles said it was easy to be human. Nothing happened every day. And every day was the same.

Only the changing light on the crumbling white

walls of the church and the hollow deep chimes from its tower signaled the passing of time.

On a hillside above the church, near a tiny cemetery decorated with makeshift wooden crosses Padre Julian Serra sat with his oil paints in the sun. When he became hot, he would move to the shade until he became cool and then would move again to the sun. Villagers smiled to themselves for they could tell time by his sitting, each lasting exactly a half hour.

Serra's face was rippled like a dried-out peach, the deep lines and his startling white hair accentuating his advancing years. He was sixty. But in spite of a delicate constitution, a slight build, and a trace of a limp which had developed in childhood when a broken bone failed to heal properly, he owned the admiration and trust of his people. To comfort a parishioner, he needed only to smile or flash his dark brown eyes with their own brand of power and gentleness, two qualities that sometimes shone through in his paintings.

Today he recorded the present in a landscape of little adobe huts from the village and, as always, flicked instinctively at the flies that buzzed around his head. Then he put down his paintbrush and rested.

The harsh contradictions of the Yucatan are never more evident than in each day's last hour of sunlight. Sparks fly during these moments when light and shadow collide and repel like magnets of opposing poles.

When light and shadow collided in that measureable point in time on this particular day, December eighth, a stillness fell over Las Cumbres like a rush. For long moments nothing in this sudden still life moved, disturbed not even by the cricket's chirp or the hum of a fly. There was only the beat, the quiet pulsating beat of the sun's light preceding an apocalyptic moment when the world burned in negative image and an invisible flash of black lightning simultaneously signaling beginning and end.

A shrill cry carried across the churchyard. The villagers, dressed in their cool white rags, abandoned their private silences and looked up fearfully, for there was no mistaking its terror. One by one they bolted for the church. In a moment three dozen or so hovered near the entrance shouting at Ramon Diaz, a young farmer, who balanced himself precariously on the ledge of the steep bell tower.

Thrusting his arms wildly in the air, he screamed madness as heavy droplets of sweat ran down his feverish face.

"If America dies, we all die!" he shrieked. "If America dies, we all die! I will not murder children in their sleep . . . no more . . . no more . . . no evil . . . no more."

Diaz was barely conscious of the people below. His black hair was matted with perspiration and his eyes were blazing wildly. The children who had not yet learned fear were amused and giggled. But one boy of eight, Ramon's son Luis, had learned early and was terrified.

"Father, come down," he cried. "You frighten me."

Many of the peasants were stunned into silence. Some tried to coax Ramon Diaz down. One stooped old man taunted him.

"Jump you fool," he shouted cruelly. "Show them how crazy you really are."

Another man, unknown to the villagers and dressed in a lightweight tan suit, stood apart from the crowd. Leaning against a dusty black automobile—one of the few that had ever come to Las Cumbres—he watched

Diaz in silence, with small dark eyes obscured by heavy brows and thick lips the color of his suit. Sergio Grijalva was in his middle thirties, a few inches over six feet with a tightly-drawn, wiry build, but it was impossible to imagine him smiling. He carried his weight like a tomb and looked like the sceptre of death.

The padre put down his brush when the first cry pierced the air. One of the children shouting playfully, he thought. But when no laughter followed the cry and when he saw villagers run for the church and the figure of a man on the bell tower, the realization struck him sharply. In his panic he toppled the paints and canvas and raced down the hill crying, "Ramon! Don't move. Stay there, please stay, I'm coming!"

Diaz could hear none of them. Nor was he at all conscious of his trembling body or the ledge which seemed almost a dividing line between this very real suffering and what would surely become a memory of a village farmer who had inexplicably gone mad and was finally at peace.

The padre raced into the church and flew up a stairway to the tower, scaling three and four steps at a time, grimacing with the pain he felt in his crippled right leg and trying bravely to ignore it.

Young Luis, tears raining down his cheeks, ran up after him.

Exhausted, Serra reached the tower, his leg throbbing, heart pounding fiercely. Out of breath, he beckoned to Ramon and advanced on him slowly. Diaz backed off, frightened, whimpering like a child. Now he was cornered.

The padre stopped abruptly. Then Diaz stopped, no more than six inches from the edge. He clung to an adobe pillar as his life support. Saliva ran from his mouth, and he burst into tears. The padre leaned toward him, carefully avoiding abrupt or startling gestures.

"Ramon," he whispered, "in the name of the Holy Father, come inside. Whatever drives you to this will pass. We can talk today with God, together, you and I. Like we have done during difficult times in the past."

Something in Ramon's mind seemed to click suddenly—now he seemed to remember, and the madness in his glazed eyes dimmed a little. He let one arm fall from the pillar and reached out for the padre's hand, a comforting hand, then drew it back defensively, then slowly extended it again. They were near to touching.

Luis reached the top step and, when he saw his father, was swept up in a wave of relief. He ran to him with pleading arms, crying, "Father. I love you," sniffling to hold back tears.

With the violence of a thundering sky, Ramon again began to tremble, the look of hopeless abandonment again fell across his face as he recoiled.

He screamed so wildly, so suddenly, that Luis drew back out of fear, and the padre himself flinched. It was a piercing shriek of agony that echoed in the bell tower and spilled over the village like a brown ghost, a cry that shattered the serenity of Las Cumbres and would be remembered for a generation each time the tower bell sounded.

In the millisecond that elapsed when the priest closed his eyes and Luis drew back, Diaz let go of the pillar and furiously hurled himself over the ledge, scattering the horrified crowd below. The padre staggered backward, a reflex action by a human body in shock, nonthinking, unreasoning, instinctively fearful that he and Luis might somehow be pulled over the ledge.

The padre threw a hand over the boy's eyes and pulled him violently to his chest. They wept uncontrollably and collapsed in each other's arms.

Chapter 4

Jay Hiller marched rapidly down the long, sterile corridor and burst into the Op Center. It screamed with soft green full-spectrum lighting and ringing telephones and the clucking of an army of workers. He had a full day ahead of him: meetings with officials of the Secret Service, the FBI, and the CIA, and with the secretary of state. None of them would be too pleasant. With the exception of the secretary, they viewed him as an outsider. It did not matter that the First Lady and the Vice President had both asked him to head the interagency investigation. So far as the intelligence community was concerned, an outsider was an enemy.

It had been several years since Hiller had worked as an investigator, and certainly never when the President's life hung before him like a carrot. The stakes were inordinately high because Royce was a personal friend as well as the President. In making decisions Hiller would have to learn to put that friendship aside.

As he came through the door, Hiller spotted Phyllis Royce, the President's wife, near the Telex machines. She was an archetypical First Lady—dignified but with a good sense of humor, strong-willed but never arrogant, and, as everyone who came into contact with her knew, possessed of an acute sense of fairness. Though not physically beautiful, she had lovely, sympathetic hazel eyes and a gracious smile. Hiller was always struck by the way she retained her vitality. She looked much younger than her forty-four years, and this was all the more apparent now, when she was going through a severe personal crisis.

They greeted each other with kisses, and he looked at her with some amazement in his smile.

"Phyllis, all things considered, you look terrific. You think you could share some of your composure with me and the Vice President? We could both use a bit."

She laughed a little and said, "If you knew what was going on inside of me, you wouldn't ask that."

Hiller spied one of his aides, Jeff Brodsky, slipping out of the room and roared, "Get that Day One Report over here!"

He lowered his voice as if revealing a confidence to her and asked, "Are you holding up all right?"

Phyllis smiled. "How can I answer that truthfully? If I say yes I sound like a martyr. And if I say no—well, you've got enough to worry about."

"Never mind *me*," he said. "Look, I want you to know that although we're going to . . ."

The last words were lost in a gasp. They strangled in his throat. Out of nowhere came that cruel, familiar squeezing-off of air, that vacuum which swelled like a blowfish and pressed against his lungs. He shivered. The powerful shoulders drooped and his knees became rubbery. Blood flooded the veins and arteries in his head and his face burned feverishly, as if his flesh was on fire.

He staggered away from Phyllis and fumbled in his pocket for a plastic nebulizer. He shoved it in his mouth and sucked on it. A light spray coated his throat and numbed his senses, a sweet thankful numbing that allowed him to breathe, that dried the sweat which trickled down the back of his neck, that patched his lungs, that returned life to his sagging body—until the next time, until the next horrible time.

Phyllis had seen this before though not for several years. She remembered the last occasion distinctly—John Royce's gubernatorial victory party, from which Hiller had had to excuse himself. Now the expression on her face was a mixture of fear and concern.

"Jay," she said gently, "are you sure you're up to this?"

Hiller was fond of saying he had been given a big mouth and a Marlon Brando nose to enable him to suck in more air. But now he felt she was pampering him. He noticed others in the room too who were pretending not to notice. He was embarrassed and felt grotesque. When he finally spoke, it was with a rasp in his voice, his eyes reddened and watery.

"For crissakes, Phyllis. It's *asthma*. I don't need a wheelchair. I'll stop by as soon as I can and let you know what's doing."

He forced a faint smile and turned quickly away.

She watched him grow smaller as he weaved his way to another part of the room, stopping first at a water fountain, where he drenched his throat and his forehead. Was it possible she was asking too much? Could he survive the pace and the pressure? Phyllis was smart enough not to try to answer her own questions. She bowed her head and left.

Jeff Brodsky followed Hiller to the fountain and produced the Day One Report. Hiller snatched up the papers and ordered him to retrieve a map. He was angry at himself for his pitiful display in public. He had anticipated that his condition would be aggravated with increased activity, but not so soon. He had hardly begun. . . . He wouldn't mind the self-abuse, he thought, since he was used to abusing himself—the danger to his health, the twenty-hour workdays, the sock-laundry soup and papier-maché hamburgers or even the incredible pressure to turn over to the media and the nation some startling new shred of evidence on a daily basis. But he had to confess he was nervous and full of doubts.

The future of the nation would be affected, even altered, by what he was or was not able to do. And, given that, the course of history as well. And there was that goddamn reputation he would also be expected to live up to. During his career Hiller had developed a talent for becoming embroiled in the agency's most compelling cases. It was as if they sought him out—much the same way a movie star seems to end up in all the box-office hits.

After a decade of field work in Uruguay, Chile, Ecuador, and the Caribbean, Hiller had made headlines in 1974 when he foiled an anarchist plot to blow up and close off the Panama Canal. The following year he discovered a counterspy operating out of the State Department, and as an outgrowth of the same investigation, the CIA prevented plans for a neutron bomb from falling into the hands of two nations in the Middle East.

He was considered one of the country's finest federal investigators. But he was also an idealist—and in retrospect, he thought, maybe government work and idealism were an insoluble mixture. He had believed in America. In the throes of student unrest in the sixties, when contemporaries were either sitting in on campuses or shipping out for Vietnam, he was well insulated within the intelligence community, that is, until assassination and political corruption and war began to wring the patriotic wail out of him.

The disillusionment never seemed to end. In 1970, while working on a special project to monitor political plotting in Chile, Hiller uncovered a plan to kidnap the Chilean military Chief of Staff, General René Schneider, as part of an effort to destabilize the government and smooth the way for the overthrow of President-elect Salvador Allende.

Clearly overstepping his bounds, Hiller bypassed CIA director Wilson McAvee because of logistics and a critical factor, and got word directly to the Administration.

Hiller had anticipated the dressing-down he got from McAvee—it was something he had hardened to as the frequency of reprimands increased. But what he failed to understand was that although U.S. officials were professing a live-and-let-live policy toward the new Chilean government, the White House was secretly trying to undermine it.

When Hiller informed the then-President of the impending plot against Schneider, he had taken away the Chief Executive's most crucial defense mechanism—deniability.

If the President could not deny knowledge of the plot beforehand, then silence would make him an accomplice. Schneider had to be warned, and consequently, the kidnap attempt never materialized. Hiller was then shuffled off on another case that ranked in importance with a bill to set aside one week in July when ducks would be safe from hunters. Soon after, General Schneider was assassinated.

Hiller had run out of excuses for these things long ago. He could no more incorporate moral concession with political necessity than he could bring himself to run down a crippled cat. He quit at his peak, giving his asthmatic condition as reason for early retirement. The compromises had simply become too difficult to live with. At first he had thought he could change the system. Then he realized that he had to get out before the system changed him.

Hiller's fierce idealism made him impatient with realists and pragmatists, and in Washington that netted him thrice as many enemies as admirers. He had few friends. But Royce was one of them. When the First Lady, at the suggestion of the Vice President, asked for his help as a personal favor, he never for a moment entertained a refusal. But even without considering the physical discomfort he was bound to suffer, it would be an impossible task. There would be many who, faced with a choice, would help the kidnappers before they would help him. But it was precisely that insolence that fed his willingness to work again in Washington.

Now he joined Jeff Brodsky and another aide, Jack Albaum, at the large light table near the Telex machines. Brodsky and Albaum were young and inexperienced—Brodsky especially—and Hiller could not understand why the CIA had assigned them to the case. Or to him. He liked them both because they were among the few who did not lionize him. But Brodsky was as green as they came, too eager, too sure of himself. He had been lured away from law school, which Hiller figured showed questionable judgment—a characteristic not conducive to longevity in intelligence work.

Making use of his easy smile and good looks—he vaguely resembled the Russian dancer Baryshnikov—Brodsky had prior to this been primarily giving government bureaucrats private tours of the Company's Langley, Virginia, headquarters.

Albaum, on the other hand, had a tougher shell.

With his sharp nose and weak chin and amazingly mobile face, he looked sly—sly, pragmatic and, like Hiller, a cynic. He had breezed through two years of graduate work at the University of Wisconsin and had fallen into the CIA job because it meant money and security and, he'd thought, the opportunity to travel. He had been wrong—and that reinforced his cynicism.

Albaum greeted Hiller dryly. "Hail to the Chief."

Hiller nodded at the plastic computer-coded map on the light table.

"Show me," he demanded.

"Piecing it together, we figure they came down like this, about fifty miles west of Macon, over Blackshear Lake and Tallahassee and south into the Gulf. They dropped off the radar here and here and disappeared over the Everglades."

Albaum hesitated a moment, expecting a reaction. When he got none, he continued.

"We lost them as they crossed over the Georgia-Florida border and only picked them up briefly again near Cape Coral."

Hiller studied the map and said, "The escape route is highly speculative, and you're only guessing about the Everglades."

Albaum nodded.

"It's a good guess," Hiller said. "The Everglades could be a strategic jumping off point to South America, Central America, or North America."

He looked at the faces of the two young men before him. They hid traces of adolescent smugness.

Hiller smiled sardonically. "Congratulations, gentlemen. That narrows it down to one hemisphere—at least for the time being."

Albaum and Brodsky felt deflated as Hiller drew their attention to a military delineation on the map.

"That's Fort Cherry, isn't it? Find out if anybody

down there woke up long enough to learn the President was kidnapped."

Brodsky had anticipated him.

"They said they couldn't move without orders from the Pentagon. Afraid they'd endanger his life."

Hiller shook his head and muttered to himself.

"Fucking wind-up toys. They either want to blow up this or blow up that or sit on their collective arsenal of asses. . . ."

"There's more good news," Albaum chirped. "Not a single lead came out of that hotel in Atlanta."

Hiller had expected as much.

"You don't go scooting off with the President and leave bird droppings behind for intelligence agents to follow," he said.

The kidnappers had planned well, timed well, and executed well.

"All right, find out who set up the television interview with the President. Get me a list of every subversive group in the hemisphere whose patterns fit this MO—that's 'method of operation' for you freshmen. Find out if anyone in that Atlanta crowd took movies or photographs. Talk with anyone who thinks they can provide descriptions. Our people are supposed to talk with the station that sponsored the interview with Royce—find out what they've got. Check the Bureau's subversive files and the Protective Research sections in the entire intelligence community and dig up dossiers on presidential threats. And coordinate your efforts with all crews and work banks so there's no duplication. . . ."

Hiller made a mental note to ask for reconnaissance over the Everglades, "just in case we get lucky," he said to himself.

Brodsky and Albaum moved to the cadence of Hiller's bark just as the Telex machines started rumbling and a chorus of telephones rang. A moment later a familiar voice was calling his name.

It was Fred Goss, a square-shouldered, medium-sized man with trim black shiny hair and a smile that flashed like a china setting. His perfect rows of teeth reminded Hiller of someone in a toothpaste commercial, and at forty he still looked like a handsome smooth-skinned collegian.

Nobody had risen through the Company as rapidly as Goss, from a trainee at Camp Peary to an operations officer in the Caribbean to a station chief in Uruguay and later Southeast Asia to head of the Special Operations Group within the counterintelligence division.

Early in his career he forged letters to create dissension in Cuba, implicating Cuban minister Manuel Esposito in a CIA plot to assassinate Fidel Castro and cunningly arranged for Esposito's superior to discover them. The Cuban minister was arrested and shot as a traitor, though he had never spoken to Goss or any other agent in his life.

There was no question in Hiller's mind that Fred Goss had shrewd covert abilities and was masterful at finding a weak link in any institution and infiltrating it. He put together a reliable string of spy networks in Vietnam, the Dominican Republic, Indonesia, and Greece which ultimately resulted in the overthrow of old regimes and the establishment of new ones more favorable to the United States.

Hiller would remind him, however, that all of the political changes he effected had been accompanied by an excess of bloodshed. There was a touch of fanaticism in Goss and he couldn't understand such criticism.

"When we are told to do something, we do it," he

said. "Nowhere does it say 'ask them nicely.' This isn't the Girl Scouts and I'm not Emily Post."

Hiller always remembered the words "when we are told to do something, we do it." He had seen them before in books about the Nuremberg trials.

In the late sixties, under Goss's direction, the agency investigated antiwar activities in the U.S. and compiled so much information they began to call him "the vacuum cleaner."

He used whatever means were at hand to gather material and, on occasion, acted in violation of the CIA charter forbidding domestic operations. Goss never gave it much thought and if he had he would have cited the "sleeper" clause in the National Security Act which permits "such other functions and duties related to intelligence affecting national security as the NSC may from time to time direct."

But had the clause not existed it wouldn't have mattered. He was a zealous Company man and, in the agency's view, one of the most pragmatic and productive.

Goss and Hiller first met in Montevideo, where Goss was station chief, and in spite of their vastly different approaches to their work, the two became friends.

At the time, Goss was embarking on a program to undermine the economic stability of Uruguay, proposing biological warfare and food contamination as a means of accomplishing his goal. When it became clear that Hiller had no taste for such things, Goss suggested he make the switch to the Office of Security. Following Hiller's subsequent investigative successes Goss announced, half-jokingly, that he "made Hiller into a national hero."

Several years later, Goss's passionate beliefs spilled over into Hiller's personal life. Soon after Hiller left the agency, the local print media decided to profile his career. They got more than they bargained for.

A *Washington Post* reporter, visiting one autumn afternoon while Hiller raked and piled leaves in his yard, listened to him pass a few blunt remarks that made excellent copy and pricked ears up and down the Potomac.

"The agencies are getting too big, too unwieldy, and too independent," he told the reporter. "It may already be too late for American-style democracy in America. In a few years it won't matter *who* the President is because the Chief Executive will be Wilson McAvee, the director of the CIA, or Doug Padley over at the FBI. *They'll* be determining foreign and domestic policy with independent covert actions. Almost everything they do now, they do without checking with the President. And if private citizens don't do something about it soon, there may not *be* any private citizens."

The deep rumbling of unrest from the organizational substrata caused one hell of a flap in D.C. The day the story hit the stands—page-one stuff—Fred Goss came to visit Hiller.

"What the fuck do you think you're doing with this?" Goss demanded, waving the paper as if he were beating a kettle drum. He didn't wait for a reply. He berated Hiller as if he were reprimanding a child and warned him there would be "consequences" if he "continued to play games."

Hiller looked impassively at Goss. It was an odd reaction. Far less belligerent things had been known to disrupt the sleeping grizzly in him, yet all he was moved to say to his old friend was "There's a fundamental something you don't seem to understand, Fred. The difference between you and me is that the America I believe in allows me to express this opinion. The

America you believe in makes you come here to question me about it."

Goss grew impatient and snorted.

"You're about two hundred years behind the times with this shit. Wise up, Hiller. You've been in this business long enough to know that nothing gets overlooked, nothing comes cheap, and everyone is paid for in the end."

It was meant as a warning for the future. The Company didn't take lightly his dancing naked in the newspapers.

Goss strode from the house in a wave of triumphant defiance without the vaguest regard for the passing of their friendship, or the understanding that it was Jay Hiller who had truly been defiant.

From that day on, Hiller was certain that he was on the agency's "watch list."

Now, four years later, Goss stood before him with his laughing blue eyes, and while he remembered their last encounter, it no longer seemed important. Goss flashed his toothy smile and extended a hand. Hiller took it warmly. He hadn't aged much, Hiller thought. In fact he looked better—and that made him feel tired.

"I thought they turned you out to graze with all the other cows," Goss said.

Hiller smiled sardonically. "Another warm greeting like that, Freddy, and you'll be picking up your terrific teeth with a spoon."

Then they laughed together and almost immediately went to work. It was typical of both men that they spent less than a minute getting reacquainted before attacking the problem at hand. They agreed Goss should be the one to talk with Mark Kinstrey, the presidential press secretary, since Goss did not know him personally. He was also to try to trace the television equipment used in the penthouse suite of the St. Mark's Hotel. Goss listened patiently as Hiller went down a list of field officers in Central and South American countries whom he wanted checked for information on subversive activities that might possibly provide a tie-in with the kidnapping.

Then Goss said, "You know, it occurs to me the kidnappers might never leave the United States. It would be the last place we would look for them, eh? It would save them the problem of foreign entry. It would save them the difficulty of transportation and remaining undetected while harboring the President."

Hiller looked thoughtful for a moment and said quietly, "Sure, it's possible their aircraft is domestic and they are still in the States now. But I'm banking on getting Royce back, and once he's free, it would be suicide for them to remain here, wouldn't you think?"

Goss considered the reply carefully and silently. His only response was an impassive shrug.

Chapter 5

Lynn Carlisle pulled her collar to her throat and crossed against the light. The sky was a deep gray and the December wind whipped through the city streets with a fury, lashing her cheeks to a numbing redness.

She noticed that the stores were nearly deserted, the sidewalks even more so. The city's lampposts and storefronts were, ironically, decorated with an excess of wreaths and die-cut reindeer. But America was staying indoors, huddled with their television sets and daily newspapers for some sign—no, permission—that it would be okay to celebrate Christmas this year.

In spite of the media's attempts to explode each new development as if it were the heralded rescue of the President, she was struck by what little physical impact the kidnapping actually had made on the nation. What D.C. paranoia existed wasn't immediately visible.

Lynn remembered President Kennedy as she hurried up the block to the television station. The assassination had also occurred on a day near the end of the week shortly before another festive holiday—and nothing in the country had really changed then either. Granted there was a certain somberness that drew the nation together. But the buses ran, the stores opened, there were no riots or mass arrests. The impact on her ten-year-old life, however, had been devastating. There were tears instead of Thanksgiving as the family attended the Kennedy funeral in the living room of their Merrick, Long Island, home—the last Thanksgiving they would spend together.

Soon after, an invisible veil of death fell over her life, and within two years her mother and father were gone.

The thin red lips of an expressive mouth stiffened, and worry lines creased her brow. In the back of her mind Lynn wondered what in her personal life the kidnapping might trigger.

She pushed through the glass doors of WZBZ—nerve center of the Pan American Network—and waved complacently at the guard in the lobby. In a few hours she would be on, and she hadn't yet digested the news—or her dinner.

* * *

Secret Service agent Mike Popfinger waited in one of the conference rooms of the gargantuan GOB and in twenty minutes had filled a glass ashtray on the conference table with half-smoked cigarettes. He arrived looking as though he had been beaten into the ground. Ordinarily, his steel blue eyes, light brown curls, and waspish nose were like those of a ski hero. Today the skin was lemon-colored and the eyes hollow, as if the pupils had disappeared—though some measure of anger and frustration shone fiercely behind them.

Popfinger knew what was coming, another in a series of unpleasant confrontations. As supervising agent of the Secret Service White House Detail he was dodging grenades all over Washington—from the State Department to the Treasury Department to the White House press corps. People seemed to have very quickly forgotten that he lost three of his best men trying to prevent this thing from happening, he thought bitterly. And now someone had to be cut up and fed to the media lions, so it would be *his* Christian ass. Someone would also have the sullen task of visiting the families of agents Zones and Schiano, and that would have to be him too. And someone had to meet with the special investigator, who was now late, and again it fell to him.

Then there would be a face-off with the Bureau and a grilling by Secret Service Chief Philip Eisel.

In the three years he had been on the White House Detail no mention was ever made that he had done his job to perfection. In this kind of work you only received recognition if something went drastically wrong.

Popfinger anxiously shifted the weight of his lean body from one foot to another and felt a sudden impulse to urinate. He felt sick . . . and angry. He picked up the ashtray laden with butts and slowly turned it upside down. Ashes and filter tips poured onto the carpet. Then he suddenly flung the glass object across the room. It shattered against a wall just as Jay Hiller walked in.

Hiller, prone to similar fits himself, made no mention of the outburst. There were, of course, more important things on his mind than conducting a lecture in deportment on behalf of the GOB.

After a handshake, he motioned the embarrassed Popfinger to a chair and said, "If I understand your report correctly, you're conducting your own investigation into this, up to the point where your men were killed."

"Yes, that's right. We're covering it as a murder investigation of three of our agents."

"So that you will be in constant touch with us, turning over information that might help on this end."

"Of course."

"The two Secret Service men assigned to the President when he was kidnapped were both experienced, were they not?"

"Nineteen years between them. Both good men and qualified to handle their assignments."

Hiller glared at him.

"Apparently not," he said grimly, "or they would be alive today."

"That's not a fair assessment," the agent protested. "My men had an impossible job. The President's 'mingle freely' attitude only allows us to do so much."

"Can you tell me why, in that case, only one man was stationed on the roof of the St. Mark's Hotel?"

Popfinger shifted uneasily in his chair.

"There was no reason to expect . . ." His voice trailed off and he hesitated. There could be no faking it. "In retrospect it may have been a lapse . . ."

Hiller pinched the crab's-leg wrinkle between his brows. He sighed and spoke quietly.

"Don't you find that remarkable? That the organization responsible for the security of the President has a lapse in security?"

"It's not as if we were asleep," Popfinger said defensively. "We had more than two hundred agents and officers on duty, one of the beefiest details ever assigned for such a short visit. The hotel was reinforced with double security. The west penthouse was sealed from all traffic—there was only one to-and-fro access and that was covered.

"The building had been thoroughly checked numerous times. It all happened so fast. And then the ensuing confusion—nobody could believe it. We took every precaution. Nine hundred ninety-nine times out of a thousand . . ."

Hiller shot an angry glance in Popfinger's direction. He did not want to be among those kicking the man when he was down—but Popfinger was being utterly stupid.

"We're not dealing in percentage probabilities on paper, Mr. Popfinger! We're talking about what the hell happened at the hotel! Just what the hell happened? Who advanced for you and checked out the St. Mark's? Why was one agent alone on the roof? Who okayed the conditions for the interview of the President?"

To Mike Popfinger the questions were like a hangover that wouldn't quit. It was all he had been hearing since the abduction.

"Mr. Hiller, these same conditions have existed for scores of similar interviews. There was no reason to doubt the ef—"

"The fact that the same conditions have existed for scores of interviews should have been reason enough to alter them. Have you determined how that damn television crew got guns past your hotel security check?"

"Apparently they had weapons broken down and hidden inside the body of a TV camera. All media persons were security checked in the lobby, but logistically it would have been impossible for us to take apart every piece of equipment that came through there that day."

"Have you talked to your people who were manning security stations?"

"Of course. But none of them, unfortunately, can provide anything close to a description. Their accounts of the incident in detail are in your report."

"I saw the report," Hiller said impassively. "There were more hard facts on the six-o'clock news."

Popfinger held up his hands in front of his face as if to surrender. "All right, all right," he said in a voice that signaled compliance. "Of course we're investigating these things. Of course you'll get your answers. But you *are* aware this took place less than twenty hours ago. . . ."

Hiller shook his head and got to his feet.

"In twenty hours the tide goes in and out. In twenty hours millions are born and in twenty hours millions die. I don't want the President to be one of them. In twenty hours I'd like Royce back in the White House. Twenty hours from now I expect answers. And you goddamn better well have them!"

Popfinger blinked. He knew Hiller meant it. Literally.

A meeting with CIA director Wilson McAvee was about as appealing to Hiller as an asthma attack.

McAvee was a large menacing figure with thick white hair, a towering forehead and eyes that were like slits of blue ice. In spite of his advancing years, he was tailored and barbered to perfection and had an imposing dignity.

McAvee had had an impressive career which involved him in more international political theaters than any agent in the history of the CIA. After graduating Princeton and writing a book on World War II, he took a job with the American Embassy in Berne, Switzerland, and was later recruited by the newly-formed Central Intelligence Agency. As a field officer he worked effectively in Japan, Germany, Korea, Czechoslavakia, the Soviet Union, and some of the Latin-American nations.

In the mid-fifties he pinpointed a heavy weapons pipeline from Czechoslavakia to Puerto Barrios, and played a mysterious role in moving Guatemala away from communist rule.

Two years later he uncovered a plot to assassinate the American Vice President during a visit to Colombia and was subsequently awarded the Medal of Merit from President Eisenhower.

In 1959, McAvee was transferred to the Middle East on special assignment. His job was to keep King Hussein alive.

As a supervising agent in Laos, he maneuvered the Vietnam War by bribing Laotian generals with military supplies. Those who cooperated were given arms. Those who didn't were not. He allowed the opium trade to flourish as a means of payment for valued information and fed such selected details to Washington as he deemed appropriate to support his arguments for a particular strategy.

Under John Quinlan Royce, Wilson McAvee had become czar of the intelligence community. Reorganization gave him financial, if not operational, control of the National Security Agency, the National Reconnaissance Office, the Defense Intelligence Agency and the newly established National Intelligence Tasking Center which set priorities for intelligence gathering.

The revamping had two major effects: It made McAvee the most powerful CIA director ever and, more importantly, the second most powerful man in the government. And it caused the other intelligence agencies like the FBI to guard their own domains even more zealously than before. If they had been reluctant to trade information with the CIA in the past, they now looked upon McAvee and the Company as a threat to their very existence.

Of the infamous stories and half-truths that circulated around the Capitol, one caused Hiller to remark that McAvee gave reason to doubt that man is a warm-blooded animal.

The story involved a border war between Iran and Iraq. Responding to the pleas of the Shah of Iran, the CIA funneled money and support to the rebel Kurds who were revolting against the Iraqi government.

When Iran and Iraq a few years later settled their differences, the agency cut off arms and supplies to the Kurds so instantaneously that the rebels were left helpless. The Iraqis embarked on a merciless seek-and-destroy campaign, ferreting out their enemies and slaughtering thousands—their maimed and bloodied bodies strewn across the desert, while nearly a quarter million more fled the country. But McAvee, then deputy director of the CIA, refused aid of any kind. He said simply, "CIA work should not be confused with the Salvation Army."

If McAvee seemed not to consider the value of human life, it was because to him there was a greater value to consider—the preservation of the nation as world leader. This took precedence over all, he would have argued, and dictated his thinking. By pursuing the national interest and aggressively restricting the spread of communism it naturally followed that the value of human life would be considered, he said.

When Hiller broke with the agency, he charged McAvee with being so anticommunist that intelligence reports were rarely impartial. To please their superior, agents in the field would dig up what he wanted to hear. From Hiller's point of view Wilson McAvee was a sorcerer leading an army of lemmings on a thunderous march to the sea.

Hiller and McAvee clashed in style as well as philosophy. Hiller was the kind of person who would speak his mind because it was a necessity, a physical need, and perhaps regret his tactlessness later. McAvee could speak his mind with a condescension so lethal that it seemed to presuppose anything a listener might consider saying in response.

What these two diverse personalities did share was a fierce loyalty to the President.

McAvee entered the conference room, let the door slam, and sat down without a greeting.

"I hope you'll make a mental note that *I* came to *you*," he said gruffly.

"Absolutely, if you think it's part of the job."

McAvee bristled and cooked Hiller in his gaze.

"Get on with it," he snapped.

Hiller spoke in an easy but forceful manner.

"Since I am heading up this interagency investigation, which I think you'll agree should be every agency's first priority, I would like your assurances that information picked up in the field which pertains to this case will be directed to me personally before it is distributed elsewhere. It would be an embarrassment to me and to the investigation if it appeared our efforts were uncoordinated."

McAvee gave him a quick, sharp look. He faced a dilemma. The kidnapping itself did not reflect unfavorably on the Company because it was a domestic incident. But breaking the case, saving the President's life, apprehending the kidnappers with information supplied by the CIA would put the name of intelligence czar Wilson McAvee in history books. What bitter irony that the man who might do this for him was Jay Marvin Hiller.

"Yes, you have my assurances, Mr. Hiller," McAvee said, his cold blue eyes flaring. "But let me be frank. In spite of all that guff that appeared in the press about your illness forcing retirement, the fact that you are here now reaffirms my belief that you are more precisely a quitter. I find you crude personally and rather naive politically. You're a man who has garnered an excellent reputation, largely undeserved, through manipulation of the press and through associations with the First Family. Let me say that I only *accepted* you as head of this investigation because of the unbending insistence of the First Lady."

Hiller suppressed a sudden impulse to laugh.

"Thanks for your vote of confidence, Mr. McAvee," he said evenly. "And let me say that I only *accepted* the position as head of this investigation because the American people might be more interested in *solving* this case than in covering it up."

"You read too many newspapers," McAvee said, getting to his feet.

Hiller stopped him with a gesture.

"I have another request. Realizing the gravity and urgency of the case, I would also appreciate full clearance . . ."

McAvee cut him short.

"No," he said flatly. "I said you'll get whatever we have on the abduction. But I don't want you within a mile of any other agency business. If I find you are, I'll force it all the way to the wall with you. You're operating in the Company ballpark and you'll operate under my rules."

Hiller looked thoughtful for a moment and said searchingly, "What makes you so uncomfortable, Mr. Director?"

"Nothing, Hiller. Not a thing. I just don't like gnats in my grapefruit."

Chapter 6

On December ninth, at seven thirty on the morning following the kidnapping, the gears of government began to grind.

In the old Executive Office Building, Vice President Seymour Clayton, a balding man with a slight build and a small, round face hidden behind steel-rimmed glasses, cupped his elbows in his palms and tried to gather himself together with the help of a glass of bourbon.

It had been said of Clayton that even when he was sitting still he seemed to move nervously about like a chicken. Clayton feared public opinion and the newspapers perhaps more than he feared what the kidnappers might do. He fantasized editorials criticizing him for indecision and was determined to snuff out the imaginary printed word by acting quickly.

He thought of Lyndon Johnson and how Johnson,

through a peculiar mixture of fate and politics, had willingly taken on the role of national villain. The shaken country, one might have thought, would have looked to him for leadership and strength in its most precarious hours. But that had not happened. The Vietnam War became divisive, certainly, but even more than that, Clayton thought, Johnson could not get beyond the fact that his very presence reminded everyone of the man they had seen as the young light of the nation lying in state.

Now his own presence would remind the nation of Royce. Clayton could not hope to match his personality or his popularity. He did not have what Washington columnists were fond of calling "style."

Until now, he had been an unseen and unimportant man in government, shuffled under the White House carpet into obscurity. But now all heads were suddenly turned toward him for stability and guidance.

In the first few hours following the abduction, Clayton issued directives like the Mint issues dollars. He mobilized the National Guard in Washington, imposed a curfew of ten P.M., changed it to midnight, and then later rescinded it. He organized a meeting of the Executive Committee of the National Security Council, later to be known as the Ex Comm, composed of members of the President's Cabinet and high government officials.

He declared an "Orange Alert," and nuclear-armed bombers and jet fighters loaded to the nines with missiles roared into the heavens on patrol. All armed forces throughout the world were made combat-ready. All tactical air squadrons were set to strike. Ship and submarine patrols blanketed the coasts. Special low-profile emissaries were dispatched to allied nations to keep their governments informed of American maneuvers.

Clayton's job was to keep chaos from erupting—and chaos was always just around the corner.

In New York a group calling itself the Committee for a Democratic World lit fires in streetcorner oil drums on United Nations Plaza and marched with signs reading, "Death to All Terrorists" and "Avenge U.S. Bring the President Home." For no apparent reason, the Soviet Embassy in Washington was pelted with eggs. Police and firemen in Madison, Wisconsin, called off a bitter eleven-day strike and reluctantly returned to work without a settlement. In spite of hourly radio and television bulletins on the kidnap, newspapers from coast to coast were flooded with calls requesting the latest information. Clergy in dozens of small towns conducted twenty-four-hour prayer vigils. Citizens banding together placed full-page ads in print media, some advocating might and militancy, other reason and ransom. The occasional presence of jeeps and guardsmen in the streets and the roar of military planes overhead caused many to shudder fearfully and kept current events foremost in the minds of all.

The previous evening the Vice President had spoken on national television to reassure the country and ask for prayers for the President's safe return. Then he met with bipartisan leaders, and an emergency joint session of Congress was scheduled. Special agents in the intelligence community gave hourly reports to Clayton, Secretary of State Stephen Brownell, and Secretary of Defense Paul Garrett.

Clayton planned to ask the Ex Comm to draft a "policy paper" making contingency recommendations to cover all circumstances. UN Ambassador Roger Hofstaedter emphasized to the General Assembly the need for unilateral cooperation in closing off avenues to the kidnappers, who if successful might set a dangerous precedent.

Clayton and Brownell agreed that the National Guard should remain on duty in D.C. and on maximum alert throughout the rest of the country; that double security would be in effect around the clock at all government and defense installations; and that the Vice President would make no unusual decisions without consulting the Secretary of State. This last point, Brownell was convinced, had been agreed to only as a matter of courtesy and expediency. It was Clayton's style of diplomacy. He would say one thing to circumvent disagreements and then, if he felt strongly enough, do another.

Clayton was convinced the kidnapping was a leftwing plot engineered by the Soviet Union or Communist China. And Brownell had to admit he entertained the notion himself for a few moments. But that did not make sense. And Brownell knew very well why it didn't. The problem was he could not reveal the reasons.

Hiller heard FBI chief Douglas Padley's North Carolina accent as it echoed through the corridor and grew louder. There was also a second voice—less distinctive—mumbling prudent responses.

In a moment, sitting with him was the director of the Bureau, a massive blond-haired man of forty-nine with a broad chest and overdeveloped neck and shoulders, and his chief administrative assistant, George Berkquist.

Padley's physical presence made other men feel uncomfortable, and that had nothing to do with the .38-caliber revolver he always carried hidden with him. The feeling was impelled by his size. He was six feet six and two hundred forty pounds, with an immense square-shaped head, a page-white complexion, and large round eyes, savage and colorless, like those of a fish out of water. Hiller thought if he had to choose one person he would least like to meet in hand-to-hand combat, that person would have to be Douglas Padley.

Heads turned wherever he walked, and when he marched through the GOB to the Blue Wing conference rooms everyone he passed privately held their breaths.

Padley was an enigma. As deputy director of the Bureau, there had been rumors he had used the FBI to even personal scores, had embellished his powers, and had popularized the use of tax audits by the IRS as a means of harassment and revenge.

But after his appointment to the directorship Padley abruptly became a sentinel of honor, issuing strict reforms and operational restraints and even discharging those who were slow on the uptake. Even the old rumors stopped. Those who had lost their jobs were bitter and vocal. But since no one could prove that Padley had at one time been guilty of the same kind of rule-bending that he now refused to put up with, the name-calling died out.

There were polite handshakes all around as Berkquist set an attaché case on the table and handed a copy of a one-page memorandum to Hiller.

Hiller was glad the deputy was there. Berkquist was egoless, which was rare in the Bureau, and a mellowing influence on Padley. Like soothsayers to medieval kings, his main function seemed to be to counsel wisely. Unschooled observers assumed he was the brains behind the director's brawn, and physically he fit the part—spare and retiring, with a receding hairline and sad little eyes lowered in a professor's downward glance.

But Padley considered himself just as shrewd and would have bitterly extinguished such rumors, maybe even discharged his aide, except that he did not consider him a threat.

Berkquist shifted the glasses on his nose and spoke quietly. "As we have previously stated and in accordance with FBI policy, pertinent information from the Bufiles will be filtered to you whenever applicable."

"Yeah, it's the word 'filtered' I don't like," Hiller said.

Padley challenged him immediately.

"Cooperation to you is where everyone responds to your beck and call. You seem to forget, Mr. Hiller, we have our own agents to deal with, our own part in the investigation to pursue, as a matter of first priority. We can't be responsible for you too, son." The last word was elongated with a heavy drawl and was rich in its spitefulness.

The tone surprised Hiller. Perhaps he had underestimated the impact on the Bureau of McAvee's new powers as intelligence czar. Padley's protectiveness and defensiveness could not be allowed to fester.

Hiller said, "Let me preface this by saying I have an understanding of your position and your situation. But I think the gravity of the current crisis outweighs whatever insecurities each of us may have to deal with as a result of other conditions. . . ."

Padley was shaking his head before Hiller could finish.

"I think you misunderstood me, son. *You* have an investigation to conduct. *We* have an investigation to conduct. If we can tip you off on something without disrupting the momentum of our own work we will do it, surely. And we'll expect you to do the same. Otherwise I believe it's going to be kind of like a political fox hunt. Everyone wants to bag it and become a hero. Nothing new there."

Hiller's eyes become cold and fierce.

"That is precisely the kind of competitive attitude I'm trying to guard against. What do you think this is? I'm conducting an interagency investigation into the kidnapping of the President; I'm not asking to borrow a quarter. This will not degenerate into a contest between the FBI, the Secret Service, and the CIA to see who can save America. Do you follow me?"

Padley frowned. "I follow you, son, but I'm afraid a lot of the information you already requested is classified."

"I don't give a shit if it's sealed in a time capsule," Hiller snapped. "If you give me trouble on this, Mr. Padley, I'll pin your ass to the Washington Monument."

The December sun did little to temper the bitter cold of late afternoon. Gusts of wind swept across the quad in front of the Washington Monument and blew leaves and dust in the faces of lonely stragglers.

Across Seventeenth Street the water in the Lincoln Memorial reflecting pool, usually like a mirror, beat roughly against the concrete siding.

Hiller and Secretary of State Stephen Brownell, wrapped in overcoats with upturned collars, fought the gusts for every step they took. Brownell was ill at ease and punctuated his words with awkward gestures from the shoulders. He was a short, rotund man in his late fifties with glittering eyes, crooked teeth, and slicked-back brown hair. A survivor of a light plane crash twelve years earlier, the secretary still had to fight cricks in his back and looked more like a butcher than someone who ran the foreign policy of the United States.

And now, fat-cheeked and red and breathing visible breaths into the air, he looked as if he had just stepped out of a meat locker. Brownell had a keen, penetrating mind and was credited by Royce with creating what had been considered a high point in American prestige abroad. Now he considered how tenuous that prestige appeared to be and how quickly the foundations that had been laid so carefully during the President's first three years in office could come toppling.

There was an undeniable sense of urgency. Without attracting too much attention, he had to get in touch with the Soviet ambassador and make contact with the representatives of the People's Republic of China. If Vice President Clayton began making insinuations or publicly started calling the kidnapping a leftist plot, it was sure to have a snowballing effect and would put an end to the administration's political harvest.

Brownell took Hiller by the arm and spoke forcefully.

"A lot is happening very quickly and we may not have the opportunity to talk as often as we'd like. I'll let you know of anything significant that breaks in the Ex Comm's 'war council.'

"I know you're under a good deal of pressure as it is, but I'm afraid I have to add to it. Over and above the obvious reasons for negotiating a quick return of the President, there are additional circumstances as well. For one thing, as a so-called precaution, Clayton is considering suspending civil liberties and declaring martial law. . . ."

Hiller was astonished. "Can he do that without Congress?"

"Under a provision in the Constitution governing national crises, yes."

"Jesus, Brownie! Does he think turning Nazi is going to help matters?"

"He says martial law was instituted in Canada during the kidnapping of Pierre Laporte, the municipal affairs minister, and that without it Quebec would have been lawlessness and anarchy."

Hiller shook his head. "If he's going to use that as a precedent, we'd better forget about Royce. Laporte was murdered by his kidnappers."

Brownell nodded quickly. "Yes, I know. My main concern is this: A meeting of the utmost urgency has been set for the twenty-first between the Chinese Communist Party chairman, the Soviet premier and the President. Nobody knows of it, not even the Vice President. But if he has to attend in place of the President, it could be suicide for the nation."

"What's the summit about?"

"I'm afraid I can't be specific. Just realize it is urgent."

"Is it possible news of the conference leaked and provided someone with a motive for kidnapping?"

"Of course it's possible. But it seems to me very unlikely. So far as I'm aware only the principals involved know. That means you're accusing Chernyenko or Teng Hsaio-Ping directly. And even then I don't see a motive."

"Who would stand to gain from the meeting not taking place?"

The secretary shrugged. "Nobody."

"So what you're asking me to do is perform a very quick miracle."

Brownell nodded. He had a very grave expression on his face.

"I don't like the electricity that Padley and McAvee send out," Hiller said. "It's not conducive to miracles."

"I'll ask the attorney general to talk with Padley. If McAvee appears to be giving you difficulty, it's no doubt because he feels you usurped his role as intelligence ringleader. I doubt he would carry it so far as to jeopardize what you're doing."

"Then you might want to ask why he's given me two of the greenest kids in the agency to work with," he said with a touch of derision.

"Does that matter? I mean for desk-top intelligence work?"

"Anyone new or inexperienced always costs you something."

Brownell looked thoughtful for a moment and said, "I'll speak to him."

A few minutes later, he was off to join members of the Ex Comm. Hiller lingered awhile at the foot of the reflecting pool, feeling dwarfed by the impressive structure of the Lincoln Memorial, particularly in light of the talk with the secretary.

"Do the impossible"—that was all anybody wanted. He sighed, brushing the windblown hair from his brow, and had a fleeting daydream of napping under a shade tree with a beer and a nectarine at his side. He hadn't a care in the world, and the weather was perfect.

It was so cold today that his lips were getting numb. The kidnappers would make contact soon, he thought, and they would make him move fast with no spare time to maneuver. What would they demand? What connection, if any, was there to the summit? And what could he do about any of it?

Chapter 7

In the makeup room at WZBZ, Lynn Carlisle dusted her cheeks with one last slap of powder and raced down the hallway to Studio B. She took her place behind a long desk with built-in television monitors and clipped a tiny microphone to her blouse. One of the cameramen made an offhand remark about the microphone and her breasts. She chose to ignore it.

Lynn breezed through the national edition of network news—there was only one story this day—and taped a lead-in for airing later. With the completion of the tape, Studio B turned into a playground. Lynn freed herself of the microphone and looked for an exit. Telephones rang. Cameramen shoved their huge cameras into corners and shouted obscenities. Technicians moved heavy wires or crushed paper into balls and bounced them off the heads of colleagues. The assistant news director swung Tarzan-like across the set on a rope suspended from the ceiling.

One of the sound technicians signaled Lynn from across the studio and waved a telephone receiver in the air. She weaved her way to the phone through the activity, enduring a paper ball which bounced off her forehead and which she good-naturedly fired back at her assailant.

Either the caller spoke too softly or the noise in Studio B was inordinately loud (she would later not remember which) but she had to plug an ear to be able to listen.

The caller spoke deliberately, emphasizing each word equally in a deep monotone that sounded like a primitive instrument in mourning. It unnerved her. The final words spoken were "Do you understand?"

She nodded, gasped, and threw back her head before uttering an affirmative reply. The caller hung up.

She stood holding the receiver, with the bewildered expression of a lost tourist, hypnotized by the suddenness with which the events she had just broadcast had become an integral part of her life. Was it possible or was it a prank? No, you could always tell a prankster. But why? Why her?

For a moment the voice became familiar and played again in her head. Then it was lost in the ruckus of Studio B.

The technician looked questioningly at her.

"Are you okay, Lynn?"

She made a complacent gesture and stuttered over her first few words.

"Wh—wh—what was that guy's name, the one heading the presidential investigation?"

"Hiller, wasn't it?"

During the half hour that Lynn Carlisle was broadcasting the evening news, Jay Hiller was almost constantly on the telephone. Fred Goss, special operations chief of the CIA, called to say he had learned from White House press secretary Mark Kinstrey that the President himself had initially approved conditions for the interview at the St. Mark's Hotel. It had been set up through Kinstrey's office by phone shortly before Thanksgiving by a Frank Mayberry of station WFFV in Atlanta. Hiller suggested that a visit there might be in order and Goss agreed. It was the first solid lead they had to work with.

A second call came from the lab. They had checked over the television equipment that had been impounded from the St. Mark's Hotel suite and traced it to a manufacturer in Chicago. The manufacturer told a field agent the equipment had been stolen in October from a warehouse. The agent was checking the story with police.

The phone rang again. It was Secret Service deputy Mike Popfinger. Hiller smiled a little to himself—Popfinger moved fast when he had to. In a voice hurried by apparent nervousness he told Hiller what Fred Goss had already relayed—that the Atlanta press conference had been set up by phone and that conditions had been approved by the President. The one thing he added was that originally the interview was to have taken place on the second floor. That was why only one man had been stationed on the roof.

"Who okayed the switch of rooms?" Hiller asked.

The deputy thought a moment and said hesitantly, "We proposed the switch because the balconies on other floors would have looked down on the President's suite. I don't know who on his staff gave us the final go-ahead."

Hiller's voice was surprisingly calm. "Find out," he said.

When Jay Hiller put down the receiver, his young aides Jack Albaum and Jeff Brodsky were standing at his desk with a tape recorder and faces brimming with enthusiasm. Brodsky's charmingly curious eyes flashed confidently as he pushed a button on the machine and said, "This is the only one we've received that sounds legit."

Hiller sighed, leaned back in his chair and listened to a deep throaty voice on the tape.

"The President is in good health and will be set free upon receipt of seventy-five million dollars in U.S. currency. The ransom should be placed in a black leather satchel with zippered top and left underneath the southeast viaduct of the Sousa Bridge near Anacostia Freeway. This is the only message you will receive. If you hope to see the President alive again, you will follow it to the letter."

Hiller glared into a full-spectrum light and saw colored dots when he blinked his eyes. Slowly he let out a long breath of air, making his lips putter childishly.

"Dump it," he ordered. There was a slight trace of contempt in the tone.

Brodsky looked flustered. "Why?" he exclaimed.

"Why else? It's phony."

It was then that Brodsky felt a sudden urge to land a punch. Both he and Albaum had listened to the tape a dozen times and each time it rang true. What made Hiller dismiss their deductions so frivolously?

Hiller looked them over with a penetrating gaze. He was controlled but slightly irritated and said in a condescending way, "No kidnapper interested in a seventy-five million dollar ransom is going to overlook a detail like *when* he wants it delivered."

Brodsky felt his body sag. He was so anxious for this to be the real thing that he had been careless. Albaum only shrugged and walked away. The interoffice phone buzzed and wakened Jeff from his defeat. Hiller leaned forward to pick it up.

"Yeah, that's right, I want the videodisc files *and* one thousand two hundred sixteen vertical files *with* photographs," he said sharply. "Look, I don't care if it weighs more than the Library of Congress. Get 'em over here."

One of the outside lines rang and Brodsky answered it. He listened a moment and caught Hiller's attention with a timid gesture. Hiller covered the mouthpiece.

"What is it?"

"Lynn Carlisle," said Jeff. "From Pan Am Network news. . . ."

"No interviews, for crissakes," Hiller snapped. "Tell her to speak to the press officer."

He returned to his call but Brodsky persisted.

"She says it's an emergency."

"Everything's a goddamn emergency. . . . I'll call you back," he cried, slamming down one receiver and picking up the other. Hiller listened and said nothing for nearly a full minute. And then, excited, he rose from his chair and said into the phone, "Where are you located? . . . Ten minutes! Farragut North station in ten minutes!"

At 7:28 P.M. Jay Hiller parked his car in front of a fast-food joint called Best of the Wurst and went inside the Farragut North station, where it took a moment for his eyes to adjust to the light. The D.C. Metro was hospital-clean and cold, its arched ceiling of gray stone and recessed geometry like something from a science-fiction movie.

It was odd to see it completely empty when so many times the scene had been a contest of gladiators elbowing their way to a train.

There were no greetings of the season plastered about, only billboards on the walls touting gift suggestions. One had been prominently scribbled on: "George Orwell was an optimist."

Hiller sniggered to himself and grimly thought it prophetic. Then the trace of amusement vanished. He remembered that Orwell's literary counterpart, Aldous Huxley, had died the same day as Royce's political counterpart, John Kennedy.

A long corridor led to a row of turnstiles and a glass

booth manned by a municipal guard. Hiller showed his agency ID and was waved through. He hurried down an escalator that wasn't operating and near the bottom of the landing felt a rush of cold air on his face, the pneumatic whoosh of a rubber-wheeled train forcing gusts of wind out of the station as it sped away.

In a moment he was on the platform, alone. Bright red and blue enamel tiles in chessboard pattern ran along the walls. He shuddered, imagining someone breaking a tooth on them.

Abruptly the afternoon meeting with Brownell came back to him. Presumably he was the only man in Washington to have been informed about the summit conference. Was there a connection between it and the kidnapping? And if so, what the hell could it be? Hiller paced back and forth at the end of the platform, looking around impatiently. In front of a No Smoking sign he lit a cigarette and checked his watch. The girl was going to be late.

His mind raced frantically and he began muttering to himself. This *had* to be the contact from the kidnappers. Crank calls came directly to him—they didn't bother with an intermediary. And if he guessed right, he would soon know two things: how desperate these individuals were and what they were asking.

That in itself might scatter the veil of dust and make all the difference in the world as to whether he could be assured of the President's life. At least now there might be *something* to follow, no matter how hidden, no matter how obscured.

Like the tap of a dancer or the click of a castanet, a cadence of heels echoed through the station and scattered his thoughts. A shapeless figure in a heavy overcoat, with reddish brown hair stuffed under a longshoreman's cap and a pocketbook slung over a shoulder, rushed up the platform leaving clouds of carbon dioxide in her path like a steam engine. It was Lynn Carlisle as her audience had never seen her.

"I'm sorry I'm late," she cried even before reaching him. "I had trouble getting a cab."

Hiller glanced at her amusedly and suddenly burst into violent laughter. He had trouble getting his breath and when he did finally, he said through teary eyes, "You run into a pumpkin or something? What'd you do to your face?"

Lynn flushed with embarrassment.

"It's television makeup, Mr. Hiller," she said bristling, and her tiny nose flared defiantly. "I left it on to compete with your ghoulish personality."

Her skittishness surprised him. After all, she worked in a carnivorous profession in a carnivorous town. Political journalists often spent their most productive years crawling through the heap and rubble of small town newspapers and television stations before finally getting a shot at Washington. And then with all the competition, they could get skimmed off the top in one short kill-or-be-killed season. But she was already at the top—nationally known, a network personality, with as much security as the profession allowed. Even at her age—he guessed early thirties—Lynn Carlisle had to have survived a hell of a lot worse than his mocking outburst or she would have been gone a long time.

"All right, all right. I'm sorry," he said with a frown. He touched her shoulder in a peacemaking gesture—and then felt awkward.

"Now that we're best of friends, what have you got for your old buddy?"

Lynn silently considered his apology. She smiled faintly and pulled a note pad from her overcoat.

"They want five hundred million dollars in seven

days—by December sixteenth—and will contact me later with specific directions as to where and when. Any attempt to abort their plan will . . ."

Only a few seconds had passed when Lynn's words no longer made sense. They seemed to be calling at him from far away. Hiller dropped his cigarette. Her voice became fainter until it was lost completely, lost in the sudden something that was so much more important, lost in a throaty wheeze that emanated from deep in his chest, in the violent ringing in his ears, in the dreamless desire to finally surrender his body.

Hiller felt his face flush with blood. O God, now? Why *now*? His eyes became glassy. His limbs began to tremble. There was the familiar weakness in the knees.

Blindly his fingers groped through pockets. Blindly they picked about for the nebulizer. Ashamed, he turned his back to Lynn and shoved the instrument in his mouth. The sweet mist that fell on his throat and lungs was like the breath of a sudden savior blowing air into a collapsing balloon. He felt lightheaded for a moment and bent over. But the danger had passed. Again the scale had been righted.

"My God," Lynn said, horrified. "And you *smoke*?"

"It's still *legal*, y'know," he replied facetiously. His voice barely registered. Lynn's big oval green eyes widened with concern.

"Are you all right?" she asked.

Hiller straightened.

"Yeah, yeah. A little asthma. Happens every time I have to put together five hundred million dollars in seven days."

There was a slight trace of a motherly pout on her thin strawberry lips. She resisted an impulse to touch him. Hiller must have sensed it because he became painfully aware of her sympathy. It made him more uncomfortable.

"Go on!" he cried impatiently.

"Of all things to . . . I mean, how can you do that to yourself? Why do you *smoke*?"

"I'm trying to get lung cancer so the asthma won't bother me so much. What else did they tell you?"

Lynn decided quickly to drop her crusade.

"That's it. Except that if you don't do it their way, the President dies. 'Will be *executed*,' they said."

"Great." Hiller's voice was sarcastically light.

The conditions were unrealistic: five hundred million dollars in seven days. There was no room for negotiation, no time to stall or to plot heroics, as he had expected. There was only time to get the ransom together and hope to God they would let Royce go.

They had given no information that they didn't need to, and there was no way of knowing where they were operating from. Hiller was sure these were the men. But he asked anyway, "What assurances do we have that they *are* the kidnappers?"

"They said they'll be sending proof."

He shivered and felt bumps rise on his flesh as he fantasized dismemberment. Then he quickly put it out of his mind.

"All right, since they're going to contact you again, I'll want to send some people over to your station to set up for voiceprint."

"That should be no problem."

"Did the caller give you any clue as to who we're dealing with? Did they speak with an accent of any kind? Did they mention any group claiming responsibility for the kidnapping?"

Lynn replayed the call in her head, but she knew she hadn't overlooked anything. Hiller asked questions just like the news director at WZBZ.

"The only thing that might be of help is a tape the network shot. I checked with our sister stations and learned we've got twenty-four minutes at the St. Mark's Hotel lobby just before the kidnapping."

Hiller was stunned.

"Christ, you mean nobody from intelligence called for that? How soon can I get it?"

"It should be here in the morning. If you stop by the office tomorrow we can take a look on some of the world's finest video equipment."

For the first time Hiller let the warmth shine through in his eyes. He smiled at her. Lynn liked him decidedly better than she had a moment earlier.

Chapter 8

December 10.

At 8:30 the next morning Jay Hiller called Phyllis Royce to tell her of the ransom demand and then took a cab to the Capitol to attend an emergency joint session of Congress. It was sunny and cold.

None of the usual tour groups or guides or amateur photographers pigeoned about the grounds. National Guard patrols were stationed in and around the area supplementing the Capitol Police. Newsmen and newswomen were barred from the building but hung out in the parking lot at the East Front entrance where Emanuel Springer, president pro tempore of the Senate, had promised to answer questions following the emergency meeting.

Hiller slipped around to the West Front entrance without being recognized. Two guardsmen who were telling jokes and laughing among themselves quickly passed him through. Tucked under his arm in a manila envelope was what the kidnappers had promised less than thirteen hours ago. Proof they had the President.

At Station WZBZ, Lynn Carlisle came in several hours early to get a first look at the videotape from Atlanta. If there was a way to beat the other stations and print media to relevant information on the kidnapping, she would find it. She was not going to wait until Jay Marvin Hiller issued a general press release about something her own network provided. That's not how one stayed ahead in this business. She couldn't remain one of the nation's better-known reporter/newscasters by preening her tail feathers.

She was pretty enough all right, and there were those, fueled by jealousy, who theorized that she had bedroomed her way up the ladder. But her looks had had nothing to do with her breaking open the Blue Chip congressional payola scandals of several years ago or linking former presidential aide Marsh Collyer to a multimillion-dollar land fraud scheme. Those stories were the result of quite another part of her life—a most private part—which had earned her first the network's top reporter slot, then a job as anchor on the evening news, and now just about any assignment she cared to cover. In fact, since her divorce five years ago, Lynn had dedicated so much of her life to her career—a career that consistently demanded the straight, impartial, cerebral retelling of facts—that she sometimes felt completely out of touch with her sensibilities.

In such times she fell into an uncompromising depression, locked herself away in her apartment and, after days of brooding, wondered if the reason no one important shared her life was because she was an emotional animal prowling the wrong jungle. Too old to cry, she thought, and too lonely to laugh alone.

Inevitably what brought her around was another big story, restoring her fully to a world of hard facts, deadlines, blood-letting competition, and rewards. And for all that had consumed her and made her suffer, the cause became the cure.

As Lynn Carlisle threaded a videotape player in a private viewing room, Ruppert Knapp, the general manager of WZBZ, came in with another man. Knapp introduced Fred Goss and then cast a disparaging glance in her direction. "You know you're not supposed to touch those machines," he said.

"We're in a national crisis, Rup," Lynn said with half a smile. "Union rules are temporarily suspended."

He shook his balding head in a fatherly way.

"Mr. Goss is from the interagency task force and would like to see the tape—and so would I, if you've no objection to sitting with us in the dark."

Lynn looked questioningly at Fred Goss. "I thought Mr. Hiller was coming over. . . ."

Goss said patiently, "I imagine he is—but in an investigation of this magnitude, Miss Carlisle, there's bound to be some overlap. Mr. Hiller is in congressional session this morning and I have to be in Atlanta this afternoon. Since we're working on different phases of the inquiry and are operating on different timetables, this kind of duplication will sometimes be unavoidable."

Lynn, Knapp, and Goss viewed the tape in absolute

silence. Goss took several notes and seemed to have anticipated the result. He got up, thanked her, and left with Knapp.

Lynn was disappointed. There were no scoops on this tape. She lit a cigarette, remembered suddenly that she had, eight weeks ago, given up smoking, and tossed it to the floor.

In the House Chamber, every senator and congressman grabbed for a look at an eight-by-ten photograph of John Quinlan Royce with a sign across his chest that read Kidnapped.

It rang of the huge courtroom dramas, with its Exhibit A, stenographer, speaker's rostrum, and elevated judicial bench front and center. Nine semicircular rows styled in natural mahogany to match the chamber walls, as well as dozens of folding chairs in the aisles, were filled to capacity. There were many more present than anyone had expected, what with vacationing politicians out of reach, the relatively short time since the abduction, and the logistics of getting to Washington on short notice under guard. No member of the House or Senate was permitted to travel without one, a direct order from the Vice President.

Vice President Clayton, who normally chaired joint sessions, decided not to attend, fearing that his presence might cause some senators or representatives to say things they believed he wanted to hear. He also felt his presence might prove otherwise divisive. There was no need to encourage partisan debate in this matter. Instead he would meet with the Ex Comm while president pro tem Springer took over the chair.

Springer was not entirely concerned with maintaining decorum, though it was doubtful he could have done anything about it even if he had been. Nerves were on edge. Shouts frequently erupted from the gallery. Each time, the chairman's gavel rapped for order. It was hard to imagine how Clayton's presence could have made it any more disruptive. Democrats clamored for heroics. Republicans called for restraint.

House Minority Leader Philip Basilio expressed skepticism over the evidence and cried out, "This could be trick photography or some such thing. We need more than a photograph for five hundred million dollars, Mr. Hiller."

Hiller shook his head. "What would you suggest, a finger or an ear? Would you like them to start dismembering the President?"

"Of course not," Springer interjected, "but you must realize this isn't penny ante we're talking about. This is . . . this is the future of the nation. This affects the entire sphere of American influence in the world. They'll have to give us more proof."

"That's just it, Mr. Chairman. They don't *have* to gave us a goddam thing."

"We don't even know if we can legally appropriate the money," one congressman shouted. Hiller recognized Earl Morris Kenyon of Tennessee, a moon-faced politician who believed in U.S. world supremacy and taxation without representation, and who had somehow managed to stay in office for twenty years in spite of his vigorous opposition to spending for anything but defense.

"Where would you suggest this huge sum come from," Kenyon demanded.

Hiller could not resist. "Vote for one less rocket this year, for crissakes," he said.

"That's absurd," Kenyon said with disgust in his voice. "I reiterate my earlier remark—the presidency is *not* what we are ransoming here. It is the individual who *occupies* the presidency."

"With all due respect, Congressman, you couldn't be

more wrong," said Representative William Allabone of Ohio. "It's not the individual we are ransoming, it's what the individual stands for."

Senator Richard Wainwright called out: "What the individual stands for, or what the office stands for? In effect, we *are* ransoming the presidency."

Senator Perry Jedlicker, who perceived Congress as a fraternity of the privileged, leapt on Wainwright's words with a sudden vengeance. He spoke so forcefully and so aggressively that it shocked the younger politicians in the chamber. The veterans knew what Jedlicker was doing—he had contempt for first-term senators who tried to express too many ideas in their first few years in Washington and he would intimidate them, if he could, into submission.

But Wainwright wasn't waffling. He called Jedlicker "a bully who operates on simpleminded fascist principles," and the two went at each other, shouting across the floor until they were restrained by their constituents.

Again Springer was on his gavel, but it was Jay Hiller's voice which finally commanded attention.

"I've been listening to legislative bickering for two and a half hours. We have a *man* whose life is at stake. He happens to be President and as such he represents this nation. Now, do the members of the Senate and the House of Representatives want to ranson him, or do they not?"

"Forgive me, sir, but it is not as simple a question as you pose," Senator John Link said in a slow Oklahoma drawl. "We have a lot of moral issues to contend with. There is a fundamental responsibility to the people of this country and a fundamental question that must be answered. Is any one man, no matter who he is, worth all that money? Do we kowtow to pirates and bend our knees to madmen?"

Kenyon chimed in again. "We can pay the money and still not get him back."

Hiller let his arms drop to make his exasperation obvious. He sighed and spoke quietly. "That is true. But it is also the best chance at the moment of saving the President's life."

"If we refuse the ransom, isn't it possible the kidnappers might just abandon their scheme?" Basilio asked.

Hiller looked disbelievingly at him, his mouth agape. Finally he said, "Pardon me, Mr. House Minority Leader. I realize this is the nation's capital of stupid remarks. But that is the fucking stupidest remark I have ever heard. . . ."

Laughter mixed with hushed outrage sounded through the chamber. Springer pounded the gavel. He gave Hiller a quick sharp look and introduced all the authority of his office in his voice.

"We're all aware the situation is grave, Mr. Hiller, but please, this *is* a congressional meeting."

Hiller was surprised by Springer's dignity.

"I apologize," he said, and after a brief pause added, "All right, let me put it another way. This is not a game these people are playing. This is an elaborate, well-planned, and well-executed scheme. It will not be abandoned. As I see it, whether or not to vote the ransom can be answered by asking yourselves a single question: Can we afford to let the world know we made no attempt to ransom the President of our own nation?"

Jay Hiller picked up his car at the underground parking lot and drove to WZBZ after gulping a disastrous hamburger which kept repeating on him. He felt decidedly geriatric as he rode an elevator to the second floor of the station instead of tackling a flight of stairs.

The congressional singsong of the morning played with his head the way the burger did with his stomach—both were rank and overdone. How long would it take the elected representatives of the people to realize they had no choice? They *had* to come through with the money or forfeit the drum-thumping concept of America as world leader.

In an ironic turnaround of the time-is-money principle of the nation's economy, money now meant time. Before the President could be found or a realistic hope born to a solution, Hiller had to have a little time. The only thing he needed more was a little rest. He would gladly have paid a ransom for a nap.

The elevator doors slid open, and Hiller stepped into a hallway buzzing with activity. Men and women raced up and down the aisles with such obvious determination that they reminded him of soldiers being deployed for battle. There was one familiar face on the floor—Henry Yamamura, a voiceprint specialist, who leaned against a wall in the foyer sipping coffee and watching the activity with some amusement.

Hiller greeted him and said, "You got it in already?"

"All set. Get me eighteen seconds and I'll have it traced."

"Where did you set up?"

"In there," Yamamura said, nodding to a door diagonally opposite the elevators. "Ask them to call anytime."

"Do my best. Where can I find Lynn Carlisle?"

Yamamura pointed the way.

Hiller found Lynn at a file cabinet with her back to the door, blue-penciling a wire-service story. When she turned around he registered such surprise that she had to smile to herself.

Stripped of her shapeless winter overcoat and orange television makeup, Lynn Carlisle was a very attractive woman. He suddenly felt like the clod in the movies who removes his secretary's glasses and says, "Why, Miss Jones, you're beautiful."

Now her flowing chestnut-brown hair, hidden last night by a longshoreman's cap, brushed her shoulders with subtle curls and accentuated her thin strawberry-red mouth. A tiny birthmark, barely visible, registered just left of center on the bridge of her nose. And her huge oval eyes in the afternoon light became a mysterious whitewater pale green.

She did not seem like a hustling, aggressive career woman. Now there shone a softness. More than that, the vulnerability that had caught him by surprise at the Metro station was evident in the way her voice sometimes broke, even when she was not speaking emotionally.

Lynn and Hiller greeted each other. She threw the wire story on her desk and smiled.

"Listen, about last night—I'm sorry I was so touchy . . . I was tired. I'd like to think I'm not always so sensitive. I'm sure you must have had more on your mind than my vanity."

Hiller watched her a moment with quiet, understanding sympathy and said, "I guess I could have said hello before I laughed in your face—but I'm famous for my Paleolithic diplomacy. My apologies." He smiled a little. "Let's grab some coffee and check out the videotape."

Lynn had just flipped on the monitor in the viewing room when there was a knock on the door and Jeff Brodsky walked in with a folder and a small package. Hiller, sitting with his feet propped on another chair, asked with some surprise, "What are you doing here?"

"I brought the list you asked for . . ."

Hiller looked at him, puzzled.

". . . from intelligence research files on subversive organizations," Brodsky said.

Hiller suddenly remembered and said complacently, "Oh, oh, oh, oh . . ."

He gave it a quick read. "Fine. Long as you're here, grab a seat."

He introduced Jeff to Lynn as Jeff handed him a package wrapped in wax paper.

"Brought you an avocado-and-beansprout sandwich. Whole-wheat roll," said Brodsky.

Hiller smiled. "Thanks kid, but the Wheat Germ Brigade is too late. I think I had my last meal an hour ago. Microwaveburger, pickles and relish, enriched white bun. Tasted like a brick. Nothing will ever go through my stomach again."

Jeff and Lynn laughed a little. She then called their attention to the videotape. Interiors of the St. Mark's Hotel flashed on the screen: the lobby, the front desk, the flocked walls, the boutique, a few people passing in and out of the camera's eye.

Then Lynn said matter-of-factly, "What did you think of the proposal the Joint Chiefs came up with today?"

Hiller started. "What proposal?"

"You didn't hear? It's on the wires already. I was reading it when you came in before."

"I haven't heard a thing," he said, "I've been at the congressional meeting all morning."

Lynn explained it with a certain smug satisfaction—she was briefing a federal investigator on a development at the Pentagon.

"As part of a search-and-destroy mission, the military wants to strafe the Everglades."

Hiller shook his head. "I ask for reconnaissance

planes, they give me bombers. If it wasn't so pitiful, it'd be laughable. The President has been kidnapped, so blow up the alligators."

"Why the Everglades?" Brodsky asked.

Lynn replied, "I guess because it was the last place the kidnappers were monitored."

"Jeff, one of us will have to remind those geniuses that it was also the last place the *President* was monitored."

"They don't really think the kidnappers are going to hang out there and wait for them, do they?" Jeff asked.

Hiller smirked. "I don't know what the hell they think."

The playback on the video was becoming animated. It showed newsmen jamming together, camera crews moving in, unpacking, hooking up their equipment.

"Looks like a Sunday flea market," Lynn said casually.

"Right there!" Hiller cried, leaping from the chair. "Back it up and let's see it again."

Lynn was puzzled. There was nothing there she could detect. She rewound the tape and started it a second time. Hiller crouched in front of the screen. He followed the action of the camera crews while Lynn and Brodsky tried to pick up on what he saw. But this section of the tape seemed no different from everything else they had been looking at.

"Again!" Hiller ordered. And again Lynn reversed the videotape and started it rolling forward.

"Stop," he cried, and she immediately hit the controls. Now they had a still picture of the crowded hotel lobby.

"Can we come in on this?" he asked. "You see, way in the background, by the elevators?"

Lynn fiddled with a knob, and they looked at a shot of five men carrying television equipment.

"Closer. Can you get closer?"

Lynn worked the picture. "That's maximum, right there."

"Fine. Now run that for me in slow motion. Can you?"

In slow motion they were able to see five men entering the elevators with hardware. Hiller had it replayed two more times, noting in several places the specific stills he wanted lifted from the tape. He was excited and didn't hide it. It was the first flicker of hope in what till now had been a sea of useless data, false starts, and dead ends. Hiller looked again at the freezeframe on the screen.

"Kind of fuzzy," he said, smacking his lips, "but the best we got. Jeff, I want these blown up and made into eight-by-ten glossies. Send them first to all the intelligence agencies for possible ID and match-up in their photo files.

"Tell them after they've run it through their computers, I want them rechecked individually by intelligent, functioning human beings. Second, every station chief and division head in the intelligence community is also to get copies. And third, get prints of these pictures on every goddam Telex in the country. It's time for the media to lend a hand."

Lynn had known what was coming, but she made no effort to hide her disappointment.

"Great. A real WZBZ exclusive," she said sourly.

Hiller put an arm around her. "Think of it as a sacrifice for freedom and democracy, sweetheart."

Lynn made a pained smile.

A secretary with a corsage on her blouse poked her head in the room and told Lynn she had a call. Lynn wished her a happy birthday and followed her down the hallway to a telephone. Hiller was on her heels, after tipping off Yamamura.

"If it's *the* call, stay on as long as you can," he said to her. "Give us time to trace and print it."

She gave a complacent wave, but there was a trembling in her breast when she lifted the receiver and spoke her name. The voice on the other end sounded like someone had run over it with a truck, and for the first few moments Lynn concentrated on the voice rather than the words. Then she began to understand and held her breath. She blinked. She stared at Hiller, who waited impatiently, gesturing helplessly, with his palms to the ceiling. Suddenly she was nodding.

Hiller flew down the hallway and was on Henry Yamamura's back in a matter of seconds. Yamamura had the tape recorder going and worked over a computer board quickly and skillfully, even with an audience.

In seconds he had the call amplified so that Hiller could listen in. Hiller lit a cigarette and popped it in Yamamura's mouth. He lit a second for himself. Orange and green numbers flashed across the computer board. A grid on the telescreen zeroed in on a street map. Yamamura scribbled on a pad, tore off the top sheet and held it up in the air. Hiller grabbed it and flew out the door.

A two-year-old supercharged Pontiac Puma tore out of the WZBZ parking lot with the acceleration of a torpedo. It shot across three lanes of traffic, laying bold black streaks of rubber, and jumped the divider in the middle of the road to cut off a U-turn. Jay Hiller straightarmed the horn and drove the accelerator into the floor. The car screamed down North Capitol Street, veering into oncoming lanes of traffic to pass slow-moving vehicles. He made a left onto Massachusetts Avenue in front of two speeding taxis and was nearly forced into a head-on with a trailer truck.

Hiller felt a heavy pounding in his temples. He tried not to blink. He challenged two red lights and at the second picked up a siren and a patrol car.

Now the Pontiac flew down Fourth Street into the southeast section of the city. Hiller turned a corner too tightly and smashed through a group of garbage pails, strewing the contents across the street. He pounded his fist on the horn, now in staccato, and forced a terrified black woman in a beat-up old Falcon to drive into a parked vehicle.

A moment later a German Shepherd with three legs hobbled into the road after a bouncing ball. Instinctively his foot came off the accelerator and slammed the brake. The car skidded. A dizzying rush of blood pounded in his head, and what felt like a thousand tiny fingers pulled at his flesh as the Puma fishtailed, jumped the sidewalk, and smacked into the corner of an old brick building with its rear, crumpling a fender. Ludicrously, he screamed at the dog, which stood its ground barking playfully back at him.

In another second Hiller was again on the gas pedal, squealing down the block and losing ground to the police car on his tail. He gritted his teeth and picked up the auto phone.

"Get any son of a bitch on four wheels over to the railroad yard behind the Naval Weapons Plant. We might have a peg in the presidential case. And let the PD know who the fuck they're tailing so they don't shoot me off the road."

He dropped the phone, again rode the accelerator to the floor, and took a quick hit on the nebulizer, his intoxicating elixir. He blasted through a turn near rows of tracks and railroad sidings onto a dirt road, leaving smoke clouds of dust in his wake. Then he saw it, partly hidden in the shadows of a brown wood building. His heel drove the brake to the floor. Tires bounced in and out of potholes.

Hiller threw open the door and leaped out while the car was still rolling. He stumbled once, racing to a telephone booth by the old wooden warehouse. Then, as if he had been kicked in the groin, he buckled over and angrily swung his fist in the air.

"Fucking son of a bitch!" he roared.

The patrol car careened to a halt in a tornado of dust and gravel. Two officers drew their guns and rushed up in time to watch Hiller, neck veins bulging, face bright with crimson, tear the receiver from the booth in a rage.

Delivering the kidnapper's message to Lynn Carlisle over the telephone had been a cassette tape recorder.

Chapter 9

A breeze blew across the hillside behind the church, cooling the wet faces of the mourners who listened to the padre pray for Ramon Diaz. They stood on unconsecrated ground, surrounding a lonely grave, far from the makeshift wooden crosses of blue, pink, and yellow in the church cemetery where others who had known Las Cumbres had also come to rest. Luis Diaz stood by a nondescript stone marker, in no way comprehending the sin his father had committed in taking his own life. And yet Luis believed beyond a doubt that today, like yesterday and every day before, his father would come in from the hot field at evening, and they would soak each other's heads with water from a pitcher.

Ramon Diaz had been well-liked. Though the men in the village were suspicious of him because he often refused to guzzle tequila at night, and because he would leave home mysteriously for two or three days at a time, he had won their admiration and acceptance by saving the lives of three children during a flood several years before Luis had been born.

The villagers remembered his heroics today and brought flowers. They remembered with their tears and feeble gestures of comfort: pats on little Luis's head and hugs and kisses on his fat, wet cheeks.

Maria Lopesa, a huge kindhearted woman given to floods of perspiration, who never spent a full day outside her house so dedicated was she to the task of wife and mother, took Luis's hand. She told him through her sobs that he could live with her family until his mother, who was away with no knowledge of the tragedy, returned.

Luis looked at Maria Lopesa crossly. Why should he leave his father, he would have asked. But he remained silent.

In the street not far from the church, out of view of the mourners, an old black sedan coated with a gray film of dust stood in funereal repose. Sergio Grijalva, his face masked in a Cimmerian darkness, leaned against the front of the car, pulling his fingernails along the curve of a fender.

Even with common dress to match the mourners he could not have passed for one of them. For as sad a day as it was for the inhabitants of Las Cumbres, as heavy as they were with sorrow, the spark of life still shone in their faces. In Grijalva's face there was only the absence of life, in his gaze a deathlike imprimatur.

It was as a teen-ager that Grijalva's mask of fury was etched, as a teen-ager that he learned to love the smell of fear in his fellow man.

He had nearly killed a companion in a fight that began as horseplay, then accelerated into a life-and-death struggle with knives and rocks. He was not the first to draw a weapon, but when he brought the rock down on the side of his friend's head it was with the express intent to kill. It pleased Grijalva that he had fractured the boy's skull. It excited him like nothing he had ever felt before. It did not please him that the boy had lived.

A few weeks later a man sought him out and offered him two hundred pesos to rough-up a debtor who could not pay what he owed. He took the money and methodically stalked his prey until he cornered him alone in a field. This time he did not stop beating his victim until the victim's heart stopped beating.

The padre closed his prayer book and looked down at Luis. A chill ran up the length of his spine to the base of his neck. He shivered. The vibrations of the little one's sobs went into the ground, as deep as his father's crypt, and rose again through the earth. Padre Serra could feel these vibrations through his toes.

He closed his eyes and sighed. To take away the boy's pain he would even have sacrificed his church. His arm fell gently on Luis's shoulders. He knelt alongside him and watched the last of the villagers move slowly down the hill.

Luis's small hand swept across his cheeks. He sniffled and breathed deeply through his mouth and stared at the bleak stone marker. He wanted to be left alone, but he wanted also to be nurtured and was thankful the padre was at his side.

"Luis, shall you stay with me until your mother returns?" the priest said gently. The boy tried to reply but his throat filled with a sob. He shrugged silently.

"I understand your grief, my son. And I offer you my understanding in the hope it will make your sadness a little less awesome. I know there is an overwhelming feeling of helplessness. I feel it too. And so do your friends in the village. But if you take *your* sorrow alone, you turn your back on *our* sorrow. We loved your father too, Luis. It is our grief as well."

Again Luis could not speak. He nodded and burst into tears, throwing himself into the arms of the padre, clutching with violent desperation as if he was holding his father for the last time.

Padre Serra could not help but wonder what the terror must be like for an eight-year-old living in fear of each succeeding moment and of what might become of him, haunted by the savage horror of his father's suicide and the sudden mutilation of a family that could never again be whole.

These thoughts, woven between Luis's sobs, plunged him into a sad reverie so that he was unaware of the shuffle of approaching footsteps. In a moment a man was upon them. When the padre looked up, he was immediately unsettled by a face without sympathy, by heavy brows and slanted eyes and thick flat lips of a lifeless yellow. He saw in this face abandonment and death, and he felt that if the devil indeed walked the earth, he could not look much different.

When Luis noticed him, he immediately drew back out of fear.

"I have been looking for you, Padre," Sergio Grijalva said grimly. "I need to see you. Immediately."

The priest looked at him a little fearfully and said, "You could not know because you are not from this village, but today is not such a good day, my son. The boy's father . . . he . . . he has been buried less than an hour ago—a man who was loved by his fellow man. Tomorrow perhaps the impact of this afternoon will be a little muted. Will you come see me then?"

Grijalva looked at him menacingly.

"A simple request," he said, "but I don't agree to it. I must see you now. In confession."

He spoke with such grim determination that the priest dared not entertain a refusal. He brought Luis to his quarters and put him to sleep and, after soaking his face with a wet cloth, went into the church to meet the stranger.

The padre took his place in a small booth and waited for Sergio Grijalva to begin. Why had he come to Las Cumbres on this particular day, when mourners most needed their solitude? And why was his need for confession so great that he could not have gone somewhere else? The padre wished to hurry through it and return to Luis. He did not want the boy to awaken and find himself alone. Besides, this man, whoever he was, made him quite uncomfortable.

In the confessional, there was a partition with a small sliding screen that divided the chamber and usually remained closed during confession. It could be opened if necessary from the priest's side.

Grijalva tapped on the partition with a light fist. The padre did not respond. He tapped a second time. The priest slid it open with some annoyance.

Grijalva handed him a small envelope and glared so intensely that the padre was forced to lower his eyes.

"This is your confession?" he asked impatiently.

"I need a favor for these five men," Grijalva said.

Padre Serra found five wallet-size photographs in the envelope and realized suddenly what it was the man was after. He laughed uncomfortably.

"Oh, my son, no," he said. "I cannot do that. I did it a long time ago when things were very different, when it was more necessary, and even then only for a few who were desperate. . . ."

Grijalva looked at him impatiently.

"Do it again," he said. "It will save the lives of six people."

"Six people?" the priest asked.

Grijalva nodded once. "The lives of these men, Padre. And your own," he said gravely.

Chapter 10

Phyllis Royce was not the type of woman to wait for things to happen.

She entertained at the White House as often as the President, devoted much of her time to working with handicapped children, and spoke out on political issues in ways that did not always run concurrent with her husband's views. The President encouraged her, but if he hadn't it would not have inhibited her one iota. She always spoke her mind. And, in her three years in Washington, she had disarmed many a politician with forthright observations. Unlike her friend Jay Hiller, however, she was usually tactful. Many considered her outspokenness refreshing. To this quality she added a proper stateliness that was made less intimidating by soft facial features and warm, understanding eyes.

She had first met her husband on an airplane to London twelve years ago, before he had entered politics. It was during the time she was immersed in the world of fashion design. Phyllis Butler (her maiden name) wasn't supposed to be charmed. After all, she was thinking about accepting a marriage proposal from Michael DeHaven, a Washington businessman. But no logic can be ascribed to love, and the fate of the matter was that she and John Royce fell in love.

It was the strangest of ironies that now brought a very dapper Michael DeHaven to the White House at the behest of the First Lady. He arrived in a silver Rolls-Royce a few minutes after four and, after depositing his scarf and overcoat, was ushered into the Oval Room.

Phyllis greeted him like an old friend. They had last seen each other at the President's inaugural, to which DeHaven was invited, having made a sizable contribution to the election campaign. He had since put on a few pounds, grown an attractive moustache, and become chairman of the board of Trans Continental Petroleum.

Phyllis remarked about the former two but it was really the latter that had caused her to summon him to the White House. She ordered tea with brandy for them, and though beginning deliberately and perhaps a trifle nervously, she came directly to the point. "Michael, I hope this won't make you uncomfortable and that you don't consider it a breach of friendship, but I don't know who else to turn to. . . ."

DeHaven, legs crossed holding the saucer in his lap as he sipped the brandied tea, was immediately reassuring. "Of course, my dear. Please don't make a thing of it. I know this must be an extremely difficult time for you."

Phyllis smiled a little. DeHaven was a bit stiff as always, but nonetheless goodhearted.

"There's been a ransom demand," she said worriedly, wondering if he would guess what was coming next. "Some staggering amount of money. Unbelievable. One can't even conceive. . . . And it's the only chance to save John's life."

DeHaven cleared his throat and responded quickly. "Well, how can I help?"

Phyllis shook her head and shut her eyes. She was hesitant.

"I don't know. . . . I thought . . . you're the only person I know who can touch this kind of money."

The businessman knitted his brows. "How much is needed?"

"Five hundred million dollars."

He gasped involuntarily. "That's quite a sum, my dear. Isn't the government going to . . . put it together?"

The First Lady sighed. "My own perception of it is that they won't move fast enough. Unlike the corporate world, the government isn't a monolith—it doesn't work harmoniously."

DeHaven protested gently. "But surely in an emergency like this . . ."

Phyllis Royce looked at him imploringly. It was evident as his voice trailed off that she would not argue the point further. He set down his cup on a small antique table and frowned. After several moments of deliberation he again cleared his throat and said almost impassively, "Phyllis, let me explain something to you. I hope you understand that I can't make unilateral decisions at TCP simply because I'm board chairman. I could take it to the board of directors but I don't wish to give you false prospects. They would say, 'President Royce tried to put controls on our profit margins, and his policies have cost us a small fortune.'

"Even if they *could* be convinced, they would go to the stockholders for direction. And we aren't an American company, my dear. We are a multinational. That means you are asking foreign money to ransom an American president. And I don't know what the likelihood of that is. You see, they would have everything to lose and nothing to gain. And if we lose, it means everything. It means our existence."

DeHaven looked at Phyllis, and all hope drained from her face. He lowered his eyes and said softly, "It's not my money, Phyllis. It is the corporation's. If it were mine it would be yours. For you, I will be more than happy to write a personal check for two hundred thousand dollars. That's about all I could get hold of right at the moment. I wish I had the resources, my dear. It would make me a hero in your eyes, would it not?"

Phyllis Royce smiled sadly, and though she was trying to be understanding, she could not stop herself from saying gingerly, "I'm afraid windfall profits are considered much more critical than my husband's life."

In his gray-carpeted office in the Executive Office Building Vice President Seymour Clayton loosened his tie and poured himself his fourth bourbon of the evening. He wondered for a moment what the press would have to say if they took a count on his liquor. The hell with the press, what about members of the National Security Council's Ex Comm, with whom he had been meeting at the State Department through the day and with whom he would again be meeting in half an hour? What would they think? Well, it didn't matter. He showed no effects from alcohol, and it was a welcome tranquilizer for his beleagured mind.

Clayton leaned back in his chair and sipped the drink, then set it down and clasped his hands behind his practically hairless scalp. The big questions remained unsolvable: Who were the kidnappers? And what could be done about them?

Answers were as inaccessible as John Quinlan Royce. In the Ex Comm they were having sharp disagreements—not always courteous or democratic disagreements—that became more frequent as the day wore on. Nerves were wired. Patience had been clipped.

Normally a man of saintlike forbearance, Allan B. Stigwood, the national security affairs advisor, had stormed out of the round-table discussions with the dramatic touch of upending his chair when three suggestions for compromises with the kidnappers were met in rapid succession with sarcasm and hostility. Another proposal, by General Theodore Underhill, chairman of the Joint Chiefs of Staff, called for a surgical air strike over the Everglades. It was also met with facetious enthusiasm. Clayton himself thought it would amount to little more than a military exercise. And yet, nobody came up with anything bolder or, for that matter, more cohesive.

Clayton approved Jay Hiller's request for air reconnaissance over the escape route. And if these flights turned up anything, he would reconsider Underhill's air strikes, but after that there was little enough else to put into action. It had been like trying to bite into an apple without teeth.

Now the Vice President leaped from his chair talking to himself and paced across his office as if he were about to usher someone in. "The trouble is nobody knows *what* to do," he said aloud, his voice gradually rising. "We have no precedents."

They had all come to the Ex Comm's "war council" demanding vindication and left thankful that the crisis had been "contained."

Clayton pulled the steel-rimmed glasses from his

face and pinched the skin on the bridge of his nose. He could not let it ride, permitting kidnappers to call the shots. No, that would show precisely the kind of nonleadership the press expected of him—an unfair expectation, he thought with some acidity, since he had rarely had an opportunity to prove *or* disprove himself. And yet everything he could think of had an absolute ring of hysteria to it.

At that moment he hated Royce. He knew he had not been in the President's favor for almost a year— and now, ironically, it was as if Royce had willed this predicament to give him one last chance.

Well he might fail, but he would not fail by trying to live up to Royce's expectations. He had his own view of the world and how the worst should be handled. He would not pussyfoot around with terrorists. The armed might of the nation would be ready even if he had to accomplish it by marching armies through the streets. He would negotiate from strength. He had learned long ago as mayor of Kansas City that demonstrations could be literally run off the sidewalks with a strong display of force, and every political dilemma he had since encountered was in one way or another a variation on the theme.

The stakes had escalated, certainly. But even the present crisis—a presidential kidnapping—had the same elements. Only instead of dealing with unruly street crowds, he thought, now he was sure to be facing a major foreign power.

Chapter 11

December 11.

At 6:35 of a subfreezing morning, Jay Hiller again drove his Pontiac Puma to the government employee underground parking lot and walked three blocks to the GOB's Blue Wing.

A field agent had located an eight-millimeter film taken by an Atlanta housewife of the President's arrival at the St. Mark's Hotel, and Hiller was anxious for a look.

He had grabbed four hours sleep and woke up with a dull, grinding headache, but was alert and hopeful. Today's papers all over the country, maybe the world, would be running on page one the still pictures of the kidnapping suspects gleaned from the videotape. Sooner or later someone somewhere would make the connection and provide a link. Abruptly his optimism waned, and he muttered under his breath, ". . . sooner or later."

In the Op Center Hiller made a beeline for the coffee machine and poured himself a cup. He waved a complacent greeting to the half-dozen people at their desks and tried to bum a cigarette. No one smoked.

"Fucking purists," he muttered with exasperation.

Jeff Brodsky overheard him.

"That caffeine's no good for you either," he said.

"Destroys vitamins, bad for the liver, dulls senses, taxes the heart, and destabilizes blood sugar."

Hiller screwed up his face.

"You're in the wrong profession, Jeff."

"I should be a doctor, right?"

"No. A coroner."

Jeff smiled. "You keep drinking that garbage and you'll be my first customer."

"Cadaver, kid, not customer." Hiller looked cynically at him and said, "Listen, Alfalfa, you know what's going to happen to you? You're gonna become a great double agent. But when it comes time to slip your mark the cyanide, you'll accidentally give him a multivitamin."

Jeff laughed. Hiller sipped his coffee and stared over the lip of the cup at the digital clock. It read 06:58 hours.

"You been here all night?"

Brodsky nodded.

"You know it's a good idea not to look too dedicated around here," Hiller said. "People mistake it for stupidity." He was not altogether joking.

Then he chuckled to himself over Jeff's tenacity and his boyish enthusiasm for work, health food, and one particular lady, a young Vietnamese woman he constantly boasted he would marry.

Hiller felt a fraternal bond with the kid, possibly because his very wealthy family was trying to destroy the romance and Hiller had once experienced a similar trauma. Or possibly because he reminded him of an old college buddy; both were about five eight, with thick brown wavy hair, inquisitive eyes, and a soft, almost feminine mouth. Jeff's facial appearance, however, was darker, more East European.

Maybe in time he would become hard-headed

enough to operate in the field; maybe not. He had been surprisingly helpful in the office.

Hiller checked the Telex and a desk-top computer for intelligence updates. Then, almost wearily, he asked, "What happened with the voiceprint we made at the TV station?"

Brodsky frowned.

"Absolutely zilch. The voice was electronically distorted—closest we could come to a positive identification was Donald Duck. There were no prints on the cassette or the phone booth. Tire tracks were untraceable."

Hiller nodded. "Yeah, yeah," he said, suddenly disgusted. It was getting to be an old story.

"Did we get a report from Chicago on that stolen television equipment?"

"Police confirmed the warehouse manager's story. The equipment was in fact stolen in October. Albaum will be in soon with the write-up on it."

"What about Goss? What have we heard from him?"

"First I should tell you that Mike Popfinger from the Secret Service called. He says the guy responsible for the switch of hotel rooms to the penthouse was someone named Frank Mayberry. White House Press Secretary Kinstrey gave Mayberry an okay to do that after Popfinger suggested it. Mayberry's the guy Goss has been tracking in Atlanta. He's down there now following it up and will be in touch. Also, the first reports from the reconnaissance flights over southern Florida should be in at noon."

"And the agency reports?" asked Hiller.

"In your desk—along with copies of the still photos of the suspects."

From the top drawer, Hiller took a large sealed envelope marked EYES ONLY—J. M. HILLER and a manila folder with photographs of the kidnap suspects.

The prints were fuzzy—resolution lost in the blow-up—but at least they provided a likeness.

"The photo labs come up with anything on these yet?" he asked, tearing open the sealed envelope.

"Negative."

Hiller flipped through the reports and shoved them back in the envelope. "This includes files from the Bureau *and* the Company?"

"Afraid so," said Brodsky.

Hiller shook his head and slammed his cup on the desk, spilling coffee over the photographs. He was obviously annoyed.

"Go home, Jeff," he muttered. "Get some rest while you're able."

"I'd like to see the eight millimeter movie with you. That all right?"

Hiller grunted and said, "Don't wanna miss the fuck scenes, eh?"

"If that's what you're expecting, you may be disappointed."

A slightly rumpled Jack Albaum, stooped and red-eyed, with wildcat hair, met them at the entrance to the screening room. Hiller snatched the copy of the Chicago police report from his hands and snapped, "What do *you* look so wasted about? *You* slept."

"Who says I slept?" Albaum protested.

Hiller bore into him with narrowed eyes.

"Well, maybe an hour or two," he said weakly. "But I came in early for a peek at the film."

Hiller responded flippantly, "I guess that would be okay. I've been told it's G-rated. Let me bum a cigarette and I won't charge admission. The health nuts around here are all on carob."

Before the film had run completely through, he had borrowed two more. On screen were out-of-focus shots of an Atlanta family's toothy smiles. And feet, hundreds of feet, as many angled toward the police barricades for a better view of the President, all making Jay Hiller irritable. He put a hand to his face and was again conscious of the headache.

"What is this? Last year's Oscar winner?"

From the screen a dozen arms now waved—almost mockingly—at Hiller, Albaum, and Brodsky. There wasn't much left on the feed reel of the projector. The image climbed the facade of the hotel, up columns and rows of identical windows flying American flags, to the penthouse. As the last frames sped through the film gate, there was a shot of open sky and a passing glimpse of a muddy, unidentifiable image.

There was no reason to see it through a second time; the film was completely useless. But Hiller was operating on instinct and ordered Jeff to run it again—in slow motion. In slow motion the muddy image became recognizable. Then they examined it frame by frame and it was identifiable, a helicopter taking off from the roof of the St. Mark's Hotel.

Brodsky and Albaum were awestruck. Who could have guessed there was anything in such seemingly worthless footage?

Hiller jumped from his seat, talking excitedly and pointing frantically at the image as if he was afraid it would disappear.

"What does that read? Can you see those numbers on the belly of the chopper?" He was almost shouting.

Jeff played with the focus.

"XCH-62, it looks like," Albaum said.

"Get prints of this made up right away. Jack, get a tracer out on it immediately."

"XCH-62? Isn't that the Army's retractable fuselage type?"

"Yeah," cried Hiller. "Where besides the Army could somebody get hold of one?"

Albaum knitted his brows. "Nowhere," he said timidly.

The winter's ivory-colored sun barely signaled morning, and Fred Goss was already returning to Washington on the early bird flight from Atlanta.

He had decided to spend the night when his interview with WFFV station manager Bonnie Goodwin had stretched beyond 12:15 A.M., the time of the last regularly-scheduled commercial flight to D.C. Goodwin was able to answer at least some of his questions and, notably, the riddle of Frank Mayberry finally came to a close. Goss was pleased with his thoroughness. Nothing had been left unasked. But if Jay Hiller was looking for a breakthrough, he was going to grind dust out of frustration. He shut his eyes, rested his head against the porthole window of the jetliner, and fell asleep.

Shortly before noon Jay Hiller was met at the Fort Cherry landing field by General Harry Hummerstone, a tall, slender man with parted gray hair, whose erect military bearing was overt.

Hummerstone looked like a stiff English parliamentarian—thick bags under the eyes, deep furrows around a sagging mouth—and had the habit of sucking three times on a pipe before speaking.

They were driven to the post in a Jeep by the general's driver, a young corporal who seemed terrified of his commanding officer. Hiller marveled to himself at how little military bases seemed to have changed in twenty years. Open fields, wooden barracks, recruits in khakis, the very same calisthenics. And then he was struck by the thought of how much twenty years *should* have mattered.

Twenty years ago I was a kid, he thought. And

twenty years from now I'll be an old man. Wasn't there any middle ground? Any bargain he could strike to slow the marking off of moments. There were so few hours he had savored in his youth. What would he have to show for it that meant something? And why was he—and everyone—in such a hurry to reach the end?

Like a bewildered turtle, Hiller tucked his head into his chest and marveled sadly at the magic tricks of time. Back, back . . . suddenly, he was fighting off a wave of depression.

General Hummerstone, assuming he had an audience, chatted freely about the kidnapping and how the U.S. should develop a strike force to annihilate the abductors once their identities were learned, and how that strike force could be developed at Fort Cherry. Hiller threw his head back to stave off an attack of heavy-liddedness. He did not share the officer's enthusiasm.

"We're proud of our record here," Hummerstone barked. "I don't have to tell you it's the best nationwide in the armed services. . . ."

Hiller wondered why, in that case, he was telling him.

"You get Washington to front for a tactical squad, you'll find the best men available at this camp. I can take you over right now and show you some of the finest troops of . . ."

Hiller broke in irritably, "I think you misunderstand the reason I'm here, General. I'm checking on military equipment that might have been used in the abduction of President Royce. I'm not looking for a hit squad or heroes."

Hummerstone sucked his pipe and looked sharply at Hiller.

"Now just a minute, Mr. Hiller. Whatever you may

or may not discover, I believe, will have little reflection on the base as a whole or on the United States Army. We build men here, Mr. Hiller. If there's one bad apple, you don't throw the whole barrel out."

Hiller said brusquely, "You raising apples, General? Or soldiers?"

Hummerstone returned to his pipe. He thought Hiller impertinent and wished he had him under his command. That was the trouble with Washington people, too free with their mouths. Half the country's woes could be traced to that, he was sure.

The two men entered the base office, a freshly-painted white wooden building with forest-green trim. A corporal behind a desk snapped to attention and the general put him at ease. He demanded the dispatch records for the base and the corporal began punching keys on a desktop computer.

Hiller waited impatiently, tapping out a rhythm on a desk with his fingers. Hummerstone eyed him suspiciously, sucking on his pipe.

"Just what do you expect to find, Mr. Hiller?" he asked.

"I expect to find the President," Hiller said tersely. "I remind you again, General, he was kidnapped in a helicopter that came from this base."

Hummerstone considered a reply but let it drop. The corporal was receiving a readout on the computer. Hummerstone glanced at it quickly, then read it aloud.

"Went out on the eighth . . . signed over to . . . Sergeant David C. Gilbert. Oh six hundred hours . . ."

To the corporal he added, "What company is Gilbert with?"

The corporal swallowed hard.

"Well?" Hummerstone said irritably. "Speak up!"

"Well, sir, Gilbert was with B Company," he said nervously. "But according to this he was killed in Vietnam fourteen years ago."

Chapter 12

December 12.

Lynn Carlisle was awakened just after dawn by a phone call instructing her to retrieve a small package in a phone booth one block from her apartment and to deliver it immediately to Jay Hiller. Still groggy, her hair untamed and her face full of sleep lines, she threw on a pair of jeans and a sweater and ran up the street. A man in dark glasses, parked opposite the entrance to her building in a late model foreign car, recorded her movements.

Less than an hour later, Hiller was racing up the steps of the East Front entrance of the Capitol, a brown attaché gripped tightly in hand. Exiting from the building was CIA director Wilson McAvee, wearing a natty gray-check suit and a cool self-congratulatory grin.

"Visiting the Capitol, Mr. Director?" Hiller asked, forcing himself to be charming.

"Briefing the Vice President, yes. What are you doing here?"

Jay Hiller smiled to himself. McAvee didn't waste a moment turning interrogator. Hiller could have let him in on the morning's development but felt guarded. Unless McAvee was willing to trade information, there was no point in giving up what he had. McAvee could read about it tomorrow in the daily intelligence reports.

Hiller replied simply to his question. "I'll be addressing the marathon in there."

McAvee was dissatisfied with the answer.

"What do you have on the investigation?" he said.

Hiller held out a hand as if he was feeling for raindrops.

"Royce is still out there," he said. "The Congress is dragging ass on the ransom, and we don't have a hairpin clue in a shitpile of gas. We're doing fine."

McAvee grimaced at his choice of words but seemed almost pleased. Perhaps he would privately gloat over Hiller's failure, even if it reflected negatively in part on his own department. But if Hiller failed, that meant the kidnappers succeeded—and they were probably the only entities McAvee was more contemptuous of than the special investigator.

McAvee looked at Hiller. His gaze was softer than usual but somehow still chilling, as none of the softness came from the eyes.

The director spoke calmly. "For a man who has four days left to produce five hundred million dollars, you seem unusually relaxed. You'd better start making some headway. My guess is you'll fall flat on your face. And if you do and if Royce pays with his life, I'll make sure the newspapers treat you as unfairly as they did when they made you out a hero."

Hiller gathered himself to be absolutely direct and said sharply, "You seem unduly concerned with my image, Mr. Director. If you'd concentrate less on appearances and more on consequences, you might see fit to save us time, energy, aggravation, maybe even the President's life, by giving me full clearance to files in . . ."

McAvee smiled coldly. He seemed to have been waiting for such a request.

"Good afternoon, Mr. Hiller," he said and quickly descended the steps. Hiller shook his head. He watched McAvee cross the parking lot and disappear behind a soda truck.

Minutes later Hiller was sitting in on the joint congressional session, now in its third consecutive day. For the first time in eleven years, there had been perfect attendance.

Vice President Clayton was addressing the chamber. They listened with proper dignity and afforded him all respect due to an acting-President. He urged members of Congress to give at least the appearance of unity and approve the ransom or the nation would suffer greatly with its allies. No country in the world would believe in our guarantees if we would not go to the vault for our Chief Executive, he said.

Clayton spoke so well that at times Hiller thought he was listening to John Quinlan Royce. When the Vice President completed his address, heads bobbed up and down in apparent agreement. Then as he slowly made his way up the aisle, senators and members of the House aggressively shook his hand.

Son of a bitch if it doesn't look like Clayton turned the trick, thought Hiller, fooled everybody including the secretary of state as to his charisma, capabilities, and powers of persuasion. But after Clayton had left and the floor was opened for discussion, it was as if congressmen suddenly became wild schoolchildren who had been waiting for the disapproving teacher to turn his back.

It began when a senator questioned the legality of approving a ransom demand. A member of the House argued that the money should come from the Defense Department budget. Another claimed such a move would "threaten the stability of the nation" since that money was already earmarked for defense spending.

The arguments each of them put forth came from the self-willed part of man that, when provoked, stubbornly pitches forward like a beaten fighter—fists flying in desperation, hoping he will somehow land a blow. It is the ego that overtakes logic and demands restitution. And it was the ego now, and the utter feeling of helplessness, that triggered in these senators and representatives nearly irrational attempts to overcome the vulnerability of their position.

Though perfect attendance had favored approval of the ransom because of the President's many supporters, now it merely seemed to invite a wider range of conflicting opinions as to possible courses of action.

Even President pro tem Emanuel Springer, usually a man of unwavering moderation, lost his temper. His basset-hound face vibrated with thick layers of flesh as he shouted down two senators engaged in battle on the floor. Minority Leader Philip Basilio then accused Springer of failing to perform his prescribed duties. Some leaped to Springer's defense. Tension and frustration spread across the chamber like a brush fire.

Representative Earl Morris Kenyon got up and said in his Tennessee drawl, "All this tuggin' an' bullin' comes down to one thing—the country won't fall apart over one man. That's been proven at least once since I've been in Washington. No single individual is inexpendable. Not in this country."

Kenyon's remark elicted cries of outrage from one faction, and theirs in turn ignited others. For nearly half an hour, the floor became a showcase for the most vocal and abrasive.

Finally Hiller left his seat and mounted the dais at

the front of the chamber. The session was so ill-structured, he thought, it *insured* stalemate. How could anything take on its proper import in a circus? How could peril be communicated in a room sealed from reality? The mounting pressure of events had seriously impaired congressional judgment; perhaps the latest communiqué from the kidnappers would be a blessing after all. It might force Congress to act.

After numerous false starts Hiller finally gained the floor. He leaned forward on a wooden podium and read from a prepared text in a voice pitched low, suppressing anger.

"It is a bleak hour indeed for any nation when its legislative body, involved as we are in a national crisis, is more concerned with blowing a barrage of bureaucratic bubbles and strutting political etiquette than it is with obtaining the release of its President. I can't help but wonder how many of you Capitol Hill pinworms would be willing to throw everything into the pot if your own lives were the booty in this political crapshoot."

A catcall erupted from the gallery and Springer immediately drove his gavel to the desk top.

"Mr. Hiller, I don't think your insults do very much to further your position," he said in a coarse voice. "We're talking about whether we should allow the government to bend to extortion."

Hiller ran a hand through his steel-wool hair. Now he spoke impatiently.

"Yes, well, you can argue the ideology of the crisis until the ideology becomes a religion or the crisis solves or absolves itself. And the moral issue *still* may not be decided. You can analyze the pros and cons with a computer and, rest assured, justify any answer, support any position, deliver any course of action.

"But a course of action must be decided upon.

Now! Today! You're asking for time, which is a luxury we do not have. You can split yourselves down the middle and begin a parliamentary debate that may not be decided in our lifetime, which is the timetable you appear to be using. If this persists, I think members of this legislative body should issue a statement to the American people to let them know that: 'Before embarking on a course of action, we have decided to argue the doctrines and abstractions of this case, for in spite of the impending danger to the President, any effective move must be well thought out and in line with the political theories of our government.'

"I call upon you senators, you congressmen, to act like leaders of our nation instead of like political scavengers. If you don't agree with a word I have said, at least understand this: We do not have time."

Hiller spoke the last words slowly and emphatically as if each one were a full sentence. His delivery was sobering.

Whispers and hushed conversation mounted quickly, but the tones were harsh and aggressive.

From the attaché he then took a cassette player and the cassette tape which Lynn Carlisle had brought to him.

"This communiqué was received only hours ago," Hiller said. "Nobody has heard it yet, with the exception of myself. It may help you make a decision."

Hiller pushed the fast-forward button and skipped over the first part of the tape, which gave instructions for sorting and packaging the ransom.

When he stopped and started it again, they heard a hollow voice elongating syllables and issuing commands to members of the United States Senate and House of Representatives.

* * *

> If all our orders are carried out by the appointed deadline the prisoner will be released on December twenty-third, one week after receipt of five hundred million dollars. Our hostage is in good health, though we are not inclined to give evidence of this. Any demand for such will be interpreted as a crude play for time. Inasmuch as we are not satisfied that representatives of your government are acting in good faith, for every four days approval of the ransom is delayed beginning December twelfth . . .

Hiller shouted above the voice level on the tape. "That's today, gentlemen!"

> . . . a member of Congress will be selected at random for execution.

The rest of the tape was drowned in the wave of outbursts that followed. Had one of the kidnappers somehow been transported to the chamber under a banner of truce, these senators and congressmen—representatives of the people—would have torn the flesh from his body and wrapped it in the white flag. As it was, they acted as if Hiller was an emissary and directed some of their anger at him. And yet whatever outrage was expressed was merely the crest of the wave. Almost all were on their feet, gesturing wildly, and shouting as if a heavyweight champion was about to be decked.

Instead of peaking, the frenzy grew. The chairman's gavel banged futilely, ignored by men weaned on diplomacy who were heatedly engaged in private wars with colleagues. It was a pressure cooker about to blow apart.

* * *

Less than a minute after Hiller had arrived at the Capitol to attend this consequential session, the guards at the East Front entrance stopped a delivery man making a routine drop of Coca-Cola. His name was Ted Glasky. He explained to them that the delivery entrances were sealed up for security and that he had been told to enter at the East Front.

They checked him out and okayed him. Glasky smiled appreciatively, leaned his massive weight against the dolly of cola cases and pushed it through the arched hallways to the cafeteria. He loaded the machines with practiced coordination, popped open one of the bottles, and stole a drink. Then he pulled the dolly of empty cases back to his truck in the parking lot and drove off.

In the House chamber, Senator Perry Jedlicker was spitting a war cry above the percussion of Chairman Springer's feverish thumping. Jedlicker's round rigid face was surging with blood, and his demand for vengeance was punctuated with sprays of saliva and quaking fists.

". . . and is the most outrageous attempt at blackmail and extortion, I dare say, the world has ever known. I say smash the sons of bitches! Give 'em a taste of American might. If we don't, we encourage every goddam tootle-brained psychotic in every free society to attempt the same unconscionable act. Smash them, I say, smash them with every last piece of artillery that we've got and let the democratic world see we won't be made to bend. . . ."

A spattering of cheers and applause backed Jedlicker. It was this support that triggered something in Hiller. It rose steadily and swiftly like a bubble rising in water.

His temples began pounding as he gritted his teeth. And he felt a hot flush of blood around his eyes.

"Just who in hell are you going to *smash*?" Hiller demanded through clenched teeth. "We don't know where the kidnappers are. Does that mean you'll smash *anyone*? If the kidnappers are Italian, will you smash every family eating pasta in Little Italy? If they're Mexican, will you *smash* every Chicano in a lettuce field? If they're Irish will you bomb Belfast? Will you set up a goddamned police state to *solve* things; or *smash* things? Will Fascism bring the President home? Don't give me your bereaved, maligned, bleeding-hearts-and-flowers, march-or-die patriotism. Our only chance is to buy some time. That's what paying the ransom will do."

Representative Dale Markson spoke up. "Are you suggesting we have no choice but to play into the hands of these lunatics?"

Hiller was dumbfounded. "I just don't believe it," he said with complete dismay. "If someone had asked me, I'd have sworn this was impossible—I'd have bet my life all of you would line up in favor of saving the President's life. If nothing else, you're jeopardizing your futures. You're going against what the nation needs and wants and must have. If there was any clear alternative to a ransom I would suggest it. But we haven't got alternatives. You can't just sit on your collective ass and argue ideology as a clever way of abstaining from the question."

From the back row of the chamber, Senator Lawrence Yee waved the morning edition of *The Washington Post* in the air. A banner headline identified the five large headshots on the front page as those of the alleged kidnappers.

"We *know* what they look like," he said, "Why can't they be found?"

"We're doing our best," Hiller said impatiently, "But if you can suggest stones we've left unturned, by all means . . ."

Representative Earl Morris Kenyon shook his head. "Do you think there is even the slightest reason to believe they would allow President Royce to return alive?"

Hiller sighed dolefully and pinched one of the bumps on his Brando nose.

"Let me put it the way it was once so aptly put," he said in a low throaty voice. "We are looking into the mouth of the cannon. The idea is not to pull the trigger."

The session broke for lunch without a decision. Senators and congressmen spilled into the outer hallway on the second floor and continued their vocal arguments without bothering to put up a front of decorum. There was no need. The press had been barred from the building.

Hiller dodged his way through the pack to the stairwell. He took no notice of the approving or disapproving glances around him. His mind was racing furiously. He would skip the afternoon session—there was little he could say that he hadn't already said— and await a decision with everyone else. He would have to call the secretary of state and tell him it was likely to continue stalemated.

Could Secretary Brownell and Clayton turn them around with pressure? That was doubtful. They had already exercised pressure through party lines, personal friends, and political favors past due. Was there time to devise an alternative? Definitely not. Could they bargain with the kidnappers? Not without something to bargain *with*.

An overriding sense of helplessness gripped him. He felt as if he were on a carnival ride and the attendant was refusing to let him off. The decision rested with Congress and nothing he could do could change that. But *because* of that it would be something of a relief to return to the business of investigation and not have to deal with politicians. The threat of random executions was chilling, but he never for a moment questioned the seriousness of the intent. Ironically, it was this gruesome tactic that right now provided an indeterminate amount of additional pressure on Congress to ransom the President.

Jay Hiller stood at the head of the stairs for a moment, bewildered by the thought that he was part of what might historically be remembered as America's worst hour.

Richard Wainwright, the young senator from Oregon, caught him from behind with an affectionate pat on the shoulder.

Wainwright had won a reputation in his first twenty-three months in office as a giant-killer, bumping heads with defense contractors by actively opposing construction of several nuclear breeder reactors and spearheading stall tactics on the development of a new series of laser-neutron bombs. His thin, sharply intelligent features added to his popular appeal.

Hiller had met Wainwright during a Memorial Day weekend at the "Western White House" on the Sonoma Coast. There the senator had cemented an alliance with the President by preparing the best barbecued burgers he and his guests had ever eaten.

Now Hiller and Wainwright walked down the stairway to the first floor, not quite aware that the man who introduced them was again responsible for bringing them together.

"So I'm a 'Capitol Hill pinworm,' am I?" the young politician said with a trace of a smile.

Hiller smirked, a little surprised that he had said such a thing and that it was now coming back at him.

"Sorry, Dick. You're guilty by association."

"Maybe you weren't aware of it but you sounded like a politician in there. Ever think of running for office?"

Hiller scratched his nose and laughed a little.

"Thanks, but retirement is more stimulating," he said.

Then Wainwright bit his lower lip and said gravely, "I've been trying to move them, Jay, but junior senators have very little push."

Hiller patted him warmly on the back.

"Well, push them off a cliff then, will you?" he said.

Wainwright smiled solemnly. They shook hands and Hiller went out the East Front entrance. The senator watched as a flood of reporters, who had anticipated the lunch break, converged on the special investigator with note pads and minicams. There was one man he could never envy.

Four-year-old Krissy Wainwright waited for her father at a cafeteria table, galloping impatiently in place on a chair.

"Krissy, be careful," Natalie Wainwright said absently.

"What time is it, Mommy?" she asked. And then, dissatisfied with the reply, she asked again every succeeding half minute, "What time is it *now*, Mommy?"

Senator Wainwright entered the cafeteria and almost instinctively began digging through his pockets for change. He heard the cry of "Daddy! Daddy!" across the room and looked up to see his blond-haired, wide-eyed princess with a slight pug nose rushing to his feet. He swept her into the air above his head and she let out a scream of joy. He cradled her to his chest and said, "Where's my hug?"

Krissy dutifully hugged him about the neck.

"Where's my kiss," the senator demanded playfully. She leaned her pudgy blond head close to his and kissed him twice. Then imitating the authority in her father's voice, she said, "Where's my soda, Pop?"

Wainwright laughed, put her down and led her to the soda machine. Again Krissy galloped in place.

"Can *I* do it?" she cried excitedly.

The senator gave her a coin and picked her up again.

"Where's Mommy, Krissy?"

She dropped the coin in the slot and punched a button with a round little fist. A bottle of soda slid out.

"She's over there—on the telephone," Krissy said, gathering up her drink.

She tried to open it herself but almost sent it hurtling to the floor. Wainwright helped guide the neck of the bottle into the claw opener of the machine.

The cap came loose. There was a hiss of gas escaping and Kristina's predictable giggle each time she heard that hiss. The child's laughter was the last audible sound.

One second later there was a flash of blinding white light like a sudden jagged stroke of lightning, followed by the rolling thunder of an explosion—an entire wall blew open and their bodies were hurled thirty feet across the room. A metal fragment the size of a grapefruit punctured the senator's chest, the little girl's left arm and both legs from above the knee were blown off. There were screams as fire broke out and smothered the room in smoke.

There in the cafeteria of the United States Capitol crumbling plaster fell on their multilated bodies and the shredded flesh of an American senator and his four-year-old daughter burned beyond recognition in the fiery debris.

Chapter 13

When news of the Wainwright murders hit the State Department, it was as if the Ex Comm were suddenly jolted from a deep coma. General Theodore Underhill, Chairman of the Joint Chiefs, and Defense Secretary Paul Garrett agreed with Seymour Clayton that the kidnapping of the President and murder of a senator appeared to be part of a planned takeover of the United States. Once they had mounted the argument, they had momentum enough to convince most of the others.

Only Secretary of State Stephen Brownell and National Security Affairs adviser Allan Stigwood were doubtful, and for that reason Clayton agreed to move more cautiously than he otherwise might have.

In one afternoon, the Ex Comm hammered out a course of action designed to meet the challenge of a military confrontation without needlessly provoking an adversary.

The strategic air command was scattered around civilian airports to make it impossible for an enemy to pinpoint its locations; the entire nuclear strike force was prepared for combat; the number of ship and submarine patrols monitoring American interests was doubled; combat-ready manpower was tripled in strategic areas of the world.

All members of the Cabinet, the White House staff, Congress, the Joint Chiefs of Staff, and the Ex Comm would be assigned bodyguards. All government buildings would be reinforced and secured by the National Guard and the U.S. Army. A large protective force would sentry the White House, the Executive Office Building, and the Vice President's residence.

Clayton was a step away from instituting martial law but again agreed to less severe measures: the National Guard was mobilized in every major American city; military-age men would face emergency conscription; a midnight curfew was imposed coast-to-coast. Anyone caught with a weapon in his possession, licensed or otherwise, would be arrested.

The Vice President was pleased with the "war council" and with himself. They had acted quickly, under enormous pressure, and were ready, no matter who they were forced to oppose.

He guessed privately it would be the Soviet Union, an opinion reinforced by a note received that afternoon from the Soviet ambassador. It expressed sympathy over the Wainwright murders and, in view of certain deployments of which his office was made aware, urged military restraint to avoid pointless confrontation.

Why urge military restraint and initiate counter moves before it is even clear whom our deployments are directed toward, Clayton asked himself. He reasoned it was because the Soviets already knew who the aggressor was.

An hour later, however, he received a communiqué from the Chinese ambassador in New York. It said, in part: "If your government makes certain strategic maneuvers to prepare for armed hostility, it would be irresponsible of our government not to prepare for the same eventuality. . . ."

Clayton looked over the empty chairs and the long table in the State Department conference room. He was certain one of these powers would soon begin offensive maneuvers in response to our deployments—and that by doing so, he would know who meant to march on Washington.

When Jay Hiller left the Capitol, he stopped at Gus's Big Eats for a pastrami on rye and a beer to go and arrived at the Op Center fifteen minutes later. There were messages to call Fred Goss at CIA headquarters, John Chenowith at the Department of the Air Force, and Lincoln Packwood at the FBI.

Hiller took them in order of importance, wolfing down his sandwich as he dialed the agency. Luckily, he caught Goss on his way out.

"You sound like you had a rough morning," Goss said.

"Yeah, the combination of Congress and pastrami is lethal."

"The Frank Mayberry lead dried up in Atlanta," Goss said with some exasperation. "The night before the President was lifted from the St. Mark's Hotel, Mayberry had an accident. His car went off the road, through a guardrail, and over the side of a bridge. He was alone, killed instantly. We've been questioning the people at the television station but nobody knows anything about his setting up the President's interview.

"Apparently the guy was in charge of special projects. We can't tell if he was part of the conspiracy and got shoved out, or whether they deep-sixed him to use his identity to get to Royce."

Hiller asked, "How did the police write it up?"

"Accidental fatality. Coroner says he had a few drinks but was not intoxicated."

Hiller shook his head and said sarcastically, "So he missed a turn and drove his car off a bridge? Accidental fatality, shit!"

"I've already talked to him but you might want to check with Mark Kinstrey yourself, since he had phone contact with Mayberry."

"Yeah, right," said Hiller dryly.

There was a brief silence before Goss asked, "What happened at Fort Cherry?"

"We have a lead working on the chopper that was used in the escape. What are you on to now?"

"The lab—to see if they put anything together on those photos you came up with. By the way, how the hell did you get suspect pictures?"

"They posed for them," Hiller said coyly.

Next he tried Packwood at the FBI, but the line was busy. He called John Chenowith, who gave him the results of the final reconnaissance flights over Florida. Negative.

Hiller put down the phone and tried to sort things out. The question that kept nagging him was why the kidnappers' only demand was money. If it was money alone they were after, an apolitical group wouldn't have to risk kidnapping the President of the United States. And if it was a political group, why were there no other conditions for Royce's release?

Seymour Clayton's Big Power Theory—meaning the Soviet Union or Red China—alternately seemed logical and ludicrous. Would a nuclear power risk war with the U.S. by attempting something as perilous as kidnapping the head of state? No, he could not believe that. Would a nuclear power take the same risks to support clandestinely a group with whom they sympathized? Possibly, but again the hazards seemed too great. None of it made sense. Dammit, none of it made sense and that was why he couldn't get a handle. The phone rang and jarred Hiller from his thoughts.

It was Lincoln Packwood. In a deep, soft voice he told Jay Hiller about Senator Wainwright and his daughter. And then almost apologetically said he would have to question him as part of the investigation into the senator's assassination.

Hiller put down the phone, walked slowly to the bathroom, and emptied his guts in the toilet. When he returned to his desk, he mixed himself a "Raincheck": one-third Scotch, one-third Drambuie and one-third tequila. He drank it warm, without ice, in one gulp, and remembered that an hour ago he had thought the kidnappers' threat to Congress might be a blessing in disguise.

Because of that he now felt ashamed. Why couldn't he have prolonged his conversation with Dick Wainwright by five minutes? Why couldn't he have throttled Congress into approving the ransom this morning? He sighed deeply and felt a profound sense of guilt. For the first time in as long as he could remember he wanted to be able to cry.

An old and cherished photograph from his junior year at college suddenly floated before him like an apparition made of sunlit dust. It was of a pale, underweight Jay Hiller, already a battler of chronic asthma, and two friends in front of a campus statue. One was a six-foot, two-hundred-pound, powerfully-built adolescent, whose baby-faced features showed signs of breaking at any moment into extremely attractive manhood. His name was Tom Vandewater and he wore a football jersey and a smile so broad that Hiller called it "Tom's cartoon grin."

The other friend was also aggressively built, with

thick hands and a square face, but was the shortest of the three. He owned the peculiar combination of an aquiline nose and sensitive thin lips, which were quite like a woman's. He was Charley Lohman, and he too wore a football jersey.

Both Tom and Charley were outstanding athletes—both were All-American. And Tom was considered a dark-horse candidate for the Heisman Trophy as college football's most outstanding player. Hiller envied them their football glory, their good health, their limitless futures. He also loved them like family.

The odds that Jay Hiller would outlive either one were probably fifty to one, that he would outlive both of them, perhaps two hundred to one. Which is why that photograph, tucked away with his most personal memories and laid to rest with time, had stayed with him.

In his senior year, following an exciting and successful football season, Tom was suddenly stricken with an almost unknown liver ailment and two months later was gone. The night Tom died, Jay Hiller and Charley Lohman cried in each other's arms until, with the first light of morning, they could cry only by themselves.

That summer they worked a contracting job and gave their earnings to Tom's parents, who were having problems rebounding from the shock and were consequently in economic straits.

After the summer, Jay and Charley enlisted in the Army. But Hiller was promptly given an honorable discharge after his asthma was discovered. Charley, meanwhile, volunteered for Special Forces and, on the very week of the first anniversary of Tom's death, was listed missing in action in Vietnam.

The loss of his two friends left Hiller stunned for well over a year. When he began to come out of it, government intelligence work offered him more than most options. It could take him physically far away from painful memories; it would require complete absorption in his work so that he could not dwell in the past; and it would require a certain disciplining of his emotions—something he drastically needed if he was to go on living.

Though he had tasted the bittersweet lessons of young adulthood, the cold brutal harshness of the world-at-large had not, till then, touched his personal life. No longer insulated by the university, it came as a jolt. For months on end, he woke up mornings terrified and drenched in sweat. He would remember the loneliness and uncertainty of those days for all time. It was no small memory in his life.

Jay Hiller blinked away the pain of the past with the more searing agony of the present.

He tried calling Natalie Wainwright, who had been a wife and mother when the day began and was now without family. When no one answered, he dialed Phyllis Royce and asked if she would like someone to stay with her aside from Secret Service men, soldiers, and National Guardsmen. She refused politely but sounded depressed. He tried to cheer her by manufacturing a story about a lead in the kidnapping but was not very convincing. He hung up thinking she was sorry he had called.

Hiller assembled his staff and ordered various phases of the investigation pursued aggressively and thoroughly. He wanted the labs to identify the explosives used in the Wainwright assassination. He wanted Capitol guards grilled on how the bomb got by them. He wanted terrorist groups utilizing this type of explosive checked against groups considered capable of attempting a kidnapping of the President. Investigative teams were to pore over dossiers on presidential threats for tie-ins with terrorist bombings. They were to stay in close touch with the FBI's Packwood.

When Fred Goss arrived at the Op Center, he was immediately struck by how trashed Jay Hiller looked and decided to make it short and to the point.

"I ran a check on Lynn Carlisle, since she seems to be the kidnappers' playmate of the week, he said, tossing a folder on Hiller's desk. "Pertinent data—orphaned at twelve, started working as a professional journalist at seventeen, landed national network news slot four years ago after two explosive exposés, married at twenty-two to Robert Carlisle, a Seattle attorney. Divorced two and a half years later, no children, underwent psychiatric counseling three years, voting record vacillates liberal to conservative, registered Democrat, relationships sporadic and brief, lovers apolitical . . ."

Hiller's brows went up. "*Voting* record? You know who she *voted* for?"

Fred Goss winced. "Uh . . . yes . . ." he said quietly. It was a new intelligence innovation. He had forgotten that Jay Hiller hadn't been around since its inception.

Recalling their philosophical differences over agency methods in the past, Goss quickly passed over it.

"We turned up nothing on her. Unfortunately. She's cleared."

Hiller studied him closely. "*Unfortunately?*"

Goss nodded. "It would have made things a hell of a lot simpler if she could have led us to the kidnappers, wouldn't it? Eh?"

Without understanding why, Hiller was annoyed that Goss had instituted a security check on Lynn Carlisle. In agency operations, one was always suspect until an intelligence report proved otherwise. It was a totally professional thing for Fred Goss to do. And a totally unprofessional response from Jay Hiller.

Chapter 14

If the kidnapping had bound people in the street with their fellow man in search of answers and reassurance, the assassination of a senator on top of that had the reverse effect.

People were frightened by the sight of strangers walking toward them on the sidewalk. In larger cities vandals broke store windows but did not loot. There were two incidents in Washington in which national guardsmen were challenged with bricks and clubs. Both ended quickly with tear-gas cannisters.

Suddenly it was life in a war zone. Only houses of worship seemed to offer safety, and they filled up almost daily with those seeking relief.

Every familiar streetcorner and alleyway in every American city became a potential hiding place for imagined snipers. If they would kill a four-year-old, they were capable of killing anyone. Any day, it was certain, there would be a report that John Quinlan Royce had been murdered. How could this be happening?

It undermined the very credo of Middle America—that our country was invincible, that we were a nation indivisible. Out of this shattered confidence came fear, and out of the fear, paranoia. Those venturing out of doors rarely went alone. In markets, forlorn faces gazed blankly at Merry Christmas signs as if a smile or eye contact might somehow indict them as conspirators in the abduction or assassination.

Like field mice they emerged at daylight, scurried after life's necessities, and retreated quickly to their homes. Day-to-day life had become a gauntlet of anxiety.

It was after dark when Jay Hiller left the GOB and drove to the State Department. The building was infested with guardsmen, two of whom quizzed him thoroughly before personally escorting him to the secretary's office.

In a cramped, overheated room littered with papers and books and a tangle of telephones, Stephen Brownell slumped in a chair behind an oversized desk, gazing blankly at the ceiling. He gestured for Hiller to seat himself and grimaced with pain as the gesture recalled the ever-present crick in his back.

"It's like Fort Knox around here," Hiller said sourly. "You expecting company?"

"Security," replied Brownell. "Clayton made it mandatory for every one of us. Don't be surprised if you're next."

"Ridiculous!" he said irritably.

Brownell looked surprised. "Really? I've got to say this is one time I agree with him."

Hiller shook his head. "You've got thirty armed men running around, none of whom you know. What's to stop me from putting on a National Guard uniform, coming in here with a gun, and popping you? You don't know these soldiers from Royce's kidnappers, Brownie. Who's screening *them*?"

Brownell shuffled nervously in his chair.

"I'll bring it up to the committee in the morning."

There was an uneasy silence as he tore a page from a note pad and tossed it in a wastebasket.

Finally Hiller said, "You know it looks bad."

Brownell nodded. Then he said impassively, "I don't mean to be crude, but Wainwright's death could have more to do with Congress coming through with the money than anything you or I could say. I know those men. They're not heroes."

"That says a hell of a lot for the illustrious representatives of the people—to teeter only when the gun points at each of them."

The secretary shrugged. "I heard you said as much in your address to them this morning, didn't you?"

Without waiting for a reply, Brownell straightened and slammed a fist on the desk top, causing Hiller to flinch. "Oh, damn us all," he shrieked. "I don't care if they do it out of fear—as long as they *do* it! We've got to have the President for that summit meeting. I've tested the water for a postponement and it's no go. They want Sy Clayton if it can't be John Royce."

Hiller looked thoughtfully at the secretary. "Just for argument's sake, let's say we can't get to Royce for another two weeks. Would it really make that much of a difference in Helsinki? I heard Clayton at the Capitol this morning, and he was impressive."

Brownell frowned and shook his head repeatedly. "What he says to Congress behind closed doors and what he does with world powers at a conference table over delicate issues are altogether different. It's not that the man lacks ability; he simply isn't *prepared* for this. You may see my point if I tell you that at this very minute we're deploying troops, munitions, ships, and missiles all over the globe."

Hiller looked astonished.

"You seem to be taking it extraordinarily well," he said.

"The 'war council' was nearly unanimous," Brownell said softly. He gnawed over a pen with his crooked teeth before adding, "Fortunately, what Clayton is doing can still be considered defensive. And it covers the possibility that he may be right, that there will be an attempt by some power to go against us."

Hiller shuddered. "Look, don't you think moving men and munitions all over creation is going to make Russia and China just a little bit nervous."

The secretary fidgeted with the pen and nodded.

"Yes, certainly, I'm sure there will be precautionary measures, but they won't force a confrontation unless we force it on them."

Brownell spoke with less than total conviction. He knew what he said was altogether logical—what troubled him was what it would mean if he was wrong.

A light snow was falling when Hiller left the State Department. Over the car radio he heard part of a news broadcast on Senator Wainwright but turned it off. He parked in the underground lot and got a hot meal a few blocks away, counting himself lucky to have found a restaurant open.

The streets were dark and deserted. Against the murky night sky and white flurries he could barely make out the outline of the GOB's three monolithic towers. Limp strands of unlit colored lights ran from streetlight to streetlight. Only the occasional sound of tires over the wet snow disturbed the silence. It was unlike any gloom he had ever known—beyond illusory, made surreal by every laughing window of every darkened store, by every cardboard reindeer, every wreath, tinseled Christmas tree, and plastic Santa Claus.

A week earlier the same shops had been models of animated commercialism, closing late, opening early, and briskly selling, selling, selling to the tune of "God Rest Ye Merry Gentlemen," which played ceaselessly over a network of cheap outdoor speakers.

Hiller cut through a square on the way back to the Op Center. Luminous drops of snow fell silently under the umbrella rays of a street lamp, and he was reminded of how peaceful things can sometimes be even in a large city. Even now.

In the Op Center activity was subdued. Agents talked quietly among themselves, mumbled into the telephone, buried themselves in intelligence reports. Hiller tried reading Fred Goss's report on the Frank Mayberry lead but couldn't concentrate. He glanced at others long enough to know that nothing was breaking. Nothing from the photo labs, nothing on the explosives, nothing from the presidential dossiers at the Protective Research Section. He pulled bottles of Scotch, Drambuie, and tequila from his desk, poured stiff shots in a coffee cup, and drank.

Again he considered calling Natalie Wainwright. He wanted to comfort her in some small way—be absolved of his guilt—but realized right now he was incapable of doing it. He needed comforting himself. He called Lynn Carlisle.

Lynn was watching her station's Eleven O'Clock Report on the murder of the senator and his daughter when the telephone rang. She was astonished to hear Jay Hiller and then, picking up the gravity in his voice, became concerned.

"Sorry I haven't been able to get back to you," he said. "I appreciated your bringing the parcel to me this morning."

"How *are* you?" she asked.

Hiller grunted. "I could throw up for a week." he said.

"I heard you were friendly with the senator. I'm sorry."

Hiller checked an impulse to burst into a self-mocking cackle. He poked himself in the chest with a thumb and said in a dry, coarse voice. "*This* asshole lives on, but the good die young. Christ, I dunno what makes sense anymore—ever. . . ."

"Are you working through the night again over there?"

Hiller rubbed a hand over his face. "Ah, no . . . I gotta get some sleep. Every few days I succumb."

Lynn said quietly, "Can you stop by for a little tea and sympathy on your way home?"

"Off the record?" Hiller asked.

"Off the record," Lynn said.

By the time Hiller left the GOB, the snow had let up and deposited a thin white gauze on the sidewalks. Despite a raw chill in the air, he walked with overcoat unbuttoned, footprints following him, as if in a trance. The day's events weighed on him like a tomb.

It kept coming back: If he had prolonged his conversation with Richard Wainwright . . . if the congressional session had gone on longer . . . if he had played *all* of the tape instead of only part. If, If, If. Now if the ransom was approved it would be for all the wrong reasons: on the one hand, a reaction born out of fear of personal injury; on the other, a public expression of stunned disbelief and sorrow, a eulogy of greenbacks to a young senator and his little girl.

Jay Hiller shuddered. He took the crudeness personally and was at once nauseous and disgusted. In some ways he felt responsible for the savagery in life's imbalances. Why should Richard Wainwright at forty and Krissy Wainwright at four cease to go on living, when Earl Morris Kenyon at sixty-one and Perry Jedlicker at sixty-three continued like fortresses. How brutally unjust that only the best seemed to have an aversion to long life.

Now he wondered why he had taken on such an assignment. He could have instead chosen to watch news reports in the comfort of his den, criticizing the drama with the same energy and conviction he might give to a daytime soap opera. Nothing on television ever seemed real. It would have been a way to stay out of it.

As it stood, the total of their efforts was only fragments of a confounding puzzle, and he knew better than anybody that this was the kind of business where a little knowledge was a dangerous thing. As special investigator, hadn't he already failed miserably? Wasn't Royce as good as dead?

Hiller crossed at a corner in front of an empty passenger bus idling at a red light, its driver an undecipherable shadow. It was near curfew hour.

He walked down a ramp to the underground parking lot. The clicking of his heels echoed off cold stone walls. At the end of the ramp, a neon light fluttered like a candle blowing in the wind, teasing him while lighting his way.

Outside, the bus brakes hissed, and the passenger lights went out. The bus engine roared and turned onto the ramp, flooding it with its sealed beams.

Hiller stirred from the fog and bent his body sharply around as if he were going to admonish the intruder for disrupting his solitude.

The bus suddenly growled and came at him like a lion on the attack, its savage yellow eyes blinding him. He froze in the middle of the ramp, mesmerized by the teeth he swore he saw in the face of grillwork and chrome.

Instinctively he flung himself forward and ran for his life, felt the headlights burn a hole in his back. He raced toward the end of the ramp and vaulted over a railing precisely the moment the bus thundered by. It squealed to a halt and backed up quickly, cutting off a retreat, spitting exhaust fumes and rubber, screaming as if some great tortured beast had broken loose, angling for revenge.

Hiller ran toward three parked vehicles in the center of the garage, his heavy breathing, his hurried footsteps, every noise ricocheting off cryptlike walls.

The bus surged forward. It bore down on him, rapidly accelerating, chasing him, now only yards behind. He leaped onto the trunk of one car, felt a sharp pain up the side of his leg, and dove across the hood of a second as the bus smashed into the vehicles, hurling chrome bumpers and wheels into the air like so many bowling pins.

Hiller fell to the ground and rolled under another auto, his heart pounding furiously. He wheezed, then fumbled for his nebulizer. The air passages began to squeeze close, the lungs shrank, and then came the short, choking huffs like a series of relentless dry heaves.

The wheels of the bus spun, shrieked, and ate concrete. It backed up, shifted gears and lunged forward, picked up speed as it rampaged across the garage, smashing into each parked car one by one. Hiller watched helplessly from underneath the auto as his Puma was turned into junk. He sucked deeply on the nebulizer and grabbed for a gun inside his coat. The bus turned. It squealed round and roared again, charged again, its piercing yellow eyes searching out its prey.

Now it thundered toward him at a vicious rate of speed. Like a soldier on his belly, he clawed savagely at the cold concrete, trying to scramble to his feet but a piece of his overcoat hooked to the chassis of the auto and pinned him down.

He struggled fiercely, dropping the gun and tearing his coat. And as the smoldering rubber of the huge front wheels bore down on his skull, he rolled from under the path of the rampaging bus like an unraveling carpet just as it smashed into the car, pushed it across the width of the garage, and hammered it against a wall.

Hiller staggered to his feet. The backup lights flashed and the bus roared again. It spun round and picked up speed, snorting like an angry bull. He spotted the gun, raced in front of the thundering steel menace to scoop it up on the fly, and wheeled and fired six shots through the windshield.

The engine roared again. The bus accelerated and smashed into a wall, shattering glass and metal, the driver slumped limply over the steering wheel.

Hiller inhaled deeply, trying to suck in air. His eyes were clouded, he hit again on the nebulizer, and a rush of lightheadedness passed over him. His heart pounded fiercely and his head throbbed with blood.

Until now, he had always thought it cruel that there was no harbinger of his asthma—no DEW line, no omen, no messenger to warn him of attack. But now he finally understood. It was the asthma itself that was harbinger—an omen of an early death he now knew must be awaiting him.

He stared at the ceiling, at the fluttering neon light, still gasping, swallowing, disbelieving. His senses returned slowly. For the first time, he was conscious of sweating profusely. His mouth was dry and there was a burning sensation in his throat.

Hiller stumbled to the bus, its engine still rumbling, and forced open the door. He climbed the steps, grabbed the driver by the collar and thrust a knee into his face. Then he angrily flung the body to the floor.

Hiller pulled the driver's head around to the light and lifted an eyelid to see if the man was alive. He noticed what seemed to be a loose layer of flesh on the cheek. He picked at it gingerly and peeled away several layers of a latexlike substance, revealing the assailant's true features. He was dark and olive-skinned with Latin features.

There was no identification on the body. In a shirt pocket, Hiller found an old torn newspaper clipping that included a photo of the President shaking hands with . . . Jay Marvin Hiller. On the reverse side, handwritten almost illegibly, was the word *Foxbat*. He took the clipping with him and hobbled down the steps of the bus.

In the time it took to calm himself, talk to police, and get a cab to Lynn's apartment, Hiller had chain-smoked a pack of cigarettes. When he rang her bell on the second floor of a stylish old red brick building in Georgetown after jarring open the lobby door, it was ten minutes of three.

Had he thought about the lateness of the hour or how little he knew Lynn, he never would have stood there, ragged and wired, ringing for attention. What he did think about, and what surprised him, was that there was someone he felt he could talk to.

When the door finally opened, the chain-lock was on and Lynn's heavy lids peered over it, blinking sleep from her eyes. She seemed uncertain of whether she was really awake and he was really standing there.

Lynn said wearily, "The tea is cold, and I ran out of sympathy at one A.M."

She started to shut the door.

"Gimme a break, Lynn," Hiller pleaded. "Someone just tried to pave Massachusetts Avenue with my head."

"Uh . . . are you kidding?" She was still groggy.

"I won't stay long," he said in a conciliatory tone, "but it would help me if we could talk a little."

The door opened and Lynn led him into the kitchen. She made tea, and they sat at a breakfast nook while Hiller told her what had happened.

As he spoke, she grew increasingly on edge and pulled her robe tight around her. Finally she got up and retrieved a bottle of brandy from a cabinet and downed half a glass. Hiller looked curiously at her.

"Hey, *I'm* the one who almost got it, remember?" he said with a little laugh.

Lynn paced about nervously.

"How can you be so calm about it?" she said impatiently.

Hiller shrugged. "Who's calm? When that fucking bus was on top of me, I actually felt my spirit leave my body. Why do you think I roused you out of a sound sleep? My guts are trembling inside like the San Andreas fault."

"But you're not hysterical, you're not even shaking or jittery. . . ."

"I'm *always* shaky and jittery, that's why you don't notice it now."

He could see she wasn't convinced and added earnestly, "You know what it is? I think you reach a point where you have so much to be afraid of that, at least externally, you begin not to be afraid."

Lynn said, "So you've reached that point? You have

so much to be afraid of that you're not afraid of anything?"

"*Two* things," he said. "Women and buses."

Lynn laughed. "I'll believe half of that."

Hiller watched his fingers play with the handle of the tea cup. "What bothers me so much is that it just doesn't make sense. Why kill *me?* I'm the one trying to *get* the bastards the fucking ransom."

Lynn put a shot of brandy in her glass and said, "Maybe this bus driver has nothing to do with the kidnappers. Or maybe you're getting close to something."

"Yeah," he said, frowning. "Close to getting killed."

Lynn took the glass to her lips and studied him. He struck her as randomly brutal but basically warmhearted, a brooder, a man whose sensitivities were ill at ease with his harsh texture. He was complex, she thought, and, each time she had seen him, different from the time before. But what astonished her was that it was more than just her reportorial instincts that fed her curiosity.

"You ever been married?" Lynn asked, again seating herself at the breakfast nook and resting her chin in her hand.

Hiller was surprised at the question. He gulped his tea, set the cup down, and said, "Yes and no."

"There's an original answer," she replied with a touch of derision. "Yes and no."

Hiller smiled. "I'm not trying to be mysterious," he said. "It's just that it'd be hard to explain without giving you my life story."

"Then give me your life story," she said easily.

He took the brandy glass from her hand and sipped. "Didn't you want to go to sleep?"

"It's always easier if I hear a story first," said Lynn. "Something left over from my childhood."

Hiller acknowledged her clever remark with a smile. He sighed and spoke quietly, thinking he might sound silly because it happened so many years ago, but his instinct told him to trust, and he went with it.

"I went with a girl the last two years of high school. Her name was Brenda—Brenda Romanoff. We talked about getting married and having a family—the American dream, y'know. People talked about chasing dreams and ideals. I never knew what they meant. I had my dream, I had my ideal. But there's always gotta be a villain in these kinds of confessions and in this one it was her parents. I even remember their names—George and Estelle, Estelle and George.

"They hated me—I think because they were sure I would never become a doctor or a lawyer, and anything else was beneath them. And so we ran away and got married, and they, of course, flipped out and had it annulled. A few months later, Brenda got pregnant—only I had nothing to do with it. And this time they made sure I was out of the picture. One week we were supposed to be crazy in love and the next she was married to someone else.

"I never knew what hit me. For months I walked around with the expression of a store mannequin. I'd go to cheap old movies in the afternoon and sit in the back and cry in the dark—through things like *Godzilla* and *Dracula*.

"I mean it's almost comical now, but then . . . A year later she got a divorce and—I couldn't believe it—gave up the baby. And though I'm not sure why, it made me very sad. We saw each other after that, at a bar in a bowling alley where we were both still too young to get served, but by then the world had completely turned over. We were both buried under layers and layers of emotional gauze and still-open wounds, and it was like trying to pull a dream from a past life into the present.

"I guess we must have sat there for almost the whole afternoon, and neither of us said anything. We just sat there. I wanted to tell her that in spite of everything I was sure I would always feel love for her . . . but I couldn't do it. I still hurt too much. I guess she got tired of hearing me pine away, because without a word she just got up and left. We didn't even say good-bye. The following morning I had my first attack of asthma and my last attack of lovesickness."

Hiller took another sip of brandy.

"Ever since then, in every relationship I've been in, I'm very careful."

"Caution and love? I don't see how that can work. Caution and love don't really go together."

Hiller paused thoughtfully. "I'm not so sure," he said. "Caution and passion may not go together, I'll agree with you there. But caution and love . . . ?"

Lynn studied the hard lines in his face. "So you like being a loner?"

He smiled wanly and shook his head. "I'd have to say no. I've learned, perhaps as well as anybody, that life is not better alone. But for me to go out now and compete with the young, the healthy, the handsome, seems as suicidal to me as my cigarettes and, well, my liquor. Cheers."

Hiller lifted his drink and turned away suddenly shy eyes. "I don't know," he added with a frown, "it's just that I'd get involved, and something would happen to me. I'd be different somehow. And I can't stand feeling out of control."

Lynn knitted her brows. "You mean you have to control your relationships all the time?" she asked.

"It's not my relationships I mind feeling out of control of, it's *me*."

Lynn paused a moment and chewed on her lower lip.

"Funny, but I usually feel that way—out of control. Things happen around me all the time that I can't stop, start, or change. All I can do is report it if it's news and get uptight if it isn't. Like yesterday, first my gynecologist goes out of business and then I get an obscene phone call . . ."

Hiller laughed. "An obscene phone call? That bothered you?"

"Sure it bothered me—from a *woman*. Do you want some more tea?"

"Coffee this time, no lemon," Hiller said, trying for a joke.

Lynn smirked and got the instant from the pantry. She handed him the jar with a clean spoon.

"Why did you quit CIA work when you did?" she said, pouring hot water into his cup.

"Didn't you read the newspapers? I couldn't work according to the system" he replied. "No one laughed at my jokes."

Lynn would have pressed him for an answer but at that moment she lost her grip on the pot. It fell on the cup, breaking it into half a dozen pieces. Hot water splashed onto Hiller's lap and he leaped up trying to smother a cry.

Lynn squealed apologies and pulled him into the next room despite his protests.

"Oh, God," she cried, "are you all right? Go in the bathroom. There's a robe behind the door."

Hiller tried to protest, but she nearly shoved him inside.

"Please, put on the robe. . . . I'll iron the pants for you."

Lynn waited anxiously at the door, clasping her hands like an expectant father. "Way to go, Carlisle," she muttered to herself. "You dumb klutz!"

Hiller's muffled voice came from the other side.

"Listen, after what I've been through today, hot pants is no big thing."

A minute later, Hiller came out of the bathroom holding his slacks and wearing a housecoat. Under different circumstances she might have burst into hysterical laughter at the improbable sight of a federal investigator in her night clothes, but she still smarted from embarrassment.

Hiller looked himself over and flushed a deep red. He felt ridiculous.

"Shouldn't *you* end up in *my* robe? Isn't this fucking backwards?"

"No," Lynn said gently. "I don't like fucking backwards."

She had said it as a joke, but Hiller looked at her with complete surprise, as if he had discovered something new. Just as suddenly she radiated sensuality, and the spark of something distant and inaccessible flickered in him. Her hair reflected the berry-red color of her lips; her whitewater pale green eyes were stunning. He moved close to her and their bodies tingled with the excitement of touching for the first time.

He slid his hand underneath her robe and traced the outline of her waist and hips over the nightgown as their lips pressed, as their mouths opened, as their tongues played over one another. He explored her teeth and the insides of her cheeks, and became feverish with the heat from her body. Lynn felt protected and protective, both—and thirsted for the secure warmth that would allow her to feel forever safe as a woman, alive and not afraid, alone and yet not lonely.

Down they sank into the cushion of the rug. She felt him swell near her center as slowly he undid her garments, let them slip from the soft curves of her shoulders, tasted salt from the nape of her neck.

Her breasts were like peaks of freshly-fallen snow, as salient and as cool, each with a perfect pink crest which he glistened with the wetness of his tongue. Her rapid breaths excited him, the stroking movement of her stomach, rising and falling against his own. Ever so gently with her hands, her long slender fingers, she reached down and stroked his hardness and he moaned and gently bit her lip and whined with pleasure at the rhythm she had found.

They purred softly like kittens and played with one another, childlike and unhurried. Slowly as her chestnut velvet hair spilled onto his face, lapping him gently, as their breathing became more hurried, he grew dizzy in her fragrance.

The buttery flesh of her thighs became moist and alive with invisible currents, and his hand felt for the origin of her lightly-perfumed scent. How delicious the slightly sticky coating on his fingers, how wet and warm and wonderfully willing the surrender.

Deep, deeper into the core of her world he penetrated; deeper into the forbidden fruit of her body.

Chapter 15

Only the leaves from the dense tropical scrub forest which covered the limestone earth rustled in the soft wind. It was unusually serene for a winter night, as temperatures often dropped forty degrees from mid-afternoon.

Crickets played their nocturnal symphony, mosquitoes fed, and the evening's mood seemed to breathe the former tranquility of Las Cumbres. By ten o'clock half the village was asleep, nestled in their beds with windows open.

But on a little wooded rise above a furrowed field, separated from the rest of the village, Sergio Grijalva showed no respect for the quietude. He flung open the door of the small adobe hut that for years had been the home of the Diaz family and waited a moment for his narrow hooded eyes to adjust with catlike precision to the darkness.

Then he threw himself on the room with a violent passion as if it were a mortal enemy, making no effort to camouflage his presence. He pulled jars and small clay pots from shelves and tossed them to the dirt floor. As his search grew more frustrating, his eyes flared brighter and angrier. He smashed a large chipped pitcher of water with dead bugs floating in it and completely overturned a table.

He tore books from a shelf and hurled them across

the room, at first singly, then by handfuls. Finally he upended the bookshelves. He stalked about the room like a caged animal, eyes fiery, nostrils flaring, the smell of Yucatecan beer on his breath.

He flung open cabinets, smashed vases, crushed porcelain religious artifacts in his fist. The sight of a Bible inflamed him, and he violently ripped its covers apart. With bare hands he tore a leg from a wooden chair, swinging it against glasses and bottles here, against rotten fruit there. He poked and probed.

It had to be here, Grijalva thought, this thing Diaz chose to hide with his life. And the longer it took to find, the more enraged and dangerous he became.

In the padre's quarters, the naked bulb above the large wood table laid oblique shadows on Luis's round face. He watched from a stool with huge shy brown eyes as the priest recorded his expression and colors on a canvas, dabbing here and there with a multitude of brushes.

The room was simple, with a wall of wooden cabinets, a few chairs, a large table, a large wooden crucifix over a desk with a shaded lamp, and an old easel. Dozens of still-life and landscape canvases—some completed and unframed, others unfinished or abandoned—and assorted paints, books, cans of gesso, glaze, and linseed oil, cluttered the room.

Multicolored swatches were evident on the white plaster walls where the padre had either tested a color or accidentally brushed against it with pigment. The table was usually covered by a brown cotton cloth to stifle the smell of twenty years of spilled paint impregnated in the wood, except on occasions such as this when he worked.

As a youth, Julian Serra studied painting at a small American college in southern California and loved the work of Van Gogh, Renoir, and Géricault. Oddly enough, he found the religious art of the Renaissance masters not at all to his liking.

After becoming disillusioned for a while with his own abilities, he returned to Mexico and entered the seminary, giving up the idea of pursuing art as a vocation. It was only after Padre Serra was given his own parish in Las Cumbres that he returned to his paints and canvases with renewed enthusiasm and an acceptance of his limitations as an artist.

The padre, now engrossed in the challenge of a portrait, held two brushes in his left hand, the stem of another in his mouth, and the fourth one loosely in his right as he labored over the painted lips. But he was used to painting things that did not move and quickly perceived the boy's impatience.

"Luis," the padre said gently, with the brush handle still in his mouth. "You must sit still if you want me to do your picture, otherwise you will come out with two noses and three eyes."

The boy put his hands under his thighs and sat on them. His face was pained with boredom. Serra continued to labor over the canvas but said with sudden grave concern, "This terrible thing your father has done, you are sure you don't know why he has done it?"

Luis's face dropped into a twisted frown. "No," he said sadly.

The priest looked up. He was annoyed with himself for resurrecting the topic. If Luis was bored a moment ago, at least he was not miserable.

Serra tossed the brushes on his palette with more than a trace of self-effacing anger. Then his anger gave way to a fresh desire to delve ever more deeply into the matter. It was a mystery unsolved, and perhaps a few answers would help both of them gain some understanding. Perhaps it could make the tragic event easier to live with. Thus convinced, the priest took a chair next to the boy and spoke to him gently.

"Your father said nothing to you? Nothing at all?"

Luis pulled strands of his straight jet black hair over his eyes and shook his head.

"Was he sad about anything? Was he angry about anything?"

The boy stuck a finger to the corner of his mouth and chewed on the nail. Then he replied meekly, "He argues with some men."

The padre looked at Luis astonished. "Argues with some men?" he said disbelievingly. "What men?"

The boy shrugged.

"What men, Luis?" he repeated. His voice was pressed with a measure of urgency, though he did his best to restrain himself for fear of frightening the child.

Luis shrugged again.

The padre leaned toward him. "What did they argue about? Do you remember?"

"He has a package and they want it back."

"And what is in this package?"

Luis shrugged.

"Where is this package now?" the padre said.

Suddenly Luis's eyes brightened and a smile broke across his earth-colored face. He leapt from the stool and ran to the door. There he turned and cried, "I have it, Padre. I will get it for you!"

"Wait," the priest exclaimed. But Luis pulled open the door and stretched his restive legs into a gallop. Serra hurried outside and called after him, "Luis! Wait! It is too late tonight."

But it was too late to stop Luis. No healthy, energetic youth would have heeded such a call when, for certain, the alternative was being put to bed for the night.

A little more than an hour later, a weatherbeaten old bus, rusty and gray and without a door that could close, rattled up to a corner on Merida's main square, the Plaza Independencia, eighteen bumpy miles southeast of Las Cumbres. The padre stepped down and winced in pain; it was still the most difficult movement for his bad leg.

This was a journey he rarely made anymore, for the city had, by his own estimation, grown immense, obtrusive, and indifferent.

In the generation that had passed since he first arrived, it had exploded with six times its original population. The old stone buildings for government and commerce which surrounded the square were as imposing as ever. Some dated from 1549. But the character of the area had changed.

Gleaming metal signs marked the streets, whereas once, on each corner house, a figure of an elephant, flamingo, old woman, bird, or bull had shown the way. Only a few small windmills on residential rooftops, used to pump water from a well system, still remained. Little shops that formerly boasted handcrafted fabrics and leather goods, furniture and weaving, fruit stands and fresh fish, were giving way to breweries and bottling works.

The city had begun to reek of itself. On weekends it bragged of dancing and dancing nights, splendid tequila nights, streets full of people defiant with laughter and beer. On weekday evenings like this one the night brought secrecy. Every street, every plaza and fountain, every doorway was decorated with pairs of people, for the most part very young people, talking in the shadows very closely and quietly, their arms belonging to each other.

"They should be asleep, these little ones," the padre thought a little indignantly as he hurried along a dimly lit street. And then he wondered, fearfully, whether Luis could be among them. He quickly dismissed the thought as absurd, though he was unable to contain his sense of urgency.

Where would Luis have gone so suddenly for this package of mysteries? He had guessed *here*, because Ramon Diaz had come several times a week with his son. But where? Where in the city? And if not here, then where else? He had been to the Diaz hut earlier in the day to gather Luis's things, and there was no such package there.

Serra turned up the main thoroughfare. He was appalled by the sight of a drunken Mexican Indian propped against a storefront, laughing to himself and chewing on the head of an uncooked fish.

Even more startling was the familiar figure, further up the block, of Maria Lopesa, the heavyset woman from his village, ambling across the street with her eleven-year-old son in tow. The padre broke into a trot and caught up with them in front of a liquor store.

Maria was a little bewildered to see him in Merida. After all, this was not a place he often came. She was a little embarrassed that he knew where she was at such an hour. But Serra was more concerned with imminent matters and took no notice. He was still a little winded when he spoke.

"Maria, have you seen Luis? He ran from the church a few hours ago and I cannot find him anywhere."

Maria looked sympathetically at the priest and

plucked at her flaccid double chin. Then she replied, "No, Padre. I haven't. But wait, I will ask Don Carlo."

And in a moment she was hurrying up the street to find her husband. It was then the padre realized she had probably come to fish him from one of the liquor halls.

Serra's anxious eyes darted up and down the block, and when he was certain nobody was watching, he dashed into the liquor store. It was cluttered with bottles, papers, magazines, and cheap souvenirs for tourists.

He ordered a bottle of tequila and a pack of cigarettes, which he tore open so nervously that he practically decimated the package. Finally he managed one to his lips and lit it. It was the first time he had smoked in fourteen years.

The storekeeper, a middle-aged man with dark-rimmed glasses and a short, husky build, studied the priest suspiciously as he fumbled through his pockets for change. Just then a newspaper on the counter caught his attention. He bought one, paid for the liquor and cigarettes as well, and hurried out.

Cradling a brown bag with his purchases under an arm, the padre unfolded the paper. A page-one headline made him shudder involuntarily. He swallowed hard, and a dead pale washed over his face. The words repeated in his head over and over again: "5 Suspects in U.S. Presidential Kidnap."

He looked up, unnerved, eyes darting first one way, then another. A man across the street was staring at him. From some distance away, someone cried his name. His mind raced out of control and he felt lightheaded. Things were moving toward him. He dropped the cigarette, quickly turned a corner, and disappeared into the night.

A moment or two later Maria Lopesa returned looking for the padre, exasperation written into the layers of her face. She would have told him that Don Carlo had seen Luis hurrying toward the Diaz farmland, humming quietly to himself.

Chapter 16

December 13.

When Jay Hiller left Lynn's Georgetown apartment, he was conscious of a dull pain in the groin, a result, he reasoned, of a long period of inactivity in that region followed by a night of vigorous stimulation. He did not choose to remember how long it had been. But the feelings that rushed helter-skelter through his body this morning reminded him of what it had been like to be in love. By the time a taxi dropped him at the Capitol Bus Company warehouse, he felt as if he could tackle the world.

Nine buses, identical to the one that had nearly creamed him, were parked alongside a large, rough-looking wood-and-aluminum structure. Inside were six bays, two of them with disabled vehicles. Portable heaters blasted hot air at a couple of men working under a bus. But elsewhere inside, icicles hung from beams, windows, and doorways.

"Who's in charge around here?" Hiller barked in visible puffs.

A bald head peered out from underneath a front axle and spat. "Yeh, whaddya need?"

"Your attention, for starters. I'm a federal investigator."

"Yeah, an' I'm a federal spark plug," the man snarled. "Come back during regular hours." The head disappeared again under the axle.

Hiller fished his government ID from his wallet and shoved it under the bus in the man's face. In so doing, he picked up a blot of grease on a sleeve and muttered to himself in disgust. The bald man struggled out from under the bay lift and wiped his hands on a grease-laden rag. He was big but had a soft belly, and belched frequently.

"You really work for the govva-mint?" he asked with an expression of childlike disbelief.

Hiller smirked.

"Yah, okay. Better come in to the office. Warmer in there."

If it was warmer in the foreman's cubicle, then the difference in air temperature was the difference between the coffee maker being on and off. There was grease and crumpled papers everywhere and a sign on a desk that read, "God, Guns and Guts Make America Great."

If this guy's brain doesn't work, thought Hiller, it's probably because it's frozen.

The man looked at Hiller, who was clutching his arms to his body, trying to get warm. "Whaddya need?"

"License number 2Y 7983. Bus number fifty-four. I want to know who the fuck was driving it last night."

The foreman, nonplussed, pulled open a drawer and took out a sheaf of papers. He rustled through and tore one off.

"Guy named . . . Russell Frazier."

"He works for you?"

"No. No. It was a charter. . . ." he said, smothering a belch.

"Did Frazier give you an ID? Driver's license? References? Address? Employment record? Anything like that?"

"Hey, I'm renting the guy a bus, I'm not checking him for the clap, for crissakes. . . ."

Hiller's glare told the foreman to try harder. He began riffling through the papers.

"Lessee, driver's license . . . yah. References and employment we don't need if he got credit cards."

Hiller suddenly stopped thinking about the temperature. "What's the address on the license?" he demanded.

"Twenty-six twenty-one N Street Northwest," the foreman said, looking up at the clock. "You catch up with him, you tell him to get his ass back in here. That fast-talking sonnabitch was due in three hours ago with my bus."

Hiller was already out the door but called back, "Your bus is an art sculpture in the municipal garage and that fast-talking sonnabitch is viewable at the city morgue. Thanks for the address."

The beat of the wipers slapping against the windshield sounded like an old well pump in need of oiling. The government car raced along 15th Street in a freezing rain.

The shittiest of winters, Hiller thought, punching the cigarette lighter. Cold. Wet. Dark. Perfect for what the newspapers had started calling America's Dark December. He stuck a butt in his mouth and slowed, turning onto N Street. The car crept along the avenue as he checked numbers against office buildings and small shops—2621 N Street Northwest. A tailgating auto sounded its horn. Twenty-six-oh-three, Twenty-six-eleven, Twenty-six-fifteen. The horn blared a second time. Hiller rolled down the side window as the horn rang out a third time, a prolonged blast.

He waved the driver past. There was a squeal of tires as the auto pulled around him. "Up yours, dingbat!" the man shouted as he sped off. Hiller flipped him the bird. And found what he was looking for—twenty-six-twenty-one—a gray, four-story office building with a nondescript entrance, a simple glass door, and a small sign overhead reading "Global Communications."

He parked in a yellow zone and hurried inside. On the second floor in the oak-paneled reception area a secretary sat behind a desk painstakingly painting her fingernails with blood-red polish. She was pretty in a dated kind of way, with her hair in a bun and lipstick that recalled the stark colors of the fifties. She looked a little startled to see a man in front of her.

"May I help you?" she asked without bothering to affect the corporate welcome smile.

"I'd like to see Russell Frazier," Jay Hiller said forcefully.

The secretary looked at him with an expression of bewilderment, as if he had just ridden in on a kangaroo. She seemed to examine every feature on his face. Finally she said, "Who?"

Hiller quickly grew impatient. He enunciated the name a second time, slowly and facetiously. The secretary picked up an interoffice phone.

"Mr. Langway, there's a man who says he's here to see a Mr. Frazier."

She listened attentively and put down the receiver. In a vicious tone, she snapped, "Sorry. There is no Russell Frazier at this office."

The two glared at each other. Finally Hiller said,

"I'd accept that at face value, sweetheart, except my instincts tell me you're a liar."

"I don't give a damn what your instincts tell you," she hissed, throwing her head back like a cobra set to strike. "If you're not out of here in one minute I'll have the police haul you out."

Hiller gnashed his teeth and leaned over the desk with a glint in his eye. His wallet flipped open, baring his credentials, and he shoved them in her face. He snarled through set teeth, "Tell Langway I want to talk to him. Now!" He shouted the last word. "If he refuses, I'll have his ass, and yours, subpoenaed and scrubbed till they squeak. You got that?"

The woman got up and stormed through a door leading to the inner offices. Hiller sat on her desk and pulled open one of the drawers. Quickly he rummaged through an appointment book and a few loose interoffice memos. In an interoffice directory, he checked under the *F*s for a listing for *Frazier*. There was none, but an odd entry, an extension number next to the letter *F*, caught his eye. He dialed the extension; there was no answer.

As he replaced the directory, the secretary barged in, marched up to her desk, and slammed the drawer closed. "Just what the hell do you think you're doing?" she shrieked.

Hiller patted his nose with an exaggerated motion. "You have a Kleenex I could use?"

Angrily she yanked a tissue from a box at the forefront of her desk. Hiller took it and blew his nose, unconvincingly, and tossed it in a wastebasket. He smiled sheepishly, which seemed to infuriate her more.

"This way," she said icily.

Hiller followed her down a long narrow corridor. He whistled a few bars of "God Bless America" and then said lightly, "I couldn't help noticing in your directory an extension number for *F*. What's it for?"

She was not surprised he had been through her book. She had suspected as much. But it enraged her.

"Finance," she replied coldly.

"Well, why isn't it written out like other departments? If you're going to use a letter system, how come *billing* isn't *B* and *shipping* isn't *S*?"

The secretary's jaw tensed. She breathed heavily and snarled, "Because *B* could be *bookkeeping* and *S* could be *stockroom*."

"In that case, *F* could also be *filing*, couldn't it?"

The secretary knocked on an office door. A voice beckoned, and she opened it. She looked haughtily at Hiller and left him there without an answer or an introduction.

Gordon Langway got up from behind a large desk with some difficulty and ambled toward the door to greet Hiller. He was an obese man, easily three hundred pounds, with thinning light brown hair, light brown eyes with outlandishly shaved eyebrows, and the affable manner usually associated with such an enormous body.

Langway had a double chin that looked like rubber, and the extra layer of flesh seemed to repeat itself on all his facial features, particularly his lower lip. He appeared older than his fifty-one years and reminded Hiller of two people: Babe Ruth and Alfred Hitchcock.

"Come in, Mr. Hiller. Come in."

He extended a hand in welcome. On the desk was a Lucite nameplate: Gordon Langway, Vice President, and a large plastic model of a yacht. The walls were covered with a series of framed photographs of Langway and various associates on board a boat, posing with deep-sea catches.

"Sorry for the misunderstanding, Mr. Hiller," Langway said amiably. "Secretaries are sometimes a little overprotective."

"*Yours* needs an exorcist," Hiller said flatly.

The executive let the remark pass and again seated himself. Hiller took one of two cushiony armchairs that faced the desk.

In an abrupt businesslike tone Langway said, "What can I do for you?"

"You're the *vice* president here?"

Langway cleared his throat and said, "I find the title of *president* rather pretentious, Mr. Hiller. But I *am* the chief executive officer."

"Then you should be able to give me some information on Russell Frazier."

Langway made a helpless gesture with his left hand. "If I knew who he was . . ."

Hiller pulled a photo from his overcoat and tossed it on the desk. "This asshole."

Langway took it and examined it for a moment. "No," he said. "Never saw him." Then with some effort, he leaned across the desk to return it to Hiller.

"He used this address as his own," Hiller said bluntly.

Langway made a wheezing sound and cleared his throat. "I'm afraid I can't answer for that," he replied firmly. "All I can tell you is I've never seen this man, I've never heard of this man, I don't know who this man is."

The creases in Hiller's forehead grew deeper. "That so?" he asked.

Suddenly Langway's double chin stiffened and seemed anything but rubbery. His eyes leered. "That *is* so," he said flatly. "Anything else I can do for you, Mr. Hiller?"

Hiller stood up quickly and said, "Yeah, there is one thing. . . ."

Langway smirked. "Well? What's that?"

"Find someone who knows how to drive a bus."

Jay Hiller was looking into the fresh young faces of Jeff Brodsky and Jack Albaum. In spite of his unspoken regard for them, they still seemed like junior high school kids to him.

The lines in their faces had yet to become ridges, and he imagined, perhaps a little unfairly, that they still talked about what they would grow up to be.

To Albaum, Hiller fired a rapid succession of orders. "Get an administrative subpoena and look into Langway's checkwriting habits in both his personal and business accounts. Find out where he gets his money and what he does with it. Check with IRS on his tax returns. Get a list of every phone call he's made in the past twelve months. Set up a command post near Global Communications and monitor the phones. Get photographs of everyone who goes in and out of there. Something there *has* to turn up a lead."

Without losing a beat, he turned to Jeff. "Keep in touch with the morgue to see if anyone shows up to claim the stiff. I want the lab to check the handwriting on the newspaper clipping I found on the body. Make sure they also test the clothing, the blood stains, the hair, the skin, the perspiration, the contact lenses. I want to know what that bastard ate for dinner last night. Then stay as wired to Langway as you can without putting a fix on yourself. Report in every couple of hours."

Brodsky seemed pleased with his assignment. He cocked his head and made a fist. "Easy," he said with brash confidence.

Hiller leaped on him with a vengeance. "Bullshit *easy!* This isn't a class in follow-the-leader, putz. This is the real thing. If you think I'm kidding, go take a look at the photos of what they did to that four-year-old girl."

Brodsky blinked and swallowed hard; he had seen the pictures. His eyes widened with unsettling diffidence. Hiller thought it a good idea that it remain. Then he waved the two of them away with an angry gesture.

The digital clock in the office made it blunt—half the afternoon was shot already. He guzzled a drink at the water fountain, quickly checked the Telex, and sat down to read the Day Report.

The lab had pieced together the bomb in the Capitol building and found it rigged to a cola bottle; a soda delivery had been made at the East Front entrance shortly before the explosion; the FBI was cross-examining the Capitol guards for a description of the delivery man.

Then he pored over a CIA dossier—EYES ONLY—J. M. HILLER—and picked up a phone. He was cradling the receiver under the right side of his face, tapping anxious fingers, when Fred Goss came up behind him and playfully tossed a cigarette over his shoulder.

"I just tried to call you," Hiller said, slamming down the phone. "I don't get it, Fred. This is all the crap that's available on Frazier? We've got more on my mailman, for crissakes. There's nothing in here."

Goss flashed his ivory teeth in a pained smile. "I didn't think you'd be too pleased with that," he said softly. "But what we had is there. We can't make up stuff for what we're lacking, eh?"

Hiller's brown eyes hooded. He considered Goss's reply and shook his head. "Horse shit. How much of this file went into the burn basket before they let you send it over."

"Take a break, Jay. There was nothing held back. I checked it myself."

"Does this include stuff from the Bureau?"

"No, I've put in a request for their reports. You should be getting them shortly. Also, I just received the field reports from Central and South America. Nothing in there, but I'll send them over anyway."

Hiller gnashed his teeth. "Dammit," he whispered angrily. "It doesn't make sense."

Goss sensed his frustration and frowned. "What makes you think there ought to have been more?"

Hiller looked him straight in the eye and said, "*You* figure it out. This bastard Frazier was arrested four times, once for supposedly torching the Soviet Embassy. For that alone the Company should be on the guy's ass; he shouldn't even be able to find a stall in the bathroom by himself."

Goss shook his head.

"You're looking for something that isn't there," he said, raising his voice a little. "You're assuming the guy was a hit man, that maybe he had something to do with the kidnappers. I think he just may—just may— have been a psycho."

"C'mon, Fred. Psychos don't tear your picture from a newspaper before they freak out. When someone nearly cremates me with a bus four days after I take an assignment like this, I gotta assume it's more than a nearsighted driver trying to fuck pigeons."

Chapter 17

An hour after the padre left Maria Lopesa on a Merida street, he was rushing up the wide dirt road in Las Cumbres toward the church. It was almost one A.M.

No one was ever outside at that hour, and his hurried footsteps disrupted the silent rhythms of the night. He had luckily caught a bus almost immediately and he prayed on the ride back to the village that Luis would be in his quarters already, sleeping soundly.

But the sudden cool breeze in the air was a foreboding. It was not simply the night's raw breath; it was much more severe than that. A chilly wind, swirling dust from the center of the road, floated stealthily over the adobe settlement and set upon it like an angel of death.

In between gusts the priest imagined he heard the sound of an automobile behind him. But when he turned around there was nothing. He stepped up his pace, then broke into a run and was never more relieved to reach his quarters.

He bolted the door, the first time he had done so in many years, and leaned against it, breathing heavily in the darkness of his room.

His relief did not last long, for he saw immediately that the cot was empty and Luis had not returned. The padre turned on a light, threw the newspaper on the table, and nervously tore the bottle of tequila from the brown bag. The pack of cigarettes tumbled to the floor but he paid them no mind. He grabbed a glass from a shelf and poured himself a drink, inadvertently spilling a little.

The liquor made him grimace and tears welled in his fading brown eyes, but it steadied him. He went to a drawer and took out a small envelope and paused a minute to try to think.

From it he dumped the contents, five passport-size photographs, on the wood table alongside several tubes of oil paint and the wet palette he had not had time to clean. Then he spread the newspaper out with its bold black headline and page-one pictures of five men thought to be responsible for the kidnapping of the American president.

For a moment, not knowing whether their faces would match the ones in Grijalva's photos, his heart stopped. The possibility of abetting such an unthinkable act struck more than a discordant note in the padre. It challenged all his beliefs, reproached him scornfully, and more than anything, made him frightened to be alive. Instead of eagerly awaited mornings, tomorrows had become impending horrors.

He poured himself another shot of tequila and drank. It was a drink for strength. He was terrified that the worst of his fears would be confirmed.

With hands still trembling, he fumbled with the photographs and checked them against the newspaper. Then he breathed an exhausted sigh. To his utter relief, the photos were not those of the men in the paper.

The padre looked across the room at the unfinished portrait of Luis. He put a hand to his head and rubbed his eyes and was lost a moment in silence.

A sudden banging on the church door startled him,

and he leapt up in anticipation, hoping of course that the boy had at last made his way back. He lit a kerosene lamp and carried it into the vestibule, then unlocked the huge wooden door and pulled it open, preparing to first wrap the child in his arms and then scold him for running off.

But instead of the wet-nosed shy Luis at his feet, the dark, menacing silhouette of Sergio Grijalva stood over him, taking up the entire doorway. In the lamplight he looked more frightening than ever.

He pushed his way past the padre and craned his neck to look at the high church ceiling. "You have the passports, Padre?" he asked in an ugly whisper.

Serra blinked uncomfortably. "No. Not yet. I am sorry. . . ."

Grijalva turned slowly to face the priest. He wore a smile that was positively unnerving. He knew this and enjoyed its effect on people. Then he continued in the whisper, "Would you keep the Holy Father waiting?"

The padre lowered his eyes and stammered. "I have, I have been unable to work. You see it . . . the boy, Luis, my friend . . . he has disappeared."

Grijalva's eyes, dark and hooded, gleamed with insane fury. The jaw froze and he said threateningly, "I'll put it for you simply, Padre. The sooner I get the documents, the sooner you get the boy."

Serra glared incredulously at the man before him. "What? *You* have him? What is the matter with you?" he said boldly. His voice rose stiffly and echoed in the church. "Why do you involve an innocent child? This boy has already suffered enough. Have you no compassion? What kind of man are you?"

A long steel-bladed knife sprang from the dark with alarming speed and flashed in the light of the flickering kerosene lamp. "The impatient kind," snarled Grijalva. And suddenly his powerful arms were around the priest's head as he thrust the blade against the skin of his neck. The lamp fell from the padre's grasp and shattered on the ground, though it continued to burn in a pool of kerosene.

"I said *today*, didn't I?" the bigger man roared. Then, with the speed of an attacking animal, Grijalva viciously slashed the priest behind the left ear. He let out an anguished cry and felt his knees turn to jelly. Blood rushed from a four-inch gash and flowed down the side of his face. It pulsed and throbbed, and the padre sank to the ground.

In the near-rabid darkness, Grijalva said with the lofty arrogance of Satan, "If you don't *hear*, then you don't need ears to listen. You failed once, nobody fails a second time. The documents will be ready in two days—or the painting Padre will have more in common with another unfortunate artist who came long before him."

But to his sins of violence and arrogance, Sergio Grijalva also added lies. He did not have Luis Diaz as he claimed, for earlier in the evening when the boy ran off to a tilled field thick with corn, potatoes, and cactus-like agave, singing something his father had taught, a different fate had awaited him.

Luis had become aware of the night and of being alone. He was frightened, but the song helped him feel not so alone, not so fearful.

He stomped about, from one furrow to the next, kicking stones, whining nervously, blinking when he imagined something or when he thought he heard someone behind him.

The song faded then from his lips. For a while he was submerged in a dull panic with absolutely no idea why he had come. He felt a sudden urge to cry and in fact as his breaths became shorter and more restricted, tears did threaten to fall from his eyes.

It was not as easy as he imagined it would be, even with countless lizards, unseeable at night, for company. All the furrows now looked so alike that it did not seem at all like the field his father had plowed. Just when he was ready to give it up and turn back and welcome the sight of the padre's crinkled face and enjoy a protected sleep, he saw a familiar rock the size of a gopher not ten yards from his feet. This he overturned and began digging with his hands in the earth, which was much finer in consistency than the soil in the rest of the field.

Luis hollowed out a small deep hole quickly, eager to complete his mission. Finally, his hands fell upon a sackcloth which he yanked from the dirt and unraveled. Inside was a small package, the same one he had told the padre about, the same one his father refused to give up.

Luis was flooded with a feeling of accomplishment, and his huge eyes danced with excitement. But it quickly turned to panic and a terrible pounding in his chest when he saw hovering over him like a hideous monster from a bad dream the smiling mask of fury of Sergio Grijalva. He was a vicious, confident Goliath facing a David without a sling.

The boy swallowed hard. Never had he seen anyone so huge or so darkly threatening. Suddenly Luis darted away, skipping over dead and dying crops, leaping over furrows. The pounding in his heart now beat furiously in his throat and his mind was totally abandoned to a single thought: escape. Yet somehow he could not let go of the package. Somehow he clung to it like life.

Sergio bolted after him, his long stride equalling three of Luis's. But the boy knew the terrain, and several times Sergio stumbled and broke stride. Grijalva was excited by the smell of fear in the air, and it propelled him. Even alone, he was like a pack of wolves chasing a terrified deer. He gained on Luis, and in desperation the boy dropped the parcel. But now Grijalva wanted more. He bore down on the youth and hurled his tremendous frame on top of him. Luis collapsed under the brutal thrust. He gasped and struggled and with startling reflexes sank his teeth into a bare ankle on Sergio's left leg. Grijalva let out a bloodcurdling scream and swung his powerful right arm round to the back of Luis's skull. The blow landed squarely with a chilling crack, and Luis fell unconscious.

Grijalva staggered to his feet and his left leg buckled a little. It was bleeding from the ankle. He angrily ripped the garment from the boy's back and wrapped a tourniquet round the wound. He retrieved the package and tore away the wrapping to examine the contents. His thick tan lips curled with satisfaction. Then he picked Luis up by a leg and hoisted him over a shoulder as if he were carrying a slab of meat.

Favoring the right leg a little, Grijalva walked back to the hole that Luis had dug and lowered him upside down to his chest. Then he kicked a pile of dirt into the hole, filling and packing it around Luis's head, neck, and shoulders, burying him alive with as little concern as he might give to discarding a plateful of fish bones.

Chapter 18

December 14.

The sky was weighted with gunmetal gray and the threat of thunder and lightning—its drama assimilated by the greater drama of the morning.

As a light drizzle fell, twelve Navy jet fighters in formation streaked over Arlington National Cemetery. In a moment the planes were lost inside the cloud cover—thick, smoky, gray-on-gray, the perfect impenetrable curtain—though the thundering chorus of their engines still shook the ground.

Lynn Carlisle walked slowly across the rolling hills of the cemetery; thousands upon thousands of white headstones, identically unadorned, spread out before her. She felt the tremor from the jet noise. It seemed a little like a protest. Could she write it that way? A protest from an earth not yet ready to swallow these two victims of destiny, fate, whatever one might choose to call it.

National news, the funeral. Maybe international. She was there to report it along with a battalion of other news people, government officials, and foreign dignitaries. But anyone who was there could not help being affected.

A young senator who would at the very least have exerted some measure of influence in Washington; a child who had not yet learned the cruelty and savagery of survival. Why had they been chosen? A chill rose from inside Lynn's body and turned it cold as ice. *Life makes no sense to me,* she thought sadly. *Loss seems forever linked with life.*

She was struck by her own words, as if thinking them for the first time. In truth she had thought about them almost her entire life. Certain memories would not fade.

At twelve her aunt raised her after her parents died, promising her love and security, then chronically running off with men and leaving Lynn and her younger sister to be cared for by a neighbor of whom they were terrified.

At eighteen she found herself a young impressionable journalist, at a loss to decide if publisher Walter Hoague's job offer was worth the sexual compromises he expected. Should she fuck him or tell him to fuck himself?

At twenty-four her husband asked for a divorce when she was three months pregnant, then changed his mind after she had had an abortion.

At twenty-seven Marsh Collyer, the presidential aide she had exposed in a multimillion-dollar land fraud, was found dead in his automobile of carbon monoxide poisoning.

Gruesome memories—nightmarish and cruel ghosts of the past—and here was yet another. They remained with her, at times relentlessly haunting her. Was it her delicate ego that made them stalk her like a shadow? Or her profession? She shuddered against the cold, knowing she would never have an answer of any certainty.

From a black hearse military pallbearers shouldered two flag-draped coffins to the crest of a hill about one hundred yards east of the Kennedy gravesites and rested them on chromed biers. They were accompanied by a full-dress Navy honor guard. There was no wind, but it was bitter cold, and the dampness from the drizzle matted the flags against the caskets. Ornate floral arrangements surrounded them. Someone had also placed a Christmas wreath on the child's bier. A long line of black limousines—headlights glaring, wipers smacking—followed the inner roadway to the gravesite.

Jay Hiller, who had come early and stood in the falling mist some distance away, watched the procession wind closer. He had talked briefly with the Senate sergeant-at-arms, a nervous birdlike man who had arranged the funeral, and with Fred Goss. Goss had seen too much death in his life and was hardened to it. He accepted it. He could philosophize about it. Hiller needed to be alone for a while.

He was in the mood for more sensitive eyes. Now he watched as limousine doors opened and slammed shut with the thud of well-made steel as everyone from Secretary of State Stephen Brownell to Defense Secretary Paul Garrett to ranking members of the Senate and House of Representatives began to make their way up the grassy slope.

Security was tight, on the ground and in the air. But it had to be. Shit, thought Hiller, one well-placed bomb here would annihilate the entire federal government.

He stood in silent meditation for several moments, ignoring the cold and dampness until the blond-headed giant Douglas Padley and his aide, George Berkquist, enveloped him. As always, Hiller felt like a dwarf next to the director of the FBI, who was wearing an expensive hat on his head and appeared even taller than usual.

Padley nodded in the direction of the coffins and

drawled in his thick accent, "I hear you almost ended up there yourself."

"To the disappointment of many," said Hiller. Then he quickly began to feel agitated and asked Berkquist for a cigarette. The aide shifted the glasses on his nose and studied Hiller for a moment with crafty eyes. He pulled a pack from his inside coat pocket and jostled it till a cigarette popped up. "Take two," Berkquist said. "Always happy to contribute to your respiratory condition."

Hiller took one and lit up. "What a fan club," he muttered. "You guys are so sweet I can't stand it."

"Why single us out," Berkquist asked. "You know your popularity is universal."

"Oh, yeah," said Hiller matter-of-factly. He gestured at a few congressmen walking toward the gravesite. "I'm sure if they could vote me into the grave it'd be the first time they ever agreed on anything."

Then he regarded Padley with a sideways glance and asked, "Did your people talk with the Capitol guardsmen who allowed that soda delivery?"

Padley turned his round light hazel eyes with their hypnotic gaze on Hiller. "We talked with 'em," he said with a slight trace of smugness.

"And? Anything that could pass for a description?"

Padley's mouth dropped into a frown. "Nothing I'd want to issue a parking ticket on, son. I'd say those men ought to be reassigned. Siberia maybe."

Hiller was annoyed by Padley's guarded responses. Berkquist seemed to sense it himself and added, "We're trying to work up a composite on it now. But the descriptions from the two guards contradict each other. So don't get your hopes up."

"Try to remember," Hiller said sharply, "we *are* working for the same country."

Padley rubbed his huge square face as if he had

just awakened. Then, after clearing his throat, he asked absently, "I'm curious, Hiller. Why did you refuse Secret Service protection following that mess in the municipal garage? Doesn't make sense, you know. Your life on the line like that. No one's gonna think any less of you if you travel with an escort."

"Be hard for anyone to think less of him," Berkquist chided. "He's just asking to get killed."

Hiller ignored their snickering and said, "It's not important to a lot of people, but I'm still trying to hang on to what little privacy is left in my life."

Padley's eyebrows went up. He studied the man before him for a moment. "Safety is a hell of a price to pay for privacy," he said brusquely.

Hiller winced and threw his cigarette to the ground. "Is it?" he said disbelievingly. And walked off.

Four Naval officers and a Navy chaplain made their way up the slope. Hiller saw Natalie Wainwright behind them, and his heart sank. She was bent over, veiled in black, supported by two young men who needed all their strength to hold her up. He stopped and watched them lead her to the caskets. He turned his head away and swallowed a deep lump in his throat.

A short distance away, Lynn talked with Fred Goss. She had her pad out and was taking notes, but he was just as concerned that she provide him with important information. Lynn noticed Hiller watching her and she felt a bit uncomfortable. She waved timidly, her hand barely reaching the height of her shoulders, not sure whether he would want to fraternize with her publicly. Hiller beckoned with his eyes, and after arranging a later meeting with Goss, she excused herself and joined him.

Lynn immediately saw the pallor in his face. She offered a sad sympathetic smile.

"How you doin'?" he asked.

She nodded. "Usual reaction stuff," she said. "Nothing very quotable." Lynn bit her lip and asked quietly, "Unless *you* want to . . ." She left the rest of the sentence unsaid.

"No," Hiller whispered. He was not in the mood for being newsworthy.

"I didn't think so," she said softly.

Hiller followed new activity by the coffins. Several members of the family arrived and stood solemnly while the chaplain prepared for the service, paging through a book and questioning the widow. Several times, in response, she nodded to him.

Hiller heaved a deep sigh. He felt his heart beating rapidly in his chest. "You see this kind of thing practically every day, don't you?" he asked Lynn.

"Sometimes I choose not to see," she replied quietly. "I'm not beyond closing my eyes. It can make life a lot more manageable."

"It's hard being here," he said mournfully. "It didn't have to . . . It could have been . . ." His voice trailed off.

"I know you feel that," Lynn whispered. "But it's wrong. You're really twisting your head around, don't you see?"

Hiller swallowed hard. "It's such a waste of life," he said, gazing almost hypnotically at the huge, clustered floral bouquets in front of the coffins. "What are those damn flowers supposed to do for them?"

She regarded him closely and said, "Don't belittle it, Jay. It's an expression, a gesture. It's all we can do, I mean *all* we can do, right now."

"It's such a waste of life," he repeated, as if for the first time. "Did you see the pictures of the little girl? Did you *see* them? Did you ever see a kid so damned cute in your life?"

"Jay, if I could just tell you something . . ."

He lowered his soulful eyes to her.

"I mean there's no way we can do anything now . . . I mean, to change what happened. We try, we hope, to help carry on so that in a way they really do go on living. But that's all you or I or even the President can do. They're gone—but maybe death only speeds us on to newer places. And if you can remember, she had a lot to be thankful for. She had two wonderful parents that truly loved her. Look how much better off she was to have lived a short, happy life with them than maybe a long, miserable one with others."

Hiller looked at her, at her strawberry lips now tense with concern, at the tiny birthmark just left of center on her nose, at her quiet, understanding gaze. Surely Lynn had known enough about premature death to enable her to make sense at a time like this. He was silently grateful for her solace. He wanted to touch her but dared not. He just looked deep into her eyes and found they promised everything.

When the service ended, Navy jets again streaked overhead but were lost in the sky's gray gauze. An honor guard folded and removed the flags from the coffins, which were lowered into the earth as the resonant boom of distant cannon sounded nineteen times. Then the colors were presented to the widow and mourners filed by, one by one, expressing sympathies to the family. Hiller tried for special words to ease the burden for the Wainwrights, though he doubted those words existed.

He paid his respects, turned the collar up on his overcoat, and started along the inner roadway to the parking lot. Limousine doors again slammed tight. Engines started, and one by one black cars slowly drove away.

A sharp defiant voice shouted Hiller's name and disrupted his private thoughts. The large menacing figure of CIA Director Wilson McAvee thundered down the slope and accosted him. He paused a moment to catch his breath. Finally he said, "With two days to go, some sign of progress might contribute to the public illusion that you're actually working on this thing."

Hiller fumed. "Can we wait till we get out of the cemetery before the lecture begins?"

"I'm not lecturing, Hiller," McAvee said with a touch of derision. "I'm telling you where you stand."

Hiller bore into him with burning eyes. "Before you get hung up on the public relations aspect of the case," he said, "maybe we could start with a little internal cooperation."

McAvee smiled viciously. "Don't try that smokescreen with me," he warned. "We don't make a habit of working against ourselves."

"No? Why did I have to learn elsewhere that you had a meeting last week with the President?"

McAvee's smile faded. Then he said evenly. "Our meeting had absolutely nothing to do with this case."

Hiller shook his head. "Anything that has to do with the President has to do with this case," he said. "What did you see him about?"

The director studied Hiller for a moment. "The situation in the Caribbean and Latin America," he replied.

"All right, I'll pull teeth," Hiller said angrily. "What about the situation in the Caribbean and Latin America?" His tone of voice was challenging.

"You seem to have difficulty understanding one thing," McAvee said. "The only man I answer to is the President. And he isn't available at the moment."

"So you think you've got carte blanche?" cried

Hiller. "Listen, McAvee. If you want to hinder this investigation, I think you can do a better job of it. See what kind of false information you can feed us to *really* slow us down. It will be a much shrewder approach for someone who thinks he's running an autonomous self-sustaining satellite of the United States."

Fortunately for Jay Hiller, it was Stephen Brownell who overheard him, and not an enterprising journalist. He hurried over in the middle of Hiller's outburst to cut off what surely would have been a highly contagious encounter. With a surprising, clawlike grip, he hauled Hiller away by the arm and engineered him toward the parking lot. McAvee stood his ground, his Irish face gone red, the icy blue eyes glaring ever more intensely. He watched them for several moments as they walked down the roadway, his lower lip now twitching with a violent energy.

He had nothing but contempt for darlings of the media, and Jay Hiller was the prima donna of them all. Soon, McAvee guessed, Hiller would be up to his familiar manipulations—trying to convince the press that his failures were due to the director's refusal to let him pore helter-skelter through agency files.

Well, just let him try, McAvee thought, and we'll have a few rip cords to pull ourselves.

If there was a shred of doubt in his mind about Hiller's allegations, he quickly extinguished it a minute later when Fred Goss met him in front of his limo.

"Are we holding anything back from Hiller on the probe?" McAvee demanded.

"Nothing I'm aware of," Goss said assuredly. "No reason to."

"The man's a damned incompetent paranoid," McAvee said still glaring toward the parking lot.

Goss raised his brows. "He may well be damned,"

he said, "but incompetent? I don't think there are many around you who would assess him that way."

The director shot a dark glance at his associate.

"No?" he said, raising his voice. "Then maybe the people around me don't have very astute judgment."

McAvee threw himself into the back seat of the limousine and angrily slammed the door. The car drove off, leaving Fred Goss behind and more than a little perplexed.

At the parking lot, Secretary Brownell finally unleashed Hiller and clenched his fists in a give-'em-hell gesture. With his short, jerky movements and a beige raincoat he looked like a high school football coach trying to cool off his hotheaded star quarterback.

"The last thing we need is for the media to get wind of internal disputes between you and McAvee, to top off everything else," he said.

Hiller sighed a sigh of acknowledgment. He looked off in the distance at the peak of the Washington Monument above Arlington's trees and the gray metal sky behind it.

Brownell suddenly thrust his arms out in a gesture of helplessness. "Look, McAvee is as frustrated as you are. He doesn't know which way to turn. Neither does Padley. Neither does the Secret Service. Hell, we're all in the same goddam boat—that's what you've *all* got to learn to understand. We're all doing everything we can."

Hiller shook his head. "No, I don't believe that," he said. "I think that until we get Royce back safely there must be something we can do that we aren't doing."

Brownell rubbed a hand across his full red cheeks. "Sure, sure," he said impatiently. "But are you going to put time and energy into figuring out how you wasted yesterday, or are you going to do whatever you can today. You know, I don't mind telling you there were some people this morning who weren't too pleased that you took time off to show up here."

Hiller bristled. "Yeah, well you can tell any of those cold-ass fuckers I happen to have blood in my veins."

"Okay," Brownell said, cutting him short. "What *I'm* saying is I'm worried. We're no closer today to ransoming the President than we were when this thing started."

Hiller nodded forcefully several times. "What am I supposed to do about that, Brownie?"

"In plain English, get it done," he said flatly.

"In plain English, get it done." Hiller repeated it aloud with a touch of added sarcasm. He studied the secretary and then raised his voice gradually. "In plain English I can't run a full-field interagency investigation and battle the FBI, the CIA director's ego, and the fiscal turkeys in Congress at the same time. In plain English *you're* the one with bite on Capitol Hill. You can push them around. So push, dammit! Shove, for crissakes. And don't hesitate to remind them that Senator Wainwright is here because they keep passing their shit in circles!"

Brownell lowered his eyes. On the last point, at least, he felt Hiller was hitting powerfully close to the truth.

Jeff Brodsky, meanwhile, had parked alongside the special investigator's car in the cemetery lot and was listening to the news when Hiller walked up and reminded him to loaf in the office, not in public.

"What are you doing sitting here?" he asked. "Why didn't you come up?"

Jeff shrugged. "Cemeteries don't do much for my spirits."

Hiller said dryly, "Come at night—it'll do a lot more."

Brodsky grinned his winning cocky grin. "Thanks, but my kind of spirits come in a bottle."

A paternal half-smile broke across Hiller's lips. "Yeah, yeah. Big wino here. I thought you were on holistic junk food."

"I am. Bran and bran-dy. Gin and gin-seng."

When Hiller rolled his eyes over the bad joke, Brodsky shrugged again and smiled sheepishly.

"What have you got?" Hiller asked, abruptly turning to business.

"I saw the lab report on Frazier. Didn't turn up a thing."

"Terrific! What about Langway?"

"Langway drove to Colonial Beach Marina, stayed long enough to take a leak on his boat, and returned to his office. That's the only place he's been all morning. The command post reports no activity at Global."

Hiller twisted his lips around in a peculiar way. There was no time to move cautiously. He would have to begin playing like a poker demon. He did not mind that in and of itself; in fact he rather preferred it, all things being equal. He simply did not like taking chances with someone else's life. Especially the President's.

"All right, we'll have to force things a bit," said Hiller. "Pick up old lard-ass again. As soon as he's away from his office, stop at a pay phone and call in a bomb scare to Global Communications."

Jeff looked a little startled. "A bomb scare??"

"I'll arrange everything else," Hiller said impatiently. "Just call it in."

It was shortly past four in the afternoon, nearly dusk, when flashing red and yellow lights came from out of the day's persistent heavy gray mist. Three police squad cars, sirens wailing, tore through downtown streets and rounded the corner at Fifteenth and N, followed closely by an armored truck.

When the caravan shrieked to a halt in the middle of the street, the rear doors on the truck flew open and four men in protective suits and helmets leaped out.

Past the police barricade they rushed, hauling a heavy iron box up the stairwell of 2621. The last of them, Jay Hiller, noticed that among the small crowd of people evacuated from nearby buildings was a woman wearing deep red lipstick and her hair in a bun: Gordon Langway's secretary-receptionist.

The upstairs door to Global Communications had been left ajar in the tumult of evacuation. Three of the men burst into the offices and picked through file cabinets and desk drawers.

Hiller removed his headgear and went to the receptionist's desk. He flipped through her interoffice phone directory and found the strange entry, *F . . . extension 252*. He dialed it, left the receiver off the hook, and trotted through the hallways listening for the ring.

It was distant at first, tinkling faintly, coming from another level. Quickly, he scaled a flight of steps and, in the hallway on the next floor, found a locked beige-colored door. From behind it came the incessant ringing of the telephone. Hiller took out a set of skeleton keys from a canvas gear bag and began inserting them in the lock. The sixth one slid in comfortably and caused a light metallic click. The handle turned and the door popped open.

Inside, in a room no bigger than a horse stall, was a microdot viewing apparatus and ten dozen file drawers the size of a library card-system. He took the phone off the hook to stop the ringing and hurriedly flipped through the file index, hoping for something on *Frazier, Russell.*

F . . . FE . . . FI . . . FL . . . FO . . . FOREIGN EXCHANGE . . . FOREIGN TRADE . . . FORGINGS, AIRCRAFT . . . FOUNDATIONS . . . FOX . . . The words leapt out at Hiller as if they had been shot from a cannon. FOX . . . FRANCHISING . . . FREIGHT CONSOLIDATING . . . Nothing on *Frazier, Russell.* But at least there was something!

FOX . . . FOX . . . Excitedly he pulled the appropriate microdot and put it up on the viewer. FOREIGN TRADE showed data processing codes, FORGINGS, AIRCRAFT detailed schematic diagrams . . . "FOX," nothing projected on the screen. Hiller played with the viewing system. The screen was completely black. The next thing visible came under another category—FRANCHISING.

FOX, a microdot file on FOX, only nothing was there. And the other information, for his purposes, was useless.

Hiller covered his eyes with a hand and let it fall to his open mouth. He had pulled up short again, zero on FOX, zero on FRAZIER. Did FOX pertain to the scribbled word on Frazier's newspaper clipping? Even of that he could not be sure. Was there a file under BAT?

He tried the *B*'s. . . . BANKS, DOMESTIC . . . BANKS, FOREIGN . . . BARRINGTON CORP . . . BASS INC . . . BATES COMMUNICATIONS. Nothing again. He heaved a defeated sigh. "Another dead end," he said aloud.

He replaced the microdots in the files, shut the light and closed the door. As he started down the stairwell, someone called his name. One of the bomb squad technicians met him on the stairs. He was a short man with a swarthy complexion and deep facial ridges indicating he had survived more than one close call. "We ought to get out of here soon if you don't want anybody to get suspicious," he said. "It rarely takes us this long to find the rattle, if there is one."

"Okay," Hiller replied. "Give me a few more minutes and we'll be off."

Hiller rushed into Langway's office, which seemed much larger than he remembered it, a result, he reasoned, of the obese vice president's not being there. He found an annual report on the desk and flipped through it, then checked the appointment calendar and the Rolodex. Rummaging through the wastebasket proved to be a waste, as was his effort to read the reversed images off the desk blotter using a small mirror. He sifted through papers, invoices, statements which he found in the drawers. Again nothing.

Stuffed among the papers was a photograph in a frame, a picture of Langway on a yacht with a beautiful nude blonde. Hiller cackled to himself. "Who says money can't buy happiness," he muttered.

He put the papers back in the proper drawers and was about to replace the picture when he noticed the edge of a second photo underneath. Hiller felt his heart skip an anxious beat as he hurriedly tried to remove the glass cover. His own excitement slowed him down, and he momentarily lost patience with himself. "C'mon, Yo-yo," he said. "It's a very simple device called a picture frame."

Finally the glass came loose and he tore away the top photo. Underneath was a picture of Langway and Russell Frazier on a pier with a marlin!

"Bingo, son of a bitch," cried Hiller excitedly, just as the bomb squad technician burst in.

"Hiller, we've got to blast off, so to speak," he said. "I mean there's either a bomb here or there isn't."

Hiller nodded. "Right. Have you got one of those firecrackers with you?"

"Yeah. Why?"

"Well, let's make it authentic. Prove there really was a bomb here. Blow up this fucking office."

The technician looked puzzled. "You serious?"

"Yeah, I'm serious," Hiller said. "We can tell them the device was set to detonate and couldn't be moved. Go ahead, blow it up."

The technician left no doubt about his knowledge of explosives. Less than three minutes after Hiller gave him the go-ahead, there was a thunderous roar that shook the entire building. The door to Langway's office blew out and splintered into dozens of pieces, the walls collapsed, and papers, furniture, and glass scattered like pillow feathers in the air. Black smoke poured into the hall like the steamy black breath of a forest fire.

Chapter 19

December 15.

Mark Kinstrey, the President's red-haired, energetic press secretary, readily agreed to meet Jay Hiller for breakfast in the cafeteria of the GOB. Hiller was following Fred Goss's suggestion that he personally quiz Kinstrey about what arrangements had been made for the ill-fated trip to Atlanta. But in deference to the press secretary's position, Hiller thought breakfast a good excuse to avoid a formal meeting. It was the same consideration that Lincoln Packwood of the FBI had shown when questioning him about Senator Wainwright.

Hiller knew Mark Kinstrey as a man who used the media aggressively and with a stylish Madison Avenue wit.

"I'm packaging a product," was his philosophy. "The product happens to be the President. And the idea is to get you to buy."

Before meeting John Royce, Kinstrey spent three years in Washington as a legislative assistant and impressed enough people to consider taking a shot at a congressional seat. When his sponsor, the then-senator Dennis K. Tyler, was accused of accepting stock payments from blue-chip corporations in return for favors, Kinstrey had an impossible time trying to disassociate himself from a scandal that rocked both houses of Congress for months. Tyler resigned from office following an indictment, and Kinstrey packed his bags for New York. But Governor Royce of Pennsylvania called, asked him to stop off in Harrisburg, and offered him a job.

Royce's faith paid dividends. When one editorial writer in West Virginia attacked him as "a skulking political charlatan with a decayed mind," Kinstrey fired back a reply, "Of all the arduous tasks that a governor must face, the most infuriating is having to read barely literate slop from morons who create garbage."

When Royce was a dark-horse candidate for President, Kinstrey drew attention to the campaign by instituting among the press a lottery to guess how many votes the governor would pull in each of the primaries. Even the press secretary was surprised at how much extra coverage the ploy seemed to generate.

Following Royce's election to the White House, Kinstrey found he had to tread a thin line between protecting and overprotecting the President. In most cases, he succeeded. And in one recent instance, following charges by Arizona Senator Perry Jedlicker that the President was "trying to become dictator by turning the nation into a socialist playground," Kinstrey made headlines with the retort, "Being called a dictator by Senator Jedlicker is like being called ugly by a wart."

The press secretary also learned a few things from his boss, most importantly, never to make the mistake of taking oneself too seriously, and to use humor as a political weapon. It was generally agreed that if he got another few years of national exposure as Royce's press secretary, Mark Kinstrey, the Wile E. Coyote of Washington, could probably make a pretty good run for elective office and leave the experience with Senator Tyler to the past.

Hiller considered his background as they sat down to breakfasts of coffee, toast, and scrambled eggs. Kinstrey immediately recognized the reason for their get-together and blew Hiller's "cover."

"Nothing's changed since I spoke to Goss," the press secretary said. Hiller was a little embarrassed and smiled an apology. But Kinstrey repeated what he had stated previously. "The guy from the Atlanta station—Mayberry was the name—requested the interview, and after checking with the President, I okayed it for the St. Mark's Hotel. For security reasons, the Secret Service asked to move it from the mezzanine to the penthouse, and I saw no reason to complicate the job of protecting him."

"You knew in advance the interview would be in the penthouse?" asked Hiller.

"Certainly."

"Did Mayberry?"

"Far as I know. But that hardly matters, considering what happened to him."

"Did you deal with anyone else directly besides Mayberry?"

Kinstrey thought a moment and shook his head. "I wish I had. Then I might have some idea of where the hell you should look."

Kinstrey spoke quietly and did not seem to be trying to sell anything. Hiller considered that at least as important as what he was saying.

An hour later, General Harry Hummerstone marched through the Blue Wing of the GOB as if he was demonstrating for soldiers how it should be done. He was in uniform and he was in public and to him that meant he was on parade. It was his first time in the new government complex, and though he was a little intimidated by its awesome size, he would not let it show.

Tucked under one arm in a briefcase was material that he was burning to show special investigator Jay Hiller, who had all but accused the army of facilitating the kidnapping.

Hiller was waiting for Hummerstone in Conference Room B, a small, windowless cubicle with a table that could comfortably accommodate six. The two shook hands politely, but without warmth. They sat down alongside one another and the general immediately went for his pipe. Hiller waited patiently as Hummerstone produced a tobacco pouch, stuffed the blend into the bowl of the pipe, and put the flame from a fancy gold cigarette lighter to the tobacco.

Then he sucked a customary three times on the stem, reached for the briefcase, and said. "I think you'll be very surprised to see what we have here."

"That's nice," Hiller replied, forcing himself to de-emphasize the sarcasm. "I'm always up for surprises."

Hummerstone took no notice of Hiller's remark and pulled a buff-colored folder from his attaché. "All right," the general said slowly, "what we have here is the last military photograph taken of Sergeant Gilbert. Date of photo is March 1968. Uh, he's the soldier that was killed in Vietnam, near Da Nang, you remember. June fifth to be exact. . . ."

The date was a familiar one to Hiller. "Same day Bobby Kennedy was shot," he said quietly.

Again Hummerstone seemed barely cognizant of what was said. He produced a macrostat of Gilbert's signature and laid it on the table. "Now this is the sergeant's handwriting, authenticated from military records by our handwriting experts."

Hiller rested his chin in his hand, allowing Hummerstone to move at his own pace. The general then took a red folder and, from it, another photograph. He inhaled on his pipe and said, "And this picture was taken the day before the kidnapping at the time of the helicopter equipment requisition. Compare the face in this photo with the face in the other."

Both showed men of a guarded intensity, in their late twenties or early thirties, dark complected with black hair. They looked reasonably alike. In fact, they were the same man. Or so it seemed.

Hummerstone continued. "You note the similarities. You note what seems to be very little aging during the sixteen-year span between the time both pictures were taken. This leads us to believe that they are *not* the same man."

Hiller grunted. If the military death certificate on Sergeant Gilbert was genuine—and Hummerstone assured him it was—then that much, at least, had to be obvious. He picked up a phone and punched four digits. "Will you get Rozakis up to Conference Room B." He listened for the reply and said, "Good," then put down the receiver.

Hummerstone placed a second handwriting specimen alongside the first. "This signature was made by the man in the second photograph," he said. "The handwritings are not dissimilar, but if you note the loops on the letters and the way the *t*'s are crossed, you can plainly see they were made by different people."

Hiller's chin remained in his hand as he again grunted acknowledgment. Hummerstone eyed him from aside, then he stared directly ahead and sucked on his pipe. He cleared his throat and took a third folder, a black one, from his briefcase.

There was a knock on the door and a small man with a thin, pale face entered. He was middle-aged with wild brown hair and wore glasses with maroon frames.

Hiller introduced Ted Rozakis, a lab expert, to the general and directed his attention to the material on the table. Rozakis leaned between Hiller and Hummerstone and examined the photographs closely.

"Well, this one's pretty apparent," he said quickly. "Shape of the chin is different, the mouth is much fuller here on this man, also the width of the head." He was indicating the second photo.

Hummerstone bit into the stem of his pipe. He was irritated that Hiller found it necessary to corroborate what army specialists had already discovered. He sucked a stream of tobacco smoke deep into his lungs, then exhaled slowly through his nostrils.

Hiller looked at the general and said, "Were you able to identify the imposter?"

Hummerstone replied, "No. We don't know who he is. But the forged signature, the signature that went on the equipment requisition, belonged to this man."

Hummerstone flipped open the black folder and displayed a third photograph and a third signature macrostat. "Specialist Fourth Class Joseph Martinez," he said. "Positive identification made by our handwriting specialists. Again I direct your attention to the loops on the letters, the way the *t*'s are crossed and the slant of the penmanship. However, while Martinez managed to *forge* Sergeant Gilbert's signature, this second man obviously *posed* as Sergeant Gilbert."

Hiller twisted his mouth and looked at the photo of Martinez. Judging from the face, he was probably a well-built man of Latin ancestry.

"You have this man in custody?" asked Hiller.

Hummerstone shook his head. "He disappeared the day of the kidnapping. We're attempting to trace him."

Hiller furrowed his brow and sighed softly. "No big breaks," he thought to himself.

Rozakis again leaned over the table for another look at the photos. "You want me to go with this?" he asked, a little eagerly.

Hiller nodded. "If it's all right with the general, I'd like you to take it now."

Hummerstone thought a moment and puffed into his pipe. "All right," he said quietly and began packing his briefcase. Rozakis took the photographs and stats and slipped out of the room.

Hiller got up, extended his hand, and said earnestly, "Thank you, General. I appreciate your expediting matters by promptly bringing this in. And, of course, saving time by coming yourself."

Hummerstone looked at him a little perplexed. It

was the first time he had ever heard a civil word from Jay Hiller.

The light from the television bathed the room in blue-green shadows and flickered with the changing pictures of an evening news program. The sound was turned low, barely audible, as Hiller and Lynn, on a waterbed in front of the tube, finished off the last of a peanut-butter-and-jelly dinner.

He licked the jelly from his fingers and said, only half-jokingly, "That's the best meal I've had all week. You're a great cook, my dear."

She cast a sideways glance in his direction. "Is that supposed to be a complaint?" she said with a slight grin.

"No, it's a proposition."

The grin faded. Lynn looked at him questioningly. "Come here," he said gently. She inched over, making waterbed waves and snuggled next to him, wrapping her arms around his abdomen. Hiller took her flowing chestnut hair in his hands and gently pulled her head to his face. He rubbed his nose against hers and leaned back into a pillow. She followed him and their lips touched—softly, lightly, like a sip of wine.

"You taste like peanut butter," he whispered.

Lynn closed her eyes and rested her head on his chest. She heaved a sudden deep, mournful sigh and said, "I'm glad you're here." It was spoken with a gravity that seemed inappropriate and Hiller felt it.

"Hey. What's *that* all about?"

Lynn slowly lifted her head to face him. There was a long silence. Finally she said, "It's been so long since I cared. I suddenly feel as if, as if . . . I don't know. I've messed myself up a few times. Love's never been easy for me, my kid sister handles it a lot better than I do."

"I didn't know you had a sister," Hiller said, surprised.

"Jennifer. She's only twenty-four and she's already been married seven years. But she's happy."

Even as children, Jennifer was not nearly as emotionally high-strung as Lynn. When their father was killed in a one-car auto accident sixteen months after their mother died, Jenni seemed to adjust to the tragedy more quickly than Lynn, who was emotionally unsettled for months. Once when she overheard her aunt discussing her father's death with a boyfriend, conjecturing about the likelihood of a suicide, Lynn locked herself in a room for almost three days and refused to eat or talk. It was not surprising that she would extract herself from her guardian's home at an age when most of her peers were struggling with algebra exams.

Now she looked searchingly into her lover's soft brown eyes and touched the odd crab's-leg wrinkle on his face. "You ever wish you'd done things differently?" she asked.

Hiller smiled mournfully. "Only a few thousand times," he said, with quiet understanding. "*Should* have done this, *wish* I'd done that. It's a self-orchestrated futility, you know. The past is the only part of our lives we can't change. I'll never understand why we try."

They looked at each other with sympathetic eyes, silent affection in their stares. At last Hiller said, "I confess, Lynn. I bemoan my yesterdays more than most. And somehow that neurotic devotion never allowed me to change a single minute that I'd already lived. No matter how hard I try to change the past, in the present I'm still aging, still wheezing, still a son of a . . ."

"The aging part I can take," Lynn interrupted. "It's the wheezing that worries me."

He frowned. "Well, you shouldn't let it. *I* don't. I mean, technically I've always been on borrowed time. But whoever's taking inventory upstairs must like keeping me in the fire."

Lynn was troubled. He made death sound so near. "Don't joke about that," she said sharply. She sat up and clasped his left hand in her own.

"Do me a favor, will you?"

Hiller made no reply.

"Would you make some small effort for me to see if you can stop drinking like you do. And stop smoking."

He smiled at her and said, "I've stopped three times already. I'm very good at stopping."

"So what's the problem?"

"I'm also very good at starting."

They laughed a little and fell into a new embrace. "And also good at avoiding," she added gently.

They held each other for a long time before their eyes met again, and then their hungry, moist lips, half parted, pressed together. It was the way her mouth moved, to and from his own, the way her tongue darted fleetingly over his, that made him feel strangely powerless. All he could think of was needing more, wanting more. Then he couldn't think at all. The entire moment concerned only this—that he grow forgetful, that he learn surrender's lesson. He was too much as he had been. He had to molt this skin, melt this solid ice left over from long, long winters.

He slid his hands along her back. It was smooth, warm skin. He explored her every curve, moving deliberately toward her rapidly beating heart. He felt her tremble as he cupped the full, firm breasts in his hands, felt her nipples harden between his fingers, felt himself inflamed.

He kissed her gently on the throat as she filled his ear with hot, moist breath. Her baby-smooth thighs quivered and parted and she eagerly swallowed him up, locking her legs around his waist. Their blood roared and fanned like fire. And she drove wildly against him twisting, writhing like a snake.

Then their rhythms became one rhythm, feeding each other's passion, and their bodies surged in powerfully savage thrusts. She cried out, a cry of pleasure, of feeling so complete, so filled, so vital—totally free of pain. They loved vigorously, then gently, softly and now violently, as she cried again, this time of a different need.

Lynn fought for breath, the lake of the waterbed making audible the vigor of their movements. She begged to stop and begged for more. A sudden lovely exhaustion overtook her, overtook him. They clung to each other, drenched in love's sweet perspiration, breathing hard, smiling, as they gasped for air. Their eyes were brilliant, alive. They were full of color.

"You have fantastic leverage, my dear," gasped Hiller. "I'll bet you could knock me through the dome of the Capitol."

"Me?" she exclaimed. "My God, if you keep making love like this, you really *won't* live very long."

He chuckled. "I'd rather make love like this now and die young than be eighty-six and only wish I had."

Lynn exhaled, letting out an exhausted whoop at the top of her lungs. "God, I can . . . hardly . . . breathe."

Quickly, Hiller stretched over the side of the bed and dug through his pants lying on the floor. "Here. Suck on this," he said jokingly, holding up his nebulizer.

Lynn looked at it and grinned, the spark of mischief shining in her grin. She slid down the length of his torso and fondled him and said, "I think I'd rather suck on this."

A groan emanated from the well inside his abdomen, and Hiller grew dizzy with pleasure. The last thing he remembered before surrendering was the silhouette of his lover partly obscuring the face of Walter Cronkite on the television screen.

When he awoke an hour later from a lover's snooze, Hiller felt so rested he wondered for a moment if he had not slept round the clock. "Perish the thought," he said to himself, for that would be his funeral. McAvee, the press, Phyllis, not to mention his own conscience, which was beginning to weigh on him already for having taken an overly long dinner break.

Though he tried to slip off the waterbed without waking Lynn, who had fallen asleep nestled tight against him, it was beyond his athletic capabilities. It bucked, it sloshed, it had a mind of its own. She stirred, and he cringed. He saw that he had awakened her.

"I'm sorry, baby," he said softly. "I've never learned how to ride one of these."

She smiled a sleepy smile.

"Go back to sleep," he whispered.

Lynn's smile faded as she watched him pull on his trousers. She studied his movements, hitching up the belt, fumbling with his socks. It had been so beautiful. Why was she suddenly starting to feel so empty? She lifted her head from the pillow and whispered in an almost childlike way, "You're not going, are you?"

She said it pleadingly, but with little hope.

"I hardly like the idea," Hiller said regretfully, buttoning his shirt. When he looked down, her thin strawberry lips were curved in a frown.

"Hey, what's the matter?"

Lynn shook her head. He sat down on the bed next to her and lowered his voice. "What's the matter?"

"I feel alone," she whispered. "Suddenly . . . it all frightens me."

Hiller sighed. He put his left hand under her chin and looked into her wide light-green eyes. "You're making it hard for me to be a tough shit," he said. He paused a moment looking for some indication she would be okay.

"You don't have to be insecure on my account. I'm not running because I want to."

When she made no reply, he got up and said, "I bet your television audience never saw you like this."

Lynn looked as if she would burst into tears. "I need you to stay," she cried suddenly. There was desperation in her voice.

"This is not my life I'm living these days," Hiller said evenly. "You *know* that."

He went into the next room and took his coat from the sofa.

"I'll try to buzz you later," he called out. There was no answer.

"Lynn? Okay?"

She did not respond. He poked his head into the bedroom and saw her sitting, legs folded under, with her head sunk into her chest and hair hanging in front of her eyes. Then she looked up at him and said bitterly, "You just get up and leave like some vacuum cleaner salesman."

"What is going on with you?" he said in disbelief. "You're determined to bust my chops."

Her voice rose and cut him off. "You come over here, get your rocks off, and split! What am I supposed to do?"

Hiller frowned. "Look, when this is over . . ."

"When this is over," she shrieked, "go pay for your quickies at some slophouse in the city."

He looked at her and sighed, shaking his head. Then he went to the door and called back at her. "If I don't see you, your Christmas present is under the sofa."

"I didn't get you a damn thing," Lynn shouted bitterly.

Hiller turned the doorknob and said softly, almost to himself, "Hmm, that's what I got last year."

Lynn heard the apartment door close and footsteps recede down the hallway. At first she felt a trembling inside, and then a hollowness in her stomach that made her feel a little sickened. She sobbed once and then violently slammed a fist into the waterbed. There was a sudden rumble, followed by dripping and then a sloshing sound. Suddenly the lining burst and water gushed onto the floor. As she sank into the rapidly deflating waterbed mattress, Lynn burst into tears.

Chapter 20

It was just after nine when the taxi coasted to a halt on the darkened street. Hiller paid the fare and got out and watched the cab pull away. He stood there shivering in the middle of the road until the red taillights disappeared around a corner.

Goddam, it was cold. He flipped the collar up on

his overcoat and looked up and down a wide dead-end street with unpaved walks. To one side, a cluster of trees fell off into a grassy slope. Behind them in the distance, a few streetlamps from a highway burned.

But on the other side, an eight-foot Cyclone fence surrounding a huge asphalt parking lot stood between him and the coliseumlike structure of the Robert F. Kennedy Memorial Stadium.

The lot and the stadium were dark and had been since the last Redskins home football game eleven days ago. Without thousands of automobiles and sports enthusiasts it looked cold and gargantuan. The setting made him shiver almost as much as the temperature.

Hiller cupped his hands and blew into them to get his fingers working. He grabbed onto a section of the fence and stuck a toe into the diamond-shaped wire grating. It had been twenty years since he climbed one, and he knew it as he awkwardly flung himself over the top. When he dropped the last five feet onto the asphalt he was puffing, thinking about how easy it used to be.

He walked briskly across the lot with the peculiar feeling that a thousand eyes hidden in the night were watching him. His own were fixed on one of the many entrances to the ball park. Faintly, from a distant street, a siren wailed—the only sound accompanying his footsteps.

When he reached the main gate, he struggled over a second chain link fence and wavered before entering the dark concrete catacombs. He moved slowly to give his eyes time to adjust. Violet spots danced before him, then ghosts seemed to dart out and behind concrete pillars. Suddenly a shadow stirred and his heart skipped. It was the movement of his own overcoat.

On one of the pillars, obscured by the darkness, was a sign he had trouble reading. He stopped a moment, stuck a cigarette in his mouth, and struck a match. The sudden glare made him blink. Then he read the sign and snickered. "Anyone Going on the Field or Interfering with Play Will Be Ejected from the Ball Park."

A sudden noise from behind startled him and he whirled around. "Put out the match," a clear, cool voice said in commanding tones. He relaxed when he recognized it.

"Smokey the Bear?" Hiller asked facetiously.

"It makes me nervous," the voice replied. Then in the draft-blown flickering light of the tiny flame, the slim figure of FBI Deputy George Berkquist stepped from the shadows. Hiller let the match fall to the ground and watched it go out.

"Aren't we being a little overcautious?" he asked. "Concrete doesn't burn."

Berkquist folded his arms across his chest and said, "Considering I could get blown away for giving you the weather, no, we are not being overcautious."

Hiller privately acknowledged his point. He put the unlit cigarette in his breast pocket and took out an envelope which he tossed at Berkquist. It landed at his feet. Berkquist shifted the glasses on his nose and bent over on one leg to pick it up. A microlight appeared in his hand as he opened the envelope and examined its contents, several thousand dollars. The light went out.

"Isn't it time we renegotiated the agreement?" Berkquist asked. "It's been a long time since we worked. Inflation, you know what that's like, the same bread can't take care of what it used to."

Hiller felt disgusted. He tried to control his anger, but his voice gave him away. "I've had it to here these last few days," he said, making a sharp slicing motion across his forehead. "If I have to be rolled for a patriotic gesture I guess I can handle it."

Berkquist bristled and came back at him. He was annoyed that Hiller saw it only from his own point of view. He was doing a damned courageous thing and that should be understood. "Cut the red, white, and blue bullshit," he snapped. "The information is free, chief. As always. The money is for risking my life. I have a family."

Hiller considered a challenge but decided to let up. Berkquist had always come through for him. There was no reason to belittle his help—even if the installment seemed to make it a little less altruistic. Every man had his own values and motivations, why should he consider his own purer?

"Sorry, George," he said. His tone was conciliatory. "You want a Christmas bonus, you got it. Okay?"

"Fine."

"You now have my attention as well as my money."

Berkquist peered into the darkness around him. He was not entirely comfortable. There was a bit of an echo in the catacomb, and the stone-cold chill in the air was numbing. It was no small step helping Jay Hiller; to do so meant going against Doug Padley. Every word he would utter would be visible as he breathed, lingering like an incriminating message written in the air.

Berkquist began in a whisper. "There's no record of a *Foxbat* in the Bufiles. Or Central Intelligence. Or the Secret Service. And I couldn't get anything to help ID the photo from the army—you know, the guy called Martinez. So I suspect it's an alias."

"What is Global Communications a cover for?"

"We don't know about Global itself, but . . ."

"Great!" Hiller cried in a sarcastically light tone. "The only information you've got is no information, and for this you want a bonus. This isn't a poker game, George. I don't pay to see what kind of cards you're holding."

"There's more," Berkquist said softly.

"More what?" Hiller asked. "Soapsuds?"

"Your would-be assassin—the one who tried to flatten you in the municipal garage—Frazier—has an arrest record that would choke a tapeworm."

Hiller frowned. "Yeah, I already know that."

"But do you also know that he's never spent a day in jail?"

Hiller was startled. It meant that Russell Frazier certainly was no off-the-wall psychotic. And it proved that he had to have been connected to someone extremely powerful politically. Maybe Gordon Langway was that person.

As if he had read his mind, Berkquist said, "What I was going to tell you before was we traced Langway to a Florida mob. His real name is Giovanni Lambino, a kingpin with the Righetti Family in Miami. . . ."

Hiller's eyes widened. Jesus, he would have to get Jeff Brodsky off him immediately. With that kind of organization, Langway was obviously a lot more dangerous than he had estimated.

Berkquist went on. "And I'm sure you might also find interesting,"—here he injected his own bit of biting sarcasm—"that is, if you don't already know it, the fact that your Mr. Frazier was a Beretta soldier and took part in the Bay of Pigs invasion against Cuba."

Hiller's mouth fell open. Son of a bitch! A link! At last, a link, a direction, a means of narrowing down a limitless ocean of exhaustive reports spanning the entire world. Now, at last, he had a starting point—the Caribbean, Cuba—and somehow it led to Atlanta and President John Quinlan Royce and himself in Washington. Now, maybe, just maybe, he might be able to fill in some of the dots under the question marks. His sudden restless energy caused him to break into a broad smile.

"Merry Christmas, George," Hiller said excitedly.

"Merry Christmas, chief," the slender man replied.

Earlier that evening, in suburban Virginia, a light blue Ford made a right turn onto a narrow street, a safe distance behind a gleaming black Mercedes.

The neighborhood had a rural flavor, wooded in spots, with several hundred yards of rolling lawn and foliage between homes, with only an occasional streetlight, and unpaved walkways. Christmas carols came one after another on the radio in the Ford. Jeff Brodsky, his mind on the vehicle ahead, was aware only of the presence of music. But when it was apparent he no longer had the benefit of street traffic to camouflage his car, he turned it off.

Now the Mercedes ground to a halt at an interesection with a dirt road. Brodsky recognized the crossing. It led to the Colonial Beach Marina, where yesterday he had tailed Gordon Langway from his office. He pulled off to the side, killed the headlights on the Ford, and waited about half a minute in the shadows before continuing.

Following Langway at night seemed more perilous than in daylight when the docks were full of robust fishermen. Jeff's youthful energy began to give way to anxiety and his breathing became quite shallow. He turned onto the unpaved road and, about a block short of the marina parking lot, shut off the ignition, allowing the car to drift to a halt behind a cluster of tall shrubs.

From under the front seat, he took a pair of high-powered binoculars and got out of the car. The Mercedes was parked already at the foot of the wharf;

two other cars with fogged windows were at opposite ends of the lot. "Saltwater sex," he thought to himself. They were having a hell of a lot more fun than he was.

Through the binoculars, Brodsky recognized the back of Gordon Langway's fat hatless head and his dark ponderous figure sweeping down the pier. He stopped at the last berth and looked around, then boarded a cabin cruiser. For several minutes, Brodsky keyed on the vessel bobbing in the waves. Finally, a light in the cabin went on.

In the freezing chill of the harbor, Jeff began shivering and losing control of his fingers. He pulled a pair of leather gloves from his jacket and slipped into them, then returned to the binoculars to see Langway reappear on deck holding an obviously large weighty bucket. He struggled to lift it and after considerable effort dumped the contents overboard. It looked to Jeff as if several medium-sized fish were being returned to the sea.

Langway went back in the cabin, shut the light, and came out with a package tucked under his arm. He locked the door and hurried down the pier to his car.

Brodsky had to think quickly. If he moved his car, he might be spotted and arouse suspicion. If he stayed put, Langway would see him when he drove the Mercedes out of the lot.

Langway's car engine gunned to a start and the headlights flashed. Jeff threw himself into the Ford and slid down on the front seat. Like the other two vehicles in the lot, this one too could be passed off as a lovers' nest. The headlights on the Mercedes swept around as its driver negotiated a U-turn. The beams fell momentarily on the Ford and Brodsky held his breath. Then it straightened out and sped up, spitting small stones and dust from under its wheels.

Jeff heaved a sigh and dropped his head in an almost prayerful position. "Now what?" he wondered. Now was decision making time. Should he find out as much as he could as Hiller instructed? Explore the unguarded cabin cruiser? Or lay back and be cautious as Hiller warned, and follow Langway?

He put the binoculars back in the car, took a flashlight from the glove compartment, and walked across the parking lot to the pier. He stopped and looked around. In spite of the bitter temperature, there wasn't much wind. But the yachts and fishing boats groaned in their slips—old, wet wood bumping against old, wet wood—creaking like attic doors.

The smell of salt was sharp as Jeff stepped onto the wharf, timidly at first, and then walked briskly down the ramp to the last berth. A large maroon and gray cabin cruiser pitched and yawed there. He turned the flashlight on the lettering on the stern. It read: "Phoenix–Ft. Lauderdale, Florida."

Brodsky boarded and tried the cabin door. It was locked. With the flashlight, he looked over the starboard bow where Langway had emptied the bucket. The beam fell on several dead fish floating limply in the water. It was one of the weirdest things he had ever seen.

He moved around to the port bow and through a sealed window explored the inside of the cabin. He directed the flashlight to a lacquered pinewood table and was astonished to see a mess of papers left unattended. Something there could help, of that he was certain.

Suddenly Jeff leaped from the deck onto the pier and bolted for the car. Talking about heroics was one thing, executing them was something else. He would follow Hiller's warning and not take chances. Besides he had a beautiful girl friend to think of.

Brodsky threw open the door on the Ford and pounced on the radiophone. In his excitement, he fouled up the code and had to repunch. Jack Albaum answered his call at the GOB.

"Jack, this is Jeff," he said hurriedly. "Is Hiller back yet?"

"Negative," replied Albaum, "so feel free to yawn if you have to."

"Do you know where he is?"

"Negative again, JB. Can *I* take your order? The special today is lasagna."

Brodsky could not control his impatience. "Shit," he whined. "Can you get someone down here immediately! I'm at the Colonial Beach Marina, at Langway's boat. I think we have a chance to head in on something."

"Okay, clear. Sending. You can relax."

"Try to dig up Hiller, will you? And get him over here."

"Stay cozy, sweetheart."

Brodsky put down the phone. He considered returning to the boat. No, he would stay in the car and wait, maybe turn the car around and run the heater a little.

The engine on the Ford came to life, the lights went on. He threw the car into gear and suddenly froze. A slender figure in a raincoat was walking toward him in the beam of the headlights. The belt was cinched tightly at the waist, and long dark hair spilled out from beneath a kerchief.

"What the hell is a woman doing here alone?" he asked himself, bewildered.

She drew near, shoulders hunched, her features lashed to a healthy crimson by the raw chill. She lowered her attractive face to the side window and, holding a cigarette in one hand, said in a low, sexy voice, "I don't have any matches and I'm absolutely dying for a smoke. Could I get a light?"

At first he thought she was a hooker, going through her usual routine to break the ice. Then he remembered the cars and the fogged windows and he smiled to himself—the after-sex cigarette. He had once gone with a woman who simply went into hysterics unless she had a smoke after a screw.

Jeff punched the lighter and rolled down the window. Rarely had he seen eyes as alluring as the ones now looking into his own. God, she was lovely, and he wondered what the guy she was with was like. The lighter popped out and he held it, glowing, near her face. She touched his hand lightly, inhaled, and threw her head back to blow away the smoke.

"Merry Christmas," she said in a deep soft voice, and then smiled. As he complacently returned the lighter to the dash, he was struck by a nagging question, one that quite suddenly seemed all that mattered: Why didn't she use the lighter in her own car?

He had no time to guess. He saw a shadow move to his right and a sudden flash. He thought of dropping to the floor—something shiny—a fleeting vision of, for some inexplicable reason, a university—a flash and a handgun and an explosion at the passenger window. A bullet tore through the glass and smashed into his face between the bridge of his nose and his left cheekbone. He was dead instantly.

It was a few minutes past ten when Hiller arrived at the White House. Outside, the Washington Monument and the lawn fountains, seen from the South Portico, were ablaze. Inside, the lobby was decorated with braids of holly, Christmas wreaths, tree ornaments, bows, and poinsettias with branches sprayed white, as well as strands of unlit Christmas lights. All this had been strung during Thanksgiving but the mood in the Executive Mansion had since grown darker.

The First Lady greeted Hiller with a mournful smile and a warm hug and led him up the stairwell to the second floor. His pace was noticeably slowed.

"Tired, tense, and ashen," Phyllis Royce said, assessing him the way a mother might her son during his first time home from college. "I must say I've never seen you worse."

"That's because you didn't see me yesterday," Hiller said, pulling off his overcoat. Phyllis chuckled.

There was something about the remark she appreciated—its lightness, perhaps its glibness. It made her feel less like pitying herself, something she was certain she had been guilty of in recent days.

At the top of the stairs they entered a hallway with a vaulted ceiling and blue floor-length drapes. It had been tastefully redecorated with antique furniture from a private collection in Phyllis's family.

"Brownie is here," she said quietly.

Hiller managed a tired smile. "Good," he said, not really meaning it. The secretary of state's presence meant he would have to remain alert.

In the Oval Room, Hiller greeted Brownell, who was seated comfortably in a well-cushioned beige lounge chair sipping a cordial. The smell of anisette was in the air.

Knowing him as she did, Phyllis asked, "What would you like for holiday cheer?"

"Mix a little Scotch, tequila, and Drambuie," Hiller said gratefully.

Phyllis frowned and shook her head. "I'm sure that does wonders for your asthma."

He grinned sheepishly. "Actually gasoline is the best thing, but I'm trying to cut down because of the fuel thing." She threw him a quick admonishing look as he sank into an arm chair letting out an exhausted sigh. Then she slipped out of the room.

Brownell, who had been gazing above the mantel at a portrait of George Washington, lowered his eyes as if in empathy. He took a sip of his drink and set it down next to Phyllis's on a blond antique coffee table.

"There's a message at your office from me," the secretary said. "I wanted to let you know that I've got to make a move. In the next twenty-four hours, if something doesn't break, I'm going to brief the Vice President on the Sino-Soviet conference."

"In the next twenty-four hours, the ransom deadline lapses, Brownie. In the next twenty-four hours, the Vice President may *be* the President."

Both men fell suddenly silent, ill-at-ease with that very real possibility and with their utter helplessness. Finally, Brownell asked quietly, "You think they'll go through with it then?"

"The kidnappers? Shit, yes. What choice did we leave them?"

"And I'd almost begun to feel the worst was over."

Hiller sighed. "There's no way the Soviets will agree to a summit postponement?"

"Postponement?" cried Brownell and he forced a laugh. "Hah! They think we're trying to stall. They're not even convinced we didn't set up the kidnapping as a ploy, so we could buy one delay after another. No, flatly no, they will not agree to a postponement."

Hiller rubbed a hand over his face. "Wonderful," he quipped. "To add to that, though I'm sure you remember, unless the fraternity of fools at the Capitol okays the ransom, another one of them will get hit tomorrow. I hope and pray the beefed-up security forces don't lull them back into their usual comatose states. We had security when they got to Wainwright. We had security when they got to Royce. Those clowns have got to remember that it's a hell of a lot easier to score when the bastards we're dealing with don't give a damn exactly who it is they tap out."

Brownell lifted his arm to check his watch. Then he twisted his round face into a grimace and said, "Well, it's ten thirty now. And they're still at it. Wouldn't surprise me to see them go through the night."

"It's never a good sign when it takes this long," said Hiller wearily. He shifted in the chair, and both men said nothing for several moments. Hiller found himself looking around the room at a number of portraits of former presidents.

As if suddenly remembering something urgent, he raised his voice a little and said, "Wasn't the Bay of Pigs invasion engineered from the Cuban side by the anti-Castro Berettas?"

Brownell considered the question thoughtfully. "Yes," he said finally. "Why do you ask?"

"What is our relationship with the Berettas?"

"For several years we trained and funded them . . ."

"Through the CIA, I know," said Hiller interrupting. "But what's our status with them *now*?"

Brownell shrugged, fighting off the perpetual kink in his back. "Last summer the President ordered Central Intelligence to cut off financial support, as a means of establishing new inroads with Cuba."

Hiller's juices were flowing now. He suddenly was not the least bit tired. "There was opposition to the idea if I remember," he said.

The secretary rolled his eyes and formed a perfect O with his lips, blowing a breath of air. "There was opposition all right," he said, making it clear that that was an understatement. "Moderates and conservatives in Congress, the FBI, some members of the Cabinet, the CIA, the Joint Chiefs . . . That didn't leave too many in John's corner—myself, Defense, the liberals, and the Vice President, even though he was *personally* opposed to it also.

"McAvee argued—convincingly—that if we stopped supporting the Berettas, Castro would embark on a campaign to eliminate them. He said that we couldn't afford *not* to continue backing them."

Hiller said suddenly, "I think the Berettas kidnapped the President."

Brownell looked at him, surprised, and shook his head. "A group that couldn't survive without our help kidnaps the President of the United States? That's pretty farfetched. They don't have the organization."

"You said we stopped supporting the Berettas last summer."

"So?"

"So if they can't survive without our help, how is it one of them tried to kill me the other day?"

"You're certain he was a Beretta?" asked Brownell.

"Positive."

The secretary tugged on his left ear. "All right, so now he's a hit man for someone else," he said. "Isn't that what happens to most of them? I don't know what else to tell you about that."

Phyllis entered the room and brought Hiller his drink. He touched her hand gently, accepting the glass, but continued at Brownell.

"Come on, Mr. Secretary," he said a little excitedly. "Isn't it possible that . . ."

"Brownie, telephone for you inside," Phyllis said. "Sorry for the interruption."

Brownell got up to answer the call, and Hiller slumped impatiently in his chair. He was anxious to rally support for the theory, and there was no better ally than the secretary of state.

The First Lady sat down and Hiller asked quickly,

"Did John ever talk to you about anything called Foxbat?"

She smiled slightly and said, "No. I'm sure I would have remembered a name like that. What is it?"

Hiller snickered. "What it is at this point is a good question." He took a huge gulp from his drink. When he set it down he saw Phyllis's eyes were vacant, her lips fallen into a frown.

"You must be feeling a hell of a lot of pain," he said gently. He reached out and clasped her hand in his, and she gave him a forced smile.

"The sleeping pills take care of a lot," she said. "Even when I can't sleep I seem to be less prone to dwelling . . ."

Secretary Brownell suddenly burst into the room, gesturing awkwardly and excitedly with his arms. His face was animated, his fat cheeks flushed. "We have a shot at it," he cried. "The ransom has been approved."

Chapter 21

December 16.

Only hours after congressional approval of the ransom, every morning newspaper in the country had thrown a banner headline across the front page—"Half Billion in Nick of Time," "Congress OKs Ransom at the Wire"—and rushed special editions to the street. By the time Wilson McAvee got to his office a little past seven, a few were already waiting for him.

It was the number two story, however, that he was most interested in: the murder of a young agent working on the investigation under Jay Hiller.

McAvee put on a pair of wire-rimmed reading glasses and gleaned each account carefully. Then he fell back in his chair and stared at the ceiling. He seemed to have come to a decision when the intercom buzzed. Deliberately, the white-haired director leaned across the oversized mahogany desk and pressed a button. A woman's voice told him Jay Hiller was waiting.

The thick veins in McAvee's neck bulged involuntarily as he prepared himself for the first meeting of the day. He tossed the newspapers in a wastebasket and placed a single file folder in front of him. Then he stood up and straightened his jacket as Hiller came through the door.

As usual, McAvee did not greet him. Instead, with an extended index finger he pointed to a chair on his right as if he were ordering a dog to a corner. Hiller struggled to control the petty anger surging in his blood and, pretending not to notice the gesture, took a chair to McAvee's left. The director stiffened but said nothing. He sat down and opened the folder.

Hiller was nearly dazed; heavy gray sacks hung under his eyes, exhaustion threatened to unravel him. Informed of Jeff Brodsky's brutal murder after leaving the White House, he stayed up through the night trying to work. On two occasions he hurried to the privacy of a rest room and, to his own great surprise, broke down. As he had always done during emotional moments in the past, he struggled to control his sobbing by biting down on his tongue. This time he was unable to stop until he spit blood.

Hovering over a sink at one point, he saw in the

mirror what appeared to be a grotesque man: red-eyed, emaciated, tears streaming down his face. His heart leaped into his throat before the image faded. Quickly he turned on the faucet and buried his face in a pool of cold water. What was happening to him? Was he so changed from yesterday that now, suddenly, he felt free to grieve? The Jay Hiller of old had faced death every day of his career, had seen many colleagues get blown away, some with even less of a reason than Jeff Brodsky. His reaction had always been fatalistic, outwardly unemotional, a disquieting acceptance of reality.

Even when his father, lonely and embittered, died on the floor of a cheap tavern in Detroit surrounded by drunken middle-aged men, he had not cried. He had not cried openly since Tom Vandewater's death.

But the death of Jeff Brodsky made him feel something he could not understand. It made him feel *powerful*—because he became strangely uncaring about his own life. And with that power and abandon, he was suddenly freed. Unlike pain, fear and caution were too imprecise to matter. The inhibitions born of such things now seemed foolish. They would play little, if any part at all, in his destiny. He could cry now. There were no more barriers to hold him back.

And so he wept freely—for his father, for Charley Lohman, for Jeff, for that day in his life when, at thirteen, his parents calmly announced they were separating after seventeen years of marriage. He had begun to weep then, only to have his father respond with an angry speech on manhood.

Hiller's mother, Margaret, moved to San Diego and remarried with a talkative but modest life insurance salesman, who was the antithesis of her first husband. Frank Hiller lived out his days in the same small rented two-bedroom house in the suburbs of Detroit where he had tried to raise a family. Except for occasional visits from his son, he spent his time asleep or in bars.

Jay Hiller wept for all of them now. And he wept, selfishly perhaps, for himself as well—mourning, for the last time, a generation of years that to him meant half a lifetime wasted. He had succeeded at what he had chosen to do in the past but, somehow, that mattered so little in the present. What was tragic was that he believed he had stopped dreaming and, worse, felt incapable of dreaming. He had said this twice to Lynn, and each time she had glared at him unsympathetically, disbelievingly. Then he had corrected himself and said that his dreams had become quite simplified, that he had but one dream.

He had been speaking a personal truth. Now, in the turmoil of his middle years, when his body would no longer do what he wanted it to do, when that inability was a constant reminder he had given away those foolish youthful years too freely, he did have one dream: He simply wanted to forget. Why that eluded him with such ferocity, he could not understand.

McAvee leaned back in his chair, which creaked under the weight of his body, and slowly removed his glasses. He tapped them rhythmically in his left palm. In a remarkably gentle voice he said, "Jeffrey Brodsky was killed while on an assignment that in my opinion he never should have been on."

Hiller did not trust the soft side of Wilson McAvee. He had rarely seen it before and did not know what it meant. Or if it was genuine. He preferred dealing with what he knew of the man.

He stared across the room, at the warm brown drapes and the soft light of a living-room-style floor lamp and said, "With the benefit of hindsight, I'd have to agree with you—he should not have been on that assignment. However, considering our manpower and what had to be done, he was the logical choice."

McAvee cleared his throat and replaced the eyeglasses. He looked at Hiller in silence, impassively. But there was something about his manner, even now, that Hiller perceived as mocking, as if the man were fighting back a sardonic smile with his tongue pressed against the inside of his cheek. Oddly, for the first time since beginning work on the kidnapping, Hiller could detect no anger in him. He wondered why. Was it because the ransom had been approved? No, he thought, more likely it was because McAvee knew the press would crucify him once they learned Brodsky was a neophyte. And it was inevitable they would learn. He could count on that. Thus, the media which had created and perpetuated myths about the abilities of Jay Hiller would be compelled, to some degree, to dismantle them. McAvee appreciated the irony.

Finally, the director spoke. His voice was calm. "Jeffrey Brodsky was not the logical choice—though you may think so—because of his inexperience and because—"

"You sent him to me, presumably to aid in the investigation," Hiller interrupted, "and I used him. I used him in the way I thought would be most beneficial and within his capabilities. Perhaps if I hadn't felt so hamstrung throughout the investigation it might not have been necessary. But it *was*, unfortunately."

McAvee furrowed his long brow and looked coolly at Hiller. He wore the look of a poker player confident of his cards and satisfied with life.

Ironic, thought Hiller, A man with no character has all those character lines on his face.

The ridges disappeared as McAvee leaned forward on his elbows. "That'll be all," he said abruptly, with a wave of his hand. He closed the folder on his desk and picked up the telephone receiver. It was a very brusque dismissal.

A minute after the special investigator had left for the GOB, McAvee was talking with Phyllis Royce. Following a brief exchange of pleasantries, he drew on his most paternalistic telephone manner and said in a deep, gentle voice, "Phyllis, I've given it every consideration and I've decided to replace Jay Hiller on the investigation."

Though it had always been lost on Hiller, the First Lady was fully aware of Wilson McAvee's charm—tall, physically attractive, a distinguished man of sixty-four. An Ivy League graduate who had spun round the world on dozens of occasions, he had stories and experiences from the most remote corners on earth and could mesmerize a roomful of people with them on the rare instances that he allowed himself to be a social animal. But the fact that Phyllis Royce was aware of his powers probably worked against him now. She was on guard.

"I'm sorry, Wilson," she replied with conviction that surprised him. "I wanted Jay Hiller at the beginning of this thing and I'm not going to change horses . . ."

"You heard about the boy last night?" McAvee asked softly but with sudden grimness.

"Yes, I heard. I am horrified by it. And it shuts down much of the hope I had in the wake of the ransom approval. But I don't see how you can argue that it is an indication of some gross shortcoming in Jay."

"Phyllis, let's say I have access to a more complete picture," he said sternly.

"No. I don't buy that one. I'm sorry."

McAvee clenched his teeth and considered his alternatives. "You know I have nothing but the greatest respect for you, my dear," he said, returning to his original paternalistic approach. "But I'm afraid I'm going to have to go ahead on this even if it means going against you."

"You do, Wilson," she said forcefully, "and I'll go to the press and the television stations with it. I promise you that. I'll tell them that you went ahead against my wishes."

McAvee heaved a sudden exasperated sigh. Such a maneuver would clearly make him into a villain. "Must you be so dogmatic about it," he said, obviously vexed. "Why are you binding my hands?"

"I don't see that I'm being unreasonable," Phyllis replied. "I'm doing exactly what I think John would want done. I'm going by instinct. I have to trust that. If it doesn't work, there will be no one to blame. Can you understand? I'm sorry, Wilson. I hope you can understand."

The First Lady put down the receiver, realizing she had sounded committed and in complete control. What she felt now was neither. If anything, she was feeling lost.

Douglas Padley and George Berkquist sat in the corner of a small Italian restaurant in Georgetown and ordered lunch. The director of the FBI wore a self-congratulatory half-smile as he downed a Bloody Mary. In whispered tones he said, "One of the good ol' boys came up with an extremely entertaining report this morning. Seems as if special investigator Hiller, who fancies himself almighty and holier-than-thou, has a weakness after all."

Berkquist shifted the glasses on his nose and continued to listen.

"You know that flashy TV dame?" Padley drawled. "What's her name, Carlotta? Carlisle? Well, I've had her on the watch-list for a while and you'll never guess what we came up with—Hiller's been boffin' her . . ." His light eyes brightened and he laughed devilishly in anticipation of Berkquist's reaction. "We can roast the son of a bitch!"

Berkquist looked at Padley, unimpressed. He furrowed his brow and shrugged. "Will that serve our purpose?" he asked impassively.

The director pulled back just a little and looked askance. "Well sure! What do you mean? Why, McAvee would tear the white hairs off his chest for somethin' like this!"

"I don't think it'll do us any good to let that out. Say we do and Hiller gets flogged out of town. What happens then? Then we get Wilson McAvee right where you don't want him: running the investigation with ever more power and glory!"

Padley put a finger to his mouth and chewed the nail. "Shit," he muttered. "Is that a foregone?"

Berkquist shrugged again. "What do you think?"

Padley nodded. "Frying pan to the fire. So what do we do with this? It's too good to let go."

The corners of Berkquist's mouth broke into a slight grin. "Sell it to the *National Enquirer*," he said.

The director frowned. "Come on, George. Dammit."

"Sit on it then. There's plenty of room in the Bufiles on Jay Hiller for something like that. Maybe someday you'll have a chance to use it."

Outwardly, Berkquist again was the voice of reason, weighing the situation and its elements and offering sound advice to the director. Privately, he was a little disgusted by the childlike glee Padley exuded over a crumby little piece of dirt.

At ten minutes of eight that evening, Jay Hiller started onto the Dulles Airport access road from Dolley Madison Boulevard in Fairfax County, Virginia, eleven miles from downtown Washington and fourteen miles from the drop point.

In accordance with instructions on the tape from the kidnappers, he drove a 1978 white Plymouth station wagon along Highway 123 (Dolley Madison Boulevard), which had been closed to traffic from McLean to the Capital Beltway throughout the day.

Escorting him were eight vehicles—two municipal police cars and two government cars in front, two municipal police cars and two U.S. Army cars behind. All were heavily armed. At two-mile intervals along the entire route police vehicles monitored Hiller's progress. If he missed a checkpoint by more than sixty seconds, an alert would be broadcast. In no way could he fail to arrive at the appointed time.

In the afternoon Hiller had listened another half-dozen times to the distorted voice on the tape:

> The money must be in Federal Reserve notes in denominations of fifty, one hundred, and five hundred dollars, [it commanded,] with no more than eight bills bearing consecutive serial numbers. They must not have been issued prior to 1973 and not more than eighty million may be in uncirculated bills. The money will be subjected to an intensive and sophisticated examination including tests for marking, shaving, spotting, irradiating, counterfeiting, and cutting. Equal amounts should be placed in each of ten standard-size suitcases and delivered by investigator Hiller in a 1977 or 1978 white Plymouth station wagon to Dulles Airport at eight fifteen P.M. of the appointed day.
>
> The airport is to be closed to all traffic throughout the day. Leave one runway lighted—all others dark. No one is to be in the control

tower. Our instructions must be carried out precisely. Do no attempt to use tracking devices. We have means of locating them instantly. Anything done contrary to our specifications will threaten the life of the hostage.

Again Hiller had asked the lab to try for a voiceprint identification. Again they were unsuccessful.

Unnerved as a prisoner on death row, he had then triple-checked arrangements for the evening. To prepare the ransom, fifty-seven people were required; to locate the required vehicle, another twelve; additional police numbered 196; airport security 116. None of them could afford to err.

At the junction with the access road fourteen miles from Dulles International, Hiller left his eight-car escort behind. He swung onto the highway going west and accelerated to fifty mph. There were two lanes in each direction, separated by a wide grass divider. The bare, bony branches of young oak trees and a few Virginia pines landscaped the wide shoulders. No taillights led the way, no glaring headlights traveling eastbound. This road, too, was closed to outside traffic.

Along the way he had plenty to think about. The instructions on the tape had been detailed and explicit—letter-perfect and flawless. He expected no danger, but there was also five hundred million dollars in the back of the automobile, and that made him nervous.

During the day, the CIA and the FBI had come up with daring plans to bust up the ransom drop. They considered homing devices and dusting the money to induce sleep or illness, but each had been rejected as too risky. For one thing, there had not been time to formulate anything that promised to be more than a long shot all-or-nothing proposition. For another, there was no way of knowing whether the emissaries at the airport would be the directive forces behind the kidnapping. Conceivably, the government could coordinate a last-minute offensive at great danger to the President as well as to its special forces, and wind up corralling half a dozen "errand boys." That would seal Royce's fate, certainly, and would not bring them any closer to the real kidnappers. The only thing they agreed to risk was tracking by radar, and Hiller had very little hope it would help.

Now he passed a sign on the side of the road: Dulles Monitors CB Ch. 9. Then, from four miles out, he caught a glimpse of the darkened air-traffic-control tower between the trees. The gargantuan main terminal of cement and glass with its wide concave roof loomed in the distance like an enormous fireplace grate. Only a few of its lights were visible, probably those of an auxiliary system, as the main power supply had also been ordered shut down.

Hiller was about a mile away when he swung onto an unlit road that led away from the terminal building toward the runways. With the exception of the headlights, which were intentionally aimed low (he was expressly forbidden to use high beams), he found himself shrouded in a sudden curtain of darkness, and shuddered.

As he drove through an open chain link gate onto an unlit asphalt runway, Hiller turned off the heater fan in the car. It had been on high to compensate for the subfreezing temperature, but its grinding noises added to his anxiety.

He followed the digital runway signs until he came to one: 2L-9R. He replayed the tape and followed orders explicitly: Kill the headlamps in favor of parking light; slow the car to a crawl.

Then he swung onto a second runway. Strung out before him now were two rows of evenly spaced red lights, stretching as far as he could see on both sides. He drove between them past another digital sign, 7L-2R.

His mouth dried up and he began to feel his pulse banging like a hammer against his brain. He could not quite understand his nervousness. He anticipated no confrontation.

He was conscious of moving down the main runway apron at an absurdly sluggish pace, of being able to count the runway lights that ordinarily streaked past porthole windows of landing jetliners. Finally the long luminous row ended, and he was again in a dense black night under a dark sky littered with stars. But there was something else, something that suddenly engulfed him the way a canyon is engulfed by cliffs. Hiller leaned forward against the steering wheel and squinted in an effort to decipher the shadows. What he saw took his breath away.

At the end of the darkened runway, which intersected diagonally with another, in an enormous semicircle, five huge jets loomed ominously over Hiller's minusculed car. Until this moment he had had no idea man could feel so insignificant inside an automobile. He swallowed hard and turned off the engine. His eyes darted from one jet to the next. All was perfectly still in the darkened cockpits.

Hiller turned on the interior light so his movements would be conspicuous. Cautiously, he got out of the station wagon and went around to the luggage door in the rear. He unlocked it and pulled out the first two of ten suitcases.

They weighed enough to contain bricks and caused sharp pains in his shoulders. His face reddened as he lifted them. He struggled to the plane nearest him and flung them onto an extended baggage belt. He repeated this four more times, loading two suitcases onto each aircraft. Finally, rubber-legged and exhausted, he fell against the car and watched helplessly as hundreds of millions of dollars disappeared into the bellies of the jets. Then the belt mechanisms themselves were drawn in and, finally, huge cargo doors lowered, sealing up the undersides.

For a full minute, Hiller stood there—his mouth ajar—unmindful of the chill. Save for his own rapid breathing, there wasn't as much as a muffled voice. Then a jet engine screamed so suddenly that he trembled with a burning rush and his heart skipped. A second and third engine-roar quickly followed.

The whining was so high-pitched the ground shook, and Hiller was forced to cover his ears. When the other jet engines joined in the teeth-jarring chorus, he threw himself into the station wagon and started it up. Just as the first plane thundered into a roll, he sped off—tires screeching. One of them could crush him like an aluminum beer can if he hung around too long.

At a safe distance, he pulled over, made a ninety-degree turn, and rolled down a window. He saw each of the jets scream down the red lighted runway and leap into the black sky in rapid succession. Each of them banked sharply upon take-off and flew off at low altitudes in a due-east direction.

Chapter 22

The lights inside Padre Julian Serra's quarters in the church were ablaze. Two days had passed since Luis ran off, and the priest believed his only chance of seeing him again was to make good the work on the passport documents.

He was hunched over his desk, wearing extraordinarily thick glasses with a powerful magnifying capability. And with a special cutting tool and a precision tweezerlike apparatus that seemed as if it belonged in dentistry, he deftly replaced an old photograph on a passport with one of the five new ones. He was careful and meticulous in his retouching but very ill at ease. Every so often he would unscrew the cap on a bottle of tequila, pour himself a glass and drink it dry, then rescrew the cap.

Now he placed the passport forgery under a sophisticated microscope and examined it. This was an instrument he had not used in thirteen years, not since he—of all people—had been recruited to forge documents for Jews trying to flee the Soviet Union.

On rare occasions he had used his artistic gifts to forge *cedulas* for a few well-meaning and penniless Mexican migrant workers. The high quality of his work, however, gave him some notoriety. One family particularly had aroused his sympathy and convinced him to take part; not, as the mysterious contact from the Israeli underground who sought him out had believed, the sizable contribution they would make to his church.

The incident concerned a family named Rosenzweig which had been given permission to emigrate to Israel, where it was hoped the youngest of two children would be able to receive specialized medical attention for a bone disease. Rosenzweig, himself a doctor, was unable to obtain the necessary treatment for his daughter in Russia. His wife and son departed for Israel first, to arrange for housing and the girl's entry into a hospital.

However, the following week in Moscow, the physician found his papers abruptly confiscated and revoked. Authorities also refused to allow the ailing girl to join her mother and brother. The official reason was that Rosenzweig's professional services were required in the USSR, though no excuse was given for denying the child an exit visa.

The padre had accepted the entreaty because the story struck a human chord, and because no one would be harmed as a result of what he would do. But he had to make more than certain his work was exceptional. If it was not, there would be far greater consequences than the separation of a family and a child's crippling pain.

For Julian Serra, the story had a happy, if somewhat delayed, ending. Almost a year after, a short letter came to him from the Rosenzweig family in Israel. But it was written in Hebrew, and it took the padre another seven months to find someone who could finally translate it.

It said: "We have heard of your remarkable abilities from a trusted friend and are forever in your debt. Your name will always live in our hearts. May God grant you life and peace and may His light always shine upon you." It was signed, "Dr. and Mrs. Gregory Rosenzweig."

At the bottom of the page, scrawled in an eleven-year-old hand, were these words: "Dear Father, Thank you for helping me to feel so much more alive. We are celebrating Passover next Tuesday and I would like to invite you to our Seder and give you a big hug and wine. I'm sorry I couldn't give you more advance notice. I send you all of my love and appreciation. Alicia Rosenzeig—P.S. I say prayers for you every Monday, Wednesday, and Friday."

The padre rested his eyes and smiled wanly remembering the story. He found it astonishing to think that the girl today would be twenty-four, and a woman. He had no regrets about what he had done then. But now he worked under base threats of violence—so he thought—to an eight-year-old hostage.

The padre unscrewed the cap on the tequila and took a veteran's drink directly from the bottle. The hours passed slowly, arduously. It was true—he feared this man Grijalva more than he feared death. Not so much for what Grijalva might do to him, but for what he might do to a defenseless boy.

Padre Serra sighed deeply, his sad brown eyes again lowered. Suddenly they fixed on a two-day-old newspaper and began to dart back and forth from the passport photographs to the front-page pictures. He hastily spread the five forged passports alongside the paper and was noticeably unsettled as he focused on the eyes and mouths. Then with an artist's sketch pen he began drawing on the newspaper pictures, changing hair styles, adding facial hair to this one, a pair of glasses to that.

The sudden fierce beats in his breast came from panic. The padre was stunned, as incapable of clear thought as if someone had shaken him suddenly from a sound sleep. The newspaper pictures of the kidnap suspects now matched those in the photographs! All it had taken before to make this unapparent was a clever disguise.

He tore the special glasses from his face, rushed to a cabinet, and pulled out a thick green towel from a drawer. Wrapped inside was a .22-caliber revolver. His head began to spin, and his mind was racing furiously. Could he ever seriously think of using such a thing? Frantically, he dismissed the notion as a temptation by Satan. But was he otherwise helpless? He returned the gun and towel to the drawer and angrily slammed it closed.

The violent pounding in his chest escalated as he stormed to his desk and viciously scattered tools, passports, paper, and microscope to the floor. He flung open the door in the vestibule burning with rage and ran into the brisk winter night.

A short time later the padre hobbled up the little wooded rise above the tilled field and went into the Diaz hut. Had he expected to find a trace of Luis there, he certainly would have come sooner. But in fact the boy had told him he would never go home without his father.

Now the padre went anyway, not because he expected to find anything, but because he did not know what else to do.

He entered the open door and struck a match to light an oil lamp. He was startled to find the place a shambles. Books were strewn about, torn at the spines; furniture broken and upended; a mattress sliced open and feather stuffing emptied on the floor.

The padre shook his head gravely. Las Cumbres had never known such darkness as in the last few days. He bent down and took a fallen crucifix in his hand. He put the cross in its former place on a wall

THE FOXBAT SPIRAL 233

above the bed, righted a table, and picked up a few books. As he set them on a chair, a paper fell from one of the volumes. The padre took it up and held it near the lamp. In the flickering gray shadows he read a note in the jagged, nervous hand of its author:

"Because of my ways, I have led myself to destruction and my family to disgrace. There can be no forgiveness for me, for in spite of the horrible end I am about to come to, I would make the same mistakes a second time if God, in His infinite mercy, gave me another chance.

"I cannot face the good Padre in confession, so I pray that setting this to paper will act as my confession and save my soul from Hell.

"I have for many years helped a group of extremists in their smuggling trade. Though the money was dirty, it helped me provide for my family. But now these extremists go beyond my own greed and I cannot continue. They tell me I have no choice, but there they are wrong. I have one choice and I have made it.

"None of this matters, for I have learned accidentally of their frightening plan. I have photographs to prove their guilt, but I cannot give these pictures to the authorities—for they would murder my son. It is certain they will try to kill me and I am prepared for my end. But I beg that Luis will know none of this and will not curse his father."

It was signed "Ramon Diaz."

The impact of the note caused the padre to fall back a little and hold his breath, his gaze fixed in space with inward-seeing, disbelieving eyes. But gradually the expression on his thin peach-rippled face changed from shock to grim resolution.

He folded the paper with Ramon Diaz's confession and lifted the glass cover on the oil lamp. Then he set the letter to the flame, and in seconds it was ash.

Nothing he had seen in the house drove the padre from the narrow dirt path leading back to the village. And yet, in his sad bewilderment, he was powerless to check his impulse as he stumbled toward the plowed fields nearby.

Later, he would have said it was Luis's spirit that had beckoned him, crying out to be put to rest. But as he groped across rows and rows of unwatered crops, the earth thick and crusty, his heart sped up. The chill in the air was like ice, and the stillness, unlike the serenity of a summer evening, was the stillness of dissolution.

Though the wind was quieted, the smoke of his breath burned fleetingly before him as if to remind him that all breaths are fleeting. And in another moment he saw how true this was. As he stepped over another furrow, amid the shadows of agave plants he thought he saw the carcass of a small animal near his feet. It was partly cloaked in gray tatters, the head horribly submerged in earth, twisted at the neck as if it had been broken. At once it was grotesque and pathetic and not an animal at all—it was a child's body, blue and colorless at the same moment, so cold that when the padre touched it, a chill shot up his fingers.

He trembled when he saw it, and even without looking more closely he knew he had found Luis. With all urgency he flung himself at the body, clawing at the earth with his long nails, part of him believing that so young a human being is never called so early.

"Luis!" he cried in a sudden delirious panic. "Let me help, my son. Let me help."

He freed the boy and paid no mind to the finality of the lifelessness written in his face. He brushed the dirt from his hair and cheeks, from his eyes and lips. He took Luis's tiny icy fingers and breathed quick hot breaths on them. He felt his own violent thundering heartbeats in the back of his neck, in his temples, in his throat, and believed they were . . . yes, it was Luis's heartbeat, yes!

The Padre's lips trembled in a swift hopeful exuberant smile—yes, it was Luis, alive! And then the curled lips lost their power and collapsed into a sob, and he whispered barely audibly, "Merciful Mother of God . . ."

The priest's prayer was smothered as a series of rapid animallike breaths escaped from his throat. Then the breaths gave way to a shrill cry. He had come too late.

Someone could have cut off both his legs and the pain would not have been as great. He clutched the body, continuing to try to warm its hands and fingers and toes, swallowing his heart a thousand times over—and plunged recklessly into despair as if he were a carcass thrown to an open pit of wolves.

Chapter 23

A freezing wind blew off the mysterious dark water of the Potomac River, thirty miles from the mouth of Chesapeake Bay. The boats anchored in the harbor rode the choppy sea and slammed against the moorings on each new wave with repetitious moaning.

Jay Hiller drove onto the shoulder of the dirt road near the entrance to the marina parking lot and got out of the Plymouth station wagon. He had driven two hours from Dulles International after making the ransom drop to get here, something he felt he had to do if only in deference to Jeff Brodsky.

The preliminary coroner's report detailing the path of the fatal bullet from just under the left eye through the back of the skull had been brutal. In addition, there were gunpowder burns on the victim's face and slivers of window glass embedded in the flesh.

The information tossed restlessly in Hiller's mind as he packed a flashlight and walked across the deserted lot to the pier. There were no cars here tonight.

The air was even colder than at the airport. With the collar up on his unbuttoned peacoat, he watched whitecaps break against the wooden pilings and tried to imagine what the last ten minutes of Jeff's life must have been like.

"The poor, sweet son of a bitch," he said softly. And suddenly shivered against the wind. Pulling his arms tight around him, he walked briskly to the end of the wharf and boarded Gordon Langway's cabin cruiser.

Hiller tried the cabin door, which was locked. With the flashlight he dug through utility boxes on the deck, explored hatches, and, underneath a tarpaulin, found a ten-foot boathook. On the port side he came across an unlocked cabin window.

Working quickly, Hiller slid the boathook through, but the rocking motion of the vessel made him lose a firm grip, and the steel-hook end of the pole plunged into the center of a lacquered pinewood table. He tugged and pushed and, at last, dislodged it, but not without scoring a chunk of wood the size of a half dollar.

Again he extended his arm and the boathook through the window, across the width of the cabin to the door and, after flirting with the lock for several minutes, finally caught the latch and sprang it open.

He raced around to the starboard side and went in, taking care to relock the door and close the window. In a wastebasket he found a soap label, an unused blank envelope, a notice about an increase in rental space on the marina, tissue paper, and a day-old newspaper. He flipped on a cassette tape deck built into the wall and listened to ". . . stocks down sixteen cents per share on the American exchange, down five cents per share on the New York exchange . . . trading was light . . ."

He turned it off and went into the head, smelled three small glass bottles in the medicine chest, broke open a bar of yellow soap in the sink and examined it, and squeezed a tube of toothpaste, feeling for a possible hidden object. He went back in the cabin and ran across a few cigarette butts and three spent matchsticks in an ashtray. The word *GLOBAL* was burnished on the stem of each match.

Hiller took the unused envelope from the wastebasket, dropped the butts and matches in it, and jammed it in an inside coat pocket. At that moment, there was a sudden stirring outside coming from the gangway. He froze, then a key slid into the lock in the door. He was close to panic as he bolted for the shower stall.

The cabin door pushed open and a big man wearing a black parka came in, slamming the door behind him. The sound of his movements were heavy, as if he was wearing thick boots. A light went on. He moved deliberately about the cabin, sensing something alien. Then he noticed the boathook on the floor and the divot in the table. He drew a long fishing knife from a leather holster on his belt and looked around anxiously, throwing open a closet and then the door to the head. It sprang back at him and he kicked it open a second time.

The light from the cabin poured into the bath. The

man's eyes fixed on the broken bar of yellow soap. He suddenly turned and rushed out.

Quickly, Hiller freed himself from the shower stall and scrambled to the deck. Between windy gusts, he heard angry voices and the staccato marching of several men on the dock growing menacingly louder.

His heart was racing now. He lowered himself over the side of the boat, scratching and clawing his way across a rim on the stern onto a beam underneath the wharf. The thunderous stomp of boots now rattled directly above his head as the men boarded the vessel. They were shouting at each other in a foreign tongue. The fierce chilling breezes and the noise of beating waves and the boats groaning in their slips made the language indecipherable, but it sounded like Spanish.

Three men, two of them strapping, the third shorter and thinner than the others, combed the deck, then stormed into the cabin continuing their gruff vocal outbursts.

Hiller, balanced on the crossbream, inched his way toward the mooring lines of the boat. He slipped the stern line from a bollard, wormed his way backward, and did the same with the breast and bow lines. With one arm clinging apelike to a strong piling, he leaned his weight into the vessel and pushed it from the pier. Aided by the choppy water, it began to drift out.

Hiller started to climb onto the wharf when his eyes caught the bizarre and peculiar sight of several dead fish floating on the surface of the water. They all bled at the gills, which seemed to have been pried apart. He climbed down to a lower crossbeam and, after many frustrating attempts, scooped up one of the fish and pinned it under his arm. The fish was so cold it was impossible to hold with bare hands. With measurable difficulty Hiller struggled back to the top of the pier, privately congratulating himself on his rekindled physical abilities. He removed his shoes to silence his footsteps and raced down the dock to his car.

By the time Jay Hiller got back to the GOB, the red and green numerals on the center's digital clocks read "00.51." He felt like a sponge that had been left sopping wet, and his nerves were the frayed end of an electric wire. But in that now-familiar office complex of insurance-company charm on the second floor of the Blue Wing, a minor surprise awaited him. Ted Rozakis, the lab expert, had reported to Jack Albaum on General Hummerstone's photographs and left Hiller this account:

"Suspect in Exhibit C, identified by Hummerstone's staff as Specialist 4th class Joseph Martinez (who forged equipment requisiton at Fort Cherry) is the *same man* in question in the second photo Exhibit B. Here he is made up to look like Sergeant Gilbert (Exhibit A). It is our conclusion that Martinez not only forged requisition but also posed as Gilbert and, therefore, is integrally connected to the kidnap plot. After rechecking with Moore and Wingate here, we have absolutely no doubts."

Albaum had already instigated an interagency check on Martinez through the National Crime Information Center's computer network as well as through subversive files at the Bureau and the Company, Justice's Criminal Division, the Defense Intelligence Agency, the Secret Service's Protective Research Section, and the computers at the National Security Council. But before Hiller's face had a chance to brighten, Albaum dumped the news that the exhaustive effort had produced thousands of possible leads.

Because Hiller was convinced there was a tie-in with Russell Frazier, he returned to the task he had begun a day earlier—viewing slides of Beretta soldiers from the combined intelligence service files.

Though the official FBI report on Frazier had finally come in, information in it was flabby, confirming suspicions that Douglas Padley was indeed holding back. And while Albaum and the others in the office threw themselves into the awesome job of checking the new interagency data—all tied up with the Caribbean, Cuba, and the Bay of Pigs—Fred Goss hunted for Gordon Langway, who had vanished after Brodsky's murder.

In a screening room away from the glare of full-spectrum lighting, Hiller sat on a chrome-and-vinyl chair with his feet propped on another, watching faces and code numbers change every few seconds. He was fatigued but kept himself awake by busying both hands—in the right, a remote control for twin slide projectors; in the left, a coffee cup filled with Scotch, tequila, and Drambuie. Opened bottles of each sat nearby on a wooden table.

The first projector showed a single slide—Joseph Martinez—on a small screen. The second threw its bright beam on a larger screen while the click-clack of slides monotonously slipped in and out of the film gate, not matching, never matching, the face of Martinez. In several hours, Hiller had seen hundreds of faces, hundreds who at one time or another had been connected with the Beretta movement. What if Martinez had had no such connection? What if his Beretta theory was the wrong box?

"Shit," he mumbled; he could not stand it anymore. Hours ago he had dumped a half-billion-dollar package and had not gotten a scrap of a clue in return. "Not a fucking thing," he said audibly just before vomiting out a sudden violent cough. He breathed with no small amount of effort and his eyes grew heavy. His mind drifted toward sleep. Though too tired for images, the thought of that beer, his eternal shade tree, and nectarine, soft grass . . . His head sank into his chest, and he fell off in a small, sweet slumber. Only minutes later, an invisible force jarred him like a child tugging on his arm for attention, and his head sprang up with wide, surprised eyes.

Hiller sighed, put his drink—which was precariously balanced—on the floor and rearranged himself in the chair. Jack Albaum tiptoed into the screening room so as not to disrupt him but was so quiet that a sudden movement startled Hiller and caused his heart to leap.

"Dammit to hell, why don't you make some noise," he whined, "so I know it isn't *spooks* coming out of the walls."

Albaum smirked at the use of the word, a synonym for CIA operatives. It didn't matter that he had surprised Hiller and was reprimanded for being too quiet. Probably he would have been scolded if he had come in making noise.

Albaum privately nursed the tiny humiliation and said, "Here's what the lab turned up on Charlie the Tuna."

Hiller looked perplexed as he took a blue file from his aide. "Wha—?"

"That dead fish you brought in," Albaum reminded him. "You wanted it checked, not cooked, if I remember correctly. That wasn't a lox now was it?"

Hiller blinked hard. He was not in the mood for Albaum's wise-assing. The aide recognized this and backed off, thinking privately, "I've got no desire to rattle Caesar."

Hiller studied the report and nodded. "Traces of heroin inside the body cavity," he said, a hint of a smile breaking the corners of his mouth.

Albaum looked at him a little absentmindedly. "Which means?"

"Which means unless that fish was a junkie we can assume that Gordon Langway is trafficking. If you hear from Goss, let me know *immediately*. I'm sure this walrus-ass executive can lead us to the kidnappers."

Albaum said, "You know we've sent people out to the marina, to his house in King George, and to Global Communications but nothing's come out of there."

"I know, I know," Hiller said impatiently. "As usual, everything has been covered. But he's got to come out of his hole some time, and I want to be ready with a club when he does."

"Anything else?"

"Just *that* for the time being."

Albaum left the report and headed for the phones at his desk. Then he stopped abruptly and poked his head back in the room. "Oh, I know you'll be thrilled to hear that radar tracked the planes from Dulles after you made the drop and lost them to a jamming system about forty miles east of Annapolis."

"Naturally," Hiller said facetiously, and he took the coffee cup from the floor and swallowed most of his drink. Then again he pushed a button on the remote control unit and a new face jumped on the screen, a round olive-skinned face with large black eyes, but a face obviously unlike Martinez's.

Several minutes and slides passed before his eyes and another sudden noise from behind disrupted him.

"Now what?" he cried with some exasperation, anticipating another intrusion by Jack Albaum. But when he turned around, he was astonished to find himself glaring at the withered expression of a female face. Never had he seen Lynn Carlisle like this—

hesitant, timorous, the color in her usually lovely oval eyes a drab olive. Always, in the past, her vulnerability had been appealing, persistent, had somehow seemed an attribute. Now it lacked audacity. Now she stood there, with pale skin, looking demolished and in a fog.

Her eyes seemed to beg something, but it was not forgiveness. *That* she could ask for. She wanted nurturing, cradling, and was afraid of her need. Fearful not because she might seem deceptively childlike, but because rejection was so possible.

Now if she were refused, too many doors could close. She would be forced to deal forthrightly with her insecurity, her fear of isolation, with her well-camouflaged self-contempt. All those fires of the subconscious would become live demons threatening her parameters if she were turned away and made to feel once again that she had to traverse the world alone.

Finally she gathered herself and said with a tremor in her voice, "I . . . uh, about last night, I came to say . . . If I had thought . . . I mean, I knew, I'm *aware* . . ." She stopped and seemed a little irritated with herself.

Then she said uneasily but earnestly, "I'm sorry."

Having spoken it—awkwardly—her expression changed to one of hopeful anticipation. The most difficult test for Lynn had been reaching this point, and Hiller could see that now she felt relief.

Though he did not show it, secretly he was pleased to see her. He would have easily confessed his sadness over their imbroglio to a willing ear. But the frustrations of the week had taken their toll, and the bands of his temper threatened to snap. They had been stretched even further by the emotional turbulence of their last night together and it stirred the wild grizzly within him, the barest, coarsest, and most primitive of his instincts. Then he did the last thing he wanted to do—he gave it all back to her.

"Sorry? Why do you say you're sorry?" he said bitterly. "Because you heard about Jeff Brodsky? Or because you know I should have been there with him instead of getting head from a great cocksucker."

The moment he uttered it, he regretted it—the words were spoken almost involuntarily. They were a culmination of many things, not the least of which was an illogical resentment for her small part in his not being where he felt he should have been. This was no time for love. Why did it offer itself now when he could afford to give it so little? Where was it those many lonely Sunday afternoons when he walked through streets and parks fantasizing romance? Or those empty nights by the stereo, sipping drinks to help make being alone bearable? Why did she make him care at the precise time in his life when he could not afford to do that? Yes, he cared and yes, he wanted her—but just now, at this moment, he was not free to enjoy the wanting.

The brutality of his words made Lynn recoil as if she had been struck in the throat. She struggled to find something to say but had neither strength nor will to battle him. Hiller could not hold her gaze. He lowered his head ashamedly, realizing he had yielded to impulse and cut her down. When at last she spoke, Lynn's voice was a tiny whisper, but it was chilling.

"Even *you*, I didn't think, would come down *that* hard." She turned brusquely and hurried out the door.

Hiller could not bring himself to go after her. He was anchored to the chair by his own remorse, resigned unhappily to letting it pass as another personal failure. But he found himself tossed suddenly into a strange undefinable frenzy. At last he leaped up and raced into the hall. But when Lynn heard him coming, she broke into a run.

He cried out in vain, then charged after her and caught her from behind. "Wait a minute," he pleaded. "Let me say . . ."

Lynn struggled to free herself. When she could not, she suddenly swung around and landed an opened hand across his cheek. He looked at her with astonishment as his face flushed. She cocked her hand to strike again, but he seized her wrist with a fierce grip.

"No!" she shrieked. "You son of a bitch! You can cheapen anything, but you can't be God. Who do you think you are? You, you vicious . . . I know what you think, I know the kid was killed! I'm sorry he was killed! But it has *nothing* . . . *nothing* to do with us! If I never existed, you *still* couldn't have taken his place. You can't maneuver the past with guilt, no matter what you'd like to believe. What do you want—a bullet in your head to make your guilt disappear? Well, you don't need *me* for that."

The words stung like so many blows, and Hiller winced with the pain of spoken truths. He lapsed into silence, feeling unclothed and defenseless, and dropped his arms limply at his sides as if he had reluctantly agreed to take abuse. When he finally spoke, there was sorrow in his voice.

"I don't know how to explain myself," he said quietly. "But if you drive a nail into me—and I felt you did—my impulse is to do the same. I've always lived by an-eye-for-an-eye. I never learned any other way; I've never known any other way. Sure, I tried to beat down our intimacy, make it less important than it's been because . . ." Here he stopped and thought a moment and sighed briefly.

"Because I do care and because the more I care the harder it seems to be able to survive. And in spite of what it may look like on the outside, I *am* hurting, Lynn. I'm hurting over everything that's happened. I can't excuse myself for my vulgarities or my irrationalities or my belligerence. Anyone around me is going to experience the fallout when I feel squeezed."

Lynn glared at him with penetrating eyes, with a strange mix of understanding and mistrust. Though her huge eyes seemed sympathetic, almost warm, her mouth was twisted in a hard frown. Then she shuddered and so suddenly burst into sobs that Hiller was completely disarmed. She fell against his chest and he encircled her with his arms.

"You son of a bitch," she cried without a trace of anger. "Why can't it be simple? Why is it so painful and impossible?"

He was puzzled by her outburst but whispered reassuringly, "We're all learning, Lynn. You have to believe it will be all right."

"What have I done that's so wrong," she sobbed, "that my whole life should be falling apart. I can't see myself clearly anymore. Tell me what I'm doing wrong."

"Hey—it's not that bad," he said gently.

"It is," she protested through tears.

He whispered again, "Sometimes things look like they're falling apart because there are so many missing pieces to the puzzle. There's nothing we can do about that. You do what you can with what you have. The multitudes all feel cheated—we, each of us, are learning how to live. It isn't easy, but it's the only game there is."

Lynn took little comfort in Hiller's reply. The fact that everyone felt tortured did not make her own suffering easier to live with. But she found reassurance in his warm embrace, which she needed when the tears involuntarily came again. She tried to stifle her sobs but that only caused each succeeding ripple to back up and finally break forth in convulsive waves. She stayed buried in his arms and cried for a full thirty minutes.

Chapter 24

A frail hoary figure stood over Luis Diaz's broken body and administered the holy sacrament of Extreme Unction. He was a ghost, this man, stooped and beaten and ready at any instant to sever himself from an honorable past and refute God's justice.

He had all kinds of blasphemous thoughts, which he struggled to put out of his mind—and they intensified the implausible nightmare of the last few days.

Yet something forceful stirred in him for which he gave thanks but which he also cursed. It was outrage and it changed him, made him uncertain and intemperate and somehow more whole. It gave him courage and, at the same time, made him irresolute. He was aware of his physical limitations, but inside, there was nothing left. Inside, he felt he had begun to die, and that dying had given him a more complete understanding of life.

With great difficulty, he bore the child's body to the church and in the late night hours dug a new grave on the hillside. There he buried the boy with no witness, alongside the place where he had laid his father to rest.

The padre then went into his quarters and drank the last half of the bottle of tequila. He took the newspaper he had bought in Mérida several days earlier and rode the last bus of the night to the city.

When he could not find a long distance office that was open, he went to the police station and tried to prevail upon a sleepy-eyed sergeant to let him make a call. The officer, a portly olive-skinned man who was having trouble holding his tired head in his hand, smiled through his moustache after hearing the priest's incredible excuse for needing a telephone—that he had information about the kidnappers of the President of the United States.

"Sure, Padre. Sure, Padre," he said patronizingly and noted the smell of liquor on Serra's breath.

"You must believe me," the priest implored. "I can pay you for the use of the telephone. But let me make this call."

The sergeant grinned and said through half-closed eyes in a voice that was meant for a child, "I do believe you, Padre. I do believe you. I *always* believe padres. And this time is no different. But you know we have the rules here just like you have the rules at your church . . ."

The sergeant lifted his head, which required all his effort, and looked a little agonizingly at the man before him. He yawned and said gently, "Now please, Padre, go. Please go. . . . There is . . . understand . . ."

He yawned a second time and closed his eyes in mid-sentence. Then his head sank into his chest and, after a minute, bounced up suddenly with the greatest look of surprise on his face. Again his lids grew heavy as he muttered something inaudible.

Quietly, the padre sat down in a corner on a wooden bench. When the officer was at last asleep, he picked up the telephone and made a long-distance call to the District of Columbia.

The luminous digits on the investigation room clock read "03:14." Jay Hiller continued to work with the Beretta slides as if time did not exist. Though he moved sluggishly and his brain seemed to take forever to examine each face on the viewing screen, his eyes remained opened out of sheer determination.

Lynn Carlisle, however, was not of the same resolve. Exhausted physically from chasing down stories on the approval of the ransom, the dramatic drop at Dulles, and the Brodsky murder; exhausted emotionally as well from two days of anxiety, she had kicked off her shoes, pushed two vinyl chairs together, and curled up under Hiller's jacket.

But before that, with a sad smile, she gently took the coffee cup from his hands, set it down on the floor, and kissed him. His tender responsiveness to this simple expression did more to calm her than an hour of discussion about their adversities. In a matter of minutes following, she was sound asleep.

Later when Hiller wanted a cigarette, rather than chance waking her he fished one from a desk along with a book of matches. As he stood before the viewing screen taking drags in between a couple of yawns, his mind drifted. He thought about the cigarette between his fingers, about the smoke that floated up in front of the beam of the projector, about what happened to the smoke after it reached the ceiling. What if that smoke was a dream? What if life was smoke? What if there were never any *ifs*?

He looked at Lynn. Though she slept in an awkward position, she did not stir. One leg had crept out from under his jacket. She lay cuddled like a child. He smiled and recovered her carefully.

Then he picked up his cup and grimaced at the taste of room-temperature coffee. Whether Lynn had dumped the last of his drink and replaced it with coffee or he had done so himself, he could not recall. He returned his attention to the viewing screen and punched the remote control. A new slide jumped into position and another face flashed on the wall. Hiller took a weary look and hit the button again. Then his mind seemed to click into place. He reversed the machine to the previous slide and blinked hard. He was astonished to find himself looking at a photo of a dark-skinned moustachioed man with clever black eyes, a photo that appeared to match the master slide. The name of this man was Eduardo Morales.

"There it is!" cried Hiller. His eyes darted back and forth between the two faces. He felt the heat of excitement rush to his head and, in his exuberance, tossed his half-filled cup at the screen. The coffee splashed in the air and the cup shattered against the wall, but Hiller already had the phone in his hand.

"Get me the secretary of state," he said excitedly.

The operator told him there was a long-distance call coming in, did he want to take that first?

"Well, who the hell is it?" he snapped. "Who?"

There was some banter as Hiller tried to learn the nature of the call, but the operator said she was sorry, all she knew was that the call was from a priest.

"For crissakes," he grumbled. "At this hour? What the hell do *I* need to talk to a priest for? Where's the call coming from?"

Hiller shook his head. "Mexico? All right, all right. Put him on," he said impatiently. There were several clicks on the line before the faint accented voice of Padre Julian Serra came through, asking for special investigator Jay Hiller.

"Yes, Father. What can I do for you?" he replied.

Chapter 25

December 17.

The three huge Pratt-Whitney engines on the government medium-range Lear jet awoke with a sudden scream as a two-man crew readied it for an urgent trip to the Yucatan peninsula.

The early morning sun was white and still not high enough in the sky to melt the frost on the porthole windows of the plane or the windshields of several airport equipment vehicles stationed near the hangars. The temperature and gusty winds brought the windchill factor in the unprotected areas to minus twelve degrees.

Stephen Brownell had driven Jay Hiller to the airport to a special runway gate, and while it would have been permissible to ride the final two hundred yards to the plane, Hiller insisted on walking the rest of the way. He had been sitting so much, he said, that his legs were becoming vestigial organs. The secretary of state was not of the same mind, particularly since Hiller had awakened him at four in the morning—although the double-barreled news of the slide identification and the Mexican priest's phone call was the best he had heard in a long time.

Reluctantly, Brownell parked the car alongside a

blue and gray hangar and followed Hiller into the freezing morning air.

With his head tucked deep into his overcoat, his gloved hands over his ears, the secretary said sharply, "You've got to be crazy wanting to walk in this. What's the matter with a nice warm car?"

"It's too easy," replied Hiller, who was carrying a brown leather attaché and stepped along at a brisk pace with his overcoat unbuttoned as usual.

"You know we are far from being out of the woods . . . I hope your decision to fly off to Mexico like this is beneficial."

Hiller smiled wryly. "It's got to be beneficial. It's warmer."

Brownell frowned. "Very funny," he said. "You really know how to hurt a guy."

"I promise I'll bring back some tequila to warm you up."

"Wonderful," the secretary grumbled absently. For a moment he said nothing else. Then his tone changed to absolute seriousness. "Listen, Jay. Have you thought this out? I'm not sure it's such a good idea for you to be out of Washington just at this point. The kidnappers specifically wanted *you* to make the drop at Dulles. What if they specifically want you to do something else?"

"I'm only going to be away for . . ."

A gust of wind forced the two men to stagger a little and Hiller had to raise his voice. ". . . for the day! Just say I've gone south for a holiday and ask them to leave a number where I can get back to them."

He glanced over at Brownell and saw that his quip went unappreciated. The secretary returned a look of harsh intensity. Hiller straightened up and shrugged; his lightheartedness quickly vanished. Then he said impassively, "If it goes as we expect, Royce will be safe in a week or so and then we can pull out all the stops, go after them with everything possible. Look, you're the one who wants him for the summit. Well, that's in *less* than a week. This is your best shot.

"Even beyond that, I'm trying to cover it on the contingency that it doesn't go as we expect. What if Royce is never released? Or what if he's released and the trail to the kidnappers is so dry that we've got nowhere to go. At least now they are all operating ensemble. We may have a chance to bag them. Afterward, it'll be like hunting snakes in the Amazon. Where would you begin?"

"Well, at least take some people with you."

Hiller shook his head. "I don't think it's necessary. I'm more mobile alone. If I turn up anything, believe me, I'll ask in droves for help. This priest, this call from heaven, this may be the one bolt of lightning I've been looking for. He has the identity of the kidnappers, I'm sure of it."

Brownell considered this a moment and said guardedly, "If he does, then I doubt he'll remain alive long enough to give it to you."

That was something Hiller preferred not to dwell on. As they approached the restricted runway, the noise of the jet engines rang in the air and Hiller, too, clasped his hands to the side of his head.

"Did you talk with McAvee this morning?" Hiller shouted.

Brownell nodded vigorously. "McAvee assured me the Berettas are inoperative."

"Then he lied," Hiller said flippantly. "I identified Martinez as a Beretta this morning—Eduardo Morales."

Brownell regarded Hiller's accusation as out of line, but he could not help thinking how few men would have been brazen enough to make it. "Look, Jay. I'm aware that you and Wilson McAvee despise each other," the secretary said sharply. "But he has always been loyal to the President, he has always been the President's man. I think you may be letting your personal feelings gray your judgment."

The two men stopped walking near the foot of the metal stairwell to the jet cabin and faced each other.

Hiller composed himself to be absolutely direct and said, "We all agree the Berettas couldn't do it alone. Well then, *who* could help them do it? I keep coming up with the same answer."

Brownell rubbed his fat red cheeks to warm them and looked intensely at Hiller. "We don't *know* the Berettas engineered the kidnapping. That's *your* theory. Stop making it fact," he said a little indignantly. "All we know is that Martinez played a part in the abduction and was once a Beretta."

"Yes, and you forget Russell Frazier, who was once a Beretta too. And now you're going to tell me that it's pure coincidence that they happen to be alumni?"

There was no doubt Brownell was troubled. It showed clearly on his thickset face. He looked Hiller squarely in the eye and said, "You realize the implications of your accusations, don't you?"

Hiller gave a quick nod. "I think so," he said grimly. There was more than a note of fearful uncertainty in his voice.

The small jet received immediate clearance for takeoff from the traffic-control tower and, a minute later, roared down the runway and lifted up into the sky like a feather. The Potomac, winding its way through the urban forest, glistened magically, as Washington with its elongated morning shadows quickly receded below.

Hiller took a moment to watch before he pulled the

file on Eduardo Morales from the leather attaché. Since Morales had been a Beretta and since the Company had funded Beretta operations against Castro since the early sixties, there was extensive information:

At fifteen he had fought with Manolo Ray's People's Revolutionary Movement, a resistance group inside Cuba. Later, a soldier he had met in the movement brought him to the United States, where he joined Cuban exile forces organized to overthrow Castro under Operation Mongoose.

By nineteen he was actively involved in the Bay of Pigs operation and took part in the invasion. After its dismal outcome, he became a driving force in organizing the Beretta movement and, by the late sixties, was so single-minded in his pursuit to overthrow Castro that he was considered a risk for any other type of CIA-funded operation.

In 1967, when the "war" against Cuba suffered from benign neglect and the White House was more interested in containing Castro than overthrowing him, Morales initiated strikes against the island, sponsoring over 300 clandestine missions, setting sugar fields ablaze, bombing factories, trying to dismember the economy.

The violence he perpetrated he did with undue fervor, but he considered unnecessary violence self-destructive. That was an indication to Hiller that Morales was a careful planner and, consequently, an exceedingly dangerous man.

Hiller returned the file to his briefcase and yawned with an accompanying groan. There would be a car waiting for him at the airport in the Yucatan, then a rendezvous with a most unlikely connection. He shook his head at the irony.

One of the members of the flight crew brought

Hiller a cup of coffee, which he drank gratefully. His mind was dizzy with the possibilities of the next twenty-four hours, but the rest of him begged for sleep.

When he actually felt his heart speed up from the hit of caffeine, he decided to give himself a break. He pulled a pillow and blanket from the overhead rack, stretched out on a convertible lounge, and was asleep almost before his head hit the pillow.

Shortly after Stephen Brownell returned to his office from Washington National Airport, Wilson McAvee paid him a visit, ostensibly to clarify what the CIA would try to do to pick up traces of the kidnappers.

After twenty minutes, the director turned to Brownell and, out of the blue, said caustically, "I want to do a sweep on Hiller but Phyllis Royce won't go for it. She told me she'd plead her case to the papers . . ."

The faintest bit of a smile crept onto the face of the secretary. He had to admire the First Lady's grit.

"But if you were behind me," McAvee continued, "we'd have no trouble weathering the flak."

Brownell immediately felt agitated by the remark, though he could not help but marvel at how these two men could work for the same things and yet feel such hostility for each other. If McAvee took over now, he would create a "can't-lose" situation for himself. Any wrong could be blamed on his predecessor. Anything right he could take credit for.

"What would you have to gain by replacing Hiller now," the secretary asked impassively.

McAvee's impatience showed immediately. He wanted Brownell in his corner. "He isn't getting us anywhere," he said gruffly. "I should be in there. Every time a day goes by I feel compelled to get him out. I can't give him access to the files, and if I were heading up the investigation that would be no problem."

Brownell knitted his brows and said, "Is there information in the files that Hiller doesn't have that would help?"

McAvee seemed a little perturbed. "Uh, no," he said, "but—"

"All right, I understand your frustration," Brownell interrupted. "But the drop was made only yesterday, and unless you know of something that I don't, I don't really see where Hiller has failed on something tangible. It's an impossible task. You know that as well as I do."

"It's the intangibles that he's missing."

"Oh? I thought intuition was his strongest trait. At least that's what your intelligence reports on him say."

McAvee pointed a warning finger at the secretary. "Three dead," he said grimly. "The senator and his daughter. And one of my agents—a kid, for God's sakes. And you mark my words, Brownie. If Hiller stays on, it'll be four. And that fourth will be the President. You mark my words."

Brownell considered the warning, and the weight of the remark did not go unnoticed. He raised a hand and made a cautionary gesture.

"Let's wait a little more and see," he said quietly.

Chapter 26

The hollow deep chimes from the church tower struck eight times. And though the chilling temperatures from the night were rapidly giving way, the morning was oddly dark. No pale gauze of light and shadow spinning an early mist, no air tasting of black, black coffee with cinnamon sticks. The air was heavy, the light a brooding gray.

Several blocks from the church, parked on the dusty road in the black automobile which added to his sepulchral presence, Sergio Grijalva took three things from under the front seat—a flashlight, an optical magnifier, and a .22-caliber revolver. He pocketed the first two items and carefully loaded each chamber of the gun. He had been careful to stay away from the activity of Las Cumbres and just as careful not to make himself too conspicuous now. Most villagers had assumed he was someone who simply had business with the padre.

Grijalva checked his watch. He stuck the gun inside his belt, got out of the car and, concerned about the safety of the package he had stolen from Luis, locked it in the trunk. Then he walked slowly toward the church.

Inside its crumbling white walls, a half dozen people—women in scarves, with rosaries—knelt in pews silently praying. Had the padre elected to tell the villagers of Luis's murder, there surely would have been a fuller congregation and perhaps a vigilante group fired for revenge. But inexplicably, he had told no one.

Instead, he tried to throw himself into the morning tasks and was hearing the confession of a young doe-eyed peasant girl, though he felt decidedly uncomfortable waiting in the close air of the tiny chlorine-green chamber, knowing what he knew was coming.

But even the padre was not prepared for the latest sacrilege from Grijalva as he burst into the confessional and forcibly removed the terrified girl. He seized her by the arm and with his terrible hooded eyes had her whimpering and praying for mercy.

Grijalva looked contemptuously at her and snarled, "You're forgiven for your sins. Now get out!"

With that, he took her place in the darkened booth and slammed the door behind him. The padre could not contain himself and said grimly, "It would have been another few minutes. You should have waited—"

"Don't tell me what I should have done," he said forcefully.

Unseen by the padre, Grijalva then took the gun from his belt and fondled the cold steel. "Where are the passports?" he demanded.

The air in the booth seemed to grow thick and hard to breathe, as perspiration, cold as ice, formed on the priest's brow. He was dizzy and lightheaded; pounding blood rushed to his face. Had he known that this man held a loaded gun on him, he could not have been more frightened.

"The passports!" Grijalva demanded again.

"The passports," the padre said nervously. "I have them." He fumbled around clumsily. "They are here. . . ."

Grijalva grew impatient, at the same time relishing

the priest's anxiety. It was that delicious smell of fear that enticed him so.

"What's the matter?" he snarled. "You seem nervous."

The padre made no reply. His head was swimming with nightmares—images—Ramon Diaz leaping from the tower; Luis Diaz, whose radiant face had been, like a ripening fruit, lying cold and half-buried in a field. Beads of sweat ran down the side of the padre's face. His breaths were short, shallow. He clutched the passports with trembling fingers and knew, for him, that this must be the end.

Impatiently, Grijalva slammed a fist into the confessional screen and jarred him from a daze. "Open this damned thing!" he roared.

The priest slid the screen open and handed him the documents. Grijalva received them eagerly and examined them with the flashlight and optical magnifier. But the padre could not bear the sight of the man's ghost-lit face and quietly reclosed the screen.

"Where is Luis?" he asked in an emotionally strained voice.

Grijalva continued to check the passports and did not respond.

"Where is the boy?" the priest repeated.

At last, Sergio Grijalva, a man whom the padre had called a walking tomb, spoke up. "You are truly an artist," he said. The voice was derisive, but contained a note of admiration for his ability.

Serra tried to say something but choked on his words. Then he began quietly to sob.

Though he could not see Grijalva attach a silencer to the nuzzle of the weapon and slowly lift the gun, the padre seemed to know that death was at hand. Because he had previously helped desperate people, and did what many said was an admirable—if illegal—

thing, this man had sought him out for his own base purposes and wrung from him cooperation by blackmail and kidnapping. The cruel irony was that but for the padre's original act of compassion, none of this would have followed.

Now Grijalva's thick, tan lips parted and he spoke again mockingly. "Rest assured, Padre, your talents will not go unappreciated. And since you are so concerned about your little friend, I think it's time the holy father went to heaven. The boy awaits you."

Then he aimed the gun and there was a sudden explosion. A bullet smashed through the confessional screen and cries went up from inside the church. But it was a bullet Sergio Grijalva had bet his life would never be fired. It came from the priest's side of the booth, from a gun in the padre's hand, not more than a second or two before Grijalva's .22-caliber revolver would have gone off.

For a moment Grijalva's head was suspended in a normal upright position, in spite of the fact that his forehead was shattered by the bullet and little fragments of bone and tissue were sprayed across the chamber.

For a moment, the expression on the face seemed to indicate that the bullet did not matter. The mouth contorted, the lifeless eyes remained open and challenging. It enraged him that the priest would try to defy him and the hands even seemed to lunge forward threateningly.

But seconds later, the body sank, as bloody flesh was disgorged from the top of the skull. The rear of the confessional was covered with abstract patterns of skin, bone, and dark blood which ran down the wall as thick as the padre's spilled paints. A horrible reddish gauze blurred the air, together with the smell of blood, quite dense, and impossible to breathe.

Serra was stunned. Holding the smoking gun as casually as he would a brush, his first dazed feelings were of vindication: the iron yoke had been lifted. Grijalva's vicious threats meant nothing anymore in the drab light of this sudden present disorder.

But it was a momentary feeling at best, and very soon after, his confusion took over. He staggered out of the confessional looking like a ghost, with white hair tousled and dark brown eyes wild and blazing. He did not dare look toward the pulpit. The pews hid the frightened eyes of those who had been in prayer. And his own eyes now sought their private sanctuary.

He stumbled to the rear of the confessional and threw open the door. There he took a deep breath, removed the passports and a set of keys from the corpse, and staggered backward in his haste to retreat. Grijalva's body, with its cruel black eyes wide open still, clutched the revolver as if he expected to be awakened soon from this inconvenient sleep.

The padre's stooped figure turned away from those eyes and stumbled out of the church with the appearance of a beggar who had stolen from the poor box.

Outside he welcomed the temperate heat of the sunless morning. The heat was a comfort for cold blood. And everything around him now felt cold. The full impact of the terrible event was imperceptible amid the turbulence of his present struggle. He was sheltered from reality by bewilderment and fear.

As he ran up the street, the morning still was strangely dark. Heavy gray clouds were gathering in the sky—stranger still because rain this time of year was rare. Unwatered land, parched and cracked, baked in December dust—that was Las Cumbres.

The padre fought with several keys before one slid into the lock on the door of Sergio's autombile. He threw himself behind the wheel, started the engine, and hurriedly drove off, unmindful for the moment that by his own hand he had stained the church with the blood of another human being.

By midafternoon the sky hung low with brooding gray clouds, threatening the coastal land that for months had been dry and rainless. Even the jungles had a fawn-colored film of dust.

An old Willys Jeep, having banged in and out of chuckholes over fifty-five miles of impossible dirt roads, thumped to a halt at a dead end. Jay Hiller got out of the vehicle and considered the jungly wasteland before him. A narrow footpath led into its lush configuration, completely disappearing behind thick vines and unfathomable terrain.

He took a slip of paper from his shirt pocket and reread directions. Then he grabbed a light jacket from the front seat of the jeep and, following the path a bit squeamishly through tropical brush and vine—sometimes balking at sounds he had never before heard—Hiller reached a clearing on the tip of a delta which, at high tide, looked over the waters of the great Gulf.

Now, however, with the tide fallen back, he faced a muddy plain with several strange island jungles perched in the distance. One that Hiller thought truly spectacular would have taken most of the day to row around. Its trees rose into the air some sixty feet, with aerial roots literally growing out of the marsh and supporting dense green leaves and reddish brown bark and branches. He had never seen such a thing, growing—no less—in salt water. It seemed unbearably peaceful to him as he watched a frigate bird skim along its perimeter hunting for food. The sound of the distant surf was a soothing whisper against a natural sea wall of thousands of great rocks. And as each wave advanced, it dislodged the rocks, tumbling them into a fine thunder.

A half hour passed slowly with Hiller slapping at thirsting mosquitos. As the afternoon advanced, occasional north winds began to whip, the tide surged forward, and Hiller's patience—along with the temperature—started to drop rapidly.

He put on his jacket and again looked around. There was still no sign of the priest. He knelt down and scooped a handful of clay and smelled it; his mind raced back to the first thing Stephen Brownell had said to him when he planned this rendezvous: The kidnappers would kill the man before they ever got a chance to meet.

Hiller considered a second possibility—that the Mexican priest with startling information had never existed, that the telephone call had been a pretext to get him out of Washington. He even thought about an admittedly wild notion that Wilson McAvee was responsible for throwing him the bait in order to maneuver and take over the investigation.

He tossed down the wet clay and stared at the mysterious island jungle in the distance with its strange fingerlike roots. He shook his head in disgust. That was it, he thought dejectedly. The day was getting on—the priest was two hours overdue. He could not wait any longer.

Hiller wiped his hands on his trousers and walked briskly back to the footpath in the thicket. He was demoralized and fed up with himself. An entire day lost. An agent in the field would have to be assigned to track down the padre, *if* he existed and *if* he was still alive. But just as he was ready to admit that Brownell's prediction smelled like prophecy, a lean figure with unkempt white hair stepped from the shadows of the brush nervously pointing a gun.

His face immediately gave him away as a tortured man, with rippled features taut and dark brown eyes remorseful. They had become increasingly so with each hour that had passed since morning.

Padre Serra recognized Hiller from a picture in the newspaper and lowered the weapon. Then his entire body sagged as if he no longer was forced to balance some unseen oppressive weight.

"I am Father Serra," he said after a long sigh. "I am relieved that you are here, my son."

"First time a priest ever said that to *me*, Father. I'm glad you made it. Frankly, I'd begun to think you wouldn't."

Serra nodded. "I have been running all day," he said nervously. "I had to make certain it was you. And . . . to be safe . . ."

Hiller looked at him sympathetically. "You are all right then?" he asked.

The padre did not respond to the question but instead reached inside his garment and anxiously relinquished a package he had found in the trunk of Sergio Grijalva's car. "This is what they murdered an eight-year-old boy for," he whispered.

Hiller tore the brown wrapping from a corrugated box the size of a paperback novel. Inside were several dozen cellophane bags of white powder and a small envelope containing tiny strips of microfilm and three photographic negatives. He held the negatives to the light and readily identified John Quinlan Royce behind a hand-lettered sign reading "Kidnapped."

Then he ripped apart one of the cellophanes, stuck a finger to the powder, and touched it to his tongue. The padre looked at him inquisitively. Hiller scooped up another handful of wet clay. "Two kinds of Mexican mud, Father."

Serra was puzzled.

"Heroin," replied Hiller.

Again examining the negatives, he asked, "Are these the pictures you told me about on the telephone?"

The padre shook his head. From a pocket, he took the five passports and gave them to Hiller. "These are what I told you of. Make these forgeries or you will die, they said. Well, die then I will. I was ready. What can they hope to win? Threatening an old man with death is like offering him peace. But then they took the boy, a child made fatherless by these same cruel men. Animals! What could a boy have done to them? Nothing. But they slaughtered him like one would stamp out the life of an insect."

Hiller lowered his eyes, feeling helpless. "I'm sorry, Father," he replied sadly. "A lot of young lives have been sacrificed."

Both men lapsed into silence. Hiller studied the forgeries and was taken by the craftsmanship, though the only face he recognized was the one he had identified that morning as Eduardo Morales.

"You were in contact with these men?"

"No. Not these men, one who worked with them. But he is now dead."

Hiller looked questioningly at the padre. He perceived the weight of his remark in his unsteady voice and in his awkward glance.

"What about the others?"

Serra shrugged. "I don't know. I have never seen them."

"Then you have no idea where they are? Or even if they are in Mexico?"

The padre shook his head.

"The one that approached you, what name did he give?"

"He never said, but there were some papers in his car. The name was Sergio Grijalva."

"Did this Grijalva ever mention anything called Foxbat?"

The padre's eyes widened with surprise. "You have heard of it?" he asked, astonished.

"More than that. Tell me . . ."

The priest screwed up his rippled face and said, "Few people outside this province would ever have reason to hear of it. What is it you wish to know?"

"I'd like to know what the hell it is for starters."

Without hesitation, the priest said, "It is a Mayan cemetery."

"A Mayan cemetery? What else can you tell me about it?"

"The myth, the legend . . ."

He paused, but Hiller gave him silent encouragement to go on.

"A great civilization was buried there. And though each day the tide comes in and washes over the graves of our ancestors, none of the graves have ever been disturbed. And it has been like this for centuries.

"The first man buried was a Mayan king, who had been kidnapped and murdered by Spanish conquerors. His people retrieved the body, but they were afraid that the Spaniards would come again, seeking the power of kings, and ravage the dead. To protect him in death, as they could not in life, his people were borne to this secret place by the mythological diety, Zorromurciélago, a beast with the head of a fox and the wings of a bat. There they guarded him with their lives until their own deaths . . ."

Hiller was aroused and broke in excitedly. "Where is this place? How far from here?"

The padre was puzzled. "How far?? You are looking at it."

Hiller's eyes darted all around. His confusion was evident.

"Over there," the padre said. "The mangrove trees."

It struck Hiller as ironic, almost laughable, that the mysterious island jungle he had been captivated by, with its elevated roots and skeletal configuration, was the perfect setting for such a myth. "Can we get a closer look?" he asked.

"If we must," the priest replied softly. He was resigned to it if need be. He had anticipated the request but was anything but eager. "The island's magic is still magic. It is still protective of its king. You may think that ludicrous coming from the mouth of a priest, but it is what I believe. There is no way to explain what happens there. Zorromurciélago is an island of mystery; it is a mirror of the moon, a handmaiden to dark waters.

"You would ask if I have been there and though I never dared to enter, once at nightfall I rowed in a hollowed-out stump canoe to its edge. Never have I known such quiet as that, the way the water made no sound but the liquid whisper of my passing.

"And suddenly I was filled with a thousand sweet memories. And the past rose before me like a great fire and in the smoke I saw a pale mist of faces from another lifetime. They were old faces and young faces, and strangely, all the faces were the same. And I began to see all the faces were *mine*. And they melted into the face of my father and my grandfather and my great-grandfather. And I began to see how we are all part of the same. Clearly I saw how we all belong to each other. . . ."

Hiller blinked hard and lapsed into silence. The man spoke beautifully, humbly, and it moved him.

The padre regarded him quietly and said, "But as peaceful as it was at its edge, the legend is of its turbulent bowels. Men who have entered are known to have gone mad. Some did not come back. Another was said to have strangled in the mangrove roots. There are cottonmouths sunning themselves and the swamp is full of quicksand. Only fools, they say, tempt such forces. And you are still of the mind to go?"

Hiller gathered himself and said, "I've always been a fool, more often than not. I can't help thinking, Father, that one more time is not gonna make a hell of a lot of difference. We have to go."

The padre acceded. He would go, of course. Not heedless, but regardless.

Chapter 27

Dusk came rapidly of the failing gray light of the afternoon. Already the temperature had dropped significantly, and mosquitoes abandoned the air as Hiller and the padre threaded their way toward the mangrove jungle across dry spots, their pace slowed by the thick mud of a now-dampening shore.

Hiller heard in the distance the sound of a muffled engine, elusive and imprecise, at first like a motorboat at sea, then disappearing beneath the distant thunder of a wave. He was more intrigued by the sucking sound his footsteps were making in the wet sand and with thoughts about his curious companion. He noticed Serra's limp and thought better than to ask about it. Like his mangrove island, the man was a contradiction. Yet something about him invited trust:

the warmth of his eyes, the expressiveness of his mouth, his humility. He had the feeling the padre talked down to no one, that he treated everyone as a comrade. Unlike any he had known, this cleric did not preach answers. Like his fellow man, he too struggled with the questions.

Hiller was about to toss off a complacent remark about the surprising chill when a sudden flash of light from above and shattering thunder startled them. It began like a prelude to the expected tropical storm. But the ground shook and a steel mammoth rumbled out of the clouds, blades whirling through the air, an intense white beam shooting out of its head like a luminous eye scanning the ground.

The padre and Hiller froze, bewildered by the improbable sight of a helicopter over the remote coastline. They shouted to each other and could hardly be heard above its harsh, drilling engine. Then the spotlight swept dangerously near them and both men were suddenly jarred to their senses. They bolted for the thick mangroves, but with his lame right leg, the padre had difficulty over the heavy footing. Sharp pains shot up through his hip. The beam from the helicopter swept round and caught him in its glare. Machine-gun fire erupted, kicking up clots of mud several feet behind him.

Hiller, racing hard, shouted to his companion, "Haul ass, Father. . . . Please!"

The padre darted from the beam of light. The chopper swooped down and grew thunderously loud, its white eye combing the marshflats, seeking prey for its guns. Hiller felt the updraft as the helicopter bore in on him. He suddenly darted to his right as another burst of gunfire slammed into the wet ground, eating at his heels. His head was pounding viciously; the blood gushed through his veins. Faster. A little further. If they could just reach the mangroves . . .

The helicopter circled around and seeded the area with bullets. The beam of light again found the priest. There was a sudden staccato fury and the padre went down hard. The pain was awful, sharp and pulsating. His right hip throbbed fiercely. It was oppressively hot, and yet he was shivering.

Hiller immediately raced back to him, skirting the circular sweep of the spotlight. He got the padre to his feet as the old man tried to shoo him off.

"It is . . . silly for you to stay with me," he gasped

"C'mon, Father," Hiller said sharply. "Don't give me a hard time." Then in a more encouraging voice, he added, "You're not that bad off. You'll be okay."

He shouldered him as gently as he could and stumbled toward the swamp, hampered significantly by the extra weight and the heavier footing. The chopper completed its loop, banked sharply, and flew at them again, its guns splattering random bullets as if it were dusting crops. Hiller dug for the tree line, gulping air. His eyes felt as if they were bulging from their sockets. Twenty yards away, fifteen, ten . . . The copter roared in . . . five yards, three . . . its guns blazing, mud clots kicked into the air, licking at their feet. They dove for the safety of the trees and flung themselves under the mangroves. Bursts of machine-gun fire skimmed past them only a few feet away, and then faded.

Hiller gasped frantically for breath, air filling his lungs momentarily, then gulping again for more. He dared not waste a second. He struggled to his feet, lifted the padre, and moved him several yards deeper into the swamp. A moment later the helicopter thundered in and raked the area again with bullets. The two men dropped to their knees and scrambled for cover underneath the thick aerial roots of the red trees. Then the sound of the guns ceased and the noise of the helicopter drifted away.

Hiller collapsed against a tree root, wheezing. He pulled his nebulizer from a pants pocket and took a long hit. Then he offered it to the padre. After some urging, the priest reluctantly took a shot and, for just a moment, closed his eyes.

It made him forget the pain. He looked at his bloodied fingers and thought to himself, it had not taken long for the Almighty to pass judgment on him. That morning, he had broken the Sixth Commandment. And however sure he felt that it was justified, in the eyes of God, he was indefensible.

With a single irrational act he had thrown away his life's work. Look how much effort it now took merely to stay alive. Look how he scrambled through marsh and roots so desperately trying to live. Now he paid penance. Now his body was distorted; became an utterly foreign thing. He paid the price of the sinner and now every thought was sated with longing to go back and undo what he had done.

The padre lifted his head and watched Hiller take two handguns from his jacket and load them. Then he said in the most morose tone Hiller had ever heard, "Today I have seen Death from within the fire of Satan's eye, and it fills me with terror."

Hiller was startled by the utter futility of the remark. He knelt down, tore off part of his shirt, and fashioned a bandage twisted about the limb to slow Serra's bleeding wound.

"I'm scared too, Father," he said. "Believe me." Then, after a pause, he added, "Many years ago, I had a good friend who fought in the Vietnam War—he said they used to tell each other dirty jokes when it looked real bad and that would help 'em through. Know any good dirty jokes, Father? It wouldn't offend me if you told one."

The priest made no reply.

"You okay?"

The padre nodded, but he was obviously in pain.

"Soon as they set that eggbeater down, they'll have us trapped in here. You're not packing any miracles, are you?"

Serra looked at him with tired, mournful eyes. "There is a path along the mangrove trees—like this," he said and he drew a spiral in the mud with a finger. "It forms a spiral to the center of the swamp. If we follow it, we will avoid the quicksand. But as I have told you, this is a Mayan cemetery. I do not know what else we will find."

Hiller quickly considered their dilemma. "I think we'd better take our chances with Mayan spirits and mythological deities," he said grimly. "They may be more human."

In front of them lay quite an obstacle course—a crisscross puzzle of roots everywhere shooting out of the marsh, some swayed enough to form a low canopy under which they could wind; others narrower and lower might be skirted or climbed. Though it was impossible to move through the path rapidly, the long banana-shaped leaves of the jungle were thick and, with nightfall, at least provided cover.

Hiller and the padre struggled into the labyrinth, stooped like a pair of monkeys weaving through the mangroves. A murky green haze, almost like a tinted fog, came from the bowels of the swamp. Every inch of earth was covered with thick, smotheringly green vegetation—clinging, creeping things that seemed to breathe.

"This may not be so easy," Hiller said with fearful uncertainty. "I'm beginning to understand why the tourist season here is short. I can't see ten feet in front of me."

The padre winced with pain as he spoke. "Have faith, my son. I am certain that God is with you."

"If He is, Father, that's a first."

Hiller stopped to give the padre a brief rest, but when they heard the sputtering sound of the helicopter again drawing closer, they moved on.

At that moment, perhaps fifty yards from the edge of the jungle, the chopper hovered, preparing to land. Its overhead blades whirled, blowing debris across the marsh, tearing leaves from the outer shelf of trees. Then its runners touched soil and immediately the engine shut down.

A door flung open and a small gang of people in dark jungle fatigues charged toward the swamp with weapons and flashlights. They broke into twos and threes and went in at scattered points.

Hiller and the padre continued to claw their way through impossibly heavy growth. It was rapidly getting colder and the tide was beginning to come in. Already their shoes were thick with mud and the dampness seeped through, numbing their toes. Hiller tried to straighten up and bumped his head on a root. He winced and stepped to the side and felt a surprisingly firm grip on his arm.

"Not another foot," the padre said, "or I am afraid it will be the end."

With that he picked up a fallen branch and tossed it in Hiller's path. In a matter of seconds it was sucked into soft earth by an awesome invisible force that seemed alive and hungry for more.

The demonstration humbled Hiller. "I didn't see the Don't Walk sign," he said soberly.

"Stay along the path of the trees," the padre ordered.

Hiller frowned. "Some path," he muttered to himself. It was barely delineated. Then he began pulling down thick branches and vines and set about camouflaging the route they had just covered.

The padre watched uneasily but as he tried to speak he coughed violently—a deep, dry cough that came from the hollow in his chest. He took a moment to breathe deeply and finally said hoarsely and with difficulty, "Please, my son. Do not slow up because of me. I have lived my life. If it ended right now, it would not be premature."

Hiller snickered a little. "You got a short memory, Father. *You're* the one who's been helping *me*, remember? Sit tight. Maybe this jungle rot will encourage them to take a little detour, like the one I was about to make before you collared me."

Just then the priest began to tremble, and his heart suddenly thumped erratically inside his chest. He shivered and sank to his knees, then felt hot flashes, and his face drained of color. Hiller peeled off his jacket and covered him with it. He felt the padre's forehead burning and then brought him to his feet.

"I'm sorry. . . . I won't be much help now," the older man said faintly.

"Let's try to find you a spot where you'll be reasonably safe." Hiller shouldered him and they stumbled farther into the spiral. Finally, Serra begged to lie down.

Hiller sat him against a tangle of roots and tried to make him comfortable. But the tidewater was several inches deep by now and it was impossible to keep warm and dry. He realized he would have to get him out of there soon.

"Dammit, Father," he said, trying to light a spark.

"You don't expect *me* to give last rites to those goons out there, do you?"

The padre made no reply. Hiller knelt down and fixed his eyes on him. "Listen, Father," he whispered. "I'm going back. If I can snipe at them, we may have a chance."

Then he placed an automatic weapon in the priest's lap. "Use this if you have to. I'll tie a handkerchief around my arm so you'll recognize me from a distance. Just make sure when you shoot, it's not me you're shooting."

Gravely, Padre Serra shook his head. He did not touch the gun. "I could not . . . I did . . . I have already taken a life."

"I know, Father," he snapped. "I also know these men are out to kill us. Dammit, they don't give a damn about you or me and they didn't give a damn about that boy. Think of him, Father. Try to think of him."

The priest closed his eyes. There was something in his old wrinkled face that made Hiller believe he never wanted to open them again.

The old man's lips were trembling. "It does not matter," he said grimly. "It is too late for my life to be of value. . . ."

Jay Hiller brought his face to within inches of the padre's. "It may be too late for sainthood," he whispered. "But you can still make it as a conventional mortal hero. Settle for that, Father. Millions would be grateful to you."

Hiller got up and started back over the spiral path, crouching under a canopy of jungle roots which had begun to stain the water a tea-colored red from the tannin in its bark. When he was not absolutely sure of firm footing, he climbed onto the mangroves and scaled them as if they were a playground edifice. At one point he slipped and would have fallen into a small clearing—which was surely quicksand—but for a thicket of jungle vine which he clung to desperately while regaining his balance.

At last he reached the spot he had camouflaged earlier and patiently waited under a dense curtain of roots and vegetation. Almost without thinking he tugged on a vine and felt an icy rush of horror when it dangled momentarily, plopped in the shallow water in front of him, and slithered off. He shuddered. It happened all too fast to tell whether it was a cottonmouth, but in any case Hiller figured it cost at least a year of his life.

He would be more cautious now, would turn his eyes in all directions and be certain a leaf was a leaf and not a crawling nocturnal jungle creature. In his visual hunt he inadvertently came upon something that felt cold, like stone, covered by dense foliage. He dug through it and was astonished to find himself suddenly looking at a primitive stone carving of a strange animallike figure, perhaps two feet high. Etched into its mysterious, bold anatomy were the wings of a bat and the head of a fox. The eyes were most astonishing of all. Though also carved from stone they seemed to exude energy. They were remarkably alive, seemingly capable of more than seeing—capable of perceiving.

So hypnotic was the power of this stone that Hiller was not immediately aware of a few beams of light scanning the area nearby and was startled by the sudden noise of someone approaching. Through the configuration of roots three armed men stole out of the murky green night of the jungle, their faces lit like yellow ghosts by the overglow of flashlights.

They took cautious steps, stopping only yards in front of Hiller. With the subtle movement of a nocturnal animal he slipped the gun from his belt and felt for the trigger, holding his breath while tiny nerves, stretched to the point of snapping, threatened to come unraveled.

The first man to pass through an arch of roots directly before him was as fierce-looking as any he had seen—muscular, with sunken eyes and cheeks, moustached, with a vicious-looking mouth, but surprisingly short. The second, an inch under six feet, with a drooping head and puffy eyes, was older and heavier than the others. Hiller perceived him as less aggressive, less like a leader. The last man was the most ill-at-ease and kept whispering sharply in Spanish. Had Hiller the chance to check them against the photos in the forged passports, he could have identified Michael Callejo and Diego Saldise cutting short with angry gestures a reluctant Armando Rodriguez.

With catlike alertness Callejo stopped at the wall that Hiller had baited with clusters of vines and growth. There was another harsh whispered exchange between Callejo and Rodriguez, a man familiar with Bolivian jungles, whose instincts sensed danger. Hiller let out a long, slow breath; his head was pounding like a hammer. He tried not to think of asthma. If it came now it would surely be fatal.

Callejo continued to move cautiously. Without knowing, he flirted dangerously near the quicksand. If he would just take that step . . .

Then in a sudden moment, so violently did a bloodcurdling shriek shatter the night that Hiller was practically frightened out of hiding. There was a commotion and a furious clutching for vines and roots, and in seconds Callejo was up to his waist in quicksand, screaming crazed orders at Rodriguez and Saldise. They abandoned safe ground and rushed to the edge of the pit. Callejo could not reach their outstretched arms. His eyes almost exploded out of their sockets; his shouts became more crazed. Again and again he groped for them.

Saldise clung to a mangrove root and stretched his body over the pit, extending a rifle as far as possible. Rodriguez then anchored Saldise. Callejo, now up to his chest in a muddy tomb, clutched onto the gunbarrel. It was enough to prevent his drowning.

At the same time, Hiller crept out from his hideaway, the brackish water now covering the soles of his feet. Had it not been for Callejo's panic they surely would have heard him stirring. Carefully, he raised his gun and aimed. He pulled the trigger and fired three times. One hit squarely into the neck of Armando Rodriguez, killing him instantly. The second shot went wild. The third struck Saldise in the leg forcing him to let go of the mangrove and plunge sidelong into the quicksand. Callejo and Saldise thrashed helplessly, shrieking for help with the last of their breaths and hastening death with the frenzied desperation of their final convulsive moments.

On the ground nearby, a flashlight threw an eerie amber beam over the murky grave shared now by two savage men.

From afar a web of roots and branches suddenly glowed with light as heavy rapid footsteps of someone treading a path through shallow water drew closer. Hiller slipped behind a tree and poised his weapon. Suddenly one of them came alone out of the brush looking anguished and impatient. This man was Carlos Lopes, who nervously swung his gun and flashlight one way, then another, listening keenly to the haunted sounds of the jungle.

Hiller aimed carefully, again timing his breath with the squeeze of the trigger. It was an easy target. He aimed at the light just as Lopes came upon the fallen rifle of one of his comrades, and fired. The gun and flashlight flew out of Lopes's hands as the bullet pierced the center of his chest, hurling him against a thicket of mangrove.

But there was another explosion. It came from behind Hiller and shattered the tree bark not more than a foot from his head. Before he could scramble for cover a second shot rang out and hot metal tore into the fleshy part of his arm above the elbow. The pain was agonizing and burned viciously. His knees became soft and he stumbled backward into a cluster of vines.

He clung to his weapon with numbed fingers, fully knowing it was his only chance to survive. Though the blood in his arm pounded tremulously and his body begged to rest, he took staggering steps through a tunnel of roots and retreated toward the padre.

He was the hunted now. And the sheer boldness with which the hunter tore through the labyrinth, savage in his pursuit, was terrifying. He was Eduardo Morales, whose reptilian features seemed more at home in this smothering growth than on a city street.

The hunt plunged deeper into the spiral, to the point where Hiller thought he earlier had left the priest. A frenzied fear gripped him. Had the padre moved? Or were the mangroves playing tricks? He swayed with a rush of lightheadedness and grabbed hold of a root to steady himself. His eyes were glazed, and for a moment he had trouble seeing. He breathed hard and at once tried to quell the breaths that might give him away.

But the minute Hiller stilled his movements, Morales did the same. This man did not tread carelessly through the marsh, inviting death with a lighted flashlight. Behind a wall of thick leaves his eyes blazed with fury. He tuned in to sound—to the natural rustling of thick vegetation in a faint wind, to the night language of the swamp, to the swelling tide, to the false stirring of a man who would be the target for revenge.

Hiller listened, too. And though they were separated by less than fifteen yards, neither was certain of where the other lurked, neither dared more than one infrequent step at a time.

Again the swamp had fooled Hiller. For very nearby, obscured by the olive blackness of the night and partly hidden by flora, the padre lay slumped against the very same tangle of roots, ruined with guilt for his sin against God. So lost was the padre in his shrinking world, so deadening was the pain in his side, that he had heard nothing in Hiller's absence— not the gunfire, nor the drama that now unfolded at his feet. His spirit had fallen to ashes, merely the portal of suffering that he brought to himself, he thought remorsefully. How much worse was he than a common murderer who had no pretensions about his worth.

The padre stared despondently at the weapon in his lap. At last he took it up and began muttering a prayer. That whisper fell on the keen ears of Eduardo Morales. With considerable effort but as a gesture of renunciation, Serra feebly tossed the gun away. It splashed in muddy water a few yards in front of him.

The reflexes of Eduardo Morales were so razor-edged that in the space of seconds he whirled toward the noise and fired several times. Three shots caught the padre in the chest and slammed his body against twisted roots.

Jay Hiller saw the flicker from a gunbarrel fifteen yards to his right and fired at it until the gun was empty. Then there was another shot, a wild one, which came from behind trees, and the sound of a man writhing with his last agonizing breaths. Finally Morales stumbled into a clearing, clutching his stomach, and pitched forward face down into a pool stained with tannin and human blood. His lungs and nostrils quickly filled with water as air bubbles rose to the surface, gently popping.

Hiller turned the body over and looked into Morales's still-open eyes. As distant and as vacant as they had grown, there lingered even in death a glint of fury. But there was no mistaking the face. It was the face he had identified in Washington only that morning—a morning and a face that seemed a hundred years away.

It was then that he caught sight of the lifeless body of the priest slumped against the intertwined roots and went to his side. Hiller exhaled a mournful sigh. He knelt and cradled the padre in his arms and, after a long moment, whispered sadly, "I haven't prayed since I was a kid but I'll pray for you, Father . . . I pray you find your rest."

Then he shivered—the dampness long ago having seeped through to his feet—and tried to make himself warm, pulling his jacket from Serra's body and slipping it over his shoulders. He was growing dizzy and weak. There was a long silence, rudely disrupted by the high-pitched laugh of a jungle creature that seemed to be mocking him. It caused Hiller to start.

Exhausted, he slumped against a tree and was aware of little else except, of course, the excruciating, relentless burning in his arm and a loss of sensation from shoulder to fingertips. His mind would not work. He could not think clearly other than to rest and plan to drag his body back through the mangroves, over the open marshland before the tide became too high, and hope to make it to the jeep. He caught his breath and gathered strength but was so dazed and bewildered he was unaware of a dark figure tearing through the foliage. He came from behind and gruffly hauled Hiller to his feet, frisking him and carelessly searing his bloodied arm with a fierce grip. Hiller gasped involuntarily.

It took a moment before he realized that the man confiscating his nebulizer along with personal belongings and tossing aside his gun was none other than Fred Goss!

"Surprised, Hiller?" Goss asked with a self-congratulatory grin.

Hiller clutched his arm and said feebly but without flinching, "It always surprises me to see English come out of an asshole."

Goss smiled, baring all his teeth, but it was unmistakably a smile full of hate. Suddenly his powerful arm swung round and the pointed barrel of a gun landed squarely on Hiller's ear. Hiller sank to his knees. A harsh shriek—painful to hear—whistled through the inside of his skull. It was as if the jungle spun round, hurtling blurred images at him, one atop another.

"You can cheaptrick all you want, hot shot. It's over for you."

Goss's voice sounded to him like a jackhammer—every word pulsating violently in the drum of his ear. Warm blood trickled down the side of his face.

"It may be over for me, Goss," he said wearily. "But you're finished. I guarantee there's nothing left for you."

"Nothing left?" Goss roared with forced laughter. "This is just the beginning. This is the start of a new America. This is the end of letting the rest of the world pass us by. Myopics like you can't see we've grown weak. Well, weak governments have to be propped up by the strong. The country isn't a leader anymore. Fat bureaucrats are afraid to challenge our enemies—the nation's being run by idealists who put morality before might. The best governing bodies manipulate the weak, not pander to them. *Manipulate* the weak—without the law—for the common good."

Hiller looked up at Goss through dazed eyes, but his mind began to think again. Could he have known this man for so long without knowing he was a lunatic—as warped and as sick as the fascist precepts he personified? No. He knew. He had to have known.

Defying obvious pain, Hiller finally said, "Your sick, perverted sense of patriotism will do more to sell us down the river than a hundred nuclear bombs . . ."

Goss cut him off. "Idealistic horseshit," he said contemptuously. "That's what made this country knuckle under in the first place. Royce and his idealism. *He's* selling us down the river, cutting off the Berettas, wooing Castro, meeting secretly with Communists. Yeah, that's right, I know about the summit in Helsinki. I don't give a damn what they're willing to talk about—they can't be trusted. And neither can Royce.

"Thank me, Hiller—I'm preserving the free world. I'm turning the country around. I'm saving the damn nation!"

"Am I supposed to salute, genuflect, or a make a burnt offering? Look at yourself, Goss. You're a morbid cancer, but a short-lived one, I swear. Brownell is turning the agency on its ear right now—picking you and McAvee apart."

Goss's jaw stiffened. "McAvee?" he snarled. "McAvee has nothing to do with this. McAvee is Royce's toad. *I* developed the Foxbat Account. *I* saved the country. And I'll have no problem handling Brownell."

His arrogant boasting both astounded and enlightened Hiller. "Kill him off too, Goss? Like you did with the senator? Like you did with the kid in the agency? Murder, drug running, kidnapping—all part of your new America?"

Goss's eyes flared with anger. "You don't see it, do you? That's why people like you have to be shoved aside. The end justifies the means. Pragmatism, Hiller. Pragmatism works. Idealism is just paper."

Hiller looked at him with disbelieving eyes. "I pity you," he said disdainfully. "Your delusions of grandeur are so desultory that when you're through feeding on the world at large you don't even realize you've begun to chew on your own cock."

Goss moved forward menacingly and stopped short. His face was twisted into rage. "You know what I find so disgusting about people like you? You never know when you're beaten. You couldn't win this one—and still you keep trying. Even now, when it's all over. But I've got something special for you, Hiller. To make it hurt. Turn around and take it up the ass."

Hiller did not move and his expression remained unchanged. Goss, anticipating the next moment, now wore a grin of smug complacency. Then the grin faded and he roared, "I said turn around!"

Hiller looked over his shoulder and instantly went numb. There was no way he could have been prepared. His mouth fell open in stunned disbelief. Addressing him squarely, with the sullen face of a pallbearer, limply holding herself up, was Lynn Carlisle!

Hiller felt the blood surge in his neck, then slowly, painfully, descend into the pit of his stomach. He was drained and he stooped against a tree as if there was no breath left in his body.

Lynn's eyes were glassy. She tried to speak, but when no words came she raised her eyes to him imploringly. Hiller turned his head away and bent over as if to vomit. He choked once, spitting up bloody saliva, and shuddered as the banging persisted in his bloodied ear.

"What a fitting ending," he thought bitterly. "Payment for trusting. Restitution for caring. And, after all—betrayal."

He had been the perfect idiot, allowing sentiment to slip back into his life through that little chink in the door. His head spun in a dark, milky fog. His brown eyes, drained nearly colorless, were eyes of abandoned hopes, and annihilation.

He coughed once, and the cough exploded into a horrible wheeze. Again that unyielding weight played with his life. With unearthly power, it squeezed down on his chest, slowly forcing air from his lungs. His face turned red with pounding blood, throbbing like a flood against the inside of his skull.

He heard Lynn's insistent voice calling as if from the bottom of a well. "Give him the inhaler."

Again air was a gift, given in small packages, and again Hiller was a child at Christmas, wanting more. There was Lynn's voice again, more commanding this time. "Give him that thing! He needs it to breathe."

And Goss's mocking reply, "He won't be doing too much more of that."

He taunted Hiller, holding the nebulizer loosely in one hand. "You want it? Come get it."

Hiller stumbled forward as Goss smiled coldly. He enjoyed watching the infamous special investigator grovel like a beggar with a cup. Then with sadistic relish he dropped the nebulizer in the water at his feet. As Hiller tried to fling himself down, Goss slammed a heavy boot on it, and the plastic body cracked apart. Hiller fell pitifully to all fours and concentrated on slowing the wheezing—his breath sounding like the measured breath of a dying animal.

He heard Lynn's wild shouts at Fred Goss, who now hovered over him like master over dog. Short of a miracle, it *was* over—Goss's victory complete. Still, if he had it in him to believe in miracles, now would have to be the time.

Calling on the last of his strength with the last of his will, Hiller threw himself at Goss and drove a fist into his groin. He reeled backward with a cry of anguish and the two men tumbled into the water, arms flailing. They struggled savagely, each driven by a vicious hatred.

Goss pulled free, staggered to his feet, and grabbed for his weapon. Three shots exploded through the air—two of them suddenly blew apart a man's stomach. Fred Goss collapsed to his knees, staring dazedly at Lynn Carlisle, who—still trembling—clutched a newly fired gun. It was the one he had confiscated earlier from Hiller and had carelessly thrown aside.

Goss's eyes were filmy, vacant, totally bewildered, and his usually unlined features were twisted into disfigurement. Then a most amazing expression crept onto his face. He *smiled*. As if he had just been beaten at something by a young pupil, he smiled with flashing teeth. But there was more ice and cruelty in that smile than in any expression of contempt Lynn had ever experienced.

Finally, Goss's eyes clouded over and he blinked—one final time—before slamming forward into the wet ground.

Hiller sucked hard deep breaths of air through his mouth and nostrils. Was what seemed to be happening actually happening? Of that he could not be sure. Wasn't it more likely a nightmarish hallucination brought on by severe asthma? But no matter how hard he blinked through wide, glassy, disbelieving eyes, the image of Lynn Carlisle stood frozen before him.

Everything about her was in disarray—her face drawn and sheet white, her chestnut hair limply fallen in matted strands, pale eyes faded, without mystery. Even the tiny birthmark at the bridge of her nose was strangely unappealing. She was like a waif shivering in the cold. She seemed to beg with all her being, but for what was unclear.

It was several minutes before Hiller could utter a word. At last in a strained, raspy voice, he said only, "Why?"

Lynn tried to reply but could not choke down her sobs. With tears streaming down her face, she said in a broken voice, "Could I say anything, *anything* . . . that would make sense to you? I didn't know . . . I didn't know what I was a part of . . . ever . . ."

Hiller glowered and said bitterly, "Sure, sure. You never knew . . ."

Lynn shook her head vigorously. The tears flowed more freely now, and she said entreatingly, "It's true. I didn't know. I swear to you I didn't know. . . ."

"Oh, yeah. You just figured agency work was a little cat-and-mouse, a little kiss-and-tell. That's all, right? And picking me out, well, that was beautiful, that was really gonna get you points. . . ."

"No," she protested nervously. "No, that wasn't how it was at all. It . . . it's not what you think."

"No?" he roared. "Don't make me out a fool! Tell me, Lynn. How many men have you fucked for information? How does it feel being an undercover whore?"

The remark stung like a slap. "You really know how to be so cruel," she sobbed. "I've made a mockery of my life, but I never pretended . . . about any of it.

My feelings, they were always real . . . I do feel love for you."

"Then what the hell did you think you were doing?" Hiller said sharply. "Just what the fuck did you think it was all about?"

Lynn put her fingers to a cheek to wipe away tears. Her hand was trembling. "I was told it involved a matter of national . . . security. You were investigating the abduction . . . they . . . they needed to know . . . I mean they . . ."

"They! They! Who the hell is 'they'?"

"Goss. . . . He said there had been some . . . difficulties . . . with you in the past. . . . They . . . He . . . The agency couldn't be too careful on . . . something like this. . . ."

"So you agreed to be a pawn. An informer!"

Lynn groped for an explanation and shut her eyes, agonizing. Finally, she said softly, "I never saw it that way. There was always an exchange. The little I gave them . . . it never seemed like it amounted to much. It seemed like the difference between a million lighted candles and a million-and-one. I couldn't see how I mattered at all."

Hiller looked at her sharply. "You *chose* not to see."

With a faint moan, her head sank. "I chose not to see," she repeated, barely above a whisper. "I *couldn't* see. I didn't know what it was like from the outside looking in. After . . . it was as if it wasn't *them* at all—after the first time, it was . . . almost like working with any other contact."

"After the first time?" Hiller exclaimed. "How many others have you worked? How long have you been at it?"

Lynn stammered. "They came to me four, I think four years ago—after I broke the congressional payola story. They needed help and I had access to sources. And the perfect cover."

Hiller was astonished. "What happened to the great reporter in you? In all that time, it didn't occur to you to ask questions, to find out what the goddamned hell you were doing, what you were contributing to?"

She hesitated a moment, and he snapped impatiently, "Well, *didn't* it?"

Lynn fought off another wave of tears. "I . . . I'm not you," she whispered. "I can't challenge the world the way you do. Sure I asked questions. I got answers. For security, for national security. Whatever it was, they always made it a little blurred. And that satisfied me because truthfully I was afraid. I was afraid to know more. Even today, I had no idea you'd be here. I believed . . . they were pursuing a lead. It was a shot at a story . . . so I came."

Hiller gasped in disbelief and held his pounding head as if he feared it would break apart. "The all-American girl innocently and aimlessly wandering about the Machiavellian web of American intelligence work."

Their voices fell silent for a long while. Lynn lowered her anguished eyes and smothered another sob. She looked lost within her own body.

"I'm tired, Jay. I'm very tired. I've gotten old very fast and nothing I do can change that."

Hiller regarded the pathetic expression on her face and shook his head sadly. "I don't get it, Lynn," he said softly. "What was in it for you?"

She looked at him a little surprised and replied curtly, "You *know* what was in it for me."

The moment she said it, it began to make sense, though it struck Hiller as peculiarly vulgar and rendered him speechless.

Was it really possible? In exchange for her cooperation, Lynn Carlisle—nationally-known television personality—received privileged information that sometimes led to blockbuster exclusives. And while rationalizing that she and the agency were "sources" for each other, the fact remained that cooperating with the CIA provided her with an insurance policy for a successful career.

Written on Lynn's face was the guilt of a thousand years. She understood for the first time how privileged information had led to the suicide of Marsh Collyer, the former presidential aide exposed in a Carlisle exclusive on land fraud—an exclusive she might not have had on her own. She had upset the delicate balance between corruption and compromise, and it was more than she could bear.

Lynn turned her shattered body away from Hiller. "I feel lost," she said tearfully. "I'm . . . I'm sorry, God knows, for your hurt—and the others. I can't change anything I've done. But whatever role I played, I was . . . a small part . . . interchangeable with anyone out there. . . . I was afraid to let go of it. But I'm just a little person, Jay. So it hardly matters."

"Lynn," he said gently. "Little people are *all* that matters."

She covered her mouth with a hand and said in a hollow voice, "Wait for dawn. Follow the spiral path to the center of the swamp. The President is there. He's okay."

She started through the mangroves.

"Where are you going?" Hiller asked.

Without looking back she said, "I'm through."

He cried out anxiously. "Lynn! . . . Lynn!!"

She stopped and turned around. But in that long moment she could not look in his eyes and so did not see in them the willingness to comprehend, to understand her pain and allow compassion for her wretched self-destruction.

Certainly, more ordeals awaited her—humiliation by her peers, the shame of a public trial, degradation in prison, the bitter irony of harsh media coverage—all of them certainties. None of them could she bring herself to face. It was these absolutes that overcame her and made her unaware of all else. And so, without warning, in full view of the last man she had loved, she turned away, stuck the metal barrel of the gun in her mouth, and pulled the trigger.

The noise was jarring. Hiller staggered a few steps and fell stunned against a mangrove with such force one might have thought the bullet had struck him. As dark as it was in the milky jungle night, he swore that he saw clearly the bullet exit through the back of her throat and carry with it fragments of muscle and disgorged blood.

It was a nightmare he would see replayed every night for the rest of his life.

Chapter 28

December 19.

The cold wind whipped across downtown D.C., but streets were again grinding with activity. With less than a week before Christmas, the citizenry in Washington and the rest of the country was cramming a month's worth of shopping into six days.

Traffic on Pennsylvania Avenue moved steadily. Though some drove past number 1600 on the way home from department stores hoping for a glimpse of the President, most were content to look in on their televisions or read newspaper accounts of the remarkable rescue of John Quinlan Royce.

A red-and-gray taxi—one of many in the area— pulled up in front of the Treasury Building and the driver and passenger gazed with the fervor of foreign tourists across East Executive Avenue at the East Gate to the White House. The entrance and portico were well-guarded by details of Secret Service agents, who also walked the streets outside the grounds and populated the tumultuous press conference in the Situation Room of the White House.

Several CIA field officers were in the area on special assignment—an insurance measure instituted independently by the director.

Inside, the Executive Mansion was buzzing with foreign and domestic press. Special agents had been assigned the specific task of checking the authenticity of the seventy-odd select members of the press corps. Once their credentials had been verified, they were to be reconfirmed through a second source by a second agent.

In other times it might have caused resentment between members of the fourth estate and the Secret Service, but not in the wake of Dark December. Spirits were running high—how else *could* they run—it was the biggest story of the decade and it had a dramatic and successful conclusion.

Jay Hiller was a hero, though it seemed far less important to him than to almost anyone else in Washington. The price had been too great. He was weak from his wounds—his arm still confined to a sling—and the mental anguish and emotional upheaval had been devastating. He responded to gestures of attention with tired eyes and to the clamor surrounding him with uncharacteristic embarrassment. His skin was pale, he had lost a lot of weight, and he reacted to questions from the media, even lighthearted ones, without a trace of humor.

By contrast, the President was effusive. He was a man who counted himself lucky to be alive and he wanted to savor his vitality. His blue eyes glistened, and though there was a noticeable absence of color in his skin, a result of confinement for more than a week inside a windowless capsule the size of an outhouse, he had a ready smile for everyone. His spirit was childlike, and he had a renewed appreciation for the many around him, most noticeably for Vice President Seymour Clayton, who had tried to beg off from meeting the press, but whom Royce had insisted share the spotlight.

Mark Kinstrey handed out miniature American flags with press releases that typified the bouyant mood. One announcement began, "If you think the kidnapping was something, wait till you see what we've got in store next year!"

The press room atmosphere was decidedly informal. Royce and Clayton wore casual light-colored suits and Jay Hiller was tieless, a blue sports jacket draped over his shoulders. As they came in to meet the media, applause broke out spontaneously. Television minicams whirred and dozens of photographers crowded in, their motorized cameras rapidly spinning off shots.

With Royce between them the trio shuffled to the front and took places behind a wall of microphones and a lectern bearing the presidential seal.

When the tumult finally died down, the Chief Executive spoke first. Grinning broadly, occasionally nodding to a familiar face here and there, he said, "I would just like to state that, although the press corps and the President of the United States have been traditional adversaries of sorts, none of you have ever looked better to me. Whatever you might be able to criticize me about from now on is going to sound very much like a serenade. I am pleased—pardon the understatement—I am *elated* to be here today to field your questions, catch your darts, write your stories."

There was a smattering of laughter. One of John Royce's techniques for winning over White House correspondents was to recognize the individual priorities of the press and invite the differences to become part of a readily accepted tug-of-war. The reporters who laughed now were laughing at how easily the President picked up where he had left off.

"But rather than recapitulate all the details that you already have in the press releases, why don't we open it to questions from the floor."

Nearly every hand in the room shot up. Royce called on a silver-haired woman near the front. "Mr. President, would you tell us how you were treated by your abductors and what thoughts were running through your head in those first hours."

Royce replied immediately. "I was not physically abused, though I confess I've eaten better food, spent more enjoyable evenings, and lived in more comfortable places. A ten-foot capsule buried in marshland isn't exactly the White House."

He paused a moment before continuing. "My thoughts? My thoughts were . . . my wife . . . things I would have liked to have done, feelings of inadequacy, prayer. Mostly personal, I'm afraid. I hope you don't find that disappointing."

Another reporter called out, "What was your diet, what were you given to eat?"

"A rather limited selection—bread and milk. I tried complaining and called down several times to room service but no one showed. One positive aspect was that I lost a few unnecessary pounds which I'll try to keep off."

"Were you ever permitted out of the capsule?"

"No. But I had plenty of time to do pushups and think about my golf score."

Laughter erupted from the gallery, and when the President smiled ear-to-ear, camera bulbs flashed again. Then he took a question from the rear of the floor.

"Were you aware your abductors were members of the Beretta underground?"

The President shook his head. "Not until it was over. I thought of twenty or thirty groups that might want to kidnap me. The trouble was I'd been so disagreeable to all of them, I couldn't eliminate anybody."

A second chorus of laughter echoed through the air. Mark Kinstrey was delighted. There was every indication Royce would be enjoying a second honeymoon with the media—and during an election year!

A young woman journalist in the first row then cried out above the din. "I'd like to ask Mr. Hiller if he can explain Lynn Carlisle's role in this? How was it she happened to be on the marshes?"

Hiller felt himself tense up. The question came from someone he immediately recognized as the same physical type as Lynn and roughly the same age. And he detected in her rigid delivery just a faint touch of skepticism and professional jealousy.

He tried to reply impassively, but he was nervous. "Miss Carlisle followed me there hoping for a story. As the press release states, she saved my life and forfeited her own. She was a heroine. I owe her a great debt, and I think the nation owes her a great debt."

The young woman spoke again. "But how did she know where you would be?"

"Uh, I don't know," he said hesitantly. "She was a good reporter."

Another question came from the middle of the floor in a well-modulated male voice. "Are you saying that without her help the kidnapping and ransom might have successfully been carried out?"

Hiller nodded vigorously. "Absolutely. Without her help and the help of Father Julian Serra . . . several other people . . . my entire staff deserves an awful lot . . ."

The President spoke up. He had a hand on Jay Hiller's shoulder. "Let me interject one thought here. There is no minimizing the contributions of Miss Carlisle and Father Serra. However I believe the special investigator is being a little modest. In my opinion, even without their help Jay Hiller would have gotten me home safely."

"The President's confidence is flattering," he said with a sad smile. "But I'm afraid I don't share his assessment. What I was able to do was the result of their help, the work of hundreds others, and a hell of a lot of luck."

As Royce gave him an affectionate pat on the back, another question came at Hiller. "Last week, there was an attempt on your life by a man identified in your report as a Beretta. Have you been able to determine why the kidnappers counted on you to raise five hundred million dollars and were at the same time trying to kill you?"

Hiller heaved a deep sigh which sounded like a huff when he leaned too close to the microphones. He said patiently, "The attempt on my life was not instituted by the Berettas but by section chief Fred Goss, who felt that with my agency background and some information I had stumbled on I threatened the ultimate success of the plot. Because the attempt failed and resulted in clues that aided our investigation, he was forced to change his method of operation.

"The reason we couldn't get anywhere for so long was that Goss was aware of every move we made, withheld information, led us in the wrong direction, and countered us wherever possible. When I met with Father Serra, who would provide conclusive physical evidence, Goss knew he could not take any more chances with me."

The reporter pursued his question. "But the man who made the attempt on your life was a Beretta, wasn't he?"

Hiller nodded. "Yes. He was sent to Washington, sheltered by a crime syndicate and, in Morales's absence, acted under orders from Goss, who was responsible from his end for keeping the lid on. Goss and Morales were the architects of the kidnapping and were responsible, incidentally, for hiring the man who tormented Father Serra in the Yucatan."

Outside the White House in the red and gray taxicab across the street from the East Gate, an obese man with browless eyes, bundled in a heavy winter overcoat, leaned toward the front seat and gave the driver a detailed street map.

The man at the wheel took it in gloved hands and tossed it onto the front seat. He picked up a black leather case from the floor, then slowly unlocked the ends and snapped open each latch.

"I don't know," the driver said, surveying the area. "Look where we are, daylight, out in the open like this . . ."

"Don't worry about it," the passenger reassured him. "We'll be all right. I have an understanding on the matter. Nobody is going to bother us."

Press questions came in rapid succession from the floor of anxious reporters, each jostling for a quote that would make a natural lead for their stories.

The President talked of harrowing moments in the St. Mark's Hotel, detailing his ordeal and admitting that he still felt a little fatigued.

To questions about his personal reactions to the kidnapping, Vice President Clayton nervously replied that he was, like everyone else initially, shocked and disbelieving. He acknowledged feeling first more than a little scared and then a sense of outrage, coupled with fear that the nation was heading for an inevitable confrontation with a major foreign power. He refused to say which country or countries he had anticipated, but that much was obvious to everyone in the room.

Then a bearded reporter in a brown striped suit brought up a question about the various references to "Foxbat" and President Royce deferred to Jay Hiller for the answer.

Like all questions being asked today, he would have preferred to let it go unanswered. But he took a moment to compose his thoughts and finally responded, "Zorromurciélago is the name of a Mayan cemetery in the Yucatan marshland where the President was being held. It translates from the Spanish to 'foxbat' and was used as a code name by Fred Goss and the Berettas—*fox* for the first part of the plot, the kidnapping and ransom of the President. The second half of the scheme, code-named *bat*, alluded to the subsequent planned assassination of Cuban Premier Castro."

"But why kidnap the President?" the reporter asked. "Especially in view of how incredibly risky it would be."

"Desperate men will always take great risks," Hiller said simply. "I believe they thought of it as a matter of survival."

The reporter persisted. "But why the *President*?"

Jay Hiller shrugged. "No doubt because they could hold up a sum that no other human being on the face of the earth would command . . ."

Royce started to interject. Both he and Hiller knew there was another reason for the kidnapping—to keep the President from strategic talks with the Soviet Union and Communist China. But at all costs he did not want the press in on that. Once they found out, he would have little chance of attending the summit conference with a free hand. There would be plenty of time for congressional debate later. And so he stuck to the one official reason for the kidnapping—money.

"Don't forget that by utilizing the enormous ransom," the President said, "the Berettas could continue to finance their strikes against Premier Castro. And as you know, I had long ago ordered a halt to funding them. They had no capital to speak of."

The silver-haired woman reporter in the gallery asked, "Mr. President, that being the case, how were they able to bring off the abduction?"

Royce hesitated and said in a low voice, "Jay, you want to handle that?"

Hiller responded promptly. "Fred Goss, obviously far exceeding his authority, provided the kidnappers with weapons, intelligence information on how I was operating, aircraft which—in most cases—could not be traced. He placed Eduardo Morales in the regular Army under the pretext of being a CIA operative. And funds. He also supplied them with funds."

"In direct violation of a presidential order?" the woman asked.

Hiller made a pained smile. "Goss was clever about it," he said. "He used Global Communications executive Gordon Langway as a funding conduit. Money went to Langway and he funneled it to the Berettas. Langway also provided muscle when it was needed and, with Goss's help and the privileged information Goss could supply, was able to traffic drugs in and out of the country. He also stood to gain enormously in Cuba if the Berettas were successful."

"Has Langway been apprehended?" came a question from the rear.

In the cab across from the East Gate, the burly passenger went over a street map with the driver.

"You're certain of the route?" he asked.

The driver turned malevolent eyes on Gordon Langway. It was a routine assignment as far as he was concerned.

"All right, all right," Langway said, throwing up his hands. He leaned back in his seat and nervously scratched the layers of excess flesh under his chin. The driver opened the leather case on the front seat and fondled a Remington 700 BDL caliber 243 Winchester like a prizewinning Great Dane. It was equipped with a Redfield 3 x 9 variable scope with Accu-range, a heavy barrel and Harris bipod, and would shoot half a minute of angle. He set the bore sites for point of impact dead on at 150 yards and checked the second-hand sweep on his watch.

This was the precision of Ted Glasky, a powerfully built man in his mid-thirties with receding dark hair, crooked teeth, and deep-set eyes. Part of his routine included lubricating these eyes, which he did religiously at half-hour intervals. He unscrewed a plastic bottle and squeezed five drops into each pupil. He blinked hard and took up the gun.

One block away, a late model gray van was parked at the southeast corner of Lafayette Park. Two tall wiry men worked in the rear of the van. One had a clear view of the taxi through a high-powered scope and the rear one-way windows. The other operated a wireless telephone.

"This is Mother," the man on the phone said. "They're setting up. We can move in on them at any time."

"Stay with them," came the cool unexcitable reply. "But remain at your station at this time." It was a voice familiar to the men in the van. It belonged to the director of the CIA, Wilson McAvee.

In the White House, a news reporter at the rear of the pressroom, frustrated by what he felt were all-too-general responses to his questions, tried to redirect one to Jay Hiller.

"Mr. Hiller, by saying that the CIA was permitting drugs to enter the country, aren't you in fact indicting the—"

The President bristled and cut in sharply. "No. Let me interrupt here. And let me emphasize—*section chief Goss* was allowing drugs to enter the country. The CIA was not! Director McAvee was not!"

"Mr. McAvee had no knowledge of what was taking place?"

"He did not," the President said flatly. Then he took a question from a thin bald man with thick glasses in the fourth row whom he recognized as a *Sun-Times* reporter. The man rose to his feet and asked, "How many agents in the Central Intelligence Agency were involved?"

"We can't answer that at this time," Royce replied.

"An investigation is being conducted to determine to what extent those acting on Fred Goss's orders were involved. Thus far, we are aware only of instances where agents merely followed the directives of their superior and had no involvement in the plot."

The young woman who reminded Hiller of Lynn Carlisle spoke up again. "Mr. President," she said in an austere tone. "In view of the significant part played in the kidnapping by a high-ranking agency official, is it likely we'll see major reforms of the CIA and/or its charter?"

Royce shook his head and said easily, "I don't believe major reforms are needed simply because one fanatical individual—and, possibly, a very few accomplices—in the agency acted on his own. . . ."

Hiller was horrified by the President's remark and began shuffling impatiently as Royce continued to speak.

"We can still be extremely confident of the way our system functions."

But the young woman in the gallery persisted. As Royce sent a private signal to Mark Kinstrey, she raised her voice for emphasis. "In view of all the clandestine activity on domestic soil and what they were able to effect—in your own words—a very few people had brought—"

Kinstrey suddenly broke in from across the room. "Ladies and gentlemen, members of the press, I'm sorry—we'll have to end it here! We wish you all a wonderful Christmas and New Year's but we are already twenty minutes over. And the President has a lot to catch up on."

There were a few mild protests, but most resigned themselves to chumming with each other or trying to catch Royce on his way out. The Chief Executive strolled from the chorus of microphones and huddled briefly with the Vice President. The two shared a private joke and broke into laughter as photographers clicked off shots.

Television cameramen began disassembling equipment, and journalists near the front of the room tried to get in a question or two. Then the President and a troubled Jay Hiller headed for an exit. Others cornered Clayton and fired queries at him. The young woman reporter fought through the crowd and caught up with Royce at the door. Kinstrey tried to dismiss her politely, but the President called him off and invited her question.

"Mr. President, doesn't it concern you that just a very small number of fanatics were able to operate on such a broad scale?"

The President gave her a winsome smile. "Of course it does. I didn't mean to leave you with any other impression. And we're giving the matter considerable study," he said. "But what happened reflects very little if at all on the structure and the charter itself. I think that much is evident."

She began a rejoinder and he immediately retreated. "Please excuse me. There's an enormous amount of work waiting, and I'm looking forward to getting at it. It's going to be like a day in the country, breathing intoxicating fresh air."

With that, the President went out the door. Jay Hiller followed, and Mark Kinstrey stayed to fend off the press.

In the anteroom Stephen Brownell greeted Royce with a broad grin and a vigorous handshake. Though they had spoken on the phone immediately upon his return, they had not seen each other. Their exchange was warm and sprinkled with good-natured ribbing, but Hiller was seething over some of the President's remarks to the press.

Brownell greeted Hiller with a heartfelt smile and snatched up his limply held left hand. With a nod to the other in the sling, the secretary said with some measure of admiration, "Didn't I tell you not to go to Mexico, you tough old son of a bitch."

Hiller forced a pained smile.

"I sure am glad to see you," Brownell said, his eyes dancing brightly. Hiller blinked. He was touched by his forthrightness.

"Good to see you, too, Mr. Secretary," he said quietly.

The President loosened his tie and chimed in cheerfully. "What do you think, Brownie? We ought to get him a Medal of Honor, a Purple Heart, and a McDonald's hamburger?"

Before Brownell could voice agreement, Hiller spoke up sharply. "John, what the hell was *that* all about?" he said, motioning to the press room. "What happened to the announcement about putting Central Intelligence under the State Department?"

Royce looked at Hiller with a worried expression. Following a private two-hour conversation with Wilson McAvee, he realized he had promised more than he could deliver.

"I can't do that—not now, not overnight, certainly not without jeopardizing our national security."

Hiller eyed him suspiciously and almost seemed to be jeering when he said, "Our poor, beleaguered, propped-up sense of national security, always the rationale for intelligence abuses. How does reforming the Central Intelligence Agency jeopardize that?"

"It's unfeasable at this time," the President said flatly. "The system makes it necessary to handle it this way."

"The system doesn't make it necessary to perpetuate

power perversions. That has more to do with who's *abusing* the system."

"The way you see it," Royce said with a little exasperation, "everyone is waiting in the bush for the opportunity to overthrow us. What you have to consider is that there are certain armatures of the government unavoidably linked up which even you may not fully comprehend and which are better left untampered with."

"Here we go again. Every time something is brought into question, we're subjected to those dark, cloudy, undefinable political vagaries."

Royce shook his head slowly. "You don't seem to want to understand."

"Oh what the hell's the matter with you?" Hiller snapped. "It's *you* who don't understand. Can't you see the damned organization is so big that no one can control it anymore? McAvee can't control it. *You* can't control it. If this nightmare has meant anything at all it's that the present intelligence setup itself is a threat to national security. Without provisions for checks and balances we'll always be in danger of finding ourselves in a police state!"

"Look, Jay. There are things here of which you have incomplete knowledge at best. I know I owe you a lot—but this is different. It doesn't matter that you're a friend. It doesn't matter that you saved my life. What matters is that I'm President and I have to make pragmatic decisions."

Hiller was stunned. The two glared at each other while Brownell seemed to have retreated diplomatically to a neutral corner.

"Well, well, well," Hiller began scornfully. "After all of this, you're still bullshit politicking your friends."

Royce lowered his eyes and said imploringly, "Will

you let *me* run the damn country. Is it so hard for you to trust?"

"Blind faith, is that all you want? Leave your brains at the voting booth, friends, and *I* will lead you on to bliss and fulfillment." Hiller punctuated the last sentence by digging a thumb into his own chest.

"I can't tell you any more than I've already told you," the President said. "You'll just have to go on that for now. Look, why don't you put your energies into thinking about the reception tonight? How many times will you have a chance to be guest of honor at the White House?"

Hiller regarded Royce bitterly. "You'll excuse me, *Mister President*. There's an enormous amount of work waiting and I'm looking forward to getting at it. It's going to be like a day in the country, breathing intoxicating fresh air. . . ."

With that, Hiller brushed past the startled President and went out the door, with no thought of the overcoat he was leaving behind. Royce heaved a long, exasperated sigh. Brownell watched a moment and then stepped from the shadows with a frown on his face.

The President clasped his elbows in his hands, pacing about and looking at the floor. There was no doubt he was troubled.

"Brownie," he finally said sadly. "Can you get him back for me?"

Chapter 29

Jay Hiller strode into the uncomfortably cold bright afternoon from the South Portico and made his way past the tall white columns down the long path to the East Gate. The winter wind blew against him like the day's events—and both were chilling. He was saddened by a new realization, one that seemed to be the latest in a line of realizations about people for whom he had cared.

He was struck by the thought of how vaporous relationships seemed to be, how with the same fleeting vitality as a breath of wind, they could blow away into nothingness. Like smoke rings. Like vapor. The illusion had been that there would always be something to hold on to, but he had learned otherwise. His mind raced back to Padre Serra, who had lost the will to live, and to Lynn, who had never learned how, and to himself who, he was certain, had failed more miserably than either of them.

They had at least tried to solidify life with passion. The padre embraced religion, fervently devoted his soul to it, and yet stepped outside its parameters when he felt violated. Lynn loved her work, being driven constantly by the challenge of a story, and wanted so desperately to feel secure at it that she unwittingly compromised everything. It was a passionate if painful decision, worth the torment of knowing her exclusive had come not because of her prowess as a journalist, but because she had sold herself to a clandestine agency in exchange for the next day's front page.

And now John Quinlan Royce, whose moral, cultural, and economic platform had swept him into office, disavowed his ideals too when scrutinized under the keen eye of pragmatism.

Jay Hiller could not wait to get home. He felt heavy on his feet and he planned to stretch out in his living room and imagine that it was spring and he was under a shade tree with a beer and a nectarine. That peace might allow him to forget the pain of December.

Was he an anachronism—so out of step? Anathematized? Why couldn't *he* integrate his beliefs with the world at large in a practical sense? Why were there no limits to *his* idealistic nature? He shook his head and sighed longingly and plunged into a wave of despair. These questions he asked himself—as he had done in the past—again and again.

There were never any answers.

In the gray van in front of Lafayette Park, the two men watched Hiller leave the White House and walk toward the gate at East Executive Avenue. The agent on the wireless, his ruddy complexion darkening with concern, spoke anxiously into the phone.

"Subject has left the White House," he said. "Proceeding east to exit."

A voice returned impassively. "Remain stationed."

Ted Glasky blinked the excess fluid from his eyes and slid toward the front passenger seat of the cab. He braced himself against the bipod and steadied the barrel on the sill of the open window. Through the sniperscope, he focused first on the hatchmarks, then on random targets, skipping from the roof of the guardhouse to the spine of one of the Secret Service agents standing nearby to the head of Jay Hiller walking toward him at the East Gate.

As an anxious Gordon Langway sat motionless in the rear of the cab, Glasky began to slow his breathing.

In the van, the ruddy-faced agent swallowed hard and began to squirm. His companion only shook his head subtly. Then he picked up the phone and said excitedly, "This is Mother. Subject coming into range. They are committing!"

Again, the voice came back in a commanding tone. "Remain stationed."

The agent shut off the wireless and said anxiously, "What the hell's he waiting for?"

"I don't know," the second man said quietly, returning for another look through the high-powered scope. He bit his lip and hesitated indecisively a moment, then suddenly snatched up the phone from his comrade.

"Mr. McAvee," he said in a voice that compelled attention. "If we're going to do something, we'd better do it now."

There was no immediate reply. "Start up the truck," the agent with the scope ordered. But just as his companion got up and scrambled toward the front, the same impassive voice came back on the phone. "Remain stationed."

The hatchmarks on Ted Glasky's sniperscope crossed at Jay Hiller's throat. Glasky lowered the weapon just a slight bit and slid a restless finger over the trigger. He was ready now.

As Hiller neared the gate, a voice shouted at him

from behind. He turned and saw the short rumpled figure of Secretary of State Brownell rushing from the South Portico with the overcoat he had left behind. Hiller smiled at the improbable sight of the head of the State Department running after him with his clothing, fat and thoroughly uncoordinated.

The secretary caught up to him and draped the coat over Hiller's shoulders. Puffing and red-cheeked, Brownell said in a way that was clearly maternal, "Keep that wounded wing warm. We don't want you to land on your back with pneumonia."

Hiller smiled kindly. "Does my health and welfare now fall under the Department of State?" he asked jokingly.

Brownell's eyes flickered, and still out of breath, he replied, "We're *all* concerned about you, Jay."

Hiller's smile faded. He anticipated a lecture from the secretary, carefully rephrasing the President's words. But he thought wrong. Brownell simply asked that he think about the pressures Royce was under, that Jay Hiller try to take it easy on himself, particularly after his ordeal, and that he consider him a friend he could always call on. Hiller thanked him and they shook hands warmly.

He watched Brownell amble back to the White House, touched by their brief conversation. He raised his left hand and made a small gesture—a sad, friendly wave which Brownell could not see. Then he ducked his head into his overcoat and continued toward the East Gate.

A hundred yards away, in the taxi in front of the Treasury Building, a finger on a rifle stirred. There was a loud report, and a bullet exploded against the wind.

An agonizing pain suddenly gripped Hiller at the base of his throat and he was puzzled by the sensation. But it was brief. His legs buckled and fell out from under him. The sky rose up before his glazed eyes and there was a glimpse of something darkly red and indiscernible. As he fell he heard a violent thunder and tires screaming and he wondered—if *wonder* is the proper word for a sudden assault of passing images—if his brain were not exploding out of his head.

There were shouts from afar as the ground slammed against his spine. Nothing was making sense. He struggled to get up—why had he fallen?—and discover what the commotion was about. But when he could not move, he grew frightened.

Thick warm sap collected in his throat—lodged there—tasting like blood. He coughed once and spat up, choking vociferously. It was impossible to breathe. His stomach and chest rose and fell with alarming rapidity. He was seized by panic. He could not swallow, fluid filling in his throat . . . suffocating him . . . changing him. . . .

A blurred silhouette hovered over him—more noise . . . panicked footsteps . . . shouts . . . cries of *ambulance!*

The sky was white, formless. The sky was colorless, like his eyes—tiring, like his eyes—falling.

He heard nothing, saw nothing. He felt so impossibly weak and unknown. He thought of unknowable things—of a point in paradise, light-years away, through mystic cycles of fire and light, this point so verdant, so remote, so overwhelmingly beautiful, so incredibly near hell. White sand fine as talcum, transparent blue water and white gleaming coral reefs beneath. He existed in the sea. He *was* the sea—timeless—or for unknown lengths of time, turning brown, lying asleep in the sun, or napping under a shade tree with a beer and a nectarine. And then was being carried off by many arms, by years of memory.

He was confused. A natural place. He was an imprecise man in a precise world, a precise man in an imprecise world—he was whole and he was nothing.

He was, at last, at peace.

In seconds, Ted Glasky dropped his rifle on the seat and started up the cab. It screamed out of its berth leaving half a tube of rubber in the street. But in comparison his reaction time was slow.

A moment after the sniper's gun had ushered a new horror into the nation's Dark December, Wilson McAvee's voice broke across the wireless in the van in the same phlegmatic tones.

"Proceed to objective," came the order to his two startled agents.

Immediately, the gray van roared across Pennsylvania Avenue signaling other vehicles stationed along nearby streets. Two black limousines tore out of Hamilton Place on the south side of the Treasury Building and blocked the south end of East Executive Avenue. Two others shot out of Madison Place behind the van and drove toward the oncoming red and gray taxi. Five agency vehicles plugged the intersection at Pennsylvania and East Executive. Two more came up from the rear at South Executive Avenue.

Glasky had not gone fifty feet when the van and two cars bore down on him, forcing him onto the curb. The sniper and his passenger flung themselves out of the cab and tried to run. But two agents in every vehicle—a total of twenty-four men—leaped onto the street with guns poised, and before Glasky and Langway had gone ten steps they were cut down by a hail of gunfire that continued for a full twelve seconds, until every chamber in each of those weapons had emptied.

It had gone exactly as Wilson McAvee had planned. Like any scheme, this one also had its drawbacks.

Many government people would insist on a fitting memorial. Dozens of the nation's most respected individuals would bow their heads and pay tribute to the man who brought the President home. He would have to stomach a week or so of what he felt were outrageous lies, biographical bullshit, and public relations fodder.

There would be sprawling newspaper obituaries and endless electronic eulogies.

But it would also be the last time Wilson McAvee would have to read about Jay Marvin Hiller.

Dell Bestsellers

- [ ] TO LOVE AGAIN by Danielle Steel $2.50 (18631-5)
- [ ] SECOND GENERATION by Howard Fast $2.75 (17892-4)
- [ ] EVERGREEN by Belva Plain $2.75 (13294-0)
- [ ] AMERICAN CAESAR by William Manchester ... $3.50 (10413-0)
- [ ] THERE SHOULD HAVE BEEN CASTLES
  by Herman Raucher $2.75 (18500-9)
- [ ] THE FAR ARENA by Richard Ben Sapir $2.75 (12671-1)
- [ ] THE SAVIOR by Marvin Werlin and Mark Werlin . $2.75 (17748-0)
- [ ] SUMMER'S END by Danielle Steel $2.50 (18418-5)
- [ ] SHARKY'S MACHINE by William Diehl $2.50 (18292-1)
- [ ] DOWNRIVER by Peter Collier $2.75 (11830-1)
- [ ] CRY FOR THE STRANGERS by John Saul $2.50 (11869-7)
- [ ] BITTER EDEN by Sharon Salvato $2.75 (10771-7)
- [ ] WILD TIMES by Brian Garfield $2.50 (19457-1)
- [ ] 1407 BROADWAY by Joel Gross $2.50 (12819-6)
- [ ] A SPARROW FALLS by Wilbur Smith $2.75 (17707-3)
- [ ] FOR LOVE AND HONOR by Antonia Van-Loon .. $2.50 (12574-X)
- [ ] COLD IS THE SEA by Edward L. Beach $2.50 (11045-9)
- [ ] TROCADERO by Leslie Waller $2.50 (18613-7)
- [ ] THE BURNING LAND by Emma Drummond $2.50 (10274-X)
- [ ] HOUSE OF GOD by Samuel Shem, M.D. $2.50 (13371-8)
- [ ] SMALL TOWN by Sloan Wilson $2.50 (17474-0)

At your local bookstore or use this handy coupon for ordering:

**Dell DELL BOOKS
P.O. BOX 1000, PINEBROOK, N.J. 07058**

Please send me the books I have checked above. I am enclosing $_____
(please add 75¢ per copy to cover postage and handling). Send check or money order—no cash or C.O.D.'s. Please allow up to 8 weeks for shipment.

Mr/Mrs/Miss _____

Address _____

City _____ State/Zip _____

THE SUPERCHILLER THAT GOES BEYOND THE SHOCKING, SHEER TERROR OF *THE BOYS FROM BRAZIL*

THE AXMANN AGENDA

MIKE PETTIT

1944: Lebensborn—a sinister scheme and a dread arm of the SS that stormed across Europe killing, raping, destroying and stealing the children.
NOW: Victory—a small, mysteriously wealthy organization of simple, hard-working Americans—is linked to a sudden rush of deaths.

Behind the grass-roots patriotism of Victory does the evil of Lebensborn live on? Is there a link between Victory and the Odessa fortune—the largest and most lethal economic weapon the world has ever known? *The Axmann Agenda*—it may be unstoppable!

A Dell Book $2.50   (10152-2)

At your local bookstore or use this handy coupon for ordering:

| Dell | **DELL BOOKS** THE AXMANN AGENDA $2.50 (10152-2)
P.O. BOX 1000, PINEBROOK, N.J. 07058 |

Please send me the above title. I am enclosing $_____
(please add 75¢ per copy to cover postage and handling). Send check or money order—no cash or C.O.D.'s. Please allow up to 8 weeks for shipment.

Mr/Mrs/Miss_____

Address_____

City_____ State/Zip_____

BY REASON OF INSANITY

Shane Stevens

author of *Rat Pack* and *Go Down Dead*

"Sensational."—*New York Post*

Thomas Bishop—born of a mindless rape—escapes from an institution for the criminally insane to deluge a nation in blood and horror. Not even Bishop himself knows where—and in what chilling horror—it will end.

"This is Shane Stevens' masterpiece. The most suspenseful novel in years."—Curt Gentry, co-author of *Helter Skelter*

"A masterful suspense thriller steeped in blood, guts and sex."—*The Cincinnati Enquirer*

A Dell Book $2.75   (11028-9)

At your local bookstore or use this handy coupon for ordering:

| **Dell** | **DELL BOOKS** BY REASON OF INSANITY $2.75   (11028-9)
P.O. BOX 1000, PINEBROOK, N.J. 07058 |

Please send me the above title. I am enclosing $_____
(please add 75¢ per copy to cover postage and handling). Send check or money order—no cash or C.O.D.'s. Please allow up to 8 weeks for shipment.

Mr/Mrs/Miss_____

Address_____

City_____ State/Zip_____

DOWN RIVER

PETER COLLIER

An American family lives in a brutal world where survival is all.

"Explodes in a life-reaffirming mission so powerful it leaves the reader's heart in his throat."—*San Francisco Herald Examiner*.

"Brilliantly conceived, beautifully written. Nothing less than superb."—*New York Times*.

"A skillful blend of William Faulkner and James Dickey, author of *Deliverance*. Gripping, moving. A very contemporary tale."—*The Houston Post*.

"A book primarily about family, about continuity, about belonging. A true lyrical touch."—*Newsweek*.

A Dell Book $2.75 (11830-1)

At your local bookstore or use this handy coupon for ordering:

| Dell | **DELL BOOKS**
P.O. BOX 1000, PINEBROOK, N.J. 07058 | Downriver $2.75 (11830-1) |

Please send me the above title. I am enclosing $ _____
(please add 75¢ per copy to cover postage and handling). Send check or money order—no cash or C.O.D.'s. Please allow up to 8 weeks for shipment.

Mr/Mrs/Miss _____

Address _____

City _____ State/Zip _____

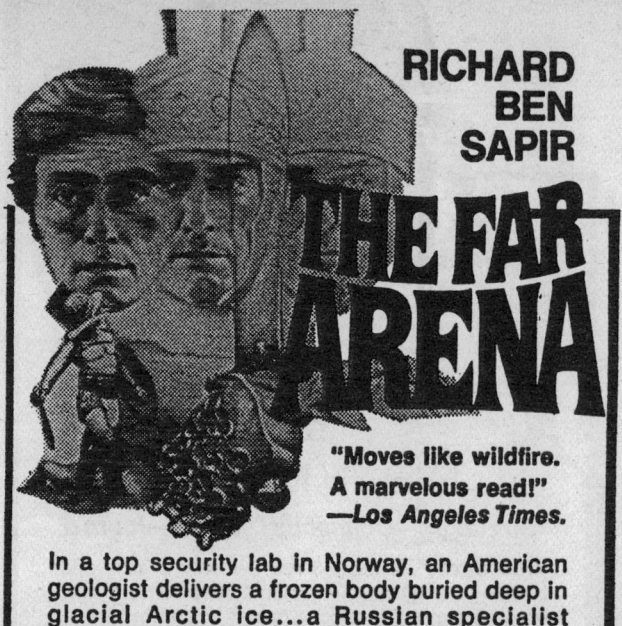

RICHARD BEN SAPIR
THE FAR ARENA

"Moves like wildfire. A marvelous read!"
—*Los Angeles Times.*

In a top security lab in Norway, an American geologist delivers a frozen body buried deep in glacial Arctic ice...a Russian specialist achieves the ultimate cryogenic breakthrough ...and a beautiful nun witnesses a resurrection beyond doubt. And Eugeni—premier gladiator of Rome—awakens from a sleep of centuries to face an utterly new and altered world.
"Riveting. Has all the earmarks of a bestseller."
—*Library Journal.* A Dell Book $2.75 (12671-1)

At your local bookstore or use this handy coupon for ordering:

| Dell | DELL BOOKS
P.O. BOX 1000, PINEBROOK, N.J. 07058 | The Far Arena $2.75 (12671-1) |

Please send me the above title. I am enclosing $_____
(please add 75¢ per copy to cover postage and handling). Send check or money order—no cash or C.O.D.'s. Please allow up to 8 weeks for shipment.

Mr/Mrs/Miss_____

Address_____

City_____State/Zip_____

A beautiful woman at the pinnacle of power can commit many sins. Only one counts— getting caught.

INDISCRETIONS

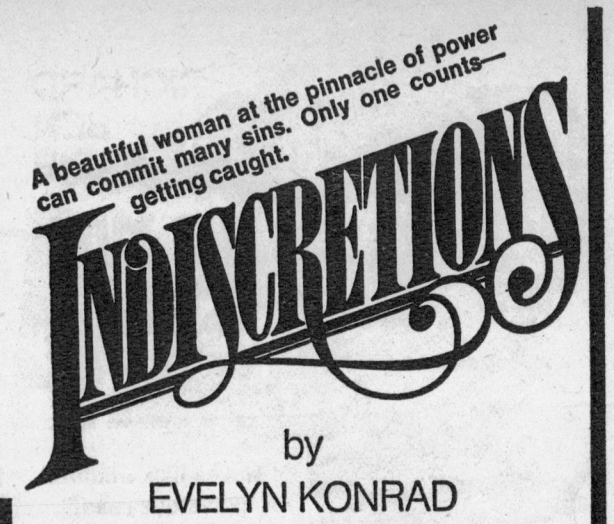

by
EVELYN KONRAD

"Sizzling."—*Columbus Dispatch-Journal*

"The Street" is Wall Street—where brains and bodies are tradeable commodities and power brokers play big politics against bigger business. At stake is a $500 million deal, the careers of three men sworn to destroy each other, the future of an oil-rich desert kingdom—and the survival of beautiful Francesca Currey, a brilliant woman in a man's world of finance and power, whose only mistakes are her *Indiscretions*.

A Dell Book   **$2.50**   **(14079-X)**

At your local bookstore or use this handy coupon for ordering:

| **Dell** | **DELL BOOKS**
 P.O. BOX 1000, PINEBROOK, N.J. 07058 | INDISCRETIONS $2.50   (14079-X) |

Please send me the above title. I am enclosing $_____
(please add 75¢ per copy to cover postage and handling). Send check or money order—no cash or C.O.D.'s. Please allow up to 8 weeks for shipment.

Mr/Mrs/Miss_____

Address_____

City_____ State/Zip_____